FREEFALL

FALL

RODERICK
GORDON

BRIAN
WILLIAMS

Chicken House
Scholastic Inc./New York

Library of Congress Cataloging-in-Publication Data

Gordon, Roderick.
Freefall / Roderick Gordon, Brian Williams. — 1st American ed.   p. cm.
Summary: As fourteen-year-old archaeologist Will and his friends plummet down a subterranean pore, they face
deadly creatures and discover a strange fungal shelf, which not only reveals artifacts from ancient civilizations, but
clues to a lost land at the end of the Earth.

ISBN 978-0-545-13877-2

[1. Adventure and adventurers — Fiction. 2. Underground areas — Fiction. 3. Archaeology — Fiction.
4. London (England) — Fiction. 5. England — Fiction.] I. Williams, Brian James, 1958– II. Title.

PZ7.G6591Fr 2010   [Fic] — dc22

2009022424

10 9 8 7 6 5 4 3 2 1   10 11 12 13 14

Printed in the U.S.A.   23
First American edition, January 2010

The text type was set in Vendetta.
The display type was set in Squarehouse.
Interior book design by Kevin Callahan

J
Gordon
Main

In order to arrive at what you are not
You must go through the way in which you are not.
And what you do not know is the only thing you know
And what you own is what you do not own
And where you are is where you are not.

from *East Coker, Four Quartets*
T. S. Eliot (1888 – 1965)

■ ■ ■

Just passing through, 'till we reach the next stage.
But just to where, well it's all been arranged.
Just passing through but the break must be made.
Should we move on or stay safely away?

from *From Safety to Where…?*
Joy Division (1976 – 1980)

PART 1

CLOSER, FURTHER

I

"**HERRRRRPH,**" Chester Rawls groaned softly to himself. His mouth was so dry it was a few moments before he could actually speak. "Aw, Mum, leave off, will you," he finally managed to say, but not unpleasantly.

He felt a tickling at his ankle, just like his mother would do when he'd failed to react to his bleeping alarm clock and haul himself out of bed. And he knew that there would be no respite from the tickling until he threw back the blankets and began to get himself ready for school.

"Please, Mum, just another five minutes?" he pleaded, his eyes still shut tight.

He felt so snug that he just wanted to lie there for as long as he could, savoring every second. In truth, he would often pretend that he hadn't heard the alarm, because he knew his mother would eventually come in to make sure he was up. He treasured the moments when he'd open his eyes and she'd be sitting there, perched on the end of his bed. He loved her breeziness and her smile, as bright as the morning sun. And she was this way every single morning, no matter how early the hour. "I'm a morning person!" she would proclaim cheerfully. "But your grumpy old dad, it takes several cups of coffee before he's himself." Then she'd imitate a mean face and push her shoulders forward and make growling noises like a wounded bear, and Chester would do the same and they'd both laugh.

Chester grinned at the thought, but then his sense of smell kicked in with a vengeance, wiping the smile from his face.

"Eww, Mum, what's that? It's gross!" he gasped, unable to explain the stench to himself. As if someone had turned off the TV, the image of his mother was gone. He immediately became very anxious and opened his eyes.

Darkness.

"What?" he murmured. It lay all around him, impenetrable and unbroken. Then he caught something out of the corner of his eye — a faint glow. *Why's it so dark in here?* he asked himself. Although he couldn't see even the smallest thing to confirm that he was in his bedroom, his mind was working overtime to convince him that he really was there. *Is that sunlight coming from the window? And that smell . . . has something boiled over on the stove downstairs? What's going on?*

The odor was intense. It was sulfurous, but at the same time there was something just beneath it . . . the sour tang of decay. The combination filled his nostrils and made his gorge rise. He tried to lift his head to look around. He couldn't — it was held by something — and, for that matter, so were his arms and legs; his whole body felt as if it was stuck fast. His first thought was that he was paralyzed. He didn't cry out, but took several quick breaths to try to quell his terror. He told himself he hadn't lost any sense of feeling, even in his extremities, so he probably wasn't paralyzed. He was further encouraged that he was able to wriggle his fingers and toes, albeit only very slightly. It seemed as though he was lodged in something firm and unyielding.

The tickling at his ankle came again, as if his phantom mother was still there, and her tenuous image flickered back into his mind's eye again.

"Mum?" he said uncertainly.

The tickling stopped, and he heard a low and mournful sound. It didn't sound quite human.

"Who's that? Who's there?" he challenged the darkness.

What came was quite unmistakably a meow.

"Bartleby?" he yelled. "Is that you, Bartleby?"

As he uttered the cat's name, the events at the Pore flooded back to him in a vivid rush. He gasped as he remembered how he, Will, Cal, and Elliott, with a huge hole behind them called the Pore, had been trapped by Limiters. "Oh God," he whimpered. They'd been facing almost certain death at the hands of the Styx soldiers. It was like a scene in a bad dream, one that refused to dim even after waking. And it all felt so fresh to him, as if it had happened only minutes ago.

More memories came back.

"Oh God!" he murmured, recalling the moment when Rebecca, the Styx girl who had been implanted in Will's family, revealed that all along she'd had an identical twin. He remembered these twins mocking Will so mercilessly, taking such cruel pleasure in disclosing their plans to wipe out swaths of Topsoilers using the deadly virus, Dominion. Telling Will to give himself up. And then Cal, Will's baby brother, stepping out into the open, wailing that he wanted to go home.

The hail of bullets that had cut the boy down . . .

Cal was dead.

Chester shuddered, but forced himself to recall what had happened next. The image of his friend, Will, came back to him — he and Chester were reaching out their hands to each other, and Elliott was shouting, and they were all linked together by a rope. Chester knew at that instant that there was still hope . . . but why? *Why was there hope?* . . . He couldn't remember. They had been caught in a desperate situation, with no way out. Chester's mind was so muddled it took him several seconds to order his thoughts.

Yes! That was it! Elliott was going to try to take them down the inside of the Pore. . . . There was still time. . . . They were going to escape.

But it had all gone so very wrong.

Chester squeezed his eyes shut as if his retinas still burned with the fiery flashes and the searing whiteness of the explosions when they'd been bombarded by the Styx Division's mighty guns. He relived the feeling of the ground quaking beneath him. And then another memory resurfaced — the hazy image of Will being flung into the air right over his head . . .

And over the edge of the Pore.

Chester recalled his blind panic as he and Elliott had tried to stop themselves from being dragged over by the combined weight of the brothers' bodies. But it had been in vain; they were all bound together; and the next thing he knew they were hurtling, all four of them, into the dark vacuum of the Pore.

. . . the sensation of the rushing, unceasing wind, which snatched away his breath . . . flashes of red light . . . incredibly intense heat . . . but now . . .

. . . but *now* . . .

. . . now he was supposed to be *dead*.

So what was this? Where . . . where was he?

Again came a meow, and Chester felt warm breath on his face.

"Bartleby, that *is* you, isn't it?" he asked falteringly.

The animal's huge domed head, barely visible in the darkness, was inches away from him. Of course, it had to be Bartleby. Chester was forgetting that the cat had leapt after his felled master, Cal, and gone over the side at the same time as the rest of them . . . and here he was now.

A damp tongue rasped against Chester's cheek.

"Geddoff!" he bawled. "Stop it!"

Bartleby licked him even more vigorously, clearly delighted to be getting a reaction. "Get away from me, you stupid cat!" Chester shouted in growing alarm. It wasn't just that he was powerless to stop the animal; Bartleby's tongue was as abrasive as a sheet of sandpaper, and being licked by him was actually quite painful. Renewing his efforts to free himself, Chester struggled furiously, all the time hollering at the top of his lungs.

The shouting did not deter the animal in the slightest, and Chester was left with no recourse but to hiss and spit as savagely as he could. It eventually worked, and Bartleby backed off.

Then there was just silence and darkness again.

He tried to call out to Elliott and then to Will, although he didn't know if either had survived the fall. He had the most horrible feeling in the pit of his stomach that he might be the only one left alive, other than the cat, of course. That almost made it worse — the idea that it was just him alone with the giant slobbering animal.

A suggestion struck him like a cricket ball to the head: By some miracle had he landed in the very bottom of the Pore? He remembered what Elliott had told them — that not only was the opening a mile across, it was so deep that only one man, so the story went, had managed to climb back out of it. As much as the invisible substance he was stuck in would allow him, Chester trembled uncontrollably. He was in his worst nightmare.

He was buried alive!

Jammed in some kind of body-shaped shallow grave, stranded in the guts of the earth . . . How was he ever going to get out of the Pore and back up to the surface again? He was farther down now even than the Deeps — and he'd thought that had been bad enough. The prospect of returning home to his parents and to his nice predictable life was growing ever more distant.

"Please, I just want to go home," he gabbled to himself and, beset by alternating waves of claustrophobia and dread, he broke out into a cold sweat.

But as he lay there, a small voice in his head told him he couldn't just give in to his fear. He stopped gabbling. He knew he had to liberate himself from whatever held him like quick-setting cement and find the others. They might need his help.

By a process of tensing and relaxing and squirming, it took him ten minutes to partially work his head loose and gain a measure of free movement in one shoulder. Then, as he contracted the muscles in his arms, there was a disgusting sucking sound, and one of them was suddenly released from the spongy, clinging material.

"Yes!" he cried. Although the movement of his arm was limited, he took a moment to feel his face and chest with his hand. He came across the straps of his backpack and undid both buckles, thinking it might help him in his bid for free-dom. Then, as he concentrated on freeing the rest of his body, heaving and grunting, he became hotter and hotter with the exertion from these micromovements. It was as if he was breaking free from a mold. Nevertheless, it slowly seemed to be working.

Many miles above Chester, at the top of the Pore, the old Styx stood peering into it while water fell in a constant drizzle around him, and somewhere in the distance packs of dogs howled.

Although his face was deeply lined, and his hair flecked with silver, age had not brought frailty to this man. His tall, thin body was stretched as tightly as a bow under the long leather coat buttoned up to his neck. And, as the light caught them, his small eyes glittered like two beads of highly polished jet. A sense of power emanated from his whole being; it seemed to pervade the darkness around him and hold it in his thrall.

As he gestured with his hand, another man stepped up beside him, so that the pair of them stood shoulder to shoulder on the very edge of the void. This second person bore an uncanny resemblance to the old man, although his face was as yet unlined, and his hair so black and tightly raked back that it could easily have been mistaken for a skullcap.

These men, members of a secret race called the Styx, were investigating an incident that had taken place a short time before. An incident in which the old Styx had lost his twin granddaughters, who had been swept over the edge of the void.

Although he knew there was little chance that either of the girls was still alive, the old Styx's face revealed no trace of sorrow or anguish at their loss. He fired orders in a staccato bark.

There was a renewed flurry of activity as the Limiters around the Pore obeyed him. These soldiers, a specialized detachment that trained in the Deeps and undertook clandestine operations on the surface, wore dun-colored fatigues — heavy jackets and bulky pants — despite the high temperatures prevalent at that depth in the earth. Their lean faces were impassive and intent as some of their number used the light-gathering scopes mounted on their rifles to probe the depths of the Pore while others lowered luminescent orbs on cables to check the upper reaches. It was unlikely that the twins had managed to stop themselves from plummeting to their deaths, but the old Styx had to make certain.

"Anything?" he barked in his own tongue, a nasal and rasping language. The word echoed around the Pore and carried up the slope behind him, where other soldiers, with their usual efficiency, were already dismantling the large field guns that had caused so much destruction in the very spot he now stood.

"They've obviously perished," the old Styx said quietly to his young assistant, then immediately shouted orders at full volume again. "Concentrate all your efforts on finding the phials!" He was counting on the fact that one or both of the twins had had time to unhook the small glass vessels hung around their necks before they were taken over the edge. "We need those phials!"

His uncompromising gaze fell on the Limiters who were crawling around him as they combed every inch of the ground. They were painstakingly checking under each piece of shattered rock and sifting through the churned-up dirt, which still smoldered from the residue of the explosive in the shells that had struck there. Every so often this residue ignited and small flames would rekindle and sprout from the ground, then vanish just as soon.

Shouts of warning rose up, and several Limiters threw themselves back as a strip of land farther along the Pore broke away with a low rumble. Tons of rock and soil, which had been loosened from the shelling, detached and slid into the abyss. Regardless of this close call, the soldiers simply picked themselves up and resumed their duties, apparently unruffled by the event.

The old Styx turned to contemplate the darkness at the top of the slope.

"No question that it was her," his young assistant said, as he, too, looked up the slope. "It was Sarah Jerome who took the twins over with her."

"Who else could it have been?" the old Styx snapped, shaking his head. "And what's remarkable is that she managed it even though she was mortally wounded." He turned to his young assistant. "We were playing with fire when we set her against her sons and, put bluntly, we got our fingers burned. Nothing is ever straightforward when it comes — *came* — to that Burrows child." The boy was no more likely to have survived the drop than his twin granddaughters. He fell silent with a frown, drawing a long breath before he spoke again. "But tell me — how did Sarah Jerome make it down here? Who was responsible for the area?" He thrust a finger at the upper slopes. "I want them to answer to me."

His young assistant bowed his head to acknowledge the order, then left.

Another figure immediately appeared in his place. It was so distorted and hunched it was difficult to tell at first glance whether it was actually human. From beneath a shawl stiff with filth, a pair of gnarled hands twitched their way out into the light. With birdlike movements, the hands lifted up the shawl to reveal a head horribly deformed with bulbous growths, so numerous that in places they seemed to grow one upon the other. Limp tufts of dank hair framed a face in which two perfectly white eyes were set. Devoid of irises or pupils, they swiveled about as though they were able to see.

"Condolences, 'n' that, on the loss of . . . ," the figure wheezed, trailing off in a respectful silence.

"Thank you, Cox," the old Styx responded, now speaking in English. "Every man is the architect of his own fortune, and *un*fortunate things happen."

In a sudden movement, Cox swiped at the string of lacteal saliva dangling from his blackened lips with the back of his wrist, smearing it across his gray skin. He held his spindly arm in midair, then, with a jerk, raised it farther up his face and tapped the melon-sized growth on his forehead with a clawlike finger.

"At least yer girls did for Will Burrows and that sow Elliott," he said. "But yer still going to purge the rest of the Deeps for the last renegades, ain't yer?"

"Every last one, using the information you gave us," the old Styx said, then shot him a knowing look. "Anyway, Cox, why do you ask?"

"No reason," the shapeless lump replied, quick as a flash.

"Oh, but I think there is. . . . You're worried because Drake has thus far eluded us. And you know that sooner or later he'll come after you, to settle the score."

"'E will, and I'll be ready for 'im," Cox proclaimed confidently, but a snaking blue vein throbbing under one of his eyes told otherwise. "Drake could throw a spanner —"

The old Styx held up a hand to silence him as his young assistant double-timed it back with three Limiters in tow. The trio of soldiers formed a row and stood rigidly to attention, their eyes set straight before them and their long rifles at their sides. Two of them were youthful subalterns, the third an officer, a grizzled veteran of many years' service.

His fists clenched, the old Styx walked slowly down the short row, stopping as he came to the last man, who happened to be the veteran. He turned fully to him and, with their faces separated by mere inches, the old Styx held the position for several seconds before dropping his eyes to the man's battle tunic. Three short cotton threads of different colors protruded from the material just above the veteran's breast pocket. These bright threads were decorations for acts of bravery — the Styx equivalent to Topsoiler medals. The old Styx closed his gloved fingers on them, tearing them out and then flinging them in the veteran's face.

The veteran didn't blink, didn't show the slightest reaction.

The old Styx stepped back, then gestured toward the Pore as casually as if he was waving away a bothersome fly. The three soldiers broke from formation. They leaned their rifles against each other in a pyramid. Then they unbuckled their bulky belt kits and deposited them in a neat pile before the rifles. With no further command from the old Styx, they trooped in single file to the edge of the Pore and, one after another, stepped straight into it. None gave as much as a cry. And none of their comrades in the area stopped what they were doing to watch as the three soldiers pitched down into the abyss.

"Rough justice," Cox said.

"We demand nothing less than excellence," the old Styx replied. "They failed. They were no use to us any longer."

"You know, the girls might just 'ave survived," Cox ventured.

The old Styx turned to give Cox his full attention. "That's right — your people really believe a man fell down there and lived, don't they?"

"They're not *my* people," Cox grumbled uncomfortably.

"Some myth about a glorious Garden of Eden waiting at the bottom," the old Styx said playfully.

"Load of guff," Cox mumbled, and began to cough.

"You've never thought of giving it a try yourself?" The old Styx didn't wait for an answer, clapping his gloved hands together as he swung around to his young assistant. "Send a detachment to the Bunker to extract samples of the Dominion virus from the corpses there. If we can reculture it, we can keep the plan on track." He cocked his head and smiled evilly at Cox. "Wouldn't want the Topsoilers to miss their day of reckoning, now, would we?"

At this Cox exploded with a cackling laugh, spraying milky spittle into the air.

■ ■ ■

Chester refused to allow himself even a second's rest. Whatever it was that had him in its grip, it felt oily next to his skin, and as he continued to struggle, he became all the more certain it was the source of the foul stench. While he was straining to get his second arm out, his other shoulder abruptly came free, and then all of a sudden the top half of his torso pulled clear. He roared in triumph as he sat up with a loud sucking sound.

He quickly felt around in the pitch black. He was completely hemmed in by the rubbery substance, and he found he could just reach the very top, where it seemed to level off. He tore off small strips from the sides around him — it was fibrous and greasy to the touch, and he hadn't the faintest idea what it was. But whatever it was, it seemed to have absorbed the impact of his fall down the Pore. Crazy as the idea appeared, it was probably the reason he was alive now.

"No way!" he said, dismissing the notion. It was just too far-fetched — there must be another explanation.

The lantern that had been clipped onto his jacket was nowhere to be found, so he quickly checked through all his pockets for his spare luminescent orbs.

"Blast it!" he exclaimed as he discovered his hip pocket torn and the contents gone, the orbs with them.

Talking rapidly to himself to keep his spirits up, he attempted to get to his feet. "Oh, give me a break!" he wailed. His legs were still firmly wedged in the spongy material and he couldn't stand.

But the gummy substance wasn't the only thing holding him in place.

"What's this?" he said as he discovered the rope tied around his waist. It was Elliott's rope; they'd used it to daisy-chain themselves together at the top of the Pore. Now it was restricting his movements — to his left and right it was firmly set in the spongy material. Without the use of a knife, he had no option but to attempt to unpick the knot. Drenched in the oily fluid, his hands kept slipping off the equally saturated rope, making the task difficult.

But with much fumbling and cursing, he eventually managed to undo the knot, then enlarge the loop around himself. "At last!" he bellowed and, accompanied by a sound like someone finishing a drink through a straw, he extricated his legs. One of his boots was left behind, stuck solid in the material. He had to use both hands to tug it out, putting it back on before he scrambled up.

It was at that point he realized how much every part of his body hurt — as if he'd just finished the toughest rugby match of his life, perhaps against a squad of particularly belligerent gorillas. "Ow!" he complained as he rubbed his arms and legs, also finding that there were rope burns around his neck and on his hands. With a loud groan he stretched his back, peering up above to try to make out where he had fallen from. The strangest thing was that, after the start of the fall, when the air had been rushing against his face so hard he could hardly breathe, he didn't really remember very much until Bartleby had brought him to by nuzzling his ankle.

"Where *am* I?" he said repeatedly, remaining in the trench. He noticed a couple of areas of very dim illumination, and although he didn't know what was causing them, the relief from the darkness made him feel slightly better. His eyes adjusted further, until he could also vaguely make out Bartleby's fleeting silhouette as the cat circled around him like a prowling jaguar.

"Elliott!" Chester called. "Are you there, Elliott?"

He noticed that, as he shouted, there was a definite echo coming from his left, but nothing at all from his right. He yelled several more times, each time waiting for a response. "Elliott, can you hear me? Will! Hello, Will! Are you there?" But no one answered.

He told himself he couldn't stand there all day, simply shouting. He realized that one of the points of illumination was in fact coming from quite close by and made up his mind to try to reach it. He clawed himself out of his pit. Because he was soaked in the slippery fluid, he didn't risk getting to his feet, but kept on all fours as he moved over the springy surface. He noticed something else as he went: He felt strangely buoyant, as if he was floating in water. Wondering if this was because the knocks to his head had made him a little dizzy, he told himself to concentrate on the job at hand.

He inched forward with small, deliberate movements, his fingers extended toward the light. Then the glow seemed to catch the underside of his outstretched palm — and he realized it was coming from something embedded deep in the rubbery material. He rolled up his sleeve and stuck his arm into the hole to retrieve it.

"Yuck!" he said as he pried out the light, his arm coated in the unctuous liquid. It was a Styx lantern. He didn't know if it had been his or had belonged to one of the others, but that didn't matter right now. He held up the lantern to assess his surroundings, his confidence building to the point where he decided to get to his feet.

He found he was on a grayish surface — it wasn't smooth by any means, but striated and pitted, with a texture somewhat akin to elephant hide. His light revealed that there were other things stuck in it, varying from small pebbles to substantial chunks of rock. They had evidently hit the material with some force and penetrated it, just as he had.

He lifted the lantern higher and saw that the ground stretched away on all sides in a gently undulating plateau. Treading carefully so as not to lose his footing, Chester went back to his hole to inspect it more closely. He couldn't believe what he was seeing, and chuckled in amazement. The light revealed a perfect outline of himself, sunk deep into the surface of the material. It brought to mind the Saturday morning cartoon with the unfortunate coyote that always seemed to end up falling from great heights and leaving a coyote-shaped impression when it hit the canyon floor. Here was a real-life Chester-shaped version! The cartoon didn't seem quite so funny anymore.

Muttering with disbelief, he jumped back into the hole to retrieve his rucksack, which took quite some doing. Once he'd freed it, he hoisted it onto his back and scrambled from the hole. Then he bent to lift the rope. "Left or right?" he asked himself, looking at the opposite lengths of the rope, which disappeared into the darkness. Picking a direction at random and steeling himself for what he might find, he began to follow the rope, heaving it out of the rubbery surface as he went.

He'd gone about thirty feet when the rope suddenly came away in his hands, and he tumbled back into a sitting position. Grateful that the subterranean rubberized mat had absorbed his fall, he got to his feet again and examined the end of the rope. It was frayed as if it had been cut. Despite this, he was able to follow the line it had left, and soon came to a deep impression in the ground. He sidestepped around the shape, playing his light into it.

It certainly looked as if someone had been there, but the outline wasn't as perfect as his, as if whoever had made it had landed on their side. "Will! Elliott!" he called out again. There was still no reply, but Bartleby suddenly reappeared, fixing Chester with his big unwinking eyes. "What is it? What do you want?" Chester growled impatiently at him. The cat slowly turned to face the opposite direction and, with his body low to the ground, began to creep forward. "You want me to come with you — is that it?" Chester asked, realizing that Bartleby was behaving precisely as if he was stalking something.

He followed the cat until they reached a vertical surface — a wall of the gray rubbery material down which water ran in rivulets. "Where now?" he demanded, beginning to think that the cat might be taking him on a wild-goose chase. Chester was reluctant to wander too far from the embedded rope and get himself lost, but he knew that sooner or later he might have to bite the bullet and explore the whole area.

Bartleby, his skeletal tail sticking out behind him, was pointing his snout at what appeared to be a gap in the wall. Water was splattering down over the opening in a continuous shower. "Inside there?" Chester asked as he tried to shine the Styx lantern through the water. In answer, Bartleby stepped through the streaming sheet, and Chester followed.

He found himself in some sort of cave. Bartleby wasn't the only one inside it. Huddled over and surrounded by discarded sheets of paper, someone else was sitting there.

"Will!" Chester gasped, almost unable to talk, he was so relieved that his friend had made it through.

Will raised his head, relaxing his fingers, which had been tightly clenched around a luminescent orb, and allowing the light to dapple his face. He said nothing, staring dumbly at Chester.

"Will?" Chester repeated. Alarmed by his friend's silence, he squatted down beside him. "Are you hurt?"

Will simply continued to stare at him. Then he ran a hand through his white hair, which was slick with oil, and grimaced and blinked one eye shut as if it was too much effort to speak.

"What's wrong? Talk to me, Will!"

"Yeah, I'm all right. Considering," Will eventually answered in a monotone voice. "Other than I've got a blinder of a headache and my legs hurt like mad. And my ears keep popping." He swallowed several times. "Must be the difference in pressure."

"Mine, too," Chester said, then realized how unimportant it was at that very moment. "But, Will, how long have you been in here?"

"Dunno," Will shrugged.

"But, why . . . what . . . you . . . ," Chester spluttered, his words tumbling into one another. "Will, we made it!" he burst out, laughing. "We actually made it!"

"Looks that way," his friend replied flatly, pressing his lips together.

"What *is* wrong with you?" Chester demanded.

"I don't know," Will mumbled. "I really don't know what's wrong, or what's right, not anymore."

"What do you mean?" Chester said.

"I thought I was going to see my dad again." Will bowed his head as he answered. "All the time all those terrible things were happening to us, one hope kept me going. . . . I really believed that I'd be back with my dad." He held up a grimy-looking Mickey Mouse toothbrush. "But that dream's gone now. He's dead, and all that he's left behind is this stupid toothbrush he nicked from me . . . and the wacko stuff he was writing in his journal."

Will selected a damp piece of paper and read a sentence scrawled over it. "'A "second sun"... *in the center of the earth?*' What does that mean?" He sighed heavily. "It doesn't even make sense."

Then he spoke in barely a whisper.

"And Cal . . ." Will shook with an involuntary sob. "It was my fault he died. I should have done something to save him. I should have given myself up to Rebecca. . . ." He clicked his tongue against his teeth, correcting himself. ". . . to *the* Rebeccas."

He raised his head, his lackluster gaze resting on Chester. "Every time I shut my eyes, all I see are her two faces . . . like they're pressing into my eyelids, into the darkness itself . . . two vile, nasty faces, ranting and shouting at me. I can't seem to get them out of here," he said, slapping his forehead with some force. "Oh, that hurt," he groaned. "Why did I do that?"

"But —" Chester began.

"We might as well just pack it in. What's the point?" Will interrupted him. "Don't you remember what the Rebeccas were saying about the Dominion plot? We can't do a thing to stop them from letting the virus loose on the surface, not from down here." With great ceremony, he dropped the Mickey Mouse toothbrush into a greasy-looking puddle, as if he was drowning the crudely painted rodent that composed its handle. "What's the point?" he repeated.

Chester was quickly losing his cool. "The point is, we're here and we're together and we showed those evil cows. It's like . . . it's like . . ." He floundered for a second as he tried to express himself. "It's like in a video game when you get a respawn . . . you know, when you get another go. We've been given a second chance to try to stop the Rebecca twins and save all those lives on the surface." He plucked the toothbrush out of the puddle and, shaking the water from it, handed it back to Will. "The point is, we made it, we're still alive, for God's sake."

"Biggish deal," Will muttered.

"Of course it's a big deal!" Chester shook his friend by the shoulder. "C'mon, Will, you're the one who always kept us all going, dragging us after you, the loopy one who —" Chester paused to draw a quick breath in his excited state "— who always had to see what was around the next corner. Remember?"

"Isn't that what got us into this mess in the first place?" Will responded.

Chester made a noise halfway between a "hmm" and a "yes," then shook his head vigorously. "And I want you to know . . ."

Chester's voice quivered into nothing as he averted his eyes and fidgeted with a piece of rock by his boot. "Will . . . I was such an idiot."

"It doesn't matter now," Will replied.

"Yes, it does. I was acting like a prize muppet. . . . I got so fed up with everything . . . with you." Then Chester's voice became steady again. "I said a lot of stuff I didn't mean. And now I'm asking you to do your exploring, and I promise I'll never, ever complain again. I'm sorry."

"That's OK," Will mumbled, a little embarrassed.

"Just do what you do best . . . find us a way out of here," Chester urged him.

"I'll try," Will said.

Chester fixed him with a look. "I'm counting on it, Will. All those people on the surface are, too. Don't forget, my mum and dad are up there. I don't want them to get the virus and die."

"No, of course not," Will replied immediately as Chester's mention of his parents brought the situation into sharp focus for him. Will knew how much his friend loved them, and their fates and those of many hundreds of thousands — if not millions — of people might be sealed if the Styx plot went ahead.

"Come on then, partner," Chester urged, offering Will a hand to help him up. Together they stepped through the waterfall and out onto the rubbery surface.

"Chester," Will said, becoming more like his old self, "there's something you should know."

"What's that?"

"Notice anything weird about this place?" Will asked, giving his friend a quizzical glance.

Wondering where to start, Chester shook his head, his mane of curly, oil-drenched hair whipping around his face and a strand catching in his mouth. He plucked it out immediately with a look of disgust and spat several times. "No, other than that this stuff we landed in smells, and *tastes*, unbelievably awful."

"My guess is that we're on a dirty great fungus," Will went on. "We've ended up on some sort of ledge of the stuff — it must be sticking out into the Pore. I saw something like this once on television — there was a monster fungus in America that stretched for more than a thousand miles underground."

"Is that what you wanted to —?"

"Nope," Will interrupted. "This is the interesting thing. Watch carefully." The luminescent orb was in the palm of his hand, and he casually tossed it a few feet into the air. Chester looked on with stunned amazement as it seemed to float back down to Will's hand again. It was as if he was witnessing the scene in slow motion.

"Hey, how'd you do that?"

"You have a go," Will said, passing the orb over to Chester. "But don't throw it too hard or you'll lose it."

Chester did as Will suggested, lobbing it upward. In the event, he did apply too much force, and the orb shot some fifty feet, illuminating what appeared to be another fungal outcrop above them, before it floated eerily down again, the light playing on their upturned faces.

"How —?" Chester gasped, his eyes wide with amazement.

"Don't you feel the, um, weightlessness?" Will said, grasping for the right word. "It's low gravity. My guess is that

2 4

it's about a third of what we're used to on the surface," Will informed him, pointing a finger heavenward. "That — and the soft landing we had on this fungus — might explain why we're not as flat as pancakes right now. But be careful how you move around or you'll send yourself spinning off this shelf and back into the Pore again."

"Low gravity," Chester repeated, trying to absorb what his friend was saying. "What does that mean, exactly?"

"It means we must have fallen a *very* long way."

Chester looked at him uncomprehendingly.

"Ever wondered what's at the center of the earth?" Will said.

2

AS **DRAKE STOLE** along the lava tunnel, he thought he heard a noise and froze, listening intently. "Nothing," he said to himself after a moment, then unhooked his canteen from his belt to take a drink. He swallowed contemplatively, his eyes peering at the gloom of the tunnel as he began to reflect on what had happened at the Pore.

He'd left before the old Styx had ordered the Limiters to jump to their deaths, but had witnessed the horrific events leading up to it. Hidden on the slope above the Pore, he'd been powerless to prevent Cal from meeting a sudden and violent end. Will's younger brother had been brutally gunned down by the Styx soldiers after he'd panicked and stepped out into the line of fire. And minutes later, Drake had been equally powerless to save Will and the rest of them when complete chaos erupted. He could only watch as the large-bore guns of the Styx Division opened up, and Elliott, Will, and Chester were blasted over the side of the Pore.

Drake had been through so much with Elliott in the Deeps that he could usually second-guess how she'd act in any given situation. And as bad as things looked, Drake had still retained a sliver of hope that somehow she had managed to anchor herself and the boys to the side of the colossal opening, that they hadn't actually dropped down it. So Drake had remained where he was, rather than do what his instincts were telling him and get away from the area, which was swarming with Styx and their savage attack dogs.

As Limiters searched the perimeter of the Pore, he'd listened out, hoping to catch the reports as Elliott and the boys were located and hauled back up. At least if they were captured, he would have an opportunity to try to free them later on.

But as the minutes ticked by and the search down by the Pore continued, he'd become increasingly disheartened. He had to accept that Elliott and the boys were gone for good, that they had fallen to their deaths. Of course, there was a decades-old story about a man who had stumbled into the Pore and miraculously reappeared at the Miners' Station, babbling about fantastic lands, but Drake had never believed a word of it. He'd always dismissed it as a rumor manufactured by the Styx to give the Colonists something to think about. No, as far as he was concerned, nobody survived the Pore.

He was also becoming increasingly concerned that he'd be detected by the Styx dogs, known as stalkers — vicious brutes whose fierceness was surpassed only by their prowess at tracking. They hadn't yet picked up his scent trail because of the clouds of smoke left over from the recent gun barrage. But the wind was rapidly dispersing the smoke and wouldn't afford him protection from the dogs for very much longer.

He'd just been debating whether he should leave when he'd heard a commotion. Jumping to the conclusion that Elliott and the boys had been spotted, he'd immediately raised himself up on his elbows and peered around the menhir he'd hidden behind. The number of soldiers with unshielded lanterns in the area allowed him a clear view of the reason for all the activity.

Down by the Pore he caught the briefest glimpse of someone in full flight, their arms outstretched on either side.

"Sarah?" he'd said under his breath.

It had certainly looked like Will's mother, Sarah Jerome, but he couldn't begin to understand how she'd managed to get to her feet and, far less, how she was able to run. Her injuries had been so severe that he truly would have thought she'd be dead by now.

But from the glimpse he got, she appeared to be very much alive as she tore over the uneven ground. Drake had watched as the Styx reacted, running toward her as they brought up their rifles. But no shots had been fired as Sarah swept two small figures over the edge of the Pore with her. She and the figures had simply vanished from sight.

"Holy smokes . . . ," he said under his breath as he'd heard high-pitched screams, assuming instantly that they had been Sarah's.

Other shouts — the shouts of Styx soldiers — rang out all across the slope and, as footsteps passed within plain sight of where he was standing, Drake had quickly tucked himself back behind the menhir. But he hadn't been able to resist a second look.

All the soldiers in the area had gathered around the spot where Sarah had jumped. A single Styx had stepped up onto a chunk of masonry and had begun shouting rapid orders at the soldiers milling around him. He'd appeared to be older than the rest of the troops and was dressed in the usual black coat and white shirt, rather than the Limiter combats. Drake had seen him around in the Colony before — he was clearly someone at the very top of their hierarchy, someone very important. And with the ease of someone used to issuing orders, he quickly and efficiently organized the soldiers into two groups — one to check the Pore, the other to comb the slope with stalkers.

Drake had realized it was time to make himself scarce.

Getting to the top of the slope undetected hadn't been difficult, and then he'd made his way out of the cavern. Once in the lava tubes, he'd moved cautiously, not least because he only had stove guns — very basic firearms.

But now, as he took a final sip from his canteen and replaced the lid, his mind was processing what he'd witnessed at the Pore. "Sarah," he said out loud, as he thought about how she'd taken the two Styx with her to the grave.

Then it clicked.

The high-pitched screams he'd heard weren't Sarah's at all.

The screams had been those of young girls. The twins! Sarah had taken her revenge on the Rebecca twins! Knowing she probably had only minutes to live, and that her two sons had already met their fate, Sarah had found the perfect focus for her retribution.

That was it!

She had sacrificed herself to eliminate the twins.

And Drake knew that the twins had had the lethal Dominion virus on them, since they'd been parading it around and taunting Will with it. They'd told Will of their plan to unleash it on Topsoilers and implied that the single phial of Dominion was all they needed. According to Sarah, one of the twins had been handed the freshly replicated virus as she'd arrived in the Deeps. Drake was willing to bet that the phial was the only specimen the Styx had in their possession. So, possibly without knowing it, Sarah had just exacted her vengeance on what was most dear to the Styx, and had foiled their plot against Topsoilers.

It was perfect!

She'd achieved precisely what Drake had thought near impossible.

Shaking his head, he took a single step, but jerked to a stop as if a current had been passed through him.

"What a fool I am!" he exclaimed. He'd completely over-looked something. It wasn't quite the perfect solution he'd first thought. Sarah had started the job, but it wasn't finished yet.

"The Bunker," he murmured, realizing that traces of the virus could still be present in the sealed test cells in the midst of the huge concrete complex. The Styx had tested the effective-ness of the virulent strain on a handful of unfortunate Colonists and renegades, and their dead bodies might still contain living virus. The Styx would know that, too, he realized. He would have to get there first, to destroy what was left.

Drake began to run, formulating a plan of action as he went. He could pick up some explosives from a secret cache on the way to the Bunker. It was likely there would still be Styx patrolling the Great Plain, but he had to get to the cells as quickly as he could. He was going to have to cut some corners — this was no time for subtlety.

Too much was at stake for that.

In the corridor of Humphrey House, Mrs. Burrows dithered, unable to make up her mind. The part of her that craved television just didn't seem to burn with its usual intensity that Saturday afternoon. She knew there was something she wanted to watch, but she couldn't quite recall what it was. She found this vaguely disquieting — it really wasn't like her to forget.

Shaking her head, she took a few shuffling steps across the green, overwaxed linoleum in the direction of the dayroom, where the only TV in the place was to be found.

"No," she said, stopping.

As she listened to the voices and the activity coming from different parts of the building, echoing and indefinite like sounds heard at a public swimming pool, she suddenly felt so very alone. Here she was in this impersonal building, with its professional staff and an assortment of troubled people, but nobody really cared about her. Of course, the staff had a clinical interest in her well-being, but they were strangers to her, just as she was to them. She was merely another patient to be sent on her way when they decided she had recovered, another bed to be vacated for the next inmate.

"No!" She thrust her clenched fist into the air. "I'm better than that!" she proclaimed loudly as an orderly marched briskly past her. He didn't even give her a second glance — people speaking to themselves were the norm in this place.

She swiveled on the worn heels of her slippers and scuffed down the corridor, away from the dayroom, as she fished in her bathrobe pocket for the card the policeman had given her. It had been three days since the last meeting with him, and it was about time he came up with something definitive. As she reached the phone booth, she flexed the flimsy piece of card with its cheap printing. "Detective Inspector Rob Blakemore," she murmured.

For a second she thought about the unidentified woman who had come to see her some months before. The woman had pretended to be from social services, but Mrs. Burrows had seen through the deception and worked out who she *really* was: Will's biological mother. And she had accused Will of murdering her brother! But this rather far-fetched claim, whether true or not, wasn't Mrs. Burrows's main concern. She was more preoccupied by two other aspects: She couldn't understand why the woman had waited until now to make herself known — waited until after Will had "gone walkabout." And she couldn't help but be impressed by the passion the woman had shown. To describe her as driven would be a rank understatement.

In the end, it was this that had shaken Mrs. Burrows from her safe, lazy world, like a blast of cold wind from an unknown country. In those brief moments with Will's biological mother, she had had a glimpse of something far removed from the secondhand life that the television provided her with . . . something so real, so immediate, and so irresistible.

She slotted her credit card into the phone and dialed the number.

As it was the weekend, DI Blakemore was, predictably

enough, not in the office. Despite this, Mrs. Burrows left a long and rambling message with the poor girl unfortunate enough to answer her call.

"Highfield Police Station. How can I h —?"

"Yes, this is Celia Burrows, and DI Blakemore said he'd get back to me on Friday and he hasn't, so I want him to call me without fail on Monday because he said he was going to review the piece of security camera footage he took away with him and try to lift a decent photo of the woman's face, from which he was going to get an artist's impression that he could distribute on the police intranet in the hope that someone might be able to identify her, and he also wanted to think about some media coverage and how that might help, and by the way, if you didn't catch it the first time, my name is Celia Burrows. Good-bye."

Having hardly drawn breath or given the girl an opportunity to say a single word in response, Mrs. Burrows slammed down the receiver. "Good," she congratulated herself, and went to extract her credit card. However, she paused in thought for a second, then dialed her sister's number.

"It's ringing!" Mrs. Burrows said. That in itself was a breakthrough because the number had been unobtainable for several months, which had probably meant that her sister had overlooked her phone bill yet again.

The phone continued to ring, but there was still no answer.

"Pick up, Jean, pick up!" Mrs. Burrows shouted into the receiver. "Where are y —?"

" 'Allo," answered a disgruntled voice. "Who's there?"

"Jean?" Mrs. Burrows asked.

"Don't know anyone called Jane. You got the wrong number," Auntie Jean said. Mrs. Burrows could hear a munching sound, as if her sister was eating a piece of toast.

"Just listen to me, this is C —"

"I don't know what you're selling, but I don't need none!"

"Noooooo!" Mrs. Burrows shouted as her sister hung up on her. She held the telephone away from her head and fumed at it. "You silly cow, Jean!" She was just about to redial when she spotted the rake-thin form of the matron bustling down the corridor.

Mrs. Burrows replaced the receiver, whipped her credit card from the slot, then stepped in front of the gray-haired woman. On the spur of the moment she'd decided what she had to do.

"I'm leaving."

"Oh, yes? Why's that?" the matron asked. "Because of Mrs. L's death?"

Uncharacteristically for Mrs. Burrows, she seemed at a loss for words. She opened her mouth but didn't speak as she remembered the patient who had contracted the Ultra Bug, a mystery virus that had swept through the country and then the rest of the world. But whereas most people were laid low for a week or two with chronic eye and mouth infections, the virus had somehow got into Mrs. L's brain. And killed her.

"Yes, I suppose that's probably part of the reason," she admitted. "When she died so abruptly, it did make me realize how valuable life is, and how much I've been missing out on," she said finally.

The matron inclined her head sympathetically.

"And after all these months with still no news of my husband or son, I've been forgetting that there's one member of my family left — my daughter, Rebecca," Mrs. Burrows continued. "She's staying at my sister's, you know, and I haven't as much as spoken to her since I've been here. I feel that I should be with her. She probably needs me right now."

"I understand, Celia." Nodding, the matron smiled at her, adjusting her wiry gray hair, which was gathered into an immaculately arranged bun.

Mrs. Burrows smiled back. What the matron didn't need to know was that over her dead body would Mrs. Burrows leave it entirely to the police to find her missing husband and son. She was convinced that the unidentified woman who had come to see her was the key to what was going on, and might even be Will's abductor. The police kept telling Mrs. Burrows they were "on the case" and "doing everything they could," but she was determined to begin her own investigation as well. And she couldn't do that in here, with just a public pay phone at her disposal.

"You know it's my job to advise you to speak to your counselor before you leave, but . . . ," said the matron, glancing at her wristwatch, "that wouldn't be until Monday, and I can see you've made up your mind. I'll get the release forms from my office right now for you to sign." She turned to go down the corridor, then paused. "I have to say I'm going to miss our little chats, Celia."

"Me, too," Mrs. Burrows replied. "Maybe I'll come back one day."

"I hope not, for your sake," the matron said, continuing on her way.

"We've got to find Elliott," Chester said as he took a few reluctant steps.

"Hold on a second." Will started to lift an arm and then made a noise, as if he was in great pain.

"What is it?" Chester asked.

"My arms, shoulders, hands," Will complained. "Everything hurts."

"Tell me about it," Chester said, as his friend managed to raise his arm all the way to his neck with another stifled moan.

"I want to see if this still works." Will began to untangle the night-vision device, which had been pushed down around his neck during the fall.

"Drake's lens?" Chester said.

"Drake!" Will gasped, immediately stopping what he was doing. "Remember what the Rebeccas said — do you think they were telling the truth, for once?"

"What . . . that it wasn't him you shot?" Chester asked hesitantly. It was the first time he had spoken to Will about the shooting on the Great Plain, and he felt distinctively uneasy now that he had.

"Chester, whoever it was that the Limiters were torturing, I honestly think I missed him by a mile."

"Oh," Chester mumbled.

Will looked thoughtful. "If they had caught or killed Drake, the Rebeccas would have rubbed my face in it," he reasoned.

Chester gave a small shrug. "Maybe he didn't escape them, and they've got him somewhere. Maybe it was just another of their nasty little lies."

"No, I don't think so," Will said, his eyes bright with hope. "What could they get from lying about that?" He looked at Chester. "So, if Drake did survive the ambush . . . and somehow got away from the Limiters . . . I wonder where he is now."

"Maybe he's holed up somewhere on the Great Plain?" Chester suggested.

"Or maybe he went Topsoil. Don't ask me why, but I got the feeling he could go to the surface anytime he wanted."

"Well, wherever he is, we could really do with his help now." Chester sighed as he scanned the darkness. "I wish he was down here with us."

"I wouldn't wish *that* on anyone," Will declared earnestly, grunting as he worked the device up over his face. He positioned the strap across his forehead and tightened it, then adjusted the flip-down lens so it was directly over his right eye. He found that the cable had come unplugged from the small rectangular unit in his pants pocket, and made sure it was connected again before turning on the device. "So far, so good," he exhaled as the lens began to glow with a muted orange iridescence.

Closing his left eye, he looked through the device, waiting for the image to settle down through a helter-skelter of static. "I think it's OK . . . yeah, it's OK . . . it's working," he told Chester as he got to his feet. The headset revealed the full extent of the fungal shelf to him as if it was bathed in a citrus glow.

"Chester, you look really weird," he chuckled as he surveyed his orange-hued friend through the lens. "A bit like a badly bruised grapefruit . . . with an Afro!"

"Don't worry 'bout me . . . ," Chester said impatiently. "Just tell me what you can see."

"Well, this place is flat, and it's pretty big," Will observed. "It looks sort of like . . . well . . . ," he hesitated, searching for a comparison, ". . . as if we're on a beach right after the tide's gone out. Sort of smooth, but with a few dunes."

They were on a gently rolling plateau that was perhaps the size of two football fields, although it was difficult to tell precisely how far it extended.

Will spotted a large section of rock a little distance away and, with several massive strides, leaped onto it. With the reduced gravitational pull, it had hardly taken any effort.

"Yes, I think I can see the edge over there. . . . It's a hundred feet or so away." From his elevated position he could just make out where the fungal growth ended. But the lens gave him the ability to see much farther than this, into the titanic void of the Pore itself. He could even make out its far wall, which appeared craggy, and shone as if water was running down it. "Chester, we fell down *one* almighty hole!" he whispered as the sight brought home to him the scale of the Pore. He was struck with the thought that it must be rather like glimpsing the sheer face of Mount Everest through the window of a passing airplane.

Then Will turned his attention to what was above them. "And I reckon we've got another ledge right over us." Chester squinted up at where his friend was looking, but nothing was visible to him through the heavy, all-enveloping blanket of darkness. "It's not as big as the one we're on," Will informed him. "And it's got holes in it." As he examined these, he wondered if they were the result of rocks and boulders slamming into it and tearing large rents.

"Anything else?" Chester asked.

"Hang on," Will said as he moved his head to get a better view.

"Yes?" Chester pressed. "What can you —?"

"Just be quiet for a second, will you?" Will said distractedly as a series of objects caught his eye. They were regular and patently not formed by nature, not even by the strange forces of subterranean nature that never ceased to surprise him. They just didn't fit in. "There's something very odd up there," he said quickly as he pointed.

"Where?" Chester asked.

"There, right on the edge of the shelf."

Several seconds passed as the view through Will's lens fizzled with static, then cleared down again. "Yes, there are loads of them. They look like . . ." He trailed off, sounding unsure of himself.

"Well?" Chester prompted.

"From what I can see they could be nets, in some sort of frames," Will said. "Which means we might not be alone down here," he added, "however far we've fallen."

Chester absorbed this piece of information, then blurted, "Do you think it's the Styx?" He was suddenly terrified that they might be in danger again.

"I don't know, but there's . . . ," Will began, then his voice dried up.

"What?" Chester asked.

When Will finally spoke again, it was difficult for Chester to hear him. "I think there's a body in one of them," he murmured.

Guessing what might be coming next, Chester didn't speak, just watched as Will began to tremble.

"Oh God. I think Cal's up there," Will said, staring in horror at the body spread-eagled on the net that Chester had no way of seeing.

"Uh, Will," Chester said tentatively.

"Yes?"

"It might not be Cal — it might be Elliott."

"Could be, but it looks like Cal," Will said haltingly.

"Whoever it is, we still need to search for the other one. If it isn't Elliott, she might still be —" Chester swallowed the last word, but Will was only too aware what it was intended to be.

"Alive," he said. He wheeled around to face Chester, breathing fast with emotion. "Listen to us! We're talking about living and dying as if we're discussing pass-or-fail exams or something. All this is messing with our heads."

Chester tried to interrupt, but Will wasn't to be stopped.

"My brother's probably up there, and he's dead. And my dad, Uncle Tam, Granny Macaulay. . . . they're all dead, too. Everyone around us dies. And we just carry on as if it's quite normal. What have we become?"

Chester had weathered such outbursts before. He yelled at Will.

"There's nothing we can do about any of that now! If those twins had got their stinking hands on us, we'd be dead, too, and we wouldn't be having this half-arsed conversation!" His raised voice resounded around the place as Will watched him, startled by his friend's precipitant anger. "Now get down from there and help me to find the one person who might just get us home!"

Will considered Chester in silence, then jumped down. "Yes, you're right," he said, adding, "as usual."

As they made their way across the fungus, the prospect of actually finding Elliott filled them both with unremitting dread.

"This is where I hit the deck," Chester said, pointing at the place where he had landed. Dropping down into a squat, Chester began to tug at the rope, which, unless it had snapped, would lead them to Elliott. As he yanked at it, it broke a line in the surface of the fungus, and both of them followed it reluctantly.

Before they knew it they came upon her. She had landed on her side just as Will had done, and her slight form had penetrated deep into the fungus.

"Oh, no. I think her face is buried in the stuff!" Chester flung himself down and tried to pull her head around so her nose and mouth weren't obstructed by the fungus. "Quick! She might not be able to breathe!"

"Is she . . . ?" Will asked from the other side of her body.

"Can't tell," Chester replied. "Help me get her out!"

Chester began to heave her up, and Will took hold of one of her legs. With a loud *slurp* she came loose.

"No!" Chester shouted as he saw the state of her arm. It was clear she had refused to let go of her rifle, with dire consequences when she'd slammed into the fungus. The rifle strap was wrapped around her forearm, which was horribly twisted. "Her arm's totally wrecked."

"Definitely broken," Will agreed hollowly as he cleared the fungal gunk away from her face, picking the remaining fibers from her lips and nostrils. "But she's alive. She's still breathing," he told Chester, who didn't seem to be able to take his eyes off the mangled limb. Nudging him aside, Will gently unwound the rifle strap from around Elliott's arm.

"Do be careful," Chester urged in a croak.

Will handed him the rifle, then undid the rope around Elliott's waist and slid her rucksack off her back, pulling her undamaged arm from the straps first. "Let's get her under cover," he said as he lifted the girl and carried her over to the cave.

They laid her down on some spare clothes from the backpack. She was breathing regularly, but out cold.

"What do we do now?" Chester asked, still eyeing her twisted arm.

"I don't know. Wait for her to wake up, I suppose," Will replied with a shrug, then sighed. "I'm going to see to Cal," he said abruptly.

"Will, why don't you just leave him?" Chester suggested. "It won't make any difference now."

"I can't do that — he's my brother," Will said, and left the cave.

Will walked around for a while, surveying the ledge directly above until he had located one of the larger holes. Then he readied himself and jumped at it. On any other occasion, the fact that he was shooting through the air like a human cannonball would have filled him with awe. But now he didn't give it more than a passing thought — what he was about to do blotted everything else from his mind.

As he soared through the hole in the shelf, he realized that he'd overdone it, and his momentum was carrying him too far. He was on a trajectory that was taking him high above the shelf.

"Whoaaaaaa!" he shouted in alarm, and began to windmill his arms in an effort to bring himself down again.

But gradually his trajectory dropped off, and he began to descend. He spotted he was heading straight for a patch of some mastlike structures that stood proud of the fungus's surface. They were thick stalks some nine to twelve feet in height, with what resembled basketballs on the ends. A voice from some remote part of his brain helpfully informed him they were "fruiting bodies"— he seemed to recall they were organs to do with fungal reproduction. But it wasn't the time to dwell on half-remembered facts from his biology lessons. As he flew straight into the midst of them, he desperately grabbed at the rubbery stalks. Although they either broke off at their bases or the basketballs on their tips detached and whizzed away in all directions, at least they helped to slow his progress.

As the last stalk came away in his hands and he cleared the patch, he finally touched down. But it was no better — he was skiing on his knees across the greasy surface on a course that was taking him toward the edge. There were no more fruiting bodies in the way to help him, so he threw himself on his chest, digging his fingers and the toe caps of his boots into the skin of the fungus. He howled, imagining he was about to shoot straight off the gently curved edge of the shelf and back into the Pore, but managed to bring himself to a halt just in the nick of time.

"Blimey, that was close," he puffed as he held absolutely still. It *had* been close — his head was far enough over the rim of the fungus that he could clearly see the one he'd just left below him.

He pulled himself back from the edge and, for a while, just lay there. "Come on," he said eventually, and got to his feet. He took very careful, controlled paces over to the frames. He certainly wasn't going to make any sudden movements after that last jaunt.

The frames were simple rectangular structures, roughly the size of goalmouths, made from what appeared to be the trunks of young trees about four inches in diameter, bound together at each corner. If they were made from wood — he couldn't tell for certain — it was blackened and charred as if it had been burned in a fire. A mesh of thick strands loosely woven together formed the netting strung between the frames. They felt rough and fibrous to the touch, and he suspected they were the skin of some plant, possibly even of the giant fungus itself. As he walked along the line of nets, he could see that many of them were torn, but the one Cal was hung up in seemed to be in reasonable shape.

Stopping before his brother's body, he forced himself to look at it, then quickly averted his eyes. He bit his lip agitatedly, wondering if he should just go back to Chester. After all, he was right: Nothing Will did now would change anything. He could just leave the body where it was.

He heard Tam's booming voice as clearly as if the big man was standing right beside him. "Brothers, hah, brothers, my nephews." Tam had uttered these words when Will and Cal, after so many years apart, and one unaware of the other's existence, had been reunited in the Jerome family home back in the Colony.

And just before Tam had sacrificed his life so Will and Cal could escape, Will had made him a promise to look out for his newfound sibling.

"I'm so sorry, Tam," Will said aloud. "I couldn't keep it. I . . . I let you down."

You did your best, m'boy. You couldn't have done anything more, came Uncle Tam's gravelly tones. Although Will knew that the voice was only his imagination working overtime, it gave him a measure of comfort.

Still he made no move toward Cal's body, debating whether to just leave it be.

No, I can't do that. It wouldn't be right, Will told himself. With a sigh, he took a step toward the net and began to test whether the frame would take his weight. It creaked a little as he pushed on it with his foot, but it seemed to be firmly secured to the fungus. He got down on all fours and moved carefully over the netting. Cal was in one of the far corners. As the fiber strips shifted under Will's weight, he took it even more slowly. It was daunting because the frame projected so far out into the void. He tried to reassure himself that even if it did give way, then he'd simply drop down to the shelf below. If he was lucky.

He edged closer to his brother's body. Cal was on his front — Will was so grateful that he was spared the sight of his face. The rope was still tied around the boy's waist, and Will took hold of it and reeled in the loose end. A quick inspection revealed that it had snapped clean through. To divert himself from the enormity of his brother's corpse being only inches away, Will began to piece together what must have happened. Cal's body had evidently been caught in the net, and the rest of them — he, Chester, and Elliott — had swung like a daisy chain onto the ledge below. Cal had acted like an anchor, and he might very well have saved their lives by preventing them from falling farther.

Will held the tattered end of the rope, at a total loss what to do next. With his head and one leg at awkward angles, his brother looked so small and broken. Will reached out and gingerly touched the skin of the boy's forearm with the tip of a single finger, then quickly withdrew his hand again. It felt cold and hard, and nothing like Cal.

Will's head was filled with vivid flashes of so many moments, as if various scenes from a film had been randomly spliced together. He remembered Cal's laughter as they watched the Black Wind from his bedroom window. This was followed by a flood of other memories from the months they'd spent together in the Colony, including the moment right at the beginning when Cal and his father had collected Will from the Hold to take him home and meet the family he never knew existed.

"I've let them all down," Will said, in a tense, muted growl through his clenched teeth. "Uncle Tam, Granny Macaulay, even my real mother," he added, remembering how they'd had to leave Sarah, mortally wounded, in the windswept tunnel. "And now you, Cal," he said to the body, which swayed ever so slightly as a breeze came in small bursts. Beside himself with grief, tears gushed from Will's eyes in a torrent.

"I'm sorry, Cal," he sobbed over and over again. He heard a low howl and, blinking away his tears, he peered down at the ledge below. Bartleby's eyes shone like two polished copper plates — they were fixed on Will. He was not alone in mourning the boy's death.

What do I do now? Will thought to himself, then asked the question out loud.

"Tell me what I should do, Tam?" This time there was no response from his imagination, but Will knew instinctively what his uncle would have done in the same situation. And Will had to be practical, just like Tam, even if it was the last thing he felt like doing. "Check if there's anything we need," Will mumbled, and without disturbing Cal's body he began to search it. He found the boy's penknife, a bag of peanuts, and some spare luminescent orbs. In one of the pockets, he discovered an unopened but misshapen bar of Caramac. It was clear from the way it had melted that the boy had been carrying it around with him for some time.

"My favorite! Cal, you were holding out on me!" Will said, grinning through his grief.

He tucked the bar away in his jacket pocket and, not wanting to turn the body over, he cut the strap to the water bladder that was over Cal's shoulder and reknotted it so he would be able to carry it. Then he unbuckled the shoulder straps of Cal's backpack and removed it. As he lifted it to one side, he noticed there were holes in it. Many small holes were punched into the canvas and, as he touched one of these, he realized with a start that his hands were covered in a sticky darkness. It was Cal's blood. Will quickly rubbed his palms on his pants. That did it — there was no way he was going to search the rest of the body.

He remained with Cal for some time, simply staring at him. Every so often pieces of rock would come whistling down the middle of the Pore in a hail, or a sudden flurry of water in shape-shifting showers would flash past, sparkling like earth-bound stars. Except for these occasional interruptions, all was so quiet and still there on the edge of the fungus.

Then came a sodden *thump* from somewhere behind him on the shelf. The whole ledge seemed to flex and judder, and the net shook beneath him. "What the heck was that? A rock?" Will exclaimed, looking nervously around. He quickly concluded that an object with some mass must have slammed into the surface of the fungus, the shock of the impact rippling through the whole shelf. It was enough to get him moving again — this was no place to hang around for long. There and then, he made up his mind what he should do next. He braced himself by grabbing hold of the netting with his hands, and he used his feet to maneuver Cal over to the very edge of the frame.

Peering down into the Pore, Will shivered as he imagined himself falling into it. Then he glanced at Cal's corpse. "You never did like heights, did you?" he whispered.

He took a deep breath and shouted, "Good-bye, Cal!" With a hard shove from both feet, he propelled his brother's body over the edge of the frame. He watched as it shot across into the Pore, hardly losing any height as it went. Like a burial in deep space, it was slowly rolling over and over in the low grav-ity, the rope trailing around it. It only began to tip downward when it was some distance away. Then its trajectory dipped, and it was falling and falling, and Will watched as it became a tiny dot that was finally swallowed by the murky darkness below.

"Good-bye, Cal," Will shouted once more, his voice also lost in the immensity of the Pore, with barely an echo from the other side. Bartleby wailed a high and pitiful wail, as if he knew that his master was on his way to his final resting place.

Filled with the bleakest feelings of despair and loss, Will turned and began to clamber over the net to return to the fungal ledge, tugging the backpack behind him. All of a sudden he froze absolutely still.

He closed his eyes and pressed his hand to his forehead, as if he was experiencing a stabbing pain. But it wasn't that sort of pain.

"No. Shut up," he gasped. "Don't!"

Something in his head was telling him that he should follow his brother, telling him that he should jump. At first he thought it was his intense guilt over Cal's untimely death — his guilt that he might have saved Cal if he had acted differently. It also occurred to him that he'd suddenly developed a fear of heights, just like Cal. But he quickly realized it was neither guilt nor fear compelling him. It was something else altogether. The voice in his head had become an impulse, which was so overpowering Will was barely able to resist it.

As if he was outside his own body and calmly looking on, Will had a vivid picture of himself carrying out the act. From this third-person perspective, stripped of all feeling, of all emotion, chucking himself over the brink made such perfect sense.

It would be the answer to everything, a clean end to so much unhappiness and uncertainty. Still frozen on the net, Will battled the impulse, frantically trying to oppose it.

"Stop it, you idiot!" he pleaded through tightly drawn lips. He had no idea what was happening to him. As the contest raged inside his head, his whole body was shaking. The urge was assuming control of his limbs, making them move, and he was slowly but surely turning back toward the abyss. But Will still seemed to have some say in the matter, and kept his hands clenched — they were grasping the net so hard they hurt, but at least they were anchoring him in place. At least he still seemed to be able to do *something* to stop this madness.

"For God's sake!" he screamed at himself, shaking more than ever. All of a sudden, he thought of Chester, waiting for him below. Whether it was this or because he'd won the raging contest in his head, he found his limbs were under his control and responding to him again. He released his grip on the net and crawled back to the ledge in a frantic hurry, terrified that his victory was only temporary.

He kept crawling for some distance before he allowed himself to get gingerly to his feet. He was drenched in a cold sweat, and very frightened indeed. He couldn't understand what had come over him — never before had he been subject to such an irrational impulse as that, an impulse to take his own life.

Below, Chester had been mopping Elliott's face with one of his spare shirts. Then, as he moistened her lips with a little water, she mumbled something. He nearly dropped the canteen. Her eyes were half open and she was trying to speak.

"Elliott," Chester said, taking hold of her hand.

She was still attempting to say something, but her voice was so weak it was barely audible.

"Don't try to talk. Everything's OK — you just need to rest," he said as reassuringly as he could, but she pursed her mouth as if she was angry. "What is it?" he asked.

Her eyes slid shut as she lost consciousness again.

Just then Will ambled through the curtain of falling water and into the cave.

"Elliott woke up for a second. . . . She said a few words," Chester told him.

"That's good," Will replied listlessly.

"Then she just blacked out again," Chester said. He noticed the change that had come over his friend. "Will, you don't look so good yourself. Was it awful . . . with Cal?"

Will was moving as if he was absolutely drained and about to drop.

"Elliott will be all right, Chester. She's tough," Will replied, sidestepping his friend's question. "We'll fix up her arm," he said, as he delved into Cal's rucksack. He lobbed the water bladder to Chester, followed by the packet of peanuts. "Better add these to our food stores," he said, then staggered over to the wall and slid down against it.

Bartleby wandered in through the waterfall and glanced at each of the boys in turn with his morose eyes, as if to make sure neither of them was Cal. He shook the droplets of water from his sagging skin, then made straight for Will, curling up beside him with his huge head resting on his thigh. Will absently rubbed the cat's massive forehead — it was the first time Chester had seen him show any real affection toward the animal.

"You didn't answer me," Chester said. "About Cal?"

"I saw to him," his friend replied inexpressively, before he closed his eyes with a long sigh, leaving Chester the only one awake.

3

AS HE TURNED a corner into a cavern, Drake came to a stop at the sight of a single soldier. "Blast!" he mouthed, quietly pulling back into the tunnel again.

From the gray-green uniform, Drake recognized that the soldier was Styx Division. It wasn't routine for these men to be deployed in the Deeps, their principal role being to patrol the borders of the Colony and keep an eye on the Eternal City. But in the past month, he told himself, nothing had been *routine*. Not only had trainloads of the fearsome Limiters pitched up at the Miners' Station, but a couple of Division regiments had also been drafted in to support them. He'd never seen so much activity.

Lowering himself to the ground, Drake nosed around the corner so he could take another look at the soldier. The man's back was to Drake, and he was resting his rifle stock on the ground. The soldier was hardly being vigilant, but it would still be too risky to tackle him. Drake grimaced. This was a real nuisance. It would cost him at least another hour if he was forced to turn back and take another lava tunnel to get to the Great Plain.

Then an engine suddenly revved, filling the cavern with

thunderous noise. Drake slid farther around so he could see what was going on. One of the Coprolites' huge excavation machines sat beyond the soldier, smoke streaming from the multiple exhausts at the rear and forming a black pall in which Drake could just about make out some bulbous forms. Coprolites. So the soldier was overseeing a mining operation.

Drake knew it was crucial that he destroy the test cells in the Bunker before the Styx reached them. Time was critical. He had no alternative but to deal with the soldier.

He rose slowly to his feet and, staying close to the cavern wall, crept toward the man. Helped by both the roaring engine and the fact that the soldier's attention was on a Coprolite emerging from the excavation machine, Drake managed to reach the man without detection. He dropped him with a single blow to the nape of the neck. Drake immediately swooped on the soldier's rifle. Pulling back the bolt to make sure it was loaded, he allowed himself a smile. He felt better now that he had a proper weapon in his hands again and didn't have to rely on his rather rudimentary stove guns.

As he slung the rifle over his shoulder, he turned to the four Coprolites standing in a group not far from where the Styx soldier had fallen. Just as he expected, they hadn't shown the smallest reaction to what he'd just done. They were completely motionless, with the exception of one who was bobbing his head in a slow rhythm, much like the bough of a tree caught in a breeze. It never failed to amaze Drake how passive and detached these gentle beings were. Master miners, they toiled to supply the Colony with coal, iron ore, and other raw materials vital to it, and in return the Styx treated them like slaves, chucking the odd consignment of fruits and vegetables their way and providing them with just enough luminescent orbs to stay alive. These orbs were slotted into place around the eye openings in their thick mushroom-colored dust suits, with the result that one could tell precisely where they were looking. And at that moment, it was anywhere but the unconscious Limiter, or Drake, or the huge machine they had apparently been about to board.

"Make yourselves scarce, guys!" Drake yelled above the noise of the engine. "Go back to your settlement. The Styx will know that a renegade did this," he explained, waving a hand toward the unconscious soldier, "so there won't be any reprisals against you. Just go home!"

Drake swung around to the steam-driven vehicle. It was a huge beast with a cylindrical hull constructed from thick sections of armored steel. Propelled by means of the three solid rollers underneath it, at the front end was a massive diamond-edged cutting wheel some thirty feet in diameter, which enabled it to slice a tunnel through the hardest of rocks.

The rear hatch was open. As Drake considered it, an idea began to form in his head. He urgently needed to reach the center of the Bunker, where he knew the test cells were situated. And that would take him quite some time on foot.

"I wonder . . . ," he said out loud. Although he'd never piloted one of these vehicles before, he had seen inside them several times, and the controls didn't look too demanding. Plus, this one was fired up and ready to go — the four-Coprolite team had clearly been about to leave when he'd clobbered their Styx overseer.

He walked toward the hatch and, stepping inside, glanced around the interior. It was all made from bare, beaten metal, dark with grime except for the areas that were regularly used, which shone like burnished steel. His eyes settled on the steering levers and the various dials beyond them.

"Worth a shot," he said, and was about to close the hatch when a set of bulbous fingers gripped the edge. The hatch swung back. A Coprolite stood there, his eye-beams shining directly at Drake.

"What!" Drake exclaimed.

This was most unusual. Although the suited figure before him looked rather sinister, with its enlarged limbs and glowing eyes, Drake didn't feel threatened. It didn't even enter his head that a Coprolite might be about to turn on him. He knew them better than that — they were incapable of hurting anybody. In any case, he'd done his very best to help them out over the years, passing them over any surplus luminescent orbs that came his way in exchange for food. Both he and the Coprolites knew this was a token transaction, because he really didn't need their food, while they most definitely needed the extra orbs.

As the Coprolite stood there, his hand still gripping the hatch, another of the strange beings joined him, then the remaining two, so that the whole team was present. Like a group of automatons that had been issued a silent command, they all began to advance at the same time.

"What are you doing? It's not safe for you here!" Drake yelled, but drew to the side, since they seemed intent on entering the vehicle.

After the last Coprolite had closed and locked the rear hatch, Drake watched as they took up their positions. Two of them slid into the seats on either side of the hatch and strapped themselves in. The other two padded to the front of the vehicle, and one of them turned to Drake. He recognized it was the Coprolite who had been bobbing his head — he was a few inches taller than the others. "You shouldn't be here. It's too risky," Drake repeated, but the Coprolite placed his bulbous hand on the driver's seat and spun it around, as if offering it to Drake.

Drake shook his head. This was unprecedented. Apart from the fact that Coprolites always kept to themselves, maintaining an almost religious neutrality, they knew too well that the consequences of aiding and abetting a renegade would mean certain death for themselves, and possibly retribution against their entire settlement. These four were endangering their womenfolk and their children. Yet they seemed to have wordlessly decided to help him!

Shrugging, Drake went to the driver's seat and eased himself into it while the larger Coprolite took the copilot's seat beside him. The second Coprolite seated himself behind what appeared to be, from the strange map spread open on a shelf before him and the row of compasses arranged at head height, a navigator's console.

Drake hesitated as he regarded the array of controls, then pushed down on the largest of the pedals by his feet. The engine revved, but nothing happened. The Coprolite by his side leaned over to push in and twist a rod on the dashboard, and the vehicle began to creep forward.

"OK!" Drake shouted over the noise of the engine, and depressed the accelerator a degree as he pulled down on the left steering lever. The vehicle began to turn ponderously. As its floodlights lit a stretch of cavern before him, he aimed at the lava tube that would take them out onto the Great Plain. He could barely see where he was going as he squinted through the several inches of pure crystal windshield. This was made doubly difficult, not only because it was badly scratched and covered in dust, but also because his view was limited by the massive diamond-edged cutting wheel mounted on the front. Several times he scraped the vehicle against the side of the lava tube, throwing himself and the Coprolites around in their seats.

Then as he cleared the lava tube and entered the Great Plain, he floored the accelerator. The vehicle lurched forward — he was surprised how fast it could traverse the moonscapelike terrain of the plain. Even over the din of the engine, Drake could hear boulders splintering as the three rollers crushed them to powder. And from the waves of intense heat on the back of his neck, he knew that the two Coprolites at the rear were continually opening the doors of the firebox to feed it with fuel and to stoke it.

After traveling a few miles, there came a sharp *crack*. Something had struck the crystal windshield. He heard the sound again, but this time the outer hull was hit, making it ring like a dampened bell. Drake realized they were being shot at.

In the headlights, Drake caught sight of a Limiter, his high-powered rifle raised. Drake laughed — it was like a mosquito trying to get the better of an elephant. He yanked down on one of the levers to alter course toward the Limiter, who loosed off another shot. But he didn't look quite so confident once he realized that the huge machine was bearing directly down on him. He turned to run, and run he did, frequently changing direction like a chased hare as he tried to escape.

Drake wasn't about to let him off that lightly. He'd already mastered the steering levers, and it was no effort to keep after the Limiter, who, growing ever more frantic, tripped and fell. Drake drove straight for him, but just at the last moment the

Limiter rolled out of the vehicle's path. His rifle wasn't so fortunate, though, and was squashed flat against the bedrock.

"Your lucky day, matey!" Drake yelled, speeding away from the Limiter as he heaved on a steering lever to get back on course for the Bunker.

A mile farther on, Drake caught his first glimpse of the Bunker wall, and very soon it was all he could see through the windshield — a thick gray ribbon stretching across the plain. He eased off the throttle, drawing up just before the wall. Uncertain what to do next, he glanced at the Coprolite beside him. The man leaned over and pushed home another rod.

The whole vehicle shook as the cutting wheel mounted on its front began to slowly rotate.

The vibrations grew and grew, so much so that Drake's vision became blurred. As the wheel reached its maximum revolutions, the Coprolite pointed at the accelerator. Drake gently depressed it, and the vehicle edged forward. The spinning wheel touched the concrete wall, its diamond-tipped teeth beginning to bite into it and spewing out huge torrents of dust. Drake watched in fascination as the wheel sliced through the wall like a hot knife through butter. Once the teeth encountered the iron reinforcement inside the concrete, the machine's incredible power was fully revealed — massive chunks of the wall were simply ripped out.

It took five minutes to penetrate the outer wall of the Bunker, and then the cutting wheel made short work of the internal partitions, slicing through them as if they were made from paper. When he thought he was far enough in, Drake steered the vehicle into a corridor and powered down, then unstrapped himself and went to the rear hatch. As he opened it, he was able to survey the full extent of the devastation the vehicle had left in its wake. The columns supporting the ceiling had been demolished, and great slabs of concrete had fallen in. At least there was no easy way for the Styx to follow after him. He turned to the Coprolites.

"I don't know how to thank you," he said.

One of them by the firebox nodded at him. Drake couldn't suppress a chuckle. For a Coprolite, that was talkative. He saluted them and then disembarked.

It did not take him long to locate the corridor of test cells that Cal and Elliott had first stumbled across. The bright lights made him blink. In complete contrast to the rest of the Bunker, which had fallen into disrepair after decades of disuse, the room was clean and startlingly white. As he walked through the central area, some thirty by sixty feet in size, he could see that along both sides were rows of doors. A quick glance through their glass inspection windows revealed that no one had been left alive in the test cells. Putrefying corpses lay in pools of their own fluid. Drake shook his head. The Styx had certainly found what they'd been looking for — if these poor guinea pigs were anything to go by, the Dominion virus was lethal and a very real threat to the Topsoil population.

The thought occurred to Drake that he could try to extract a viable specimen of the virus from one of the corpses — armed with this, it would be possible to prepare a vaccine, and the Styx plot would be thwarted. But all of the cell doors were sealed around their edges by thick welds and, short of blowing one of them open, he couldn't see how else he could gain entry.

And if he was to attempt this, apart from the fact he himself would be infected, he would be responsible for releasing the virus into the atmosphere. Then, too, there was the risk that the air currents might carry it Topsoil. He shook his head, hastily abandoning the idea, and instead investigated the laboratory equipment on a bench against the far wall of the room. There wasn't anything there that resembled viral samples.

"No time," Drake said to himself, mindful that the Styx might be along at any moment. He used all the explosives in his satchel, planting charges at the base of each of the cell doors. He wasn't going to take any chances — the heat of the ensuing firestorm would kill any remaining virus and sterilize the area, quite apart from the fact that the cells would be buried under thousands of tons of concrete and rock.

He set the fuses and ran for it. He was well away from the area when the charges went off, but it was still enough to suck the breath from his lungs and knock him off his feet. He didn't care — he was just relieved that he'd achieved his objective. Assuming Sarah Jerome had taken care of the only other source of Dominion when, as her dying act, she'd swept the Rebecca twins over with her into the Pore, the threat was now neutralized. Neutralized, that was, until the Styx could locate further lethal viral strains in the Eternal City, or develop an alternative in their underground laboratories.

Drake crossed the Great Plain on foot, taking just under two days to reach the Miners' Station, where he stowed away in one of the empty cars halfway down the train. He didn't have long to wait before it left — a few soldiers from the Division boarded the guard's car and it heaved out of the station. He was ready with the Limiter rifle if any of them decided to carry out a snap inspection of the rest of the train, but they never came. That was unusually sloppy of them.

And when the train drew into the Colony station, Drake couldn't believe his luck. As he clambered out of the mammoth car and dropped by the trackside, he was stunned that the portal was completely unattended. So it was child's play to get into the streets of the Colony. But once there, he found that a thick black smoke permeated the air. As he entered the huge expanse of the South Cavern, he was met by a strange sight. Broad columns of smoke rose up right in the middle of it, glowing with a fiery redness that illuminated the rock canopy high above.

"The Rookeries," Drake said to himself. It was clear that something earth-shattering was taking place, and he had to see it for himself. He stole closer, until he was at the outskirts.

Legions of soldiers from the Styx Division bordered the area, brandishing burning torches. Drake saw figures frantically trying to fight their way out of the Rookeries and through the solid cordon of soldiers, and heard the screams as they were slaughtered. Again and again the desperate occupants of the Rookeries, their clothes burning and their faces blackened with smoke, attempted to get through. But each time one broke from an alleyway, they were brutally cut down by the soldiers, who were wielding their scythes like the farmers of old, harvesting corn.

Other Styx, in their long black coats and white collars, strode imperiously behind the lines of soldiers, shouting orders. The systematic destruction of the Rookeries was in progress — for centuries the Styx had allowed the rebels and malcontents of the Colony's population to persist in their self-contained ghetto, but now the decision had evidently been taken to eradicate this "underbelly." Drake watched as a four-story building collapsed in on itself, and in the avalanche of old masonry he glimpsed human forms . . . worst of all, children . . . their small limbs waving helplessly as they were crushed by the cascades of limestone blocks.

There, hidden in the shadows, this toughest of men, who had survived years of hardship, both at the hands of the Styx and in the Deeps, broke down and wept. The inhumanity of what he was witnessing was almost too much for him to bear. And there was absolutely nothing he could do, just one man against so many Styx, to stop the atrocity.

With the radio blaring a Turkish station and the maxed-out heater filling the interior with scorching warmth, the minicab rocketed through the streets. As if the driver knew the synchronization of every set of traffic lights, time and time again he managed to squeeze through on the amber or just as they'd turned red. And he didn't even seem to notice the numerous speed bumps in the roads, with the result that Mrs. Burrows was bounced in her seat as surely as if she was on a runaway camel.

A heavy rain was falling, but she wound the window all the way down and leaned her head against the door frame so that it caught the rushing air. As she relished the breeze and the raindrops on her face, she let her unfocused gaze skim over the shiny-wet pavements. She lost herself in the random lines and patches of light reflected in them from the shop fronts, not really thinking about anything in particular, but feeling a sense of liberation after her time in Humphrey House.

She looked up, seeing where they were with some surprise. "Highfield?"

"Yes, the roads, they are clear tonight," the driver commented.

"I used to live here," she replied, as they sped past the turn-off that would have taken her to Broadlands Avenue.

"Used to?" the driver inquired. "No more home?"

"No," she said.

She'd sold the house at the peak of the market, and it had provided her with a tidy sum to live on. Although she no longer owned the property, she felt an unexpected tug to see it, to go back and look at the old place one last time. Even though that chapter in her life had ended, there was so much left unresolved. "No more home," Mrs. Burrows whispered, telling herself that it wasn't the time to indulge herself with a visit. She had more pressing matters to attend to.

As they drove down Main Street, there were the shops she knew so well. She saw the dry cleaner's, and the newsstand where they had bought their papers and magazines. Then she spotted that the window of Clarke's had been boarded up, as if it was no longer in business. The old-fashioned fruit and vegetable shop had been a firm favorite of Rebecca's, something Mrs. Burrows always thought rather odd when there was a perfectly good supermarket that would do home deliveries. Finally, they passed the museum where her husband had worked, but Mrs. Burrows looked in the opposite direction. For her it was a place of failure, a monument to her stifled expectations.

The cab left Highfield and very soon had reached the junction with the North Circular road. A battered white car with the stereo at an impossible volume drew up beside them as they stopped for the light. It was crammed full of passengers, and through one of the open windows a young girl fixed Mrs. Burrows with an insolent stare. Probably only two or three years older than Rebecca, the girl looked tired, with dark smudges under her eyes, and her shoulder-length hair was limp, as if badly in need of a wash. Her cold eyes were still fixed aggressively on Mrs. Burrows as she spat out a piece of chewing gum, which hit the door of the minicab.

"What you do, dirty pig!" the driver exclaimed loudly, flicking his hand at the girl. He revved the engine furiously. "I wouldn't let my little girl be doing thing like that."

The girl was still trying unsuccessfully to stare Mrs. Burrows down. "No, I wouldn't, either. I always know exactly where my daughter is — at home, safe and sound," she declared.

"Me, too, but these people have no respect," the driver said, leaning forward over his steering wheel to glare at the other car. "No respect," he repeated, as he floored the accelerator and cut off the white car, sounding his horn as he did so.

Forty minutes later, they had crossed the river and were several blocks from the housing projects where three massive apartment complexes dominated the landscape. Mrs. Burrows thought she could see which of the three Auntie Jean's flat was in, but every road they went down only seemed to take them farther away from it. The driver had given up using his *A to*

Z street guide, and was relying entirely on Mrs. Burrows to remember the way.

"This looks vaguely familiar," she said.

"South London. It all looks the same," the driver chuckled, shaking his head dismissively. "No, thank you for me."

"Wait a minute — I remember this — take a left here," Mrs. Burrows instructed him. "Yes, I'm pretty certain this is it," she said as she spotted the tower block that was indeed Mandela Heights. Then they turned down a cul-de-sac, and the minicab squealed to a halt.

"We are here," he announced.

Mrs. Burrows got out of the minicab and collected her bags from the trunk. Then she gave the driver a hugely over-generous tip.

"God bless you and all your family," he called after her as she lugged her bags into the entrance. She looked at the bank of buttons for the apartments, most of them vandal-ized, but then saw that the main doors were open, anyway. She went straight in and found, miracle upon miracle, that the elevator was working, though no less smelly than she remembered it. It shuddered up to the thirteenth floor and the doors scraped back.

"For goodness' sake!" Mrs. Burrows grumbled as she stepped over a pool of vomit directly outside the elevator.

She pressed the doorbell and waited. Then she tried again, ringing for longer this time. After a while there was a scuffling sound from behind the door, and Mrs. Burrows noticed that someone was looking at her through the peephole.

"Open up, will you, Jean!" Mrs. Burrows said to the

peephole. Still the door remained shut, so Mrs. Burrows simply left her finger on the button. It took several minutes before her sister finally wrenched open the door.

"Who the 'ell do you think you are?" she shouted, huffing furiously, the ever-present cigarette tucked in the corner of her mouth. She was wearing her old housecoat, and her gray hair was sticking up on one side as if she'd slept on it.

"Hello, Jean," Mrs. Burrows said.

Auntie Jean squinted at her, then shuffled a step back, as if this was the only way she could focus on the person standing there. "Celia! It's you!" she shouted, her mouth gaping so wide the cigarette spiraled from her lips and struck the bald carpet with a tiny display of red sparks.

"Well, can I come in, then?"

"Course, course you can." Her sister first had to extinguish the cigarette butt, which was burning a hole in her carpet. "'Ow d'you know I'd be in, anyway?"

"When do you ever go out, Jean?" Mrs. Burrows said as she picked up her bags. The hallway was cluttered with piles of discarded newspapers, as it always was, and the air smelled sour.

"You shoulda rung first, just in case," her sister said, then hacked loudly.

"I did. You hung up on me."

Auntie Jean seemed not to have heard this. "Fancy a cuppa?" she offered as they went into the kitchen. "Thought you were in that Herbert House place, with all them doctors? They let you out, then?"

"I decided it was time to leave," Mrs. Burrows said as she surveyed the appalling state of the kitchen. In the same breath, she asked, "I really thought Rebecca would've had this place spick-and-span by now. Where is she, anyway? In her room?"

Auntie Jean turned and blinked at her. "No," she said — only it sounded more like a combination of "No" and a surprised "Oh."

"What?"

"She's gone."

"What do you mean *she's gone?*" Mrs. Burrows's face blanched. She took a sudden step toward her sister, knocking a polished wooden bowl of half-rotted bananas and an over-flowing ashtray from the table.

"Took herself off yonks ago. Packed her bags and walked out, she did." Auntie Jean couldn't look her sister in the face, as if she knew she had done something wrong. "I'm sorry, Celia, but I want nothing more to do with 'er. Little guttersnipe ruined all me ciggies and poured me —"

"But, Jean!" Mrs. Burrows grabbed her sister and shook her. "You were supposed to be looking after her for me. For heaven's sake, she's only twelve years old! When and where did she go?"

Auntie Jean was slow in answering. "I told you — it was yonks ago. And I dunno where she went. I left a message with the woman from social services 'bout it, but she never called me back."

Mrs. Burrows released her sister and yanked one of the chairs from under the table, knocking more items to the floor. She sat down heavily, her mouth open, forming words but not actually saying anything.

Leaning against the sink, Auntie Jean was waving her hands

and burbling on when she stopped and said, "Then Will came by with his cousin."

Mrs. Burrows turned her head slowly toward her sister. "I'm sorry, did you just say *Will*? My son, *Will*?"

"Yes, 'e came by with 'is cousin. And they brought that lovely big pussycat, Bartleby, with 'em —"

"But Will's been missing for six months. You know that. There's a nationwide investigation going on for him and his friend Chester."

"Can't tell you 'bout no Chester, but all I can say is Will was 'ere 'bout two months ago. 'E wasn't well when 'e got 'ere, but that Cal — what a lovely boy — 'e nursed Will back to 'ealth. And Bartleby! Ain't never laid eyes on a big cat like that before, 'cept down the zoo."

"Big cat?" Mrs. Burrows said, without any emphasis. "Big cat?" She selected one of the many empty vodka bottles from the table and took it in her hand. She didn't speak for a while, simply staring at the silver-and-red label. In the silence, all that could be heard in the small room was a rattle, then a low hum, as the fridge's cooling system started up.

"It's funny, but our Bessie's been 'aving bother with 'er eldest, too. 'E 'ad a bit of an episode and . . ." Auntie Jean trailed off, realizing that her effort to divert Mrs. Burrows from the matter with family gossip wasn't going to pass muster.

Her eyes still locked on the silver-and-red label, Mrs. Burrows gave a small shake of her head, but remained silent. Auntie Jean grew increasingly agitated, until she suddenly blurted out, "Celia, speak to me! 'Ow d'you expect me to know 'e was still missing? Why ain't you saying nothing?"

Mrs. Burrows carefully replaced the empty bottle, sliding it back from the edge of the table as if it was a valuable ornament. She took in a deep breath and let it out slowly, then she raised her eyes to her sister.

"Because, Jean, right now I don't know whether I should call the police or . . . or whether I need to get you put away somewhere because you have so obviously lost the plot. Or maybe both."

Following the frantic messages Mrs. Burrows left at the Highfield police station, someone finally managed to track down DI Blakemore. He rang back, and Mrs. Burrows had a lengthy conversation with him, explaining what she'd just learned. In thirty minutes flat, he turned up with a second DI from the local police station and a team of forensic officers.

"Looks like someone's already started to strip this place apart" were his first words as he entered the hallway and surveyed the scattered letters and newspapers on the carpet.

"Oh, bloody brilliant," one of the forensic officers behind him muttered resentfully. "We've got a hoarder here, lads," he said to his colleagues. "Better call your wives and tell them you're going to be working late."

In seconds the police were searching everywhere, and Mrs. Burrows and her sister were carted off to the local station, where they were interviewed separately and both had to give statements.

It wasn't until late Sunday morning that they were brought back to the projects in a squad car. Quite a few of Auntie Jean's possessions had been bagged up and removed. The flat, although still in a state of disarray, actually looked considerably tidier than it had before the forensic team began to search it. At least the policemen had organized all the old newspapers and letters into piles and taken away the trash bags in the kitchen to check through their contents. Fingerprint powder had been left on most of the surfaces throughout the apartment, although one would be hard pressed to tell it apart from the dust that had been there before.

The two sisters, not bothering to remove their coats, flopped into the armchairs in the living room. They both looked exhausted.

"I'm dying for a gasper," Auntie Jean announced and, finding a packet close by, pulled out a cigarette and lit it. "Ah, that's better," she said after a couple of heavy puffs. With the cigarette clenched between her lips, she cast about until she found the TV remote. "'Ere you go," she said as she handed it to Mrs. Burrows, who took it from her automatically. "Watch whatever you like."

Mrs. Burrows's finger twitched over the buttons, but she didn't press any of them. "Now I've lost not only my husband but *both* my children. And the police think I'm responsible. They think I've done it."

Auntie Jean stuck out her chin as a cloud of smoke all but hid her face, "They can't think —"

"Oh, they do all right, Jean," Mrs. Burrows interrupted her loudly. "They asked me for a full confession. One of them even used the words 'spill the beans.' They've got some looney-tunes theory that my 'accomplices' kidnapped Will, but he came here after he managed to slip away from them. And don't ask me what they think I've done with Roger and Rebecca, or

Chester. I reckon they've got me down as Highfield's first serial killer!"

Auntie Jean tried to grunt with indignation, but it triggered a rather unpleasant hacking cough.

"Are you certain Will didn't mention anything at all about where he'd been?" Mrs. Burrows quizzed her after she'd managed to stop coughing.

"No, not a dickey bird. But wherever it was, I 'ad the feeling 'e was going back there," Auntie Jean said. "And 'e was taking the little lad, 'is cousin Cal, wiv 'im."

"I told you — there's no one on Roger's side of the family called Cal."

Auntie Jean blinked wearily. "Whatever you say," she mumbled. "I remember Cal didn't like it 'ere much — 'e really wanted to get down south again."

"Down south?" Mrs. Burrows repeated thoughtfully. "And you said this younger boy was the spitting image of Will?"

Auntie Jean nodded. "Peas in a pod."

Mrs. Burrows stared at the blank television screen as her mind swam with various explanations. "So, if the mystery woman who turned up at Humphrey House was Will's real mother, what if this other boy was his *brother*?" she posed.

Auntie Jean raised an eyebrow. "'Is brother?"

"Yes, why not?" Mrs. Burrows replied. "It's not out of the question. And you said Will was furious with Rebecca?"

"Oh yes," Auntie Jean said, ejecting a spout of smoke. "It was like 'e 'ated her, yet was a bit frightened of 'er, too."

Mrs. Burrows shook her head with a mystified expression. "I've got to get to the bottom of all this. It's like when I miss

73

the beginning of a movie, and I have to try to figure out what's already happened."

Auntie Jean mumbled something about needing a drink, then yawned loudly.

"And to figure out this particular story, I need to go back to where it all started," Mrs. Burrows announced as she rose to her feet. She contemplated the TV remote still in her hand. "And I certainly won't be needing *this*," she said as she chucked it into her sister's lap, then hurried from the room.

"Suit yerself," Auntie Jean grumbled, lighting another cigarette from the one that she hadn't even finished yet.

4

"**A HORSE MISUSED** on the road," the old Styx said as he bent over to examine the broad track the Coprolites' excavator had left on the ground. He followed the track with his eyes to the almost perfectly circular opening cut into the otherwise unbroken stretch of the Bunker wall. He stepped over the pieces of concrete scattered across the ground until he was close enough to touch the inside of the newly hewn passage with his gloved hand. Taking it away, he rubbed the dust between his fingertips.

A shadow glided from within the passage.

"The Coprolites would never do this of their own accord," the old Styx declared. "Would they, Cox?"

"Not in a million years," the hunched-over form agreed as it slipped, a little unwillingly, into the pool of light cast by the old Styx's lantern.

A Limiter marched purposefully down the passage. He drew to a halt and stood rigidly to attention.

"What's the position?" the old Styx asked him, switching to the nasal Styx language.

"A large explosion has caused a major collapse of the roof

over the cells and surrounding corridors. It could take several weeks to excavate them. But . . ."

"But what!" the old Styx barked impatiently.

The Limiter continued, now speaking even more rapidly. "The explosion originated by the test cells, so it's highly likely that the temperatures reached will have denatured any remaining Dominion germules," he reported.

The old Styx took a long breath, drawing it in through his tight mouth. "Then it's a waste of time. We won't find any Dominion virus there. Just leave it," he ordered.

Not able to understand the exchange but sensitive to the old Styx's reaction, Cox's pupil-less eyes rolled under the greasy hem of his hood. "Bad news?" he asked.

The old Styx took another breath and reverted to English. "Yes. And I think we both know who did this."

"Drake," Cox answered. "'E needs to be taken care of, once and for all."

"You don't say," the old Styx growled.

"We should take a last look around," Will suggested as they lingered outside the cave. "Make sure we haven't missed anything."

"Sure," Chester said. Raising Elliott's rifle, he put his eye to the scope and scanned across the fungal shelf. "At least I can see now," he added, delighted that he had something to match Will's headset and was no longer reliant on the orbs and their limited illumination.

They each went their separate way on the outcrop, searching for any more of their belongings that might have been scattered across it when they fell. As Will stepped over the springy surface, he noticed that the cat was constantly by his side. With Cal gone, Bartleby seemed to have transferred his allegiance to him, and he felt unexpectedly comforted by the creature's constant presence.

"Found another rifle over here!" Chester reported to Will.

"Cool!" Will shouted back as he watched his friend tugging something from the fungus.

After a moment, Chester added, "The sight's broken, but otherwise it looks OK."

Will continued to search around, gathering up an empty water bottle, a length of rope, and a luminescent orb that demanded a little digging out. Then he glanced over to see where Chester had got to. He was on the far side of the ledge, doing strange bunny hops as he tried out the effects of the reduced gravity. It was a ridiculous sight as he sprang up and down.

"Hey, space cadet!" Will shouted a little testily. "I think we're all done here!"

"Yeah!" Chester called back, and then came hurtling over to him. Aided by his weightlessness, Chester half flew, half ran, covering the distance with all the grace of an uncoordinated ostrich. Laughing, he came to a skidding halt after one last immense leap. "This is so cool. You're absolutely right — it feels like we could actually be on the surface of the moon!"

"More like planet Zog," Will suggested.

"But just think about it, Will. It's as if we've got extra powers, like we're superheroes or something. We can jump over buildings in a single bound and all that stuff."

"Sure, if there were any," Will muttered, rolling his eyes at his friend as they ambled back to the cave.

Taking the greatest care, Will used a length of the rope he'd found to bind Elliott's arm across her chest, securing it the best he could. She didn't stir or make any sort of sound during the process.

"That should do it," he said. "Now let's pack everything up and get out of here." He was tying the flap on a side pocket of his rucksack when Chester spoke up.

"Will," he said, "I was sorting through Elliott's stuff, and there are loads of charges and stove guns in there."

"Yes. So?" Will replied, not sure where Chester was going with this.

"Well, it got me thinking . . . are there any of those fireworks left?"

"The Roman candles?"

"No, the rockets."

Will nodded. "Yes, two. Why?" he asked.

"I was just wondering . . . If we set them off, somebody at the top of the Pore might see them and send help down."

Will considered this for a moment. "I suppose it wouldn't do any harm to try. I don't know if they'll be any good, though — the damp might have got to them." He delved around in the bottom of his backpack and pulled out the pair of rockets, then sniffed at them. "They seem to be OK," he said. "I just hope the sticks are in one piece." He fished them out, only to find that one had been broken at the end and was a little short. "Bummer," he muttered, but nonetheless slotted both of them into the bodies of the rockets.

As he and Chester walked together toward the edge of the shelf, Will experienced a resurgence of the irrational urge he'd had before, when he'd been driven to throw himself into the Pore. He slowed to a snail's pace. Much as he wanted to tell Chester about what he was feeling, he decided that he didn't want to worry him needlessly. Besides, his friend would just think he was losing his marbles — which, Will thought, might actually be the case. What he really wanted more than anything else was to turn around and head back to the cave. Instead he dropped to his knees and began to crawl. It made him feel a little more secure and in control, as if the urge would have a harder job getting him right to the brink and making him leap headlong from it.

"What are you doing down there?" Chester asked, noticing his friend on the ground.

"You should watch out — there are really strong winds by the edge," Will lied. "Wouldn't stay up there if I were you."

Chester looked around, not feeling anything more than the occasional light breeze, and shrugged. "If you say so," he replied, and also got down onto his hands and knees.

As soon as they'd cleared the overhang of the ledge above, Will suggested they stop. It was as close as he wanted to get to the void. Using his penknife, he punctured the skin of the fungus twice. "We haven't got any bottles, so this will just have to do," he said. He stuck the rockets into the holes he'd made, ramming the sticks in straight so that both of them were standing vertically.

"Make sure you get the angles right," Chester advised.

"Thank you, Professor Hawking," Will replied in a good-natured way. He made some final adjustments to the rocket with the shorter stick, which looked a little lacking next to the other one. Satisfying himself that both were aiming up into the middle of the Pore, he went to light the shorter of the two, spinning the little wheel on the lighter.

"T minus five," he announced in his best attempt at an American accent.

"Imagine if someone spots them, and they come down to get us," Chester said, his voice brimming with optimism.

Will switched back to his normal voice. "Um, Chester, two things about that: The first is that we probably fell miles, so even if they did happen to see the flares, they'd have to climb down a crazy long way to reach us," he said, glancing at the gargantuan hole before resuming his efforts with the lighter. "The second is that we might get more than we've bargained for. It might be the Styx who notice them."

Chester moved closer to Will as if to stop him from lighting the rocket. "Well, in that case, maybe we shouldn't —"

"But I want to see just how far these things go," Will said with schoolboyish enthusiasm.

"Yeah, whatever, let's just go for it," Chester agreed.

"Not sure this is going to work, anyway," Will informed Chester as the blue touch paper refused to light. "Ah, got it!" The flame finally took.

He and Chester crawled back from the rocket, watching in expectation.

With a *whoosh*, the rocket blasted off, but before it had gone any distance it veered sharply toward the side of the Pore. The shelf over their heads made it impossible for them to see how far it had gone. There was a *bang*, then the vaguest suggestion of a red glow around the Pore.

"Useless!" Will exclaimed. "Hope we do better with this one."

He managed to light it almost right away, and it shot up into the darkness, climbing higher and higher so that the boys had to crane their heads back to follow its progress.

It was just like watching a rocket soar into the night sky on the earth's surface. It had gone many hundreds of yards when it exploded with a thunderclap, and livid colors cut into the pitch-black. Red, white, and blue starbursts appeared one after the other, affording the boys brief glimpses of the sides of the Pore way up above, the stark flashes of light revealing what could have been many more fungal outcrops projecting from its walls. As the veil of darkness returned to swamp everything, the echoes from the explosion ebbed for several seconds; then, once again, all the boys could hear was the occasional howl of the wind and the soft pattering of water.

Will flipped down the lens on his headset and turned to Chester. The boy looked crestfallen, as if the bright moment of excitement had brought home how incredibly far down in the earth they were and just how serious their situation was. Will patted him on the shoulder. "C'mon, you never know . . . somebody up there might have seen it."

Alerted by the first rocket, the Rebecca twins were slowly making their way to the edge of the small fungal shelf on which they'd landed. Dressed identically in the dun-colored camouflage jackets of the Limiters, they could only be differentiated by their gait: One was hobbling and being helped along by the other as they went.

"Fireworks?" the lame twin said, and they both came to a stop on the lip of the ledge. They peered up into the darkness, trying to see more. A minute later the second rocket exploded not far above their heads.

"Yes, fireworks," the lame twin concluded. For a few moments they both listened, staring up into the Pore for any further activity. There was nothing. "There's only one person stupid enough to do that."

"Yes, *th*ubtle . . . really *th*ubtle," the other twin agreed. "Our dear *brother* ha*th th*ent u*th* an invitation, and he'll live to regret it."

They laughed, but then the lame twin swung around to her sister, all trace of merriment vanishing from her face.

"You sound utterly ridiculous! What's wrong with you?" she said without an ounce of sympathy. "You're lisping."

Her sister immediately touched her mouth. "Think I've broken *th*ome teeth."

"Take your hand away and let me see," the lame sister ordered, shining the lantern into her twin's face. "Yes, your upper incisors have snapped off," she observed impassively.

Her sister ran a finger over the two stumps. "I must've knocked them on the way down," she said in annoyance. "I'll get them *th*een to when we're Top*th*oil again."

"*If*," the lame twin said poignantly. "And what's up with your arm?"

"I think it's been pulled out of its *th*ocket. You need to fix it."

"No problem. Let me get this out of the way first," she said. She took the scythe from her sister, who was holding it in the arm that hung limply by her side. For a moment the lame twin contemplated the evil-looking weapon; some ten inches in length, its highly polished surface was slick with fungus oil, so that the light reflecting from it had a grayish hue. Quite unexpectedly, she put the blade to her lips and kissed it.

"You little darling," she said affectionately, showing her gratitude to the weapon, which was the sole reason why she and her sister weren't still plummeting down the Pore. The lisping twin had managed to lash out and catch the edge of a fungal shelf with it as they had been falling. Although they'd been going so fast that the scythe had sliced clean through the fungus, it had been enough to deflect their course toward the outcrop below.

The quick-thinking maneuver had saved them, but it was not without its cost — the lisping girl's arm had had to bear not just her weight but her sister's, too. The force on it had been considerable.

The lame twin's show of affection was short-lived. "Yuck! That's revolting!" she cried, spitting because she'd got fungus juice on her lips. She reversed her grip on the scythe and then threw it with a deft flick of her wrist. Thirty or so feet away a small clump of fruiting bodies sprouted from the floor of the fungal shelf. The scythe turned end over end once during its flight, then sank deep into the ball on the end of one stalk. That the ball was roughly the same height as Will's face would have been if he'd been standing there was probably no coincidence.

"Good *tho*t," the lisping twin congratulated her sister as the fruiting body rocked backward and forward from the impact. "But there's no *if* about it. We are going to find a way out of thi*th* pla*the*," she added.

"I know that," the lame twin said. "Now, for goodness' sake, try to stop lisping, and let me see your arm." She helped her sister from her long coat, then gently probed her shoulder.

"Yes, it's out of the socket all right. You know what happens next." She handed the Styx lantern to her sister, who tucked it tight under her armpit. Then the lame twin stepped to her side, and positioned her hands so that she had a firm grip on the upper part of the dislocated arm, on the humerus. She took a breath. "Ready?"

"Ye*th*." The lisping twin shook her head, and frowned in concentration. "Sorry, I meant to say *yes*."

With a single swift motion, the lame twin slammed the arm down against the girl's body. The humerus pivoted over the cylindrical lantern, and the arm went back into the socket again with a small cracking sound, as if a twig had been snapped. Despite the immense pain this must have caused, the girl didn't so much as whimper.

"Done," the lame twin said. "It should be OK now."

"Want me to take a look at your leg?" the lisping twin offered, wiping the beads of sweat from her forehead.

"No, it's just a str —" She stopped in midsentence as she caught sight of something in the darkness high above them. She jerked her head toward it. "Look!"

The lisping twin swept her lustrous black hair from her face and squinted.

"Yes, I see it. A light."

"It can't be the remains from that rocket. It could be —"

"A luminescent orb —"

"Or maybe . . . a lantern . . . one of *our* lanterns?"

Unspeaking, they both focused as gravity brought the point of light toward them. When it was roughly level, they saw that it was indeed a light, and that there was a man attached to it.

Neither twin needed to consult the other; they were both thinking precisely the same thing as they barked orders in unison, in their nasal Styx language.

Although he was some ways away from them, the Limiter heard them. He heard them loud and clear, just as he'd understood when the old Styx had commanded him to jump to his death. And, in freefall a little way above him, a second Limiter also heard the orders from the twins. Unfortunately the third Limiter, the senior officer, had taken his life with his scythe several miles above. The two surviving Limiters had been contemplating the same course of action, there being no reason for them to go on living. But now they had a new directive, and a very real reason to stay alive. With the skill of a pair of skydivers, they angled their arms and legs to guide themselves toward the fungal outcrop below the twins' vantage point.

The lisping twin smiled at her sister. "Fortune favor*th* the righteou*th*," she said.

"It does, indeed it does," the lame twin said, touching the phial of Dominion virus around her neck. The lisping twin also put her hand to her phial, but her one was different — it contained the vaccine.

There was no need for any further communication between the Rebecca twins. They spun on their heels at precisely the same moment and headed to the rear of the fungus shelf. They both wore the same grins. Now that they had the two soldiers at their disposal, they knew that their chances of finding a way out of the Pore with their deadly cargo had increased considerably.

Things were looking up.

AT THAT EARLY HOUR, there was very little
traffic in the Hampstead streets as Drake drove past St.
Edmund's Hospital and up Rosslyn Hill. He swung the Range
Rover into Pilgrim's Lane, racing down its full length until he
reached the end and slowed to a crawl. He parked next to a
strip of the heath known as Preacher's Hill, where the long
grass and few trees were rimed with frost, making them appear
as though they had been sprinkled with confectioners' sugar.

He reached for the key to turn off the engine, but paused as
a report came on the radio about the Ultra Bug. The announcer
was talking about how all the missed work days had cost the
economy many millions.

"Hah! They're always worried about the money!" Drake
said scornfully, his eyes closing as he leaned back against the
headrest. "They just don't get it." He yawned. He hadn't slept
properly for days, snatching the odd hour in the car when he'd
had the chance, and it was catching up with him. He allowed
his head to slide over until it touched the window, and all at
once he fell into a half sleep.

Drake was suddenly brought back to wakefulness as a
cell phone began vibrating in the bag on the passenger seat.

Drenched in a cold sweat, it took him a few moments to remember where he was. The car engine was still running, and as he listened he realized he'd missed the rest of the Ultra Bug report.

"Get your act together," he growled, furious with himself. He was still swearing as he checked the phones inside the bag until he found the one that was buzzing. He pulled it out and answered it, turning off the ignition with the other hand to silence the radio.

"Hello," he said, rubbing his face roughly to force himself fully awake.

A woman spoke, although she didn't identify herself. "Hello?"

"Yes," Drake said.

"I'm calling on behalf of —"

"No names," Drake interrupted sharply. "I know who you are. Why isn't he calling me himself?"

The voice was sad, hollow. "He's . . . he's unavailable."

"Oh dear God," Drake exclaimed, knowing exactly what the woman's words really meant. His contact was either dead or missing. So far, not a single person he'd got in touch with from his old cell was still active. His network had been dismantled.

The woman's voice became harder and more emphatic. "And don't go to the Hill Station."

"Why?" Drake asked, clenching the phone so hard that the plastic casing creaked.

"It's off-line," she said, then hung up.

Drake looked at the phone for several moments, at the small bars on the display that fluctuated with the strength of the signal. Then he flipped the phone over and removed the back, sliding out the SIM card. As he got out of the car, he dropped the card onto the pavement and ground the heel of his boot into it. He scanned the road and the area of open parkland as he went to the tailgate and opened it. From a black case he took out a handgun, quickly tucking it into the back of his waistband. Then he locked the car and strode across to Preacher's Hill. As he made his way up the slope, keeping behind the few straggly bushes, his boots left prints in the frosty grass.

Once on higher ground, he paused to survey the area again, his eyes finally settling on his destination. The Hill Station, as it had been known to the members of his network, was a large Edwardian house at the end of a row of similar properties. Drake left the grassy slope and returned to the road. Although he'd just received an unequivocal message from the caller, he had to see it for himself. But he had to be careful — they might be watching. So he walked straight past the house, apparently giving it only a casual glance. It was sufficient for him to take in the barricade across the entrance to the driveway and the sign that read KEEP OUT — STRUCTURE UNSAFE, and to see that all the ground-floor windows had been boarded up. He continued along the street for several houses, then glanced at his wristwatch as if he were late for something, and doubled back.

Upon reaching the entrance to the driveway, he effortlessly vaulted the red-and-white-striped barrier. He kept close to an overgrown box hedge along the side of the gravel drive, making for the side of the house. As he came to the entrance to the basement, he saw there was no longer a door — just a charred frame. He opened his greatcoat and took out his handgun.

He stepped cautiously through the scorched doorway, covering all angles with the gun. All that remained in the basement were the metal skeletons of desks and small pools of melted plastic from the banks of computers that had been on top of them. Everything else was reduced to ash. The walls were blackened from smoke, and the ceiling had collapsed in several places where the joists had burned through. The whole area looked as if it had been engulfed by some sort of localized firestorm.

He knew it was a waste of time to check if any of the equipment or records had survived. He backed out of the basement and returned to the car.

The Styx had been characteristically thorough: While he had been in the Deeps, the whole network had been dismantled. Drake felt a crushing sense of helplessness. The only course open to him now was to try to get in touch with one of the other cells that operated independently across the country, the risk being that he might prejudice them in the process.

But he was desperate.

"Wales it is," he said wearily, and started the engine.

"I can take her if you want," Chester offered as Will went to lift Elliott.

Will shook his head. "Doesn't make much difference, does it? It's not as if she weighs anything down here."

Chester swung the three rucksacks over his shoulders. Back on the surface, carrying such a burden would have been unthinkable, but now, as he jumped up and down several times, he was hardly aware they were there. He stooped to pick up his rifle between his thumb and forefinger, and held it out at arm's length. "Yeah, isn't that amazing? It's as light as a pencil. You're right — nothing weighs very much down here!"

With no idea where they were going, except that the cave seemed to penetrate farther into the wall of the Pore, they began to follow it.

Even after several miles, they found they were still walking on the springy surface of the fungus, which coated every inch of the tunnel around them.

Then they turned a corner and were confronted by a vertical wall of fungus. "Dead end . . . not *mushroom* in here," Chester joked.

"Very funny. It's not a dead end, anyway," Will muttered, pointing at the opening above their heads. "Dim your light for a second," he said as he put Elliott down. He flicked the lens over his eye to investigate. "Looks like it goes some ways," he informed Chester, "but I can't see what's at the top."

"Well, that's it, then," Chester replied, disheartened.

"You're forgetting something." Will took a short running start and leaped straight up the wall. He took off, disappearing from sight. Not to be left behind by his new master, Bartleby sprang after him.

"Oh, great, just leave me here by myself," Chester muttered, peering around the pitch-black. He clicked his lantern up and began to whistle to comfort himself. After a while there was still no sign of Will, and he became anxious. "Hey!" he yelled. "What's up there? Don't leave me alone down here!"

Will floated back down and landed lightly beside Chester. "There are several openings we can try. Let's go!"

"So now we can fly," Chester said. "All in a day's work, I suppose."

They encountered more of these vertical seams, and despite the fungal growth that obscured nearly everything, Will began to recognize that there was a pattern to them. They seemed to be arranged in a series of concentric circles radiating out from around the Pore. He pictured it as the geological equivalent of a pebble dropped into a pool of water, the ripples spreading out from it, and wondered if rapid cooling of the bedrock had given rise to the circular fractures.

"So the earth isn't solid at all," Will had said to Chester as they were walking. "It's more like one ginormous Swiss cheese — full of holes."

"Do you have to talk about food?" was Chester's rejoinder.

But Will was beginning to suspect that there might be, in fact, a great deal more of these seams hidden from sight, and that over the centuries they had been invaded by the rapacious growth of the fungus. It filled him with a sense of wonder that the fungus was probably one huge organism, stretching for hundreds of miles, both in a sheath inside the Pore and also through the surrounding rock.

"Do you know, we could actually be inside the biggest plant in the world," he mused on another occasion, but Chester gave no response.

They eventually came to a place where the tunnel before them split into three. They stopped to decide which fork to take.

"Well, we're really spoiled for choice this time," Will was saying.

His friend hummed in agreement.

"Look, Chester, quite honestly, I don't care which way we go," Will said. "Makes no difference to me — they all look pretty much the same, don't they?" He scrutinized the tunnels again: They were all of a similar dimension and each appeared to continue horizontally, although who knew what lay just around the corner? The boys had already been forced to turn back several times, when the way had become impassable due to excessive fungal growth or because it pinched down to crawlways too narrow for even the most determined ant to get through.

"I picked last time. It's your turn," Chester threw back at him.

"Actually, no, you didn't. Bartleby chose the last one," Will reminded him.

"Well, let him do it again," Chester suggested.

They both turned to regard Bartleby, whose head was high in the air as he sniffed, his tail swishing briskly.

"Go on, Bart, take your pick," Will urged him.

"*Bart?*" Chester asked. "Where did that come from?"

"Cal," Will said quietly.

"Oh, right, yes." Chester stole a glance at Will, wondering how he was dealing with his brother's death. But Will seemed to be entirely focused on moving through the network of tunnels, as if he had some sort of plan in mind. If he was as concerned about their current predicament as Chester was, it certainly didn't show. From the discovery of the nets on the fungal outcrop, at least they knew that there had been people down here, even if they weren't still alive. But apart from this, there was no getting away from the fact that he and Will were just wandering aimlessly along. However, Chester wasn't about to challenge his friend about it, because they had to do *something*.

"If you can't make up your mind, I'll decide which way," Will said to the cat, who seemed to be in no hurry as he continued to sample the air. Then Bartleby scampered into one of the tunnels. He had gone a little way down it when he came to a sudden halt. Following close behind, the boys pulled up just as abruptly.

Will gasped as the odor of decay hit him. "Something big died in here!"

And Chester noticed the sound his boots were making as he stepped across the tunnel. "There's gooey stuff on the floor. It looks pretty rank."

"Over here," Will whispered as he caught sight of a number of structures along the wall.

There were four wooden benches in a row against the side of the tunnel. Resembling something that might be found in a butcher's shop, they were sturdily built, their legs and tops made of thick pieces of timber. The abattoir impression was further enhanced by the fact that the benches were bloodstained and covered with what seemed to be scraps of old, dried meat, in some places a solid inch deep. A huge hatchet was buried in the top of one of the benches, as if its owner had swung it down hard, and was expecting to come back and use it again.

"Oh no!" Chester swallowed as soon as he laid eyes on the hatchet. He gave Will a horror-stricken glance.

Will's first thought was that they could have stumbled upon a tribe of subterranean cannibals, although he wasn't about to share this with his already-petrified friend. As he took a step back from the benches, he lost his footing in the debris covering the floor. He landed on his knees, just managing to keep a grip on Elliott. It gave him an opportunity to see more closely what they had been treading in.

It appeared to be a mass of hacked-off body parts, but there was nothing Will could immediately identify. "Bits of animals?" he said as he noticed a huge compound eye and the sections of shiny black articulated legs covered in bristles almost the width of his little finger. "No, insects . . . giant insects?" he croaked in disbelief. The largest intact body part he could see consisted of ten or so glossy black insectoid segments, all with legs sprouting from both sides. It could have come from some colossal centipede, but because each individual segment was two feet long, he wondered how big the whole creature had been.

"We are getting out of here. Right now," Chester said in no uncertain terms as he helped Will to his feet. "And as far the freak away as we can."

They raced back to the intersection again.

Chester was pointing down one of the other tunnels when a piercing screech made them leap out of their skins. "What the heck was that?" he whispered in the ensuing silence.

All three of them, the boys and the cat, immediately looked up, noticing for the first time that there was a wide fissure right above their heads. The screeches began again, sounding like fingernails being dragged down a very long chalkboard. Apart from the fact that the boys had no idea what was making them, the sounds themselves were painful, tearing at their nerves.

Then the echoes of the screeches died away once more.

In the lull, Chester spoke very quietly. "That's not rocks cracking or something, is it?"

Will didn't answer immediately, observing how agitated Bartleby had become.

The nerve-jarring calls came again, louder than before.

"No," Will whispered, "it's not geological. Maybe it's got something to do with all those insect parts." He continued with urgency. "Chester, get the rifle ready. And the stove guns." He began to take Elliott into the left-hand tunnel ahead of them. Bartleby was slouched low to the ground and so close to Will's feet that he nearly tripped over him.

As he trod backward from the intersection, Chester fumbled with the rifle, trying to work the bolt. He finally managed to cock it, ramming a round into the chamber. Still walking backward, he undid the flap on the pad on his hip, in which two stove guns were stored.

The sound of a rope whipping through the air took all three by surprise. The world turned upside down as Will was whisked off his feet. He held on to Elliott, desperately trying not to drop her. Something closed around him from all sides. He caught a glimpse of what it was — mesh similar to what he'd seen on the edge of the fungal outcrop. He'd been trapped in a net.

Bartleby hissed and bucked as he was bundled against Will, who found the more he struggled, the tighter the net became, until he was hardly capable of any movement at all. Over the sound of his own cries and the creaking of the net, he was certain he caught a metallic noise, as if empty tin cans were rattling against one another. With Elliott's shoulder pushed hard in his face and Bartleby writhing against his legs, he was in no position to tell if Chester had been responsible for this noise. He tried to see where his friend was and whether he'd been caught in another trap, but the net was spinning him around so quickly that everything was a blur.

The moment Chester registered that Will was in trouble, his first impulse had been to go over to help him. But he could tell Will was very much alive from his shouts, and he was more concerned by what was happening in the fissure in the tunnel roof. Rocks and soil were falling from it, as if they were being dislodged, as if something was coming. And the screeches were even louder and more numerous than before. He dropped the rucksacks from his shoulders, took a few more paces back toward Will, then trained the rifle on the opening in the roof.

It was fortunate he did.

Through the rifle scope, he saw something drop from the fissure. It fell without any noise whatsoever, like a shadow flitting across a wall. He quickly sighted on where he thought it had landed.

"What the . . . ?!" Chester spluttered.

It was approximately ten feet across, with more legs than Chester could take in at first glance. These leathery legs extended from the thick circular disk of its body. On the area of the body facing him were three patches that sparkled as if they were studded with bike reflectors. But the most striking aspect was a long stalk that protruded from above its "eyes" with a glowing tip of muted yellow light.

As he watched, the creature seemed to sink lower to the

ground, the glowing appendage bobbing gently. Then it slowly began to rise on its multiple legs.

Chester gripped the rifle. He couldn't abide anything that crawled, even at the best of times, but this monstrosity was like a physical manifestation of his worst childhood nightmares. He shuddered as wave upon wave of revulsion swept through him. "You're dead meat," he growled. "I hate —" His words froze on his lips as the creature suddenly dropped its body back down to the ground — a prelude, Chester thought, to launching itself at him.

"SPIDERS!" Chester screamed, jerking the trigger and firing. The single shot tore straight through the creature, cleaving it in two.

He watched as the halves toppled to the left and right, the legs going into a mad paroxysm of movement. With all the adrenaline coursing through his veins, Chester gave a hysterical laugh that sounded nothing like him.

Then there were no more screeching calls, just Will's shouts from the net.

Chester had just straightened up when another of the creatures landed with a soft flopping noise, precisely where the first had been. His instincts taking over again, Chester cocked the rifle, then pulled the trigger.

He was met with a sound that made his heart stop.

There was a hollow *click* as the round failed to go off. He desperately tried to work the bolt again, but he couldn't shift it — it seemed to be jammed. The beast was slowly rising up on its segmented legs. Knowing it was a waste of time, Chester tried to fire the rifle again.

Another dry *click*.

In sheer desperation, Chester did the only thing he could in the situation. He slung the rifle at the beast with all his might. The beast raised a foreleg and fended it off with a single deft flick. Chester glimpsed the rifle spinning away and heard a dull *thud* as it came to rest on the fungus-coated floor, out of sight.

Then it was just the creature and him. Chester's stricken gaze locked on to its eyes, malevolent crystal spheres that glittered under the beam of his lantern like large droplets of water. There was the faintest *hiss* as it opened its mouth, revealing a row of vicious white fangs, each as thick as his thumb.

"Oh no!" he gulped, falling onto his back as he struggled to get a stove gun out of the pad on his hip. He was still watching the creature as he managed to pry one out, dropping the second in the process. He cursed as he tried to recall what Drake had taught them about using these weapons. "Hold it in the palm," Chester said to himself, first making sure he had it pointed in the right direction. He was just curling a finger around the firing lever when the creature launched itself at him.

Chester hooked the lever straight back and released the firing mechanism. The stove gun bucked in his hand, the blast catching the monster in midair. Chester would have been hard-pressed to miss, as the beast was barely more than a few feet away from him. At such close range, its body was blown to smithereens, splattering Chester with blood.

"Barf! I am so about to hurl," Chester croaked, wiping his face and staring at the pieces of the dead creature scattered all over him. A couple of the limbs lay across him — and they were still moving. They looked like the spindly legs of a giant plucked chicken, but covered in dark callused skin and spotted here and there with coarse black bristles. Chester thought he was going to be sick as he pushed them off. Then he back-pedaled along the ground, trying to get away from the scene of the carnage. Babbling incoherently to himself, he was on the brink of paralysis, and in no shape to respond to Will's muffled, frantic calls. The only thing that kept him there and in the present was the thought that he had to rescue Will and Elliott from the trap.

Then he heard another plopping sound.

He didn't need to look to know what was waiting for him.

"NO! NOT MORE!" he yelled. In an instant he was scrabbling around on the ground in a mad effort to locate the second stove gun. But with all the body fragments and the unevenness of the fungal floor, he couldn't find it anywhere. He forced himself to look. The body of the creature was quivering slightly as it bobbed on its legs. *It's about to attack*, Chester told himself.

Then it leaped, coming straight for him.

There was a *hiss* as something fiery struck the beast. With amazing speed, the whole creature was consumed by flames. It thrashed about, screeching at an intolerable pitch.

Stunned, Chester got to his feet. He was staggering over to where Will and Elliott were caught in the net as yet another of the monsters appeared. The air seemed to sizzle as a second fiery projectile speared through it. It passed so close to Chester's head, he thought he was its target and threw himself to the ground. But in the next moment he saw that a fourth spider had been hit and was instantly engulfed by fire, falling beside the still-twitching remains of the first one.

Chester was so completely transfixed by the sight of the two burning, crackling animals that he couldn't move.

A shadowy form stepped through the smoke.

"Styx?" Chester said simply, staring up at the figure before him. It was aiming what appeared to be a crossbow of some description, with another flaming bolt already in place. But this time, it was pointed straight at Chester.

The figure moved toward him.

"But . . . but you're a mere boy," came a woman's gruff voice. She was wearing a long tattered coat, with a scarf of lighter material covering the lower half of her face.

"Are you a Styx?" Chester got out.

"What a dreadful thing to say," came the sharp response.

With a high laugh, the woman unwound the scarf. She

blew out the burning tip of the bolt and lowered the crossbow to her side.

Chester took in her wavy red hair and her full, generous face. It was a kindly face, her cheeks crinkled into a smile. Chester couldn't tell how old she was, but put her somewhere in her forties. Apart from her clothes, she could have easily passed for one of his mother's friends.

"You're lucky it was my day to check the traps, or you'd be spider-monkey fodder by now," the woman said, extending a hand to Chester. "Up you get, love."

"You're *not* Styx, then?" he asked hesitantly, looking into her eyes.

Will's mumbled cries came as she answered, "No, not Styx. Besides, I'm not the one who was trying to blast spider-monkeys with a *Limiter* rifle." Her voice was a little croaky, as if it wasn't used very often.

"It isn't mine . . . I mean . . . ," he stuttered as he tried to explain.

"Don't worry, dearie, I can see you're not a White Neck." She gazed back into his eyes. "Ah, you don't know how good that is," she said.

"What is?" he asked, taking hold of her hand and allowing her to help him up.

"To lay eyes on another person!" she replied, as if the answer to her question was obvious. She was still clasping his hand when Will shouted again.

"Um . . . my friends need help," Chester reminded her, tugging his hand away.

As Chester continued to stare at her in dumb amazement,

the woman slung the crossbow over her shoulder. Taking some sprigs of what appeared to be dried plants from the thick belt around her ample waist, she lobbed them on top of the heap of burning creatures. An intense but not unpleasant smell instantly permeated the air. "That'll stop any more of these beggars coming," she informed Chester as she bustled over to the tunnel where the net hung. Releasing a rope somewhere in the darkness, she lowered the twitching bundle of Will, Elliott, and the cat gently to the floor.

"Don't you worry — we'll have you out of there in two shakes," she said, pulling at the top of the net to loosen a tie.

Bartleby was the first to emerge, growling and baring his teeth at the woman.

"A Hunter," she said, dropping the net and clapping her hands together in delight. "Well, I never thought I'd see a Hunter again!"

Deciding she was no risk, Bartleby slunk past her, giving her a curious sniff on the way. He was much more interested in the spider-monkeys, as the woman had referred to them, and circled cautiously around their remains.

With no help from the woman, Will had extricated himself from the net. He scrambled to his feet, then rubbed his thigh. "Stupid cat bit me! Chester, what happ—" He stopped short as his eyes alighted on the woman. "Who are you?"

"Martha," she answered. "But people call me *Ma*."

"Martha?" Will said, shaking his head in disbelief. "*Ma?*"

"Yes, Ma. That's what they used to call me," she said as she studied Will. "Well, look at you. White hair and those lovely pale eyes. No question you were born *under grass*."

"What does that mean?" Chester asked, mystified.

"It means that I was born in the Colony," Will told him. "You know — under the grass — in the earth."

"Oh, right, I get it," Chester said.

Martha had noticed Elliott's unmoving form in the net. "There's another of you! What's the matter with him?" she asked, her brow crinkling with concern. "I do hope he didn't get hurt by my deadfall."

Will snapped out of his bewilderment and immediately bent to unravel the coarse netting from around Elliott. Then he lifted her out.

"Why, it's a young woman!" Martha exclaimed as she saw Elliott's face. "What's wrong with her?"

"Well, er, Mrs., er, Ma . . . Martha," Will began, launching into an explanation of how they had been hunted by the Limiters and then blasted into the Pore by their artillery.

Her arms crossed, she listened intently to him for a minute, and then raised one of her small hands to silence him.

"I'm sorry, dearie, I have to tell you, I'm not taking any of this in," she admitted, shaking her head. "Do you know when I last heard another voice?" She abruptly uncrossed her arms and, slipping her hand inside her coat, scratched vigorously at an armpit in a most unladylike manner.

"A very long time ago?" Will said, watching askance as she finished scratching herself, then put her fingers into her mouth and sucked them.

"You got that right, dearie," she said. "You had all better come with me, but I've got to collect all this food first. Looks like we're going to need every last bit. More mouths to feed now."

Will and Chester exchanged glances as she unhitched a sack from her belt, muttering something about not having any time to trim the meat off.

"So are those yours?" Will asked, pointing in the direction of the gruesome butcher benches.

But the woman didn't answer him, instead inclining her head and beaming affectionately at Chester. "You're a big, strapping lad. You remind me ever so of my son." She sighed deeply. "Would you mind holding this open for me, luvvy?" she asked as she passed Chester the sack. Then she set about gathering up all the pieces of smoldering spider-monkey and putting them inside it.

Chester mouthed, "Food?" at Will, holding the sack at arm's length and curling his lip as if he were going to be sick.

But Will didn't respond, his mounting curiosity evident as he ran his eyes over what was left of the creatures.

"It's odd. They seem to be insects or . . . or maybe arachnid, but are those shiny white objects *teeth*?"

"Yes, fangs," the coarse old woman replied as she continued to toddle about the place, picking up the grisly remains. "Along with that light they have on a stalk, they use them as lures for catching their prey."

"Fascinating," Will muttered, sticking his head without any hesitation right over the sack that his friend was finding so repugnant.

"Here we go again," Chester grumbled to himself.

"**THE DETAIL** is in the dust. . . . The detail is in the dust," Dr. Burrows repeated over and over to himself as he knelt before a half-buried human skeleton.

He was peeling back the fungus and scooping away the silt to reveal more of the bones, but stopped as he heard a distant and very faint *thud*. He had no idea what could have caused it, but he got to his feet and shouted, "Hello! Hello! Anyone there?" at the top of his lungs. Although he had traveled many miles, he'd made sure that it was always downward so that he remained close to the Pore. The last thing he wanted to do was to lose his bearings.

Then he'd struck gold. He'd spotted the skeleton and begun to excavate it.

Now, as he listened for any further sounds, all was silent. He told himself he must have imagined the noise and, shrugging, he went back to his discovery. As he tugged more of the fungus away and blew the fine silt from around the old bones, his face lit up. "What've we got here?" he said as he came across an object in the skeleton's hand. Carefully, by moving aside the phalanges — small bones that had once formed fingers — he lifted the object out.

It was a piece of pottery not unlike a genie's lantern, with a spout and a lid that seemed to be stuck in place. He picked at the end of the spout with his grimy fingernail. "The wick would have been here," he said aloud. "So you Phoenicians, or whoever you were, you used oil lamps as your light source."

Putting the lamp carefully to one side, he set about clearing away more of the loose soil, his hands shaking with anticipation, and hunger. In the glow of his luminescent orb, Dr. Burrows cut a rather sad figure, hunched over the skeleton, whistling weakly to himself. His glasses were a little lopsided — they'd been knocked about during the fall down the Pore — and the parts of his face not covered by his patchy growth of beard were scraped and bruised. His shirt was ripped down the back, and one of its arms was almost torn off, hanging by a few threads. And although he'd always been of slight build, he'd lost more weight and was beginning to resemble the skeleton he was working on.

"Bingo!" he exclaimed as he came across what appeared to be a wooden box. He yanked it out of the dirt a tad too enthusiastically and it fell apart. But in among the remnants were a series of small, flat stone tablets the size of playing cards, with rounded edges.

"Slate, and obviously worked," he observed, rubbing the uppermost tablet on his shirt to clean it. Then he began to examine it closely, finding there were some tiny letters carved into it, letters that he recognized. They were identical to the characters he'd come across in the Deeps, characters which, using his "Dr. Burrows Stone," as he'd christened it, he'd been able to translate. Despite the fact that he'd lost his journal as he tumbled into the Pore, he reckoned he could remember just enough to give him a rudimentary understanding of what was on the small tablets.

But, concentrate as he might, the tiny letters seemed to dance before his eyes, and it took him an age to identify even a few words. He removed his glasses to give them a wipe, careful not to dislodge the lenses from the twisted frame. But it didn't seem to help him see any better, and he gave up after a while. "What's wrong with me?" he grumbled as he inspected the other tablets, discovering minuscule diagrams etched into them in addition to the writing.

"Directions . . . could these be . . . directions?" he said, turning the flat stones this way and that. "Oh, I don't know," he exhaled, frustrated in his efforts to make any sense of them. He wrapped the tablets in a handkerchief and put them carefully in his pocket, then resumed his excavation of the skeleton. Other than a pair of very rotten leather sandals, there was nothing else of note.

Getting up, he continued on his way again. As his feet stumbled over alternating stretches of fungus, bare rock, and drifts of fine silt, he wondered if there were any other artifacts down there — perhaps he would find something that would tie into the map on the tablets, if indeed it was a map of this place. As he kept his eyes open for any landmarks, he realized that the fungus might be obscuring them. Depending on how much it had grown over the intervening millennia, it might be concealing all manner of things. And he wondered if perhaps the poor soul whose skeleton he'd found was there because he or she had landed at the wrong level in the Pore and become lost. If that was the case, then Dr. Burrows was also in the wrong place, and so the map would be useless.

He pulled up sharply as he remembered his own experience of tumbling down the Pore; the complete and absolute terror as the darkness had opened before him and seemed to go on forever, until he'd belly flopped onto a fungal outcrop. He hadn't been badly injured, but the worst thing was that he was so ill prepared for any further exploration: His rucksack with all his food and water, his equipment, and the journals he'd labored on for so long had all been left behind.

He began to totter along the tunnel again, his stomach rumbling piteously. If it wasn't for the lower gravity, he knew he might not have sufficient strength left even to propel himself along. He'd been drinking from streams flowing down the tunnel walls, but he needed to eat something, and soon.

Coming upon a large fissure, he looked down into it with a feeling of dread. "Always down . . . always down," he reminded himself, holding the luminescent orb before him in an attempt to see how deep it was. Having traveled this far into the earth, he wasn't going to give up now; he'd die trying before he'd ever turn back. He was determined to search for more evidence of the ancient race, and if the skeleton was anything to go by, he might not be that far from what he sought. He did wonder at times if he'd eventually find a whole heap of skeletons, the final resting place of all the misguided souls who'd perished in their pursuit of the "Garden of the Second Sun" — the subterranean paradise he'd learned about in their crumbling temple.

"Here's to a soft landing," he said, preparing to jump. He girded himself, then leaped into the center of the fissure, glimpsing tendrils of fungus on the walls and the different layers of rock on the way down. He landed with a splash in a small pool of water, bending his knees to absorb the impact and rolling onto his side.

"Made it," he said, although he didn't sound particularly relieved.

Now sopping wet, he pulled himself to his feet. It was then that he was beset by a wave of dizziness, and fell back again, unconscious.

"Dad! Dad!" Dr. Burrows heard as someone dragged him from the pool. Whoever it was propped his head up and was making sure his glasses were seated properly.

He opened his eyes and an image came into focus, then turned hazy again.

"Rebecca," he whispered feebly. "Dreaming . . . must be dreaming."

"No, you're not, Dad. It's me."

He forced his eyes to open fully, making the greatest effort to look at the person before him.

"I must be delirious."

"No, you're not. It's me," the Rebecca twin said again. She squeezed his hand hard. "There, see, I'm real."

"Rebecca? What . . . what are you doing here?" he said, still not believing his eyes.

"I heard you shouting," she replied.

Then Dr. Burrows took in what she was wearing. "Limiter . . . Styx clothes?" He rubbed his forehead in confusion.

"Yes, Dad, I am a Styx," she said without hesitation. "And

you look like you could do with something to eat." She snapped her fingers, and a figure stepped from the shadows.

"A soldier?" Dr. Burrows croaked, shifting his focus.

The man's hollow-cheeked face was emotionless as his piercing eyes met with those of the befuddled Dr. Burrows. The Limiter passed something to Rebecca.

"Here, have some of this meat. You don't want to know where it came from, but at least it tastes reasonable when it's cooked," she said, tearing off a piece and stuffing it into Dr. Burrows's mouth.

He chewed on it gratefully, studying the Rebecca twin and the Limiter as he did so.

The food was doing the trick, and he perked up immediately. "How did you —?"

"More?" she asked, shoving another chunk of the spider-monkey flesh into his mouth before he could respond.

"I don't understand what you're doing here. You should be at home," he reprimanded her, although it lost most of its effect because his mouth was full. "Does your mother know where you are?" he demanded.

The twin couldn't suppress a giggle.

Mrs. Burrows was sitting behind a microphone into which she'd been talking. Bright lights were shining in her eyes, and their heat was making her perspire. She never imagined it would be like this, her first time ever on the small screen. She was realizing a lifelong wish — she was actually appearing on television! More important, her case was finally receiving the attention it deserved.

The public appeal for information on her missing family was the last item on the police program, and she was in a large studio with people clutching clipboards and wearing earpieces, all buzzing around chaotically as if none of them really knew where they were meant to be. Mrs. Burrows had spotted that a number of the policemen on the "Highfield Family Case," as it was being called, were mulling around in the wings. When she met their eyes, they all gave her shifty looks. It was clear to her she was still the prime suspect in the disappearances, although there wasn't a shred of evidence against her. But if they didn't believe what she had told them, then why were they allowing her to make this public appeal, she asked herself. Were they hoping she'd be lulled into a false sense of security and give something away? She couldn't understand why they would go to these lengths.

Concentrate, she told herself as she read the final paragraph of the statement the police psychologist had helped her to draft.

". . . because somebody must know where they've gone or what's happened to them," Mrs. Burrows said, letting out a tremulous breath. She stared into the camera lens, as if too upset to go on. "So please, if you know anything, anything at all, you must contact the police. I just want my family back."

The red light on the top of the camera went out, and another one blinked on as DI Blakemore took over. He was wearing his best suit, and he'd got a new haircut especially for the occasion. And as he spoke earnestly to the camera, he raised a single eyebrow as if he thought he was James Bond. Mrs. Burrows had never seen him do it before. "We are now treating the circumstances surrounding the disappearances of

Dr. Roger Burrows and Will and Rebecca, and Will's school friend Chester Rawls, as highly suspicious."

Mrs. Burrows watched a TV monitor at the side of the camera that showed what was actually being broadcast as DI Blakemore continued to speak. Various photographs she'd provided of her family were flashing up, followed by a recent school picture of Chester in his Highfield High School uniform. Then DI Blakemore was on the screen again. Before he spoke, he paused dramatically, the eyebrow creeping even higher up his forehead, as if it might detach itself altogether. "This is an enhanced still taken from security camera footage." A grainy black-and-white image came on the screen. "It shows a woman we'd like to talk to in relation to the case. She's about five foot eight, of slim build, and possibly has dyed brown hair, although her natural color may be blonde or even white. She's in her early to mid thirties, and may still be in the London area. And here's an artist's rendering to give a clearer idea of what she might look like." Another picture came up on the monitor. "If you have any information in relation to this woman's present whereabouts, the hotline number is . . ."

Mrs. Burrows stopped listening as, through the glare of the studio lights, she spotted Chester's parents at the edge of the soundstage. Mr. Rawls was supporting Mrs. Rawls — she looked as though she was crying and couldn't stand by herself.

Mrs. Burrows said good-bye to DI Blakemore and the other officers. She was walking toward Chester's parents when Mr. Rawls, his arm still around his wife's shoulders, simply turned and glared at her, shaking his head. Mrs. Burrows stopped in her tracks. She'd bumped into him once or twice in the Highfield police station, but he had been very stony faced and uncommunicative with her on each occasion. One of the officers on the case had later informed her that Chester's parents, upon learning she had been zonked out on sleeping pills the evening both boys were discovered missing, were furious. They blamed her for not keeping an eye on them. Mrs. Burrows didn't accept she was at fault — Will had always gone off to do his own thing. At least it was digging, and not causing trouble down on the outskirts of town with the other kids.

But now she felt quite shaken by Mr. Rawls's reaction. By the side of the stage, she spotted a watercooler and went to get herself a drink. As she sipped the water, she heard voices coming from behind a rack of equipment.

"So you think she did it, then?" a voice asked.

"Sure. She's as guilty as sin," another voice with a Scottish accent replied. "Nine times out of ten, somebody in the family is the killer — you know that. How many sob stories from distraught relatives have we had here in the studio and, Bob's your auntie, a month later they're locked up themselves?"

"Yeah, that's true."

"Did you take a good look at her? That Burrows woman is a bitter old no-mark and no question. Typical of suburbia — full of repressed rage and fed up to the back teeth with her pointless, phony life. Probably had a little something on the side, and her husband found out, so she topped him. And her kids knew too much, so she did them in, too, while she was at it. Her son's best mate, Charley or whatever he was called, well — the poor little sod — he got himself caught up in it, too."

Mrs. Burrows edged around the equipment so she could see who was talking. One, a squat, portly man with a shaved head and a full beard, was coiling up an electrical cord as he spoke; the other, a skinny individual in a white T-shirt, was drumming his thigh with a microphone as he listened. They were just a couple of studio technicians.

"Yeah, she looked like she could be a right old dragon," the skinny one said as he scratched the back of his head with the tip of the microphone.

The bearded man caught sight of Mrs. Burrows and cleared his throat loudly. "Better check what they want in studio thirteen, Billy," he said.

The skinny man slowly lowered the microphone to his side, a confounded expression on his face. "But we don't have a studio thirteen . . . ," he said. As he glanced across and saw Mrs. Burrows standing there, he realized what his coworker had been trying to tell him. "I'm on it, Dave, right this moment," he muttered as they fell over each other in an effort to make their getaway.

Mrs. Burrows remained where she was, watching them go, the plastic cup crumpled in her hand.

PART 2

```
          S
          H
MARTHA'S
          C
          K
```

7

IT WAS QUITE astonishing to see how Martha got herself about, propelling herself down the tunnels like a ball bearing hurtling through a length of drainpipe. Contrary to her appearance, she could move with the swiftness of a leopard; it was evident that she'd lived in the low-gravity environment for some time and was completely attuned to it.

Bartleby was quietly watching her, and tried to follow her example as she rebounded from one side of the tunnel to the other. Time after time, he misjudged how much thrust was needed and hurtled out of control toward the roof or the opposite wall. Will and Chester grew accustomed to the spectacle of the hapless cat cavorting through the air, giving surprised meows as he went.

The boys were making every effort to keep up with Martha, but Will refused to go too quickly because he was worried about jarring Elliott. As their unlikely savior stopped yet again to allow them to catch up with her, they could hear her babbling to herself. It was difficult to understand what she was saying, and Will realized that she might not even be aware she was doing it.

"What can we do for the girl?" she murmured in their direction, then swiveled away from them.

"Well, like I told you, she's got a broken —" Chester began.

"What?" Martha interrupted, turning to look at him.

"You asked about Elliott. She's got a broken arm."

"I didn't ask you anything, and you've already told me that," Martha said, frowning at Chester as if he was the one who was acting strangely. "Time for another!" she announced abruptly, plucked one of the small sprigs from her belt, held it over her flaming torch until it was smoldering, then flung it to the floor. The pungent smell quickly filled the enclosed space.

"Phew!" Will said, wrinkling his nose. "That's pretty powerful. Reminds me of licorice or something!"

"Yes, it does, doesn't it? It's called Aniseed Fire." Martha gave him a knowing look. "Got the Colonist's nose, haven't you, dearie? Sense of smell like a bloodhound?"

"Well, yes, I suppose so," Will replied. "But why *are* you burning that stuff? What does it do?" he asked.

"If you don't watch it, the spider-monkeys gather in the ceiling vents and suddenly drop on top of you. The fumes from Aniseed Fire keep them away. I grow it in my garden, you know," she said, launching herself off again down the tunnel.

"Garden? Your *garden*?" Chester called after her as she sailed away. The word was so everyday and comforting in this most alien of places. "Did she really say garden?" he quizzed Will.

"Who knows?" Will whispered, looking cross-eyed at Chester, just in case his friend hadn't realized that the woman obviously had more than a few screws loose.

"Watch yourselves through here," she warned as Will and Chester caught up with her again. "The lodge is narrow and the wind strong."

"Lodge?" Chester said.

"Yes, it's narrow."

"I think she means *ledge*," Will suggested to Chester in a whisper.

They came out onto a fungal ledge barely more than three feet wide, beyond which Will could again make out a gaping void. "The Pore?" he asked himself in a whisper. But something seemed to be different about it. The air was incredibly humid, and instead of the showers of rain he'd seen before, there were clouds of steam rising in the air. And as he looked across to the other side, everything was saturated with an intense red glow — then he felt the heat on his face and knew it couldn't be the Pore.

Chester chose that moment to speak up, breaking through Will's thoughts. "Isn't that where we just came from?" he asked. "It's not the Pore again, is it?"

Martha chuckled. "No, it's not *the* Pore — it's another of the Seven Sisters. We called this one Puffing Mary." She turned her head aside and the boys heard her mutter, "Didn't we, Nat?"

At this, Chester shot an urgent glance at Will, who knew precisely what his friend was thinking. No doubt about it, they were in the hands of a rather confused old woman, who didn't even seem able to get their names right.

Keeping close to the wall, they took great care as they made their way along the ledge, which was slick with water. The limited illumination cast by Chester's light orb and Martha's burning torch gave Will the impression that this void was on the same scale as the Pore. He kept his eyes away from the darkness beyond the edge of the path, but felt himself being drawn toward it. The urge had come back, the inexplicable urge to step off the ledge that had assailed him before. The voice that wasn't really a voice but something much more powerful and deep-seated, like an irresistible desire, was trying to take control of him, to make him do it.

"No," he mumbled through gritted teeth, "Pull yourself together." He had Elliott to consider. What was he thinking? *What was wrong with him?*

After twenty minutes of slow stepping along the ledge, Will was relieved beyond words as the path swung back into another opening in the wall. As they left the void behind them, Will stumbled a few steps, knocking into his friend.

"You all right?" Chester asked.

"Fine — just tripped," Will told him as he and Chester followed Martha into a long galley, where the ubiquitous fungal growth became patchier and patchier until Will could quite clearly see areas of dark rock around him. Then, after a few more minutes, there seemed to be no more fungus at all. It was quite a novelty to feel the shingle crunch under their feet as they ascended a gentle incline.

"Here we are," Martha declared as a large cavern opened out before them. From floor to roof, some sort of curved barricade or bulwark extended a hundred feet down one whole side of it. Martha led the boys halfway along the barricade. Will could see it was formed from many vertical strips of metal, overlapping each other and welded in place. And the metal strips themselves were of varying types: some were dull, others highly polished, and a number were even perforated, with grids of cutout circles or squares along their entire length. A few stood out from the rest because they bore traces of blue or green paint.

By what appeared to be a door hung a heavy brass bell, suspended on a bracket at about head height. Martha rang the bell twice. The boys waited expectantly as the last echoes of the peal faded, but no one appeared.

"Old habits," Martha informed them as she swung open the door.

"You leave it unlocked?" Will inquired, as Bartleby scampered through the doorway.

"Yes, dust puppies aren't that smart," she replied.

"Dust *whats*?" Will said, but Martha had already gone in. As Will and Chester followed her, they were met by a fantastic sight. The incline continued before them, the cavern roof also increasing in height, and about a hundred feet away there was some sort of single-story shack. A path led up to the building, lined by beds of the most wonderful plants. As if they were luminous, the different beds gave off an almost shimmering glow of yellows, purples, blues, and reds, the cumulative light enough to imbue the whole area with their sublime and beautiful radiance.

"My garden," Martha announced proudly.

"Wow!" Chester gasped.

"Do you like it?" she asked him.

"Yes, it's just so cool!" he replied.

As the woman turned to him, she herself actually seemed to be glowing as a result of his praise. "These plants aren't just here for their looks, you know."

"Like the ones you burn?" Chester inquired.

"Yes, if I hadn't found out about Aniseed Fire, I wouldn't be around to tell you about it."

"But where did you get all these from?" Chester asked.

"Nathaniel collected specimens for me whenever he went on his expeditions. I've still got a lot to learn about their properties, but time is one thing I'm not short of."

"Who's Nathaniel?" Will cut in, unable to help himself.

"My son. He's on the hill," Martha replied, with a glance at the top of the incline by the shack. Will tried to see where she'd been looking, filled with hope that there might be someone else a little less peculiar in the place, someone who might be able to help them. "Are we going to meet —?"

"Let's get the girl inside, shall we?" Martha interrupted brusquely, closing the door and driving a single bolt home on the inside.

Chester caught Will's eye, directing him to the side of the door, where there was a welder's torch and a pair of gas cylinders on a cart, both of which were covered in some sort of creeper. It was obvious from the plants rambling over the equipment and the rust mottling the tanks that none of it had been touched in a good while. And there was no question that it was Topsoiler welding equipment.

"Nathaniel . . . did he make this barrier?" Chester asked tentatively.

Nodding, Martha turned to lead them up the path bathed in the ethereal glow.

Midway along, Bartleby skidded to a halt, his large amber eyes fixed on something. As Will stopped behind the cat, he caught the sound of trickling water. "A stream?" he queried.

Martha stepped to the side of the path. "A freshwater spring flows from behind the shack," she said as Will located the small clear stream, its swirling current suffused with purple light from overhanging clusters of small blossoms. It looked otherworldly.

"This place is wild," Will said.

"Thank you," Martha replied. "It's my little sanctuary. And I reckon the spring is why they chose this spot for the shack in the first place."

"Who was that? Who chose it?" Will asked excitedly.

"They were sailors."

"Sailors?"

"Yes. You'll see when you get there," she said.

At the front of the shack, some steps lead up to a porch. Reaching the top, Will paused to inspect one of the thick beams supporting the awning above it. "Oak," he said, running a finger over the wood, which was so old it had darkened almost to black, its surface covered in numerous runnels of wormholes. "Very old oak," he decided as he examined the shack further and saw that its frame was also made from these thick beams, and that its walls were constructed from equally ancient tongue-and-groove planking.

"So where did all this come from?" Will asked, pushing one of the planks with his foot and causing it to creak. He turned to Martha.

"We thought the sailors salvaged it from their ship. But there was no one left to ask when we first came here."

At one end of the porch a number of kegs and large trunks were stacked, and in front of a window with its shutters closed stood a bench and a couple of chairs.

The front door to the shack was ajar, and Martha elbowed it open and trundled straight in. Will and Chester didn't wait to be invited, following across the threshold. At first all they could see in the gloom was a stone hearth in which cinders glowed, and some type of stove built into one side of it.

"Put a log on the fire, dearie," Martha asked Chester. "You can dry yourselves off by it, and I'll make us a brew in a minute," she added as she lit two oil lamps hanging from the ceiling. Their yellow light revealed the rest of the room.

"Yes, of course," Chester replied, but he didn't move, captivated by the interior, which was deceptively large.

"I'll get a bed ready for the girl," Martha told Will, slipping away down a corridor. The boys listened as a cacophony of bangs and grunts immediately started up, accompanied by a load of chatter, as if Martha was talking to someone. She was clearly busy.

"Just look at this place!" Chester exclaimed as he and Will took in what was around them.

"Map chests," Will noted, spying three low-slung cupboards with brass corners against one wall. On top of the chests were a row of carved objects — Will could make out a figure with a rifle, and by it a cave cow — one of the large arachnids that lived in the Deeps. As his eyes passed over the rest of the room, he could see that suspended in the corners were all kinds of nautical paraphernalia — harpoons, ropes and pulleys, a small net, and even a ship's sextant of tarnished brass.

Then Will spotted several swords with wide, slightly curved blades, also mounted on the wall.

"Cutlasses! You've got to be kidding me!" he exclaimed. "So she's right. All this looks as though it came from a ship, and an old one at that. A galleon, perhaps?" he said to Chester. "See those beams up there." He pointed at the ceiling. "They're superancient, like they could have come from the Tudors' *Mary Rose*, five hundred years ago."

"But a ship . . . down here?" Chester asked. "How's that possible?"

"I don't know. And how did Martha get here?" Will posed just as she floated back into the room.

"Still haven't got that log on, have you, dearie?" she prompted Chester. There was nothing unpleasant about the way she was asking, as if a mother was reminding her son to get on with his chores.

"Sorry, Martha," Chester said with a smile. "I'll do it right away."

"Good lad," she said, then turned to Will. "So you're curious how I came to be down here?"

Embarrassed that she'd overheard him, he flushed, and looked awkwardly at his feet.

"I was pushed down the Pore by my husband," she said abruptly.

"Oh . . . ," Will floundered, stunned by her forthrightness.

"We were Banished from the Colony and lived in the Deeps as renegades for years. It wasn't easy, I can tell you, bringing up a young child in that forsaken place. Then, one day, I suppose my husband simply decided he'd had enough of us," she said as she opened the lid of a basket and pulled out some blankets. "You could call it a divorce, of sorts."

Martha was so matter-of-fact about it that Will began to feel less embarrassed. "Did you know any of the other renegades?" he asked. "Elliott was one of them — she went around with a man called Drake. Maybe you knew him?"

Martha straightened up with the blankets in her arms and looked at Will thoughtfully. "Drake . . . no, don't know the name. Probably after my time."

"What about Tom Cox?" Will tried. "He was like this archenemy of Drake's."

Martha tightened her arms around the blankets, her face hardening into a mask of pure hatred. "Oh, I knew that scum, all right. I've always reckoned my husband fell under his spell . . . and it was Cox told him to do it . . . to get rid of us," she hissed, her words tight, as if she was suddenly out of breath. Then her expression turned to one of despondency and she relaxed her grip on the blankets. She sniffed loudly, blew her nose on her sleeve, and continued. "Bring the girl so I can have a proper look at her."

Will carried Elliott into a small side room. Although there was a sizeable bed in the center with a pair of lank-looking pillows, it had clearly been used as a storeroom of sorts. A pile of oddments was heaped against one wall, as if Martha had just haphazardly thrown them there. Will could see a jumble of leather suitcases, an old tin trunk with ornate writing just visible on its lid, and many rolls of fabric. There was the slight scent of oil in the room as the lantern hissed gently, shedding its light.

"On here," Martha said, as she finished spreading the blankets over the bed. Once Will had put Elliott down, Martha sat beside the girl. She undid the rope that bound her broken arm to her chest and very carefully laid it out.

"She's taken a bad knock," she said as she examined Elliott's head. Turning her attention back to the broken arm, Martha burbled on to herself the whole time, and Will could only understand the odd snatch of what she was saying. "No, not a pretty sight," Martha commented, then inspected Elliott's hand, peering closely at the ends of her fingers. "But the circulation is still there. Good."

"Do you know how to fix her arm?" Will said. "Can you put a splint on it or something?"

Martha mumbled but didn't look up as she laid a hand on Elliott's forehead and then nodded, as if relieved. "No fever."

She made sure Elliott was in a comfortable position by arranging the pillows under her head, then went over to the window. She stared at something for several seconds before speaking. "I need a cup of tea."

"Tea?" Will said in disbelief.

But back in the main room, as the kettle boiled, Martha really did have something that appeared to be tea, which she spooned into a blackened kettle from a battered tin caddy. And she also had sugar, coffee, and a startling range of spices in square wooden boxes in a cupboard by the hearth.

They took their tea in chipped porcelain cups over to the table and sat in the wheelback chairs arranged around it. In the center of the table was a life-sized bust of a boy, which seemed to have been carved from a section of one of the old beams. The boy was smiling serenely as he looked skyward. And by the bust was a smaller maquette of two figures, an adult and a young child hand in hand. It hadn't been finished, and there were a couple of chisels and a little heap of shavings on the table by it. As Will studied it, he realized the larger of the two figures could have been Martha.

The new log on the fire began to burn, long red flames licking up from its underside. Their glow mingled with the yellow light of the oil lanterns in the room.

"It's nice here," Chester said as all three of them watched Bartleby make straight for the threadbare rug in front of the fire. Extending his claws, he pushed one paw then the other into the rug, over and over, pumping and kneading it as his massive shoulder blades seesawed under his hairless skin. Then, purring at an impossibly loud volume, he finally flopped down onto the rug. He rolled over on his back and stretched himself full length with a cavernous yawn.

"Bart's happy. He's found his place," Will said, grinning.

It was so reminiscent of the time Will had first seen the colossal cat at the Jerome house in the Colony that he was strangely moved. It almost felt to Will as though he was home again. Glancing at Chester, he could see that his friend, too, had forgotten all his worries for the moment. As if the boys were visiting an aunt, there was something so domestic and familiar about the situation they found themselves in, particularly with the taste of sugared tea in their mouths — even if it lacked milk.

"Where did all the stuff in this room come from?" Will ventured. "Was it really a ship?"

Martha nodded. "Most of it was here already, but Nathaniel salvaged some more from a galleon in one of the Seven Sisters," she replied.

"I thought it was a galleon," Will said, nodding. "But do you know how it got there?"

Martha shook her head, not looking at either of them. She cleared her throat so loudly it made Chester sit up in his chair, then she blew her nose on her sleeve again.

"Can you take us to it?" Will said, determined to find out as much as he could about what was down here.

"Nathaniel found other vessels, too. He would go off for weeks on end and come back with all manner of items, and then work on them here. He was so clever with his hands. All the materials for our barricade were salvaged from a metal ship."

Will frowned at Chester, mouthing the words "metal ship?" but now didn't seem the right time to inquire further —

there was something more pressing he needed to find out.

"And Nathaniel," Will asked. "Where is he now?"

Martha groaned with the effort of getting out of the chair. She waddled over to an oil lantern and lifted it down from its hook, then beckoned the boys to follow her. She paused on the porch to glance down at the various flower beds and, putting her head back, inhaled deeply through her nose. Will sniffed, too, catching not just the smell of Aniseed Fire but an abundance of other, sweeter scents. "Glorious," Martha declared, then led the boys from the porch and onto a winding path toward the higher ground at the rear of the cavern.

They were passing a bed of what looked like smoldering lupins, their tips emitting a glow that alternated between an intense red and a more subdued orange, when she said, "Mind you don't go near the Spitting Caps. They can be nasty blighters."

Neither of the boys was certain if she'd meant what she said, but they weren't going to take any chances, so both kept to the far side of the cinder track. Appearing from nowhere, Bartleby slipped in behind the boys, evidently not wanting to miss the outing.

Seconds later, they found they were standing before a carved wooden angel. It was as tall as a man, with a tranquil expression on its face and long tousled locks that draped over its shoulders and its swanlike wings, which were folded behind its back. "Nat . . . Nathaniel," she whispered. "This is where I laid him to rest." She dropped her eyes to the carefully arranged stones below the angel.

"Then . . . then he's . . . uh . . . dead," Will said, his voice hollow.

"Yes, two years ago," Martha replied huskily, her eyes still downcast as Bartleby backed up to the angel. He began to cock his hind leg. Will and Chester watched, both of them mortified at what the cat was obviously contemplating. He became aware of their intense interest in him and seemed to hesitate. Then he snorted and lifted his leg higher, and Will knew he had to do something to stop the inevitable.

"Bart! No!" he whispered, frantically making small pointing movements that the cat should leave.

Bartleby got the message. Glowering at Will, he lowered his leg and slunk away to the back of the shack. Martha appeared to be none the wiser as Will, feeling he should say something to fill the long silence, spoke up again.

"Did you make the angel for him?"

"No, it came from the ship — from the prow — but I carved his face into it . . . my boy's face," she said distantly, as she scratched the back of her head. "I chose this spot because it's where Nathaniel liked to come and sit. It was his place. And by the wall, over there," she said, tipping the lamp so the light fell on the ground past the angel, "there are other graves. Nathaniel always reckoned the men who built the shack are buried here."

She turned on her heels as if she had said all she was going to say and was about to return to the shack, when she stopped and held very still. "There's something you should know. Nathaniel was on one of his foraging trips when he fell down a crevice. He broke several ribs. The spiders swarmed. They seem to be able to sense when something is hurt or weakened, and they came at him, scores of them."

She looked at Will and Chester in turn. "Nathaniel hadn't taken enough Aniseed Fire with him, but he still managed to escape from them and get home." She didn't speak for several seconds. "I can take care of most things . . . illnesses and wounds. You have to learn fast in the Deeps." She frowned. "Nathaniel's ribs were healing and he was doing just fine when . . . when he was suddenly taken with a fever. A bad one. I did everything I could for him." She let out a quavery breath and brushed the front of her skirt with her dirt-encrusted fingers. "That's all there is to it. He was nineteen years old and my only child. He just faded away."

"I'm sorry," Chester murmured.

Martha's mouth clamped shut as though she was fighting back tears, and the silence stretched out. Although Will wanted to offer some words of condolence to the woman, he couldn't think of what to say. Then Martha spoke again, her voice steadier.

"Nathaniel was older than your friend, and strong as an ox, but there's something foul in the air in these parts. Like the spiders, it waits until you're hurt, then it creeps into you. It got a grip on him, and I just hope the same thing doesn't happen to her."

"So, let me get this straight—you've been a Styx all along," Dr. Burrows said as he sat across from the Rebecca twin.

"I'm *Thtyx* by birth. You don't *th*uddenly become a *Thtyx*," Rebecca replied, her temper flaring.

"You lisped again. Is there something wr—?" Dr. Burrows began to ask.

"Broke a few teeth when I fell down the Pore," Rebecca interrupted, now enunciating very precisely as she did her utmost to control her lisp. "And I jumped down it because I wanted to help you."

He was silent for a second or two, regarding her a little skeptically before he continued. "So, you were a Styx from birth, and Will was a Colonist. . . ." Taking off his glasses, Dr. Burrows kneaded the bridge of his nose. "But you . . . he . . . you are . . . he was . . . ," he said, his words tripping over each other. Finally, as he replaced his glasses, it was as if his various thoughts were also coming back into focus. "Then how did we end up adopting both of you?"

"Luck of the draw. You and Mum took Will in, and the Styx Panoply decreed I should be there, too, to keep tabs on him," the Rebecca twin said, giving Dr. Burrows a half smile. "Why, do you disapprove or *th*omething?"

"Well, quite frankly, yes . . . I think we should have been told," Dr. Burrows huffed.

The Rebecca twin laughed snidely. "But you didn't tell Will or me we were adopted," she fired back, playing with him. "Don't you think we had a right to know that?"

"That's not the same at all. It seems you knew all along that you were adopted — but that aside, your mother and I were going to tell you when the time was right," Dr. Burrows said. He frowned and inspected a broken fingernail as he tried to deal with what he'd just learned.

Rebecca had told him as much of the story as suited her, but nothing like the whole story. And she certainly wasn't going to reveal that she had an identical sister.

"It all seems a bit irregular," Dr. Burrows finally stated, squinting through his crooked glasses at the taciturn Limiter, who was lingering behind the Styx girl's shoulder. "We went through the proper channels for adoption, so I really don't understand how we got you as well."

"You talk about me as though you were buying a used car."

"Don't be silly, Rebecca. It wasn't like that at all," Dr. Burrows said in an exasperated tone. "I just don't understand how it could happen."

"And I honestly couldn't care less how it happened," the Rebecca twin replied, beginning to look slightly bored. "We had friends in the adoption agency. We have friends everywhere."

"But I feel as though we've been tricked . . . as though your mother and I have been horribly deceived," Dr. Burrows continued. "And I don't like that," he added categorically.

"And I suppose you don't like my people, either?" the Rebecca twin prompted.

"Your people . . . ?" Dr. Burrows began, not failing to notice the edge to her voice.

"Yes, my people. They didn't treat you badly in the Colony, did they? Are you saying you disapprove of their methods?" The Rebecca twin was bristling now, the Limiter stirring behind her.

Dr. Burrows held up his hands in alarm. "No, I didn't mean that at all. It's not my place to judge. My role is to observe and record — I don't get involved."

The Rebecca twin yawned as she got to her feet, brushing herself down. "So you're my adoptive father, yet you're saying you're not involved. How does that work?" Her mood seemed to have suddenly changed, as if her anger had been put on purely for effect.

Dr. Burrows, his mouth open but with no idea how to respond, was all at sea now. Heaped upon his chronic confusion, this person before him — who he'd thought was his little girl — was someone formidable, and although he didn't admit it to himself, he was actually quite intimidated by her. Particularly since the Styx soldier was staring at him from the shadows with his dead eyes, the eyes of a killer.

"So, Dad," the Rebecca twin said, emphasizing *Dad* as if she had absolutely no respect for the title, "I've made sure you've been fed, just like in the good old days, and I can see you're feeling like yourself again. So tell me about these," she demanded, producing the small stone tablets from inside her jacket. Dr. Burrows immediately touched his own pocket, finding it empty. "They look like a map of some sort, and that's just what we need right now," the twin went on. "You're going to find us a way out of this place, and we're going to help you to do it."

"Oh, great," Dr. Burrows replied tepidly, taking back the tablets she was proffering him.

"HI, JEAN,"** Mrs. Burrows puffed as she answered a
call from her sister on her cell phone. She was looking
flustered as she hurried along Highfield's Main Street.

"Out of breath? Yes, just been to the gym," she said, hiking
up a shoulder to stop the strap of her bag from sliding off.
She held the phone away from her ear in response to a hoot of
laughter from Auntie Jean, which was loud enough to be heard
by a man passing in the opposite direction. "Yes, can't tell you
how good it makes me feel. I've booked a month's worth of
sessions with a personal trainer. You should give it a try."

This elicited another piercing hoot, which sent a nearby
pigeon flapping away.

But as Mrs. Burrows tore along the sidewalk, Will would
have been amazed by the change in his adoptive mother's bearing. There was a lightness to her step that he wouldn't have
merited possible. She already looked years younger.

As her sister chatted on, Mrs. Burrows glanced at her watch.
"Look, there's no news from the police and I really can't talk
now. Expecting a delivery at the apartment," she said, ending
the call before her sister had the opportunity to respond.

As she came around the corner, she saw that the mover's truck was already there.

"Oh golly, sorry I'm late. Got held up," she called out as she broke into a run toward a man in blue overalls who was just about to get back into his truck. Once she'd opened up the apartment, he carried a whole batch of cardboard boxes inside. She wasted no time slicing the tape on one to inspect the contents.

"New place?" he inquired as he heaved yet another box onto the top of a pile.

"Yes, I put all this into storage until I found somewhere to live," Mrs. Burrows replied distractedly as she took out several of her old videotapes and tossed them straight into a trash bag. "Time to clean house. To really clean house."

After the man had brought in the last of the boxes, she spent the whole afternoon going through them. There were so many that there was barely any room to move around, but she eventually came to a batch that had **Bedroom 3** scrawled on them with a felt marker.

"Will's," she said as she opened the first of these. She unwrapped the white paper from the precious finds that had been on the shelves in his room — his "museum," as he had called it. There were so many Victorian pâté dishes, broken clay pipes, and Codswallop and perfume bottles that her lap was soon full of items and she had to find space on the floor for the rest.

Then she came to a box of his books and, grunting with the weight of it, lugged it over to the table by the window. At first she took each book out to check through it, shaking it by the spine to see if anything had been hidden in the pages. Finding absolutely nothing and growing weary of the process, she began to take the remaining books from the box and stack them on the table without looking inside them. Near the bottom of the box was what purported to be a *Geological Guide to the British Isles* — a book dating back to the sixties or seventies, from the outdated design of its cover. Mrs. Burrows didn't pay it any particular attention, but as she glanced at the book that had been below it in the box, she frowned. This book had no jacket, but in faded gilt letters on its clothbound cover was the title, *Geological Guide to the British Isles*.

"Two copies of the same book?" she said to herself as she picked up the one with the dust jacket again. She opened it. The pages weren't printed — instead there was handwriting on them. "Hello," she said, knowing immediately whose it was. Her husband's. Dr. Burrows's. She removed the jacket to see what was really underneath: a notebook with a marbled purple and brown cover, and stuck to the front was a label with *Ex Libris* in ornate writing and a drawing of a wise-looking owl wearing circular glasses. On this label was scrawled JOURNAL. She recognized her husband's messy handwriting again.

"So this is it. I'm finally going to find out what really happened," she announced to the many piles of boxes in the room. And she didn't once leave the table as she read the book from cover to cover, turning the pages, which more often than not had muddy fingerprints on them. "Will," she said, smiling affectionately, because she knew they would have been his.

As she progressed through the journal, she became breathless with excitement. She was at last finding out what Will and Chester had learned before they went missing. Although she knew nothing of the tunnel that the boys had re-excavated beneath her former home on Broadlands Avenue or if indeed there was any link between their disappearance and her husband's observations, she still felt she was making progress. Mrs. Burrows avidly read her husband's thoughts about the strange people he'd identified in Highfield, the luminescent orb that had turned up at Mrs. Tantrumi's house, and a local well-to-do businessman from the eighteenth century called Sir Gabriel Martineau. As she came to the section on the buildings this man had put up in Highfield old town, including the square that bore his name, she stopped to stare out the window for a few moments before diving into the journal again. Then she came to the final entries, noticing the date of one of them.

"That was the night . . . the night Roger left," she said, her voice tense. Her eyes settled on the words, *I have to go down there.* Reading to the end of the entry, the last in the journal, she came back to these words again.

"What did he mean, *down there*? Down where?"

She checked through the blank pages at the very end of the journal, making sure she hadn't missed anything. On the inside of the back cover she spotted a name and telephone number in pencil. *Mr. Ashmi—Parish Archives*, she read.

Will and Chester spent the night in the main room — Will on a pile of carpets that Martha had spread out on the floor by the map chests, and Chester on a piece of furniture she referred to as the "chaise longue." Chester's eyes had lit up when she'd first mentioned it, imagining he would be sleeping on something approximating a real bed. He was to be sorely disappointed. Once the chaise longue had been cleared, he found that it was so short his feet hung off the end, and also that its old upholstery was as hard as nails. Despite this, the soothing sound of the fire, and their fatigue, insured that both he and Will fell asleep within seconds.

They were aroused from their slumbers by Martha rattling the kettle on the hearth.

"Good morning!" she trilled in a jolly voice as both boys heaved their aching bodies to the table.

"Tea," she said as she handed cups of it to them. Then she placed a chopping board on the table, on which was a bunch of gray plant stems and a selection of white roots of different sizes and shapes. "How about some breakfast? I'll bet you're both starving," she said, as she set about slicing up the stems and roots.

Chester eyed the unappetizing mass of vegetable matter as she worked on it. "Um, really, no thanks, Martha," he moaned. "I feel a bit sick, actually."

"Me, too," Will said.

Martha frowned. "It might be because you're new to this place," she suggested. "It takes a while to adjust." As she was chopping, the knife slipped from her hand and flew into the air, where it performed a couple of revolutions. "Bother!" she said as she caught it again, and finished the job. "I remember Nathaniel and I went through the same thing."

"Low gravity," Will said. He'd watched what had happened with the knife and was nodding to himself. "Yes! Martha's right. It could be the low gravity that's making us feel like this. S'pose we just need to get used to it."

"Well, you're both going to eat, whether you like it or not. You've got to keep up your strength," Martha said, sliding from her chair and returning to the hearth, where she scraped the diced vegetables into a pan of boiling water. "A bowl of my soup is what you need," she said firmly.

"What about Elliott?" Will asked suddenly. "How is she?"

"Don't you worry," Martha said. "I checked on her during the night and she's still out for the count this morning."

"Can you do something about her arm?" Chester ventured.

"First item on my list today," Martha said, picking energetically at a rear molar with the nail of her pinkie finger. After examining whatever she'd scraped off her tooth, she sucked it back into her mouth and chewed on it with a pensive expression. Chester, who'd been observing her do this, pushed his tea away from him. If he'd looked pale before, he now turned green. He gulped loudly. "Really, no soup . . . nothing for me, Martha."

"You probably should have some," Will advised. "We haven't eaten properly for ages, and besides . . ." He glanced down at his stomach. "It might get everything working again."

"That's just a little more information than I need," Chester said.

An hour later, they all went to Elliott's room. Will and Chester hovered on the threshold as Martha gave the girl a thorough examination.

"So why is she still unconscious?" Chester asked.

Martha ran her hands over the girl's scalp and the nape of her neck, then used her thumb to lift an eyelid so she could check the pupil. "She's concussed. She's had a bad knock to the head. Anyway, better for her to be out while I set her arm. Come and help me, will you?"

The boys sidled up to Martha. She placed a pair of splints at the ready on either side of Elliott's arm. "Take these," she said to Chester, passing him a couple of rolls of linen bandages from her apron pocket. "Right. Will, go around the other side of the bed. I need you to hold her steady."

Will did as she directed. Martha then gripped Elliott's wrist and pulled several times. The boys heard clicking as the broken bones grated against each other.

"Ohh," Chester said. "Awful . . ."

From behind Will there was a dull thud.

"What was that?" Will asked, still gripping Elliott by the shoulders.

"Your friend has just passed out. Leave him there — I need you to keep the girl steady," Martha said to Will. "I've got to get this right." She pulled on Elliott's arm again, applying tension as she manipulated it. Beads of sweat formed on her forehead and she mumbled to herself all the while she worked.

"That looks better," Will said.

Martha nodded. "It's so swollen it's difficult to tell, but I think the bones are back in place now," she said. She spent a few more minutes checking the arm, then appeared to be satisfied. She carefully put the splints on either side of the arm and bound them with the linen strips, tying off each roll.

Martha straightened up and sighed, as Will also got up from the bed. He turned to see Chester, in a heap on the floor.

"We'd better get him next door," Martha chuckled.

"The *Highfield Bugle*, 19th June 1895," Mrs. Burrows observed as she leaned over the old newspaper spread open before her on the table. "So, Mr. Ashmi, what exactly am I looking for?" she called out.

Mrs. Burrows was in the Highfield historical records office, where documents dating as far back as the tenth century were kept. As no answer appeared to be forthcoming from Mr. Ashmi, she scanned the newspaper, noticing the title in faded print halfway down the page. "'*The Ghosts of the Earth*.' Now there's a headline guaranteed to grab your attention!"

"Certainly is, and that's the report you should read," came the muffled response from the far end of the basement, past umpteen tiers of freestanding shelves on which were a mind-boggling number of document bundles and boxes. Mr. Ashmi, the borough archivist, stopped delving in the box before him and stuck his head around the edge of the rack to look at Mrs. Burrows. His horn-rimmed glasses caught the sickly yellow illumination of the strip lights overhead as he spoke. "It's typical of the incidents."

"OK," Mrs. Burrows agreed. "But I hope you're going to tell me why I need to read it when I've finished." She turned again to the newspaper and began:

"*Work on a tunnel for the new Highfield & Crossly North station was abandoned after an incident in the early hours of the morning Wednesday last. The Harris brothers, the celebrated tunneling engineers from Canada, assisted by a four-man work gang, had drilled and set explosives in a deposit of sandstone. The warning Klaxon was sounded, and the area cleared.'"*

"The next bit gets to the nub of it," Mr. Ashmi grunted as he heaved a box of papers from a shelf and pushed it into the central aisle, then beetled off to another part of the basement.

Mrs. Burrows cleared her throat and continued:

"'After the detonations had been performed, the Harris brothers and the work gang, now accompanied by Mr. Wallace, the Northern & Counties Railways assistant surveyor, re-entered the excavations. As they waited for the dust to settle in order to make an assessment of the workface, they heard grating noises under their feet. They at once suspected it to be subsidence and began to withdraw from the tunnel. However, the grating noises became even louder, portending a terrible scene as strong lights suddenly shone into the tunnel from out of the very ground itself. All those present said they beheld trapdoors opening in the bedrock, from which an army of phantomlike apparitions marched out.'"

Mrs. Burrows stopped reading. "Is this for real?" she asked.

"*The Times* took it seriously enough to run it the next day," Mr. Ashmi replied from behind a rack. "Keep going."

"If you say so," Mrs. Burrows said with a shrug, then read on:

"'Mr. Wallace stated that the figures sported dark fustian or gabardine coats, and that they wore white collars around their necks. In their hands they held spheres from which issued bolts of green light. As the menacing figures began to advance, he and the work team were afeared and fled for their lives. According to Mr. Wallace, the Harris brothers did not run, courageously holding their ground. Thomas

Harris armed himself with a ten-foot iron ramrod, while his younger brother, Joshua, wielded a pickax handle.'"

"And guess what became of the Harris brothers?" Mr. Ashmi called to Mrs. Burrows, sounding as if he was closer now.

"They were never seen again?" Mrs. Burrows said, peering at the shelves nearest to her.

"Got it in one!" Mr. Ashmi congratulated her.

Mrs. Burrows gave up trying to locate the elusive Mr. Ashmi, and went back to the article:

"'Police officers from the Highfield constabulary were summoned, and shortly afterward they escorted Mr. Wallace back into the tunnel. The roof above the workface had caved in, and they beheld no sign of the Harris brothers, nor the army of phantoms. Despite further excavations, the bodies of the brothers have not been located.'"

"And they never were," Mr. Ashmi put in. "Strange, don't you think?"

"Yes, very strange," Mrs. Burrows agreed.

"Well, try this. It's also from the *Highfield Bugle*, after a raid by the German Luftwaffe in the summer of 1943." Mr. Ashmi breezed by the table, depositing yet another old newspaper in front of Mrs. Burrows.

"Why?" she said to his retreating back.

"Just look at the last paragraphs," he replied, waving a hand in the air as he went.

Mrs. Burrows sighed. *"'Report on Yesterday's Raid,'"* she read, then scanned down the article. *"'Incendiaries fell on Vincent Square . . . roof of St. Joseph's church blown off'* . . . Ah, think I've found it. . . . *'At noon, a land mine was dropped on the Lyon's Corner House, killing ten; the millinery works, killing three; and also completely destroying the private residence at No. 46, in which Mr. and Mrs. Smith and their two children, of ages four and seven, perished.*

"'However, when the bodies of the Smith family were retrieved from the rubble, the corpses of five unidentified men were also discovered. The men had evidently been in the cellar, and were described as being remarkably similar in appearance, with pale faces and thickset builds. They were dressed in civilian apparel which did not seem to be British in origin, immediately raising suspicions that they might be Nazi spies. The Military Police were called to investigate and the five corpses removed to the St. Pancras Mortuary for further examination, but they were apparently mislaid en route. The Smith family's maid, Daisy Heir, had been fortunate not to have been in the scullery at the time of the raid because she was collecting the family's weekly meat rations at the butcher's in Disraeli Street. When questioned by the Military Police, Miss Heir said that there had been no guests staying at the house, and that she had no knowledge whatsoever of the five men and how they came to be there. She could only suggest that they had been looters, who had somehow gained access into the house and secreted themselves down in the cellar during the raid.'"

Mrs. Burrows looked up from the newspaper to find Mr. Ashmi standing there. "All this is gripping stuff," she said. "But can you tell me why my husband wrote your name and number in his journal?"

"These reports are why," Mr. Ashmi replied, easing himself into a chair across the table from her. "Since the early eighteen hundreds, there have been accounts of these odd-looking squat men and also the taller 'phantoms' wearing black habits with white collars. These aren't just isolated incidents — they've occurred with surprising regularity through the past two centuries and up until the current day."

"So?" Mrs. Burrows said.

Mr. Ashmi slid some typewritten pages in front of her. "In the months before he went missing, your husband, Roger, researched these incidents with me. It took many days of work, but he compiled this list."

Mrs. Burrows turned through the pages; she had to agree that the sheer number of reports was quite extraordinary.

"Funny thing . . . ," Mr. Ashmi began, leaning forward as if he was worried that he might be overheard.

"What?" Mrs. Burrows asked, also leaning forward, but not entirely convinced she was dealing with a person in possession of all his marbles.

"I had one of these lists under lock and key in my office," he said. He drew his hands through the air as if he was about to do a magic trick. "But it vanished." He leaned even farther forward and lowered his voice. "And quite a number of the records themselves have 'gone walkabout' from my shelves in here, too. If it wasn't that I use my own rather idiosyncratic archive system — which no one else knows — I expect more of them would have disappeared."

"Oh," Mrs. Burrows replied, not sure what else she could say. As she turned her attention back to the typewritten list, she saw that there were notes jotted next to some of the reports, not in her husband's handwriting. "Is this you?" she inquired, pointing at the writing.

"No, that's Ben Wilbrahams, the American. He's also investigating these incidents, for a film or something. In fact, you should really have a word with him — he's always upstairs." Mr. Ashmi pointed a finger at the ceiling, indicating the town library on the floor above.

"Yes, right, I will," Mrs. Burrows said, not intending to do anything of the sort.

Clutching the photocopies of the newspaper articles Mr. Ashmi had insisted she take, Mrs. Burrows was glad to leave the dusty archives. She could very easily picture her husband down there, eagerly poring over the obscure newspaper reports. It brought back too many memories of the old days and her chronic unhappiness at the way things had been. All her husband had seemed to want to do was hide away in some fuddy-duddy self-fabricated world where he could pretend to himself that he was a serious academic doing something meaningful. As she mounted the steps to the ground floor, she growled with frustration. Frustration because she knew her husband had been capable of so much more than his job as the curator of the local museum, but he just didn't have the get-up-and-go to find something better, something — most crucially to her — with a reasonable salary.

She folded the photocopied papers and shoved them into her bag. Despite Mr. Ashmi's obvious conviction that there had been strange goings-on in Highfield, it was all too fanciful for her to take seriously. She wondered if her husband had been drawn in by Mr. Ashmi's infectious enthusiasm, and whether that had led him to make the wild statements she'd read in his journal.

In order to leave the building she had to pass through the library, and there she thought she spotted the man that

Mr. Ashmi had referred to: the American. Although he had a neatly trimmed beard, his hair — black and quite long — made him look as if he'd just rolled out of bed. Sitting alone with several books open before him on the reading desk, he was deftly spinning a pen with one hand, rotating it round and round in endless circles. He glanced up and, narrowing his eyes through his wire-rimmed spectacles, gave Mrs. Burrows a broad smile. As she realized she had been caught staring at him, she immediately averted her gaze and hastened toward the main door.

9

"**AVAST, YE SWABS!**" Will challenged Chester the moment his friend emerged onto the porch. Will was advancing up the garden path toward him, one hand on his hip as he slashed a cutlass through the air.

Chester grinned, then his face went blank. "I've got no idea what that actually means."

"No idea what *what* means?"

"Swabs. What the heck are swabs? Pieces of cotton wool?"

"No, I think it used to mean something really nasty, so you'd better defend your honor, you lily-livered cuttlefish!"

Will stopped brandishing the sword to admire it for a moment. "Considering it must be probably centuries old, this is in brilliant nick. You can see tiny pictures of a cross and a branch engraved on it, and some words in what looks like Latin," he said, peering at the cup-shaped piece of metal that curved from the cross guard to the pommel, and which served to protect the swordsman's hand in combat. Then he attempted to read out the inscription, stumbling over the words. "*Soli Deo Gloria.*" He looked at Chester with a shrug.

"Sorry, dear Gloria?" Chester suggested, not really paying attention as he spotted the assortment of other weapons Will

had spread out on the floor of the porch. "If it's a duel you want . . . ," he declared as he chose a long-bladed dagger and tried it out, stabbing the air in front of him. "No, that doesn't do it for me," he muttered as his eyes fell on by far the largest of the weapons, a metal pole nearly six feet long with both a lethal-looking spike and a large ax head at the end. "This is more like it," he said. "What is it, anyway?"

"That's a halberd," Will replied.

"A halibut?" Chester laughed as he weighed it in his hands. "Right! On guard!" he yelled as he launched himself down the front steps, landing just in front of Will. "Your time has come, White Beard!" he said.

Will lunged with his cutlass several times, Chester blocking with the halberd, the clash of steel ringing around the luminous garden. Then Chester went on the offensive, swinging the halberd at Will, although without much force. Taking advantage of the low gravity, Will easily avoided the weapon by leaping high into the air.

Chester continued to sweep the halberd at Will, who each time sprang high above it. After a while, Chester got the giggles and couldn't go on. "This is like one of those crazy kung fu movies where they all leap around as though they've got springs on their feet."

Will was trying his utmost to maintain his very best murderous pirate face, but couldn't stop himself from laughing, too. "Yeah, you're right. What was that film called — *Leaping Dragon, Flapping Duck*, or something like that?"

"Ready thyself, White Beard," Chester said. "Prepare to face the largest can opener in the world!" He swung the halberd again.

To avoid the attack, Will executed a perfect backward somersault in the air, landing squarely on his feet farther down the path.

"Aha!" he exclaimed, delighted with his acrobatics. "Not so easy to kill, am I, Ninja Rawls?"

"Show-off," Chester muttered.

They continued to play-fight each other, vaulting across to other paths they'd discovered between the flower beds, gradually moving their battle to the rear of the shack, where they hurtled between the rooftops of the small outbuildings.

"Let's stop a minute — need to catch my breath," Chester puffed, landing beside Will.

"Yeah, OK," Will replied, passing his cutlass in front of him in a figure eight. "This is great, isn't it?" he said, smiling at his friend.

Chester smiled back, nodding in agreement. As the days had passed, they had adjusted to the reduced gravity, and the nausea they'd experienced to begin with had all but gone. Martha looked after them well, and without the constant threat of the

Styx hanging over them, for the first time in a long while they could truly relax and enjoy themselves.

To fill the hours, they devised new activities to keep themselves occupied. Will had found an ornate ivory chess set in one of the trunks, and they would play into the small hours, drinking endless cups of tea. And Martha was only too happy to teach them about the different properties of the plants in her garden and entertain them with stories about the Colony and the Deeps. She'd been reluctant to let them use her crossbow when they first asked her, but finally gave in to their constant requests. Although it took them a while to master the weapon, they eventually got the hang of it and set up some targets by the barricade at the end of the garden. They found it amazing how true the flights of the bolts were, traveling in an almost straight line with little or no loss whatsoever of trajectory — another feature of the low gravity.

"OK, Captain Snow, let's do it," Chester said, now that he'd recovered.

"Only if you can catch *me* first," Will dared his friend, leaping clean over the roof of the main shack and landing on the ground in front of it. There he took refuge behind some bushes that, exceptionally for the garden, didn't seem to emit any light. Chester stole around the side of the shack, then surveyed the garden. Guessing exactly where Will was hiding, he propelled himself at him, wailing with his best battle cry.

Will ducked out from the bushes and onto the path, his sword up and ready to repel the attack. Chester advanced. But in the blink of an eye, something dropped in front of him.

"Wh —?!" Chester gasped.

It was Bartleby. As the cat arched his back, Will saw that all his muscles were bunched under his hairless skin, as if he was about to pounce. Bartleby edged forward and hissed at Chester with such vehemence that he dropped the halberd. As he hastily stepped backward, he tripped and fell into a border of dainty plants that let off a pinkish hue. The cat, still in a panther crouch, crept toward the terrified boy.

"Will, do something!" Chester squawked. "Call your crazed moggy off!"

"Bart! Stop!" Will cried.

Bartleby glanced at his new master for confirmation, then lowered himself to the ground. But he was still watching Chester intently, as if he didn't entirely trust him.

"Silly old cat," Will said, stroking him affectionately on the head. "What did you do that for? You didn't really think Chester was attacking me, did you?"

Chester was more than a little put out that his friend was taking the incident so lightly. "Will, I swear, it was about to go for me. It had those sick giant claws out!"

"I'm sure he wouldn't have gone that far," Will said.

"Could've fooled me," Chester grumbled as he picked himself up and retrieved the halberd. He stared angrily at Bartleby, who had begun to purr as Will continued to rub his temples. "Know what?" Chester added.

"What?" Will asked.

"I've just realized how much you two look like Shaggy and Scooby-Doo."

Will was just framing a suitably rude response when Martha called to them from the front door.

"You'd better come."

The boys trooped up to the shack and followed Martha inside. She hovered by the edge of the table, her anxiety evident.

"Martha?" Chester asked. "What's the matter?"

"I'm afraid it might have begun," she said in a flat voice. "I checked first thing and wasn't sure, but I think it has."

Will dropped his cutlass onto the table with a clatter and took a step toward Martha. "You're talking about Elliott, aren't you? What's happened?"

"Remember I told you about Nathaniel and the germule that did for him?" Martha said.

"Elliott's got the fever?" Chester gabbled quickly. "Oh no, Will, she's caught it, too."

"Now, hold your horses," Martha said, raising her dirty palms to them. "It's not definite, not yet — it might not be the same thing. But she has taken a turn for the worse, and it doesn't look good."

In silence, they all made their way to Elliott's room.

"Oh no," Chester whispered.

They saw right away that a change had come over the unconscious girl. Her face looked very shiny and flushed, and the long shirt she was wearing was soaked with her perspiration, as were the bedclothes all around her. Martha went over to Elliott and gently lifted the towel from her forehead. She dipped it in a basin of water beside the bed and wrung it out before replacing it on the girl's head.

"You said her arm was doing well," Will said, trying to look for something positive to say.

"Yes, it's the oddest thing, but her bones mended very quickly. It's as though . . . ," Martha began, then trailed off.

Both Will and Chester gave her inquiring looks.

"They would say in the Colony that she's been blessed by the preacher's touch," Martha said.

"The preacher? But I thought they're all Styx, aren't they?" Will asked, his expression one of puzzlement as he remembered the religious ceremonies he'd been obliged to attend during his months in the Colony. "That can't be good."

"Oh yes, it is — you see, the Styx are not like other people," Martha replied. "They heal in half the time that you and I do. The girl's bones have knitted together so fast I've even been able to take the splints off."

The boys had been so preoccupied with the disturbing news about the fever that they had failed to notice Elliott's injured arm was now only bound by a lightly wrapped bandage.

"But the fever," Chester said, turning to Martha. "I feel so guilty — we've left you to do everything while we've been horsing around . . . while Elliott got like this. Tell us how we can help."

"For starters, we have to keep her temperature down — the poultice on her forehead should be moistened every ten minutes or so," Martha said.

"Fine — you go and get some rest, Martha," Will said. "We'll take turns looking after her."

In a chair by the bed, Will was on his second three-hour shift, having recently relieved Chester, who'd stumbled wearily away to his chaise longue. After a while, Will caught himself beginning to doze off as he slumped lower and lower in his seat.

"Come on," he growled, then slapped his cheeks several times to wake himself up. In a bid to keep himself occupied, he began to look over the diagrams he'd drawn of how he thought the Pore and the other similarly huge openings might once have been open at the surface, but then had become sealed up. To do this he'd tried to remember everything he could about plate tectonics and what happens when there is movement between two plates. "Destructive, Constructive, and Conservative Margins," he murmured to himself.

And, in a small picture at the very bottom of the page, his imagination had run away with him and he'd drawn a galleon tipping over the edge of a huge, swirling whirlpool in the ocean. He closed one eye as he contemplated it, and found that he was whistling through his teeth. He stopped immediately.

"Holy smokes, I'm turning into my dad," he muttered as he flipped over to a clean page. He tried to jot down his observations from the last week. The trouble was that he didn't have anything new or particularly interesting to record, and his efforts soon degenerated into a series of overlapping circular doodles scribbled in the margin, which almost matched the number of times he was yawning.

An hour later, he'd discarded his journal and was hunched over a Bible with a thick leather cover, which he'd discovered in a trunk earlier that day. The dry pages crackled like old leaves as he turned them, and now and then he squinted at a sentence he thought he might be able to translate, blinking his eyes with disappointment when he found he couldn't get anywhere with it.

"Why didn't I take Spanish at school?" he asked himself as he closed the Bible. He twisted around in his chair to contemplate the chessboard set up on a small side table next to him. After a few moments, he slid his queen to a new square, but didn't take his finger from it.

"No, that's a stupid move," he grumbled, moving the piece straight back to its original position. He shot a look at his imaginary opponent. "Sorry, not thinking straight."

Elliott stirred and said something. Will was immediately at her side. "It's me, Elliott — it's Will. Can you hear me?"

He took her hand and clasped it in his. Her eyes were moving rapidly under her closed lids, and the normally pale skin of her face was a disquieting color, as if she'd been dusted with crimson powder and it had collected around all her features, particularly her cracked lips.

"It's all right," Will said soothingly.

Her mouth twitched as if she was trying to speak but didn't have the strength to draw breath. She frowned as if there was some internal conflict going on in her head, something in her febrile dreams that she was trying to resolve. Then she murmured a few words that Will could just about catch. The first sounded like "Drake"; a few minutes later she said something which could have been "Limiter."

"You're safe now, Elliott. We're all OK," Will said softly, realizing she might be reliving the events at the Pore.

Then she said Drake's name again, much more clearly this time, and her eyelids looked as though they might actually open.

"And Drake's fine," Will assured her, although he didn't know this for certain.

Elliott began to babble — to Will's ear it sounded like a bunch of numbers. Over and over she said them, at a barely audible level. He snatched up his pencil and jotted them down next to his doodles. She seemed to be repeating a string of the same numbers, but he wasn't sure he'd got all of them down in the right order.

Just then Chester shambled in.

"Can't be your turn already?" Will asked him.

"No," he replied sourly. "I just couldn't get to sleep out there."

"Why not?"

"That bloomin' moggy of yours is snoring so loudly, I swear I kept waking up thinking I was about to be run over by a moped."

"Well, just wake *him* up," Will said, unable to stifle a grin. "Maybe you should try whispering the word 'dog' in his ear. That might work."

"Yeah, right, and get my face bitten off," Chester grunted. He looked at Elliott. "How's she doing?"

"Very hot, but she's been trying to talk. She mentioned Drake, and I think she might also be having nightmares because she said 'Limiter.' And she kept repeating some numbers — I don't know what they are, but I wrote down all the ones I could hear —"

"Like these?" Chester interrupted, pulling a scrap of paper from his pocket.

Will took it from him and compared the sequence with the one in his journal — Chester's was the more complete.

"Hey, cool. But do you think that's all of them?" Will asked.

"I reckon so — she said them enough times. Suppose they must be important to her, somehow."

"Eleven digits," Will pondered. "Maybe it's a code?"

"You tell me, Sherlock," Chester replied, then yawned as he sank down to the floor at the foot of the bed, and out of Will's sight.

"Oh . . . good night, then," Will said in a disappointed tone. He'd been hoping that Chester would keep him company on his vigil. But the only answer he received from his friend was some loud snoring, which continued unabated as Will puzzled over the sequence of figures, trying to work out if there was some sort of pattern to them.

Mrs. Burrows came out of the employment agency, stopping on the sidewalk as she put the appointment cards in her bag.

"Burrows," she overheard someone saying, then, "bad business," but she didn't catch the rest.

She turned to find two young women with a gaggle of children around them. The women had clearly recognized her from the way they were staring. One of them immediately whipped her head around and began to walk off, tugging her children behind her. The other simply continued to glare, her top lip hooked in a vicious snarl as she clenched the handle of her baby carriage. She was wearing a short-sleeved T-shirt, which displayed to full effect the large crimson heart tattooed on her upper arm and some name emblazoned below it.

"Child killer," she leered at Mrs. Burrows before she heaved the stroller around and went after her companion.

Mrs. Burrows was flabbergasted.

Following the television appeal, there had been a few mentions in the tabloid newspapers, but it was all pretty low-key stuff. However, the local rags had picked up on the story, running a series of articles about her and her missing family, and then there'd been a two-page spread on Chester's parents, in which several ambiguous comments about Mrs. Burrows's suitability as a mother were made. Inevitably, Mrs. Burrows had achieved a degree of local notoriety from these.

Trying to shrug off the incident, she began to walk slowly up Highfield's Main Street, then picked up her pace. She didn't want to be late for the first of her job interviews.

10

MARTHA WAS CHOPPING up a bundle of dried plants she'd fetched from one of the outbuildings. With both hands she lifted a football-sized fungus from her basket and plopped it onto the table.

"Looks a bit dodgy," Will commented, wrinkling his nose.

"These are rare as snake feet around here," Martha said as she patted the sides of the mushroom, rather like a baker with a lump of dough. Then she began to peel away the tough outer skin as one would a very large orange. "You should know what this is."

Will nodded. It was a pennybun, but in comparison to the ones he'd seen in the Colony, this was a sorry specimen. Its skin was dry and in places ruptured, and it sagged as if it had lost some of its innards. "Has it gone bad?" he asked.

"No, it's *jugged* pennybun."

"Jugged?" Will said.

"Yes, I hang them for a couple of months. Gives them a richer flavor," she answered. She began to cut it into small sections, lobbing them into a cooking pot.

"Just looks rotten to me," Will said, nudging the end of one of Martha's chisels so it spun on the tabletop. He watched as it came to rest, then spun it again.

"Look, haven't you got anything better to do?" Martha asked gently.

"Not really," Will said listlessly.

"Are you bored because you and Chester can't play together as much as you used to?" she said.

"We don't *play* together — that's for kids. We just . . . hang out, do stuff," he said a little sharply, then checked himself, replying more civilly. "Well, we can't really, not with Elliott the way she is. It doesn't feel right."

"It's more than just that, isn't it, lad? You've got that restless look in your eyes, like Nathaniel did before he went off on his expeditions. Itchy feet," she pronounced, giving him a knowing glance as she continued to cut up the pennybun.

"Yes, s'pose . . . a bit," Will replied, then pulled himself up in his chair. "Martha, you know we . . . Chester and I . . . we can't stay here forever. We have to get back up Topsoil somehow — and soon. If the Styx go ahead with the Dominion plot . . ." He trailed off.

"I know, I know," Martha said sympathetically. "Will, I hate to be the one to tell you this, but you might be wasting your time. You might be too late already."

"Doesn't matter," Will said tersely. "We've still got to get back — just in case we can do something to stop them."

"And as far as getting back — it's never been done, and never will be. There's no way back," she said, with a thrust of her knife into a slab of mushroom flesh. "You can't climb up the inside of the Pore or any of the other Seven Sisters. It's miles. You would never make it." She paused to look directly into Will's eyes. "Don't think we didn't try."

"What about whatsisname? De Jaybo?" Will asked as Martha resumed work on the pennybun. "He managed it, didn't he?"

"Ah," Martha began, taking a moment to pick her nose. Will rolled his eyes. "You've obviously been told the story. He claimed he fell down the Pore and that he kept on going to a hidden place where he saw all manner of weird and strange things — horrible things. Another world, where there was daylight."

"Yes, I heard all that."

"Another world, with its own sun?" Martha said, shaking her head. "There were some in the Colony that said he didn't know his up from his down, and that he'd blundered out Topsoil somewhere, and all the things he said he saw were a load of old —"

"Codswallop," Will interjected, remembering the precise word Tam had used to describe the story.

"Yes, codswallop — or maybe it was just a sham," Martha agreed. "Some believed the whole yarn was put around by the Styx, to fill people with a fear of the Interior."

"My dad thought there might be something down there," Will said wistfully. "On the pages I've got from his journal, he's made notes about carvings in a temple he found, about a Garden of the Second Sun." Will couldn't stop his voice from shaking as he thought about him. "Dad must have been so excited — bet he was whistling his head off." He bowed his head, stabbed by a sudden pang of grief.

Martha rubbed her hands together to rid them of the fungus, and came around the table to him. She patted him on the back. "You've got new family now," she said tenderly. "We're together, that's what counts."

He raised his head and looked gratefully at her.

"You could do with getting out of here for a while, and we could do with some fresh meat. I've been spooning broth into Elliott, but my stocks are running low. So why don't you gather up your kit, and tell Chester we'll be gone for a couple of hours."

Chester was none too happy that Will and Martha were leaving him alone with Elliott. "What happens if you don't come back or something?" he said. "What'll I do then?"

But Will was relieved to be out of the stockade, even if it was only for a short while. As Martha led him along one of the tunnels, some sprigs of Aniseed Fire tucked under her belt and her crossbow cocked, he kicked out his legs, relishing the exercise.

"Now keep the noise down," she warned him as they dropped into a new section of tunnel. "This is spider country."

A little farther on, she raised her crossbow and slowed to a crawl. Will fell in line behind her, trying to make out what lay ahead.

"Careful," she whispered as they crept toward a junction. Martha didn't seem concerned that Will was using the lantern, so he made no effort to dim it.

Then he saw that a trap had been sprung — a net just like the one he'd been caught in. It was gathered up into a bundle and hung from the roof above, suspended by a single line. As they came nearer to it, Will could see the multiple legs protruding through the netting.

"Got ourselves a catch," Martha whispered.

Sure enough, there was a single spider-monkey trapped inside. Sensing their approach, it began to thrash its legs, sending the net bobbing up and down.

"Whoa — that's gross. It stinks!" Will said, cupping his hand over his nose.

"They do that — spew out a defensive stench. It's a last resort when they're cornered," Martha told him, drawing out her knife. She walked around the bobbing animal, chose a spot, and jabbed at it. It was instantly still.

"That's rank!" Will said as he pinched his nose, wondering if he would ever be able to bring himself to eat the meat again. But as Martha untied the net, his curiosity surpassed his repulsion. Intrigued by the creature, he let go of his nose. "Those eyes are incredible," he said, leaning over the spider-monkey to study the three circular reflective patches on its disklike body.

"They're not eyes — they're ears," Martha informed him.

"Really?"

"Yes — see the two small spines there above its fangs?" she said, indicating a pair of what Will had taken to be extra-thick bristles with the tip of her knife. "They send out the screeching sound, which the ears pick up."

"Really?" Will said again. "So it's like a bat?"

"Just like a bat," Martha confirmed, "but Nathaniel also said they use them to sniff out injured or dying creatures." Putting away her knife, she rolled the dead spider into a sack. She passed this to Will to carry, and then took them on what was clearly a regular circuit as she checked more traps along the way. In no time at all, Will was lugging around three dead beasts on his back.

Eventually they came to the wooden benches piled deep with old meat and body parts. "Hey, I recognize this place," Will said.

"You certainly do," Martha replied as she took the sack from him and emptied out the dead spider-monkeys. Then she pulled a large sprig of Aniseed Fire from her belt, lit it, and handed it to Will. "Wave it around. We've been lucky so far, but I'm not taking any risks with you here. They might swarm when I begin the cutting and they scent blood."

Will did as he was told, passing the sprig in front of him, the movement causing the smoldering fronds to glow brightly as the smell of licorice flooded the cavern.

"Sweeney Todd time," Martha said under her breath as she flipped the dead spiders onto the closest bench, then took hold of the murderous-looking cleaver. "You might want to take a few steps back," she warned Will as she raised her arm. "This can get messy."

On their return journey she announced they were going to make a slight detour.

"Because it's dust puppy season," she informed him.

Will didn't ask what she was talking about, thinking he'd find out soon enough.

She led him to a large bank of soil steeped high against the tunnel wall. Will took some in his hand and rolled it between his fingertips — it was rich and loamy, the sort of soil a gardener would die for. He watched as Martha seemed to be looking for something, then fell on a small opening. She began to dig away at it, clawing the soil with her hands.

She'd dug a good foot in when she suddenly let out a triumphant cry and plucked a wriggling object, the size and color of a newborn piglet, from the soil. She held it up by the scruff of its neck so Will could see it clearly. It had a plump little body, with four stubby limbs, no discernible eyes, but tiny white-pink ears tucked back against its head. It looked like an overfed and bald hamster. It writhed and twitched as she continued to hold it up, its pale whiskers vacillating and its mouth opening, but not making any noise.

"So that's a dust puppy," Will said in amazement. "Is it a baby?"

"No, it's fully grown."

"It sort of looks like a little Bartleby. A Bartleby kitten!" Will laughed, then blinked several times as she dangled it closer to him. He stepped back. "Ugh! It reeks, too . . . smells of —"

"Urine," Martha said. "Yes, their warrens are completely drenched in it. Somehow they can live with it."

"The odor's so strong it's making my eyes water," Will said. "Does *everything* stink to high heaven down here?"

"That's why the dust puppies are left alone — the smell protects them. But their meat is good . . . tastes like liver," she said.

"I hate liver, and that smell's making me feel ill," he replied, the thought popping into his head that Martha was none too clean, either. He'd certainly never seen any evidence that she washed herself.

As they returned to the shack, Will began to chuckle.

"What is it?" Martha inquired.

"I was thinking you'd better make sure Chester doesn't see any of this before you cook it," Will said, as he hoisted up the bloodstained sack he was carrying. "It'll put him off his food for weeks!"

Dr. Burrows was becoming desperate.

"It's no good — I need my drawing of the Burrows Stone to work out what all this means," he said, the small stone tablets spread out in front of him.

"And where did you say it is, again?" the Rebecca twin asked as she walked slowly around him.

"I told you — my journal was left behind at the top of the Pore," Dr. Burrows answered a little squeakily, indignant at the girl's constant inquisition.

"How very careless of you," she said, tapping a foot impatiently. "But you said you could remember enough to get by," she snapped.

"I said I *hoped* I could," he countered. He took off his glasses and rubbed his eyes, before replacing them again. "But I don't seem to be able to. And your constant interruptions aren't —"

Rebecca made a move toward Dr. Burrows as if she might strike him, but froze as a high-pitched squeal filled the warm air. "Sounds like another one of those absurd spider things." She flicked her fingers at the Limiter. "Go deal with it," she ordered the ghostlike figure hovering behind her. The soldier brought up his spear — a makeshift weapon he'd fashioned by binding his scythe to the end of a fungal stalk — and slipped away soundlessly.

"I don't understand. . . . How is it you can speak to him like that?" Dr. Burrows dared to ask, now that they were alone. "He's a soldier."

"Oh, he's much more than just a soldier. He's a Limiter . . . he's Hobb's Squad," she declared proudly to Dr. Burrows as she lowered herself into a sitting position in front of him. "Best, most fearless, and most brutal fighters in the world. And you love your history, don't you? You probably think the Spartans were the toughest kids on the block?"

"Well —" he began to answer with a small shrug.

"Nah, they were Boy Scouts," she said sneeringly. "You give me a full-strength battalion of Limiters, and London would be mine in a week."

"D-don't be so silly, Rebecca," Dr. Burrows stuttered. "Why do you say things like that?"

"Just concentrate on the map, Daddy, so we can all go home," she said. "Because I do so miss my homey-womey," she added in a sickly little-girl voice.

"You don't listen, do you? I think these stones might be a guide *down* to somewhere, rather than showing us a way back up," Dr. Burrows said.

"I don't care — anywhere is better than here," she barked, her voice hard as steel.

"And I also need to tie the map to something on the ground — I need to find a landmark down here that corresponds to an icon on the map itself." He swallowed noisily. "My throat is absolutely parched. Can I have something to drink?"

Rebecca shook her head. "Let's try to make some progress first, shall we?"

"But I'm thirsty," he complained.

There was a *whump* sound and Dr. Burrows started as a pair of dead spider-monkeys landed by his side. "Oh . . .

171

my . . . God," he said. "What are those? Some sort of spider? Arachnids?"

"Little Miss Muffet sat on a tuffet, eating her curds and whey," the Rebecca twin recited. "Not that you ever found time to tell me nursery rhymes. You were always too busy hiding down in your stupid cellar with your stupid books." There was genuine resentment in the Rebecca twin's voice, and she glanced at the Limiter, almost embarrassed that she'd dropped her guard and revealed her emotions, human emotions.

But Dr. Burrows hadn't heard what she said. He was nervously regarding the twitching legs of the spiders. He edged back as blood leaked from the creatures' bodies, flowing in little crimson streams through the dust by his leg.

"If you're thirsty, help yourself to some of that," the Rebecca twin offered, absolutely unaffected by the grotesque sight. "Otherwise we can have some water with our evening meal," she mocked in a schoolmarmish voice. "But we need to press on with our homework first."

11

"**H**IYA," **CHESTER SAID** as he emerged from the shack and saw Will lounging in a chair on the porch. "Martha chucked me out. She's giving Elliott a sponge bath."

"How's she doing?" Will asked him.

Yawning, Chester stretched his arms wide. "We managed to get some more broth into her," he said, then sank into the chair beside Will. "Martha's doing everything she can to keep her strength up."

"That's good. But she's not getting any better, is she?" Will said.

Chester shifted uneasily in response. Neither of them had voiced their concerns to each other that Elliott might actually die, just as Nathaniel had. The subject was almost taboo.

"No," Chester finally said.

For a while neither boy said anything as they gazed down the length of the garden, so deep in thought they barely took in the display of colors that fluxed and pulsed in the air like a scaled-down version of the aurora borealis. Will cleared his throat. "Um, Chester, something's been bothering me," he said.

There was concern in Chester's eyes. "What is it, Will?" he asked.

Will lowered his voice and looked in the direction of the door. "Martha's out of earshot, isn't she?"

"She's still in with Elliott," Chester confirmed. "Tell me, what's the matter?"

"Well," Will began uncertainly. "I know Martha's been brilliant, and she's doing everything she can for Elliott, but could we be doing more?"

Chester shrugged. "Like what?"

"We've been here for weeks now, and we've become so reliant on Martha that we haven't even considered that there might be someone else around who could help Elliott — *really* help her," Will said.

"But Martha says —" Chester started.

"I know what Martha says," Will cut him off. "But we don't really know *her*, do we? What if there are other people down here, with medicine, or someone like Imago, who could help Elliott?"

Chester looked at him blankly. "But why on earth would Martha keep that from us?" he asked.

"Because she's basically a lonely old woman who all of a sudden has got a couple of stand-ins for her dead son," Will said.

"That's harsh."

"Yes, but it's also true," Will replied. "Don't you ever kind of get the feeling that we're prisoners here? Martha tells us there's no one else in these parts, and we shouldn't risk going outside by ourselves because of the spiders, and how it's too dangerous to take us to see the ships her son found, and that there's no way back up to the Deeps, and nothing down below. . . ." He paused to draw breath. "I reckon she's doing everything she can to keep us right here." He tapped his index finger against the arm of his chair to emphasize the point.

Will was watching Chester intently, trying to see if any of what he was saying was raising a doubt in his friend's mind.

Chester gave a small nod. "So, if what you're saying is true, what then?" he asked. "We ditch Martha and trog off into the darkness? We drag a sick girl out of her bed in the hope that we might just bump into someone?"

Will blew through his lips. "Maybe I'm completely wrong and it would all be some terrible mistake, but I think we both know how this is going to turn out, don't we?"

Chester didn't answer.

"Come on, Chester, if we don't do anything, the same thing that happened to Martha's son is going to happen to Elliott. She's going to *die*. We shouldn't kid ourselves about that," Will said. "And maybe — just maybe — we can take Elliott with us and get some help for her. Maybe we *could* find a way back up the Pore and contact Drake or something, or one of the other renegades."

Chester banged his head against the back of the chair. "I don't know, Will," he murmured. "I just don't know."

"We've got nothing to lose, have we? Or rather, Elliott's got nothing to lose, has she?" Will said desperately.

Over the next week, Elliott showed no sign of improvement. Will, Chester, and Martha watched her, fed her, and tried to keep her temperature down, and on the occasions the boys were alone neither one of them brought up the subject of leaving again.

It was as if an oppressive pressure had descended over the shack, one in which it was wrong to laugh or to permit themselves to have fun because their friend's future hung in the balance, and that was all that mattered. The boys spoke in muted tones even when away from the shack, as if they might somehow disturb Elliott. The atmosphere even seemed to affect Bartleby, who spent most of the day sleeping in front of the hearth or scratching around in the land at the rear of the shack, sometimes giving himself dust baths.

When he wasn't on "Elliott Duty," as he and Chester called it, Will continued to play chess against himself. He also set himself the task of putting the pages of his father's journal in order the best he could. It was important to Will because they were his father's legacy, and it was his duty to preserve them in case he ever made it back to the surface again.

Many of the pages were badly creased, but Will smoothed these out, weighing them down to flatten them. Where Dr. Burrows's writing or sketches were faint because they had been immersed in water, Will meticulously traced over the lines to make them more legible. When he had finished, he laid out all the pages on the floor, to see if there was anything he could glean from them. But try as he might, the strange letters and hieroglyphs recorded by his father were meaningless to him and didn't offer up anything useful.

While making an inventory of what kit remained in his

rucksack, he came across his camera. Amazed to find it still worked, he now put it to use, taking a few snaps of the journal pages before placing them carefully in one of the map chests. He figured they'd be safe from the damp there, and from Martha, who had the habit of bunging anything vaguely combustible on the fire to keep it burning.

Then he went to one of his favorite haunts — a small outbuilding that housed a multitude of items Martha's son had brought back from his expeditions. The hut was crammed with trunks of nautical oddments, and Will was in his element as he opened them and sifted through their contents. He tried not to rush the task, rationing himself to one or two trunks at a time so that he had something to look forward to every day. Much of it was just scrap metal, such as iron brackets, thick pins that looked like they'd been made by a blacksmith, pulleys, and even some cannonballs.

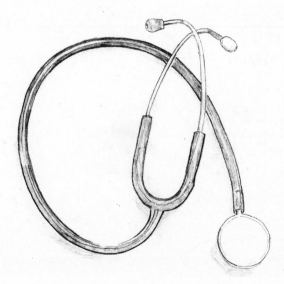

But in among all this, Will found a huge ship's compass. And in the same trunk there was a battered leather case, inside which he discovered a rather wonderful brass telescope. Will couldn't believe his luck. He immediately took it to the front of the shack to try it out. Although it wasn't much good either in the darkness or the limited confines of the strangely colored garden, Will didn't care. As he handled it, his imagination was filled with thoughts of the seafaring people who had once used it and might also have been responsible for building the shack.

At the bottom of another trunk he also found a stethoscope. It was made from a dull silver metal and black plastic or rubber, which showed not the slightest sign of deterioration. To Will's eye it looked very modern. He used it to listen to his own heartbeat, then chucked it back into the trunk, not giving it a further thought as he continued his search for more exotic objects.

12

ON HER WAY BACK from work, Mrs. Burrows dropped into the local newsstand to pick up an evening paper. She had taken a part-time position with a firm of solicitors, where she did some receptionist work, typing and general filing. It wasn't as if she needed the money — the sale of the family home had brought in much more than she'd anticipated — but the job gave her a sense of purpose again, and she enjoyed the company of the other people in the office. And since she only worked a couple of days a week, she had time to continue with her own investigation and also keep the pressure on the police to come up with results.

As she paid for her newspaper, she noticed that the shopkeeper was staring at her.

"Hope you don't mind me asking this, but are you Dr. Burrows's wife?" he ventured.

Mrs. Burrows didn't reply immediately, studying the man's face to see if there was anything in it that suggested hostility. After the incident outside the employment agency, she had grown chary of local people. She was only too aware of the looks she received while she was out shopping or on her way to the gym.

"Yes," she replied eventually. "I'm Celia Burrows."

"Ah, good. Then I have these for him," the shopkeeper said, ducking below the counter and producing a sizeable pile of magazines. He began to go through it. *Curators' Monthly* . . . one . . . two . . . er, three copies," he said, putting them in front of Mrs. Burrows. Without looking at her, he continued to speak. "I took the liberty of canceling his orders after a couple of months . . . but there are also three copies of *Excavation Today*, and some —"

"You know he's gone . . . he's gone missing," Mrs. Burrows blurted.

The man's expression turned to embarrassment, and he found it difficult to meet Mrs. Burrows's gaze as he shuffled the remaining magazines. "I know, but I thought you might like them for . . ." He trailed off.

"For when he comes back?" Mrs. Burrows finished for him. She was about to add, "I don't think that's going to happen," but decided it wouldn't be wise. The way public sentiment was against her, it might be taken the wrong way, and this man, too, might jump to the conclusion that she knew more than she was letting on. So, instead, she took some pound notes from her purse and thrust them at the shopkeeper. "Look, it's all right, just give them to me. I'll pay for them now." The shopkeeper sorted out her change in the uncomfortable silence that followed. Without waiting for him to put them in a bag, she snatched them from the counter and left the shop.

As she stepped outside, there was a flash of lightning followed by the rumble of thunder. "Great timing," she muttered as a heavy rain began to fall. She used one of the magazines to

shield her head from the downpour. As she struggled up Main
Street, the glossy covers of the other magazines became more
and more slippery, and kept sliding from under her arm. She'd
just dropped them for the second time when she spied a trash
can close by. "Sorry, Roger," she said as she heaved them all
into it.

Hurrying along, she swore as the rain showed no sign of
letting up. She'd stopped at the curb to check for traffic before
crossing the road, when she happened to look back in the
direction she'd just come.

"What the —?!" she exclaimed.

With their backs to her, two men were standing around the
bin into which she'd thrown the magazines. She could see that
they were carefully taking them back out and scrutinizing the
covers, before putting them, one by one, into a suitcase.
The men were both stockily built, and wearing dark-colored
jackets with some kind of curious shoulder mantle. They
looked like something from a different time.

For some reason, possibly because she'd been upset by the
incident at the newsstand, she was gripped by a precipitant
anger.

She had no idea who the men were. *Too well dressed to be
tramps*, she thought. Her first guess was that they were truck
drivers — not from England but the European Continent,
because of their unusual garb. On the spur of the moment,
she began to yell, breaking into a run toward them.

"What are you doing? Leave those alone!"

Although she'd thrown the magazines away, they had
been so much a part of her husband's life in the old days,

so important to him, it felt wrong that anyone else should help themselves to them. Mrs. Burrows knew she was being irrational — it wasn't as if she needed any more of Dr. Burrows's junk, her apartment was stuffed with his possessions as it was. But if he wasn't around to read them, she didn't want anyone else to get them, either. And she certainly didn't want them snaffled by people who wouldn't have her husband's appreciation for them.

"Leave them alone, you buggers! They're Roger's! Buy your own blasted magazines!" she shrieked. Through the rain she could see that both men had on flat caps and, as one of them reacted to her shouts and slowly swiveled toward her, she could make out that he was wearing dark sunglasses. That made no sense at that time of day, with the light almost gone. With another flash of lightning, she saw his face clearly. His skin was startlingly white. She skidded to a halt. "Those *pallid men*," she whispered, immediately recalling her husband's description from his journal.

Both men were regarding her now. She was close enough to see their wide jaws and grim-set mouths. The one holding the suitcase clapped it shut, and they started to stride determinedly toward her, completely in step with each other. Mrs. Burrows's anger immediately turned to fear. There was no doubt in her mind that they were coming for her.

She glanced quickly around Main Street to see if there was anyone who could help, but the rain seemed to have emptied it of people. She turned and ran, her shoes sliding on the wet pavement. She scoured the shops for anywhere she could take refuge, but of course Clarke's had closed down and it was far too late for the Golden Spoon café to still be open. There was nothing for it but to get across the road and take the side street in the direction of her flat. She would be safe there.

As she ran, the pounding on the pavement behind her was getting louder, and it was as if her fear opened up a remote corner of her mind. She suddenly remembered the incident from the previous year, when three men had forced a lock on the French doors of the living room and broken in. It had happened at a time when Mrs. Burrows was in the clutches of a chronic depression, spending nearly every hour of the day asleep in her favorite chair in front of the television.

She'd surprised the intruders, and they'd dragged her out into the hall. Then she'd surprised them some more. With the almost superhuman strength of someone not in their right mind, she'd walloped the intruders about their heads with a frying pan. They'd been scared off. The verdict from the police was that the thieves must have been watching the house from the Common, and that they were after the usual — the TV, cell phones, and any cash lying around the place.

But now, as these men pursued her, something in the way they carried themselves recalled to mind the intruders of that night.

As she reached Jekyll Street, there was a loud peal of thunder, and she hared it across the road to the opposite sidewalk. She didn't see the approaching car until it was too late. She heard the squeal of brakes and tires sliding across the wet pavement as the car slewed to a halt. Blinded by the headlights, she threw her arms around her head. The front bumper struck her, and she went over.

In an instant, the driver was out of the car and at her side.

"Jeez, I didn't see you! You just stepped out into the middle of the street!" he said. "Are you hurt?"

Mrs. Burrows was sitting up now, her wet hair in her face as she peered over her shoulder to look for the strange men.

"Where are they?" she mumbled.

"Does it hurt anywhere? Do you think you can walk?" the driver asked, his voice full of concern.

She pushed her hair back, seeing the driver clearly for the first time.

It was the bearded American from the library.

"I know you," she said.

The man crinkled one corner of his mouth as he squatted by her, his dark eyes searching her face. "You do?" he asked.

"Ben . . . something."

"Yeah," he said quizzically. "Ben Wilbrahams."

"Yes. Mr. Ashmi in the town archives said I should talk to you. I'm Celia Burrows," she told him.

He frowned, then his eyebrows rose in an arc above his wire-rimmed glasses. "So that would make you Dr. Burrows's wife," he said as Mrs. Burrows got to her feet, wincing as she tried to put weight on her left leg.

"I think I've sprained my ankle," she said.

"Look, you're completely drenched and I live right near here — at the end of Jekyll Street. Let me make sure you're all right — it's the least I can do."

Ben Wilbrahams lived in an imposing, wide-fronted Victorian house. He gave Mrs. Burrows a hand into the hall and from there into the living room. He sat her down on the sofa and lit a fire in the hearth. After fetching her a towel so she could dry herself off, he went to the kitchen to make them some coffee. Mrs. Burrows limped over to the wide marble fireplace, taking in the old paintings in the room — mostly landscapes and classically English. With its high ceilings the room was impressively large, running the full length of the house. Still drying her hair, she hobbled a few steps toward the garden end of the room. Even though it was in darkness, she could make out a number of large boards set up on easels.

She found a light switch and turned it on.

There were six boards in total, on which were pinned a mass of maps and countless numbers of small cards covered in neatly written notes. But the farthest board consisted only of photographs, and one of these photographs made her do a double take. She hopped over to it. It was a small black-and-white portrait of Dr. Burrows.

"That's from the Highfield Museum website," Ben said as he entered the room carrying a tray with cups and a French press of fresh coffee on it. "They haven't updated it yet."

"Did you ever meet him?" Mrs. Burrows asked. "My husband, Roger?"

"No, never had the pleasure," Ben Wilbrahams replied, noticing Mrs. Burrows's interest in the other photographs pinned around the one of her husband. There was a color photograph of a smiling family on which had been written **The Watkins Family.**

"The people in all those other pictures, they all went missing, too," Ben Wilbrahams said, setting down the tray.

"So what is all this? What precisely are you up to here?" Mrs. Burrows asked suspiciously as she hopped over to another board. She leaned on the back of a chair for support as she examined a map of Highfield, which was peppered with red stickers.

"You're not a journalist or a writer or anything like that?" he asked, narrowing his eyes in a less than serious way.

"Not yet," Mrs. Burrows replied.

"Good, because I don't want anyone stealing my ideas," he said. "I came across to England five years ago to write and direct an episode of a new cable TV series called *Victorian Gothic*. My episode was about London's cemeteries, and when it was finished, I never went home. That's what I do — I make films and documentaries."

"Really," Mrs. Burrows said, impressed. She thought back to her own television career and how much she had given up when she and Dr. Burrows adopted Will.

Ben Wilbrahams pushed down the plunger on the French press. "At the moment I'm doing some general research on Highfield and all the crazy — or maybe not so crazy — stories that fascinated your husband, too."

"Why don't you tell me about them?" Mrs. Burrows said.

Will sat up and rubbed his eyes, convinced he'd heard a bell ringing. If he really had heard one, he could only think it was the bell on the barricade.

From the chaise longue, where he'd been sleeping, he watched Bartleby, who seemed to have been roused, too. The cat had been curled up in his favorite place at the fireside, but was now glancing lazily at the garden. He let his head sink slowly to the rug again and promptly went back to sleep. Since Bartleby appeared to be so relaxed, Will told himself he must have dreamed it. He lay down again, also intending to go back to sleep.

Just then Chester, all in a fluster, burst in from the side room, where he'd been watching over Elliott.

"Well, don't just lie there!" he shouted.

"Huh?" Will said drowsily.

"The bell! You must have heard it."

Will hauled himself from the chaise longue to join Chester at the front door.

"Are you sure it was the bell?" Will asked as they both looked down the path toward the barricade.

"Absolutely."

"It might be Martha," Will suggested. "Maybe she went outside to check the traps."

Chester didn't need to reply — Will's question was answered as, without a word, Martha barged between them and launched herself down the front steps. Still dressed in the ankle-length, dirty white gown she usually slept in, she'd clearly gotten up in a hurry. But she also had her crossbow in her hands and, as she stormed down the path, she cocked it and drew a bolt from her quiver.

"Looks like she's expecting trouble," Chester observed.

Reaching the barricade, she checked through the peep-hole in the door. With a quick glance in the boys' direction, she unbolted the door and flung it open. As she took a step through the opening, her crossbow was trained on something, and she looked tense.

"What could have rung the bell like that?" Will pondered. "Spider-monkeys?"

"*Shhh!*" Chester hissed. "I think she's talking to someone."

"Martha *never* stops talking," Will replied. "Even if there's no one there."

"Will!" Martha suddenly cried out. "Get down here! Somebody's asking for you."

The boys exchanged bemused looks.

"Says she's your sister," Martha added.

"No! No way! I don't believe it!" Chester exploded, thumping the doorjamb. "Your sister the Styx! Those foul murdering cows have followed us here!" He turned and dashed inside the shack, but Will was already making his way down the path to the main gate, racked with curiosity, and dread.

Martha didn't look up from her crossbow, her lips tight as she spoke. "Know her?"

Will poked his head cautiously outside the doorway.

It was Rebecca.

One of the twins was standing there, her hands clasped before her and her fingers interlocked. Her face was streaked with filth and shiny with tears.

"Oh, Will," she croaked as soon as she saw him. "Help me. Please . . . please help me."

Will was speechless.

"She's wearing a Limiter's uniform," Martha spat, her fingers clenched so tightly around the crossbow that her joints were white. "She's a Styx."

Will found his voice. "Yes . . . a Styx. I told you she was a Styx," he said to Martha. Then he spoke to the Rebecca twin. "What is this? Why've you come here?"

"Oh, Will," the lame twin pleaded. "You've got to help me. She threw me down the Pore."

"Are you by yourself? Are there any other Styx with you?" Will demanded, as his brain kicked into gear. He scanned the gloom behind the girl. "Her sister might be here, or more Styx. This might be a trap," he said in a rush to Martha.

With her crossbow still aimed on the girl, Martha advanced toward her. She stopped, then glanced quickly both ways along the tunnel. "Seems clear," she whispered.

The Rebecca twin had shrunk back a couple of steps as Martha approached, and Will saw from the way she was moving that there was something wrong with her leg. She also seemed absolutely petrified by Martha. She began to babble at Will. "I'm alone . . . she's not here . . . my sister . . . she threw me down the Pore."

"On your knees and put your hands on your head," Martha barked.

"My sister . . . she . . . she pushed me down the Pore," the Rebecca twin continued to babble as she did what Martha told her.

"Why would she do that?" Will asked.

"I wouldn't go along with her anymore. She's insane. . . . I told her I wouldn't be a part of it." Rebecca was crying openly now, her slim shoulders quaking. "She's just sick, Will. She made me do those things. She made me do everything. I had to — she threatened to kill me, so many times." Her hands on top of her head, Rebecca peered up at Will, her raven hair scattered over her face.

"You must think we're complete idiots!" Chester yelled. Will hadn't even been aware that he was there. "You lying little cow!" He was so crazed with fury that spittle was flying from his mouth as he yelled. Then he whipped up his rifle and aimed it straight at the kneeling girl.

"No! Chester!" Will screamed, reaching for him. Will managed to knock the rifle just as it discharged. The bullet cracked against the rock somewhere behind Rebecca. Whimpering, she flung herself onto her side, her face buried in the dirt.

Chester was working the rifle bolt so he could take a second shot. In the heat of the moment, Will pushed him hard in the chest. He was so surprised at Will's intervention that he relaxed his grip on the rifle, allowing Will to grab it away from him.

"What are you doing? Give it back to me!" Chester demanded. He hunched his shoulders like a linebacker about to charge.

"Steady, Chester," Will said, holding the rifle across his body, ready to fend off the boy if he had to.

"She's a Styx," Will heard Martha growl. He whipped his head around just in time to see what she was intending to do. Acting on pure instinct, he jabbed at Martha's crossbow with the rifle stock. It was enough to deflect the bolt, which swished into the shingle. It had missed the prone girl's trembling body by a whisker.

"Enough! Both of you — stop!" Will shouted. "Just stop!"

Chester and Martha were both facing him now, and from their expressions he truly thought they might go through him to get at the Styx girl.

"What's wrong with you? You nearly shot her!" he cried.

Chester's voice was cold and low. "Yeah, that's right. Too right. Give me the gun back and I *will*—"

"But—" Will began.

"But what? You weren't in the Hold. You didn't go through what I did," he said. He jabbed his finger at the Rebecca twin. "That little witch was there when they were beating me! And *she* beat me, too. She was laughing like it was all some big joke." He glared at the girl. "Well, I've got a punch line I'd really like to try on her!"

Will pulled himself up to his full height. "We can't just kill her, not here, and not like this. She might be telling the—"

"The truth? That it wasn't her, it was all her sister?" Chester interrupted. "Come on, Will, get real. They're both exactly the same; they're both evil! What about Cal, Tam, your grandma? Are you forgetting that these psychos slaughtered them? And what about all the other people they killed? She has to die."

"I'm not going to let you do it," Will said. Releasing the magazine from the rifle and working the bolt to make sure the chamber was empty, he threw the weapon back to Chester. "Not in cold blood."

"Why not?!" Chester rasped. "You're with me on this, aren't you, Martha?"

Martha nodded. "All the way. You need to finish her," she urged Will.

"No," Will said, his voice breaking with the strain of the confrontation. "No. We're not like them. Killing her makes us just like them."

Chester fixed Will with a stony glare, then spat at the Styx girl before he stomped off back inside the barricade.

Martha stood motionless, holding her crossbow as if she was thinking about recocking it. "So," she said to Will, "let me get this straight. This is one of the twins you spoke about, one of the fakes who pretended to be your sister and has done everything she can to make your life a living horror . . . to hunt you down and kill you. And you're prepared to let her off scot-free?"

Will ran his hand over his long white hair several times, at a complete loss as to how to answer. "I . . . I really don't know, but . . . but we should hear what she has to say."

Martha shook her head, and smiled sourly. "Make me a promise, Will."

"What?"

"Let her say her bit — and after you've heard all her lies — you'll bring her back out here again, and finish her off yourself?"

"I . . . I . . . ," Will stuttered.

"This is how it starts." Martha suddenly looked extremely weary, her head drooping. "The Blackheads worm their way in and before you know it, you'll wake up with one of them standing over you with a knife." She took a deep breath and stared hard into Will's eyes. "I hope you know what you're doing, dearie."

Will looked confused. "No, I don't. I really don't," he

admitted. He heard the Styx girl's sobs and turned to where she lay. "Get up, Rebecca or whatever your name is. You're coming with us."

The girl didn't move.

"I said *get up!*"

She scrambled to her feet, shaking with fear, her large frightened eyes on Will.

"Martha?" Will said.

"Yes," she answered, her scornful gaze burning into the pitiful Styx girl.

"I found some leg irons in the stuff Nathaniel brought back from the galleon."

"Now you're talking," Martha snarled, seizing Rebecca's arm and twisting it behind her back. Then she shoved her roughly through the doorway and toward the shack.

Will paused for a moment to search the darkness outside before he shut and locked the door of the barricade.

Unseen by him, a Limiter slipped away, his mission accomplished. He swung his makeshift spear in front of him, ready to dispatch any further spiders unlucky enough to cross his path. "Child's play," he said in a gravelly voice as he sped down the tunnel to rendezvous with his comrade. This may have been because he already knew the lay of the land as well as he knew the lattice of scars on the back of his hand, or because the spiders and the other fauna he'd encountered so far were so easily dealt with; it just wasn't true.

13

CHESTER CAME OUT onto the porch holding a mug. He lowered himself into the empty chair next to Will and made a long *humph* noise as he crossed his legs.

"All right?" Will inquired tentatively.

"S'pose," Chester mumbled in reply, not looking at his friend. "Will . . . it's . . . ," he began, throwing him a brief glance before taking a large sip from his mug.

"What?" Will responded, knowing only too well what was coming.

Chester's drink was evidently much hotter than he'd been expecting, and he had to take a couple of rapid breaths to cool his mouth before he could answer. When he did, his speech was clipped with anger. "That twin tried to kill us . . . and you just let her off, like it was nothing."

"I haven't let her off," Will countered. "It's just —"

"It's just *what?*" Chester said, growing even more heated. "Come on, Will! You're acting like a . . . I don't know . . . like a complete wimp!"

"No, I'm not," Will objected, doing his best to keep his voice even.

"Well, I think you're making the biggest mistake of your

life." Chester looked thoughtful for a moment. "Well, one of them, anyway."

"Look, Chester, it's like this," Will said as he massaged his forehead, trying to alleviate the throbbing headache that had come on after the incident. "It would have been the easiest thing in the world for me to let you and Martha kill her."

"Yeah, so why didn't you?" Chester challenged him.

"Because afterward you'd have regretted it. Haven't you had a bellyful of all the killing? If we'd finished off the twin, we'd be no different from her and all the other Styx. We can't let ourselves sink that low."

"Don't you dare compare us with them," Chester said, outraged. "We're the good guys."

"Not if we shoot twelve-year-old girls in the face, we're not," Will said.

Chester clicked his tongue against his teeth. "Aren't you forgetting that she's downright dangerous? What if her sister's outside that barricade, with a soddin' army of Limiters? What if they're waiting for a sign from her before they storm this place and kill us all? What then?" Chester snorted through his nostrils like an irate bull.

"Why wait? They could do it any time they wanted," Will reasoned.

Chester waved his hand through the air as if brushing Will's answer aside, then he changed tack. "And as for sparing the Rebecca twin, what's that expression? Live by the sword —"

"— die by the sword," Martha interjected as she came onto the porch and deposited a metal plate on the floor by Will. "Here's your prisoner's food." As she promptly returned inside, Will noticed she had her crossbow slung over her back. It was clear she was as nervous as Chester about more Styx showing up.

Will regarded the plate but didn't make a move toward it. "Don't you think I want revenge, too, Chester? Don't you know I live every minute with the weight of what they did to Cal, Uncle Tam, my real mum, and Granny Macaulay? And if they'd looked after my dad, he might still be alive today. But shooting the twin isn't . . . isn't the answer." He thumped the arm of Chester's chair. "You're not listening to me. Look at me, will you?"

"What?" Chester asked, as he met Will's resolute gaze.

"You've got to believe me when I say this — *I have not forgiven her.* Not for one single second."

Chester gave a small nod.

Will got to his feet and collected the plate of food. "And you never know — perhaps she can help us. Perhaps she knows a way out of the Pore — so we can get Elliott some medicine. If we'd just killed the twin . . . well, she'd be too dead to tell us."

"You might have a point," Chester conceded. "So ask her for three tickets on the express train back to Highfield, will you?" He rubbed his nose with the back of his hand as he added, "First class."

"I'll do that." Will was so relieved that he and Chester hadn't fallen out over the situation. The last thing he wanted was for them to be at loggerheads again — he'd had enough of that in the Deeps to last him a lifetime. "And, Chester, I'm sorry I pushed you like that and grabbed away the rifle."

"Sure," Chester said.

Will started down the front steps, then turned to his friend.

"By the way, did you just burn your gob on that tea?" he said, breaking into a grin.

"Get out of here!" Chester laughed.

Rebecca was being kept in the dry-log store, the sturdiest of the outbuildings at the rear of the shack. Martha was taking absolutely no chances and had supervised Will as he patted the twin down for any weapons, then placed shackles around her ankles, each secured with a massive padlock. As if this wasn't enough, Martha looped a heavyweight length of chain around the manacles and one of the huge beams at the four corners of the shack — there was no way the girl was going anywhere.

"Twins," Will said under his breath as he carried the plate over to the hut. Even though he'd seen it with his own eyes at the top of the Pore, he had to keep reminding himself there were actually two Rebeccas. They'd been taking turns spying on him, one on, one off, for all those years in Highfield. It didn't really matter which of them this was, as they seemed to be indistinguishable.

Rebecca was sitting cross-legged on the dirt floor, her head hung low. She looked up as he entered. Her hair — which he'd never known to be anything but perfectly groomed — was all over the place, and her face was daubed with filth. Will was actually a little alarmed by her disheveled state — for all those years in Highfield, she'd never once let her standards slip.

Back in the Colony the Rebeccas wore the Styx uniform of a black dress topped by a white collar — a uniform that gave them an aura of immense power and authority. As Will regarded the sorry-looking specimen before him now in her torn Limiter fatigues, she didn't appear quite so powerful or commanding anymore. Whichever Little Miss Perfect this was, she had fallen a long way.

Cautiously, as if approaching a highly dangerous animal, he placed the plate on the ground before her, then stepped back.

"Thank you, Will," she said meekly. "And thank you for what you did out there. You saved my life. I knew I could count on you."

"Don't!" Will snapped, holding up his hand. "I don't want your gratitude."

"OK," Rebecca said quietly, poking at the food on the plate. "But I hope you believe me, Will. I was forced to do what my sister and the Styx told me. If I'd refused, they'd have tortured or executed me, or both. You've no idea what it's been like, living in fear for so long."

"Oh, I don't know — you and your people have given me a pretty good idea," Will said, his face expressionless.

"It wasn't up to me, Will."

"Just stop it!" he flared up, his face turning bright red as his temper snapped. "What? Do you expect me to simply take your word for everything? I'm not that stupid!"

"I was following orders," she said, quailing at his outburst. "You have to believe me, Will."

"Oh, fine, let's just be brother and sister again. We can play 'happy family,' just like we used to," he snarled mockingly. "Talk all you like, you're wasting your breath." As he spoke, vivid memories of their previous life in Highfield ran through his mind. Time after time, in the way that only a younger sibling can, Rebecca would needle him until he blew his top — exactly what she wanted him to do. And now, as his heart beat rapidly and he breathed shallow breaths, it was as though nothing had changed, despite all the terrible events he'd been through since those days.

Bartleby pranced in, his tail swishing. He made straight for Rebecca and sat himself smartly next to her. She scooped some of the dark meat from the plate and offered it to him. Will's anger gave way to surprise as the cat took it from her without any hesitation at all, as if he knew and trusted her. Rebecca noticed Will's frown.

"I nursed him in the Colony," she explained. "Bartleby was in a real state when we brought him home." She gave the cat another handful of the meat, carelessly dripping the gravy over her ragged Limiter's jacket.

How very un-Rebecca-like, Will thought to himself.

Bartleby purred as he gulped down the food. "Food equals love," Rebecca pronounced, peering up at Will.

"I have some questions for you," he said. "And if I think you're lying to me, I'll turn you over to Chester and Martha. Got that?"

She gave a single nod.

"Are you really down here by yourself?"

"Yes," she replied unequivocally.

"So your sister's not with you? Or any other Styx?"

"I'm totally alone," she confirmed.

"And you fell down the Pore, same as we did?"

"I was pushed down it," she said.

Will wasn't certain, but he thought he saw her lower lip tremble, as if she might be about to cry; but then she helped herself to some food.

"We have to find a way out of the Pore. Elliott's ill — she needs a doctor, badly," he said.

"I'm sorry to hear that, but I don't know how to get back," she answered immediately.

"What about the De Jaybo story?" Will shot at the girl. "Did he really climb out?"

"Yes, he did, though nobody knew how he did it," she replied. "I was told Dad asked to see his drawings, but was refused permission."

Will bristled. As far as he was concerned, she had forfeited any right to call Dr. Burrows her father. She sensed his annoyance, her whole body appearing to sag, as if she was suddenly overcome by grief. "I miss him, too, you know," she murmured. "I did my best to make sure he was left alone when he was in the Colony."

"You saw him there?"

"I wasn't allowed to. Oh, Will, I wish I could have done more for him."

Closing his eyes, Will pressed against his eyelids with his fingertips. His headache didn't seem to be getting any better. He longed to go back to the shack and bury himself in the oblivion of sleep, somewhere he could shut all this out.

"You have to believe me, Will — I was forced to do all those things, all those awful things. I had no alternative."

Will finally opened his eyes.

"How can I convince you I'm telling the truth?" she asked.

Will shrugged.

"What if I were to give you this?" she said. She pulled at the shirt collar around her neck with her gravy-stained fingers, then lifted out a thin cord on which hung two small glass phials. "What if I give you Dominion *and* the vaccine, as a gesture of good faith?" With a flick of her wrist, she snapped the cord and offered the phials to Will. "Here, take them. They're the only specimens we had, and . . . and now they're yours."

Unspeaking, he reached over to take the phials, then held them up by the light so he could examine the clear fluid inside. "How do I know if it's really Dominion?" he finally asked.

"Because it is," she said with a small shrug. Her leg irons rattled as she shifted her position in the dirt so she could see Will without straining her neck.

"But why would you and your sister have these in the first place. Why you?"

"Because we're important," she said casually.

"What do you mean?"

"I'm sure you gathered in the Colony that we don't have family units, not like Topsoilers do. When my father lost his life at the hands of your uncle Tam —"

"The Crawfly?" Will interrupted. "So he *was* your father!"

For an instant Rebecca's eyes were suffused with a fiery light, as if she was about to release an incandescent fury on Will. He knew then that by repeating the unpleasant nickname Uncle Tam and his gang had bestowed upon him, he'd insulted her dead father. But she blinked, and quickly looked away from Will. She was calm and collected when she resumed. "It was left to my sister and me to see the purge through with our grandfather. That's why we had the phials."

"Purge? What do you mean?" Will asked again.

"Our plot to release Dominion Topsoil, to carry out the word of the *Book of Catastrophes*."

As Will racked his brains, trying to remember if he'd seen her grandfather or heard anything about him during his time in the Colony, a question leaped out at him. "At the Pore, you and your sister each had a phial. So how did you manage to come by *both* of these?" he quizzed her.

"She gave me hers for safekeeping. The one with the black wax on the stopper is the virus. The other — with the white wax — is the antidote."

"Hold on," he said. "That doesn't make sense. If you had both of the phials, why did she push you down the Pore? Why would she do something as dumb as that?" he asked, thinking he'd caught the twin in a lie.

"Because we were having a flaming row. We fought, and she must have been so mad at me, she didn't stop to think about the phials," Rebecca said without a moment's hesitation.

"What were you fighting about?"

"I told you already — after you and the others were blasted over the edge, I was upset. I said to her that I couldn't go along with her plans any longer. That I'd had all the killing I could take. She went crazy."

"How do I know if you're telling me the truth? What if your sister and grandfather still have some of the virus left, and they're going ahead with the plot while we're stuck down here?"

"They don't. The virus you've got in that phial is all we had of it, and all that's needed for a full-blown pandemic."

"But why don't they just make some more?" Will asked, staring intently at the black-topped phial.

"It's not that simple. They might try to reengineer it, but it will take time to produce the same strain — months, possibly years. Anyway, whether or not you choose to believe me, I swear to you that phial is all there is." She paused, wiping her face with her filthy hand. "So now you have the key."

"I have?" Will said.

"Sure." Rebecca's jet-black eyes were supremely confident as she answered. "Deliver those specimens to the right people on the surface, and they'll be able to vaccinate the Topsoil population. Then if, by some miracle, more virus is manufactured and the purge is restaged, it won't have any effect — none at all. You have the power to stop Dominion in its tracks."

"Yeah, that's all great, but how on earth do I get this to the surface?" Will asked.

"You'll figure it out, Will. You were always clever like that. And when you do, you've got to take me with you," Rebecca said, "because I can be useful to you. I can tell people the whole story." Then she gave a deep sigh, glancing at Bartleby, who was napping by her side. "And I know there's no way you'll ever believe me, but I miss Dad so much. He was my father, too."

"Hurry it up, you stupid old fart," the Rebecca twin said under her breath.

"Did you say something?" Dr. Burrows asked, casting a nervous glance at the Limiter prowling in tight circles around him as he tried to work on a translation of the tablets.

"No, nothing," she replied innocently. "How's it going — nearly finished?"

"Hah!" he exclaimed. "You're asking me to do the impossible. All I've made out so far in these inscriptions is something about seven —"

"*Seven* what?" she cut in.

"I don't know. I can read the word *seven* or *seventh*, but I don't know what it's in relation to. This is really hard going — I can get a handful of words, but then I'm lost." He readjusted his glasses, peering at her as she perched on a mound of fungus.

"Oh, come on — it can't be *that* difficult," she urged him.

"I keep telling you and you just won't listen. I have to have the drawing of the Burrows Stone from my journal," he said despondently. "There are too many variables for me to do this quickly. It will take me yonks to piece it together — unless, that is, you happen to have a cryptanalyst with a high-spec computer hidden away somewhere down here."

The Limiter said something in the nasal Styx tongue to the Rebecca twin, and she nodded.

"OK," she announced, easing herself down from the fungus. "What are our options? You've got a basic map there — even if we can't read the words, we must be able to use it somehow."

"Well," Dr. Burrows began, sounding more upbeat.

"So, come on then, spit it out," she urged him, clapping her hands together. "What can we do?"

"We explore until we spot something that ties into the icons on the map. Then we might just be able to get ourselves on the right track."

The Rebecca twin considered this for a second. "So . . . let me get this right . . . you're expecting us to slog through hundreds of miles of these slimy tunnels on the off chance we see something familiar — maybe with a big 'seven' on it? Is that the best you can come up with?" she asked snidely.

"Have you got a better suggestion?" Dr. Burrows said. "We could make a start where I discovered the skeleton with these tablets. From there, we fan out in ever-increasing search radii, and we comb every last inch of the tunnels. . . . We explore them thoroughly for anything that might help us."

The Rebecca twin didn't look too convinced. "Sounds like a long shot to me," she said.

Dr. Burrows's expression turned to one of confusion. "Rebecca, why is it that all of a sudden you're so keen to help me? You weren't the slightest bit interested in my work all those years in Highfield."

"I just want to go back to my people, Dad," the Rebecca twin said, all sweetness and light. "Or at least get out of this grotty place. OK," she said, glancing at the Limiter, "let's give Plan B a try, but I don't want us to wander too far."

"Excellent," Dr. Burrows said, wrapping the tablets carefully in his handkerchief again. "And while we walk, I want to hear more about your people. I know so very little of them."

"You and the rest of the world," the Rebecca twin said. In

the Styx tongue, she added, "Thus it has ever been, and thus it will ever be."

When Will returned to the shack there was no sign of Chester in the main room. He assumed he was on Elliott watch. Will was actually quite relieved — he needed time to think things over. Bartleby padded past him and made straight for the hearth rug, where he stretched himself out in that luxurious way only cats can. "Good old Bart," Will said, and sat down on the rug next to him.

Will took out the phials, reknotted the cord attached to them that the Rebecca twin had snapped, then hung them before him, wondering if they really contained Dominion. After a while, the crackling fire gave him an idea. How easy it would be to throw the phials into it. He knew the heat would destroy the virus and, worst-case scenario, if any of it were to escape, it would be highly unlikely to get all the way up to the Topsoil population and infect it.

On second thought, though, that didn't seem like such a clever idea — he and the others wouldn't fare so well if any of the virus happened to escape the flames. He'd rather not die like the men in the test cells that Cal had told him about. Perhaps, he reasoned, it would be better to get Martha to build a fire a safe distance away from the shack and burn the phials there — just in case.

But he shouldn't overlook what Rebecca had said about delivering Dominion to the right people Topsoil and, by doing so, derailing any further attempts by the Styx to start a pandemic. In which case, he thought to himself, it would be extremely rash of him to destroy the phials.

He also realized that it was now imperative that he return to the surface with the deadly cargo as quickly as he could. He didn't know how he was going to manage it, or quite what he'd do when he got there, but he had to try.

Bartleby yawned.

"Why can't my life be more like yours, Bart? Nice and simple," Will said as he scratched the cat's whiskery chin. "Want to swap?"

The cat nuzzled against his hand and began to purr his rumbling purr. His skeletal tail slowly swiped from side to side, looking for all the world like a malnourished snake performing an act of levitation. "Good boy," Will said, and the cat slid open his saucer-sized eyes and regarded him affectionately.

"So what do I do?" Will posed to the empty room as he dangled the phials in the air, the flames of the fire visible through the clear vessels as if it was actually inside them.

Bartleby must have thought Will wanted to play with him, and flicked out one of his huge forepaws in a kittenish attempt to cuff the dangling phials.

"Whoa! No!" Will quickly snatched away the phials. "Holy smokes, that was close!" he spluttered, imagining the tinkle of glass as the phials shattered on the floor and flooded the shack with the deadly pathogen. Bartleby had stopped purring and was eyeing Will with disappointment, clearly put out that his new master was such a killjoy.

Will immediately went over to the nearest map chest and pulled open the top drawer. "Here it is," he said as he found a small leather tobacco pouch he'd spotted there before. He carefully wrapped the phials in a strip of burlap and then placed the diminutive bundle in the pouch. "Perfect. That should protect them from any knocks . . . and cats," he said to Bartleby, as he weighed the pouch in his hand. Then he frowned, falling into thought for a moment. *Chester needs to know about this*, he decided, starting for Elliott's room.

When Will entered, Chester was wide awake in the chair beside Elliott. He dipped a cloth into a bowl, squeezed out the excess water, then dabbed the girl's forehead.

"She's badly dehydrated," Chester said. "And look at her. She's getting so thin. I mean, it's not as if she was very big to begin with."

"Fading away," Will said, repeating the precise words Martha had used to describe what had happened to her son.

"Yes," Chester nodded. "Maybe what you said was right. Maybe we should just leave and take our chances outside. We'd be all right if we took enough Aniseed Fire with us to ward off the spiders. And if it all comes to nothing and we draw a complete blank, maybe Martha will take us back."

"Doubt it," Will said. "Especially if we nick her precious plants."

"Oh, I really don't know what we should do," Chester said through a sigh.

"Neither do I," Will agreed.

"Get anything useful from the Styx twin?" Chester asked, changing the subject.

"Just this," Will replied, taking out the leather pouch and unwrapping the burlap from around the phials.

Chester blinked in astonishment as he focused on what was there. "Dominion? She gave you *Dominion?*" he said loudly, then shut his eyes tight and shook his head. "No. I don't believe it. It's not the real thing."

"Want to see it?" Will said, extending his hand with the phials over Elliott's still form.

"Hello? No!" Chester declined. "I don't want to go anywhere near that stuff. And I don't want anything to do with that evil cow." He placed the cloth back into the bowl and wiped his hands on his shirt before he spoke again. "Do you really believe she's given you the actual virus?"

"I've got no way of telling. I suppose we could always try it out," Will replied. "You know, one of us act as a guinea pig."

Chester gave him a quick look, trying to figure out if his friend was serious or not.

"And we could decide which of us it should be with a game of chess," Will said, unable to keep a straight face.

Chester grinned. "Not likely. You've been practicing way too much. I'd have more of a chance with Rock, Paper, Scissors," he said. Then the smile left his face and he moved his chair around to Will's side of the bed. "OK, so straight up, tell me exactly what the Rebecca twin said."

"Well . . . for starters, she swears her sister is responsible for everything and that she was forced to go along with it." Will held up his fist, the phials in it. "She also says this is all the Dominion the Styx have got. So they can't go ahead with their plot."

Chester's eyebrows hiked up at this. "How likely is that?"

"She said that even if we don't believe her, and the Styx have got more, we should get this to the right people on the surface. They'll be able to produce the vaccine."

"Apart from the fact that we can't *get* to the surface, this all sounds like a load of bunk. I don't believe a word of what she's telling you," Chester said adamantly.

"Hold on," Will urged him. "Think it through logically. Maybe this Dominion is real, but she knows there's no way we can get Topsoil, so it actually doesn't matter if we have it or not. Or she really believes we can find a way back, and she's trying to buy her way in, because she wants to go home. *Or* maybe, just maybe, she's genuine, and she *was* forced to do everything by her sister, and this is her way of proving it to us."

Chester shook his head. "Um . . . run that by me again."

"Look, it's simple: If there's even the tiniest chance we can save tens of millions of lives on the surface, and help Elliott in the bargain, then don't we have to try everything we can to get out of the Pore?"

"If you put it like that, then yes, of course we have to," Chester agreed. "And what about the twin? Do we leave her here with Martha?"

"No, we take her with us when we go. She promised she'd spill the beans on the Styx and their plans," Will said.

Chester rubbed his chin thoughtfully. "So, we should just pack up our bags and go."

From the doorway a voice made them both jump out of their skins. "I warned you about letting that Styx girl in," Martha said. "This is what happens. This is how it always starts." Then she turned on her heel and left.

14

MARTHA NEVER said a word to either of the boys about what she'd overheard, and as much as they could in the cramped confines of the shack, they both tried to stay out of her way for a few days. Will continued with his routine of nursing Elliott, playing chess against himself, and sorting through the salvaged items in the outbuilding, but now there was the added responsibility of Rebecca.

But his and Chester's main preoccupation remained Elliott and her continued decline. It was agonizing to watch her lying there on the bed, the sweat pouring from her, and to listen to her outbreaks of feverish babbling. She was forever saying Drake's name and reciting the sequence of numbers that meant nothing to the boys.

Will became increasingly depressed, to the point that he could think of nothing else but Elliott's plight. Even when it wasn't his turn to watch her, he would frequently keep Chester company, the two of them sitting in silence together. On one such occasion, Chester spoke to him.

"Will, you can't stop yawning and you look completely done in. Why don't you go and get your head down?"

"All right," Will mumbled, heaving himself to his feet with another yawn, then shuffling off next door.

"Whassat?"

Will didn't know how long he'd been asleep, but he awoke with a start, as if someone was calling urgently to him. He sat bolt upright and looked nervously around the gloomy room. Nothing appeared to be amiss, so he strained to see if he could hear anything further, but there was only Chester's deep breathing as he slept soundly on the pile of carpets on the floor.

Will threw off the light blanket and went to check on Elliott in the next room. Deep in fever, she was rolling her head from side to side on the sweat-stained pillow, and her arms made occasional small flailing movements, as if she was struggling against someone or something. As he leaned over and felt her forehead, she was muttering, but it was nothing that made any sense to him.

"Too hot," he said in a whisper. "Come on, Elliott, you've got to beat this."

For a few minutes he watched her, wishing there was some way he could ease her suffering. Then he made his way back through the main room and out of the shack. He stopped on the porch, sitting himself down on the top step. He was grateful for the gentle breeze blowing up the slope, and he shut his eyes, enjoying it on his face.

When he opened his eyes again, the glow from the garden seemed to be brighter than ever, bathing the cavern in a glorious array of multicolored radiance. It called to mind the summer evenings when the fair had come to Highfield Common — seen from afar, the stray light in the sky above it was not dissimilar to the phantasmagoria he was witnessing now.

As his eyes roved over the beds on either side of the path, he could have sworn that some of them were growing in intensity while others were becoming more muted, as if passing the baton from one to another. The changes were enough to alter the light on the porch, chasing his shadow around the wood decking behind him.

He moved down to the bottom step and raised his hand before him so he could admire the colorful hues falling on it, which dissolved from yellow to orange and then to a palette of reds and blues, all in constant rotation. He thought of the fair again. It didn't take very much to imagine the mêlée of organ music and the old rock 'n' roll songs, the hoots of laughter and the calls of excited children rolling across the grassy fields.

"Homesick?" said a deep voice.

Will squinted, making out someone sitting a few steps behind him.

It was a man, a large man, and his profile was familiar.

"Uncle Tam!" Will said aloud, wondering why he wasn't more surprised or more frightened by what he was seeing. "But you're . . . you're dead!"

"Ah, that'll explain why I've been feeling a bit off-color recently," Tam replied wryly.

"Is this a dream? Am I dreaming?" Will asked him.

"Quite possibly," Tam answered, sliding his hand up his face and then to the top of his head, where he began to scratch vigorously. "Reckon I've got those lice again," he chuckled. "Little bleeders."

"I *am* dreaming," Will decided, and twisted himself around on the step so he was directly facing the apparition.

"Tell me what I should be doing, Uncle Tam. You have to tell me."

"You've got yourself in a pickle, my boy, haven't you?" Tam said.

Will frowned, remembering there was something vitally important he had to say to his uncle. "Cal . . . I'm so sorry about Cal . . . there was —"

"Nothing you could do," Tam interrupted as he took out his pipe and began to fill the bowl with tobacco. "I know that, Will, I know that. You only just made it out by the skin of your teeth yourself."

"But what can I do about Elliott?" Will asked as the big man scraped a match against his thumbnail and it burst into flame, lighting his face for an instant. "She's really sick and I feel so helpless. What should I do?"

"I wish I could be of assistance, Will, but I don't know this place." Tam took a moment to survey the cavern as he chewed on the stem of his pipe. "I can't give you any maps to show you the way this time. Just choose a course of action — you'll know when it's right — and stick to it."

"Please, Tam," Will begged the shadowy outline. "I need more than that."

Tam puffed out a hazy cloud of smoke that seemed to hang in the air forever, imbued with the constant cycle of different colors the plants were emitting. "Listen to your heart," he said, as the cloud finally dispersed.

"What does that mean?" Will demanded, profoundly disappointed with the response. "That doesn't help me at all!"

Tam merely exhaled an even bigger cloud of smoke, which completely enveloped him.

"What are you doing out here?" Martha asked.

"Huh?" Will gasped, jerking his head around.

"I heard voices," she said, looking out over the garden from the top of the porch.

"I couldn't sleep so I checked on Elliott, then came out here for some fresh air," Will explained.

"You didn't check on Elliott. I was with her — I would have seen you come in. Are you all right, Will?" she asked, concerned.

Will didn't answer, turning back to where Tam had been sitting. He was surprised to see Bartleby there instead, watching him alertly. "Must have dozed off," he mumbled, getting up and passing Martha as he went inside the shack, shaking his head.

When Will took his turn with Elliott later that day, she seemed to be even more restless than usual, her head tossing from side to side as she tensed all her limbs. Every so often her eyes flickered open for a few seconds. It frightened Will — he had no idea what it meant or what he should be doing. As he tried to soothe her by talking to her, her eyes seemed to look at him, but he knew she wasn't seeing him — they were lifeless and red-rimmed, and not like her eyes at all.

She began to babble and froth at the mouth, her movements becoming frantic. Then she screamed, and her whole body convulsed and locked up as if an electric current was running through it. Shouting for help, Will tried to straighten her out on the bed, but she was rigid, her back arching and her legs so tautly clenched that she was thrusting herself up from the mattress. He caught a glimpse of her face. It was no longer flushed as it had been ever since the fever set in, but completely drained of color. Deathly white.

"Help, anybody! Come quick!" he screamed.

Chester and Martha rushed in at the same time — they had clearly both been asleep.

Martha reacted to the situation immediately. She picked up the bowl of water and threw it over Elliott, then thrust the empty bowl at Chester, telling him to go and refill it. As Chester rushed off, she joined Will in trying to straighten out the girl's body.

"What is it? Why's she doing this?" Will said, so beside himself with worry that his voice was quaking.

"It's because of her temperature. It should pass," Martha told him. She was checking Elliott's mouth — the girl's teeth were clenched tightly shut. "Got to watch out she hasn't bitten her tongue," Martha said.

"Look . . . look at her eyes," Will gasped. They had rolled up into her head so that only the whites showed.

"It'll pass," Martha assured him again.

Chester thundered back in with a full bowl of water and Martha drenched the girl a second time. Elliott's body slowly relaxed, until she was completely still and the color had returned to her face.

"Poor Elliott," Will mumbled. "That was just awful."

"She was fitting. It's because she's been too hot for too long," Martha said. "It's affecting her brain."

Will and Chester exchanged glances.

"Isn't there anything we can do to stop it?" Chester asked.

"I'm afraid not. And it's likely to get worse," Martha replied. "Exactly the same happened with Nathaniel."

Mrs. Burrows had just left her apartment when she noticed two surly-looking youths hanging around by the railings in the middle of the town square.

Both had their hoods up and were wearing identical sky-blue camouflage baseball caps with oversized peaks, so it was difficult for her to make out their faces. But then one of them, the bigger of the two, who had a cigarette cupped in his hand, raised it to his mouth for a drag, and Mrs. Burrows caught a glimpse of his features.

She slowed, then crossed the road toward them.

"I know you, don't I?" she said, frowning.

"Don't think so, lady," the bigger boy replied, his manner gruff as he slung his cigarette into the gutter. Tucking his head down low, he began to swagger off with his confederate in tow.

"I *do* know you. You and Will had a set-to a couple of years ago, when he used his shovel. I had to come in and talk to the headmaster, and you were there, too, with your parents. You're Spike or Spider or something like that, aren't you?"

The boy stopped on the spot, twisting his head around to regard Mrs. Burrows. "Spider? What sort of name's that?" he spat. He curled the side of his mouth in what was probably intended to be an insolent sneer, but it looked more like he was about to sneeze. "The name's Speed, lady, *Speed*." Then, as what Mrs. Burrows had said registered, he frowned and began to study her with more interest. "Will . . . Will Burrows. You're Will's mum?"

"That's right," she confirmed.

Speed exchanged a glance with his companion, Bloggsy, then strolled back toward her. "I thought you'd been put away somewhere," he said insensitively.

"I was. Went through a rough patch, but I'm through it now."

"My stepdad got all tweaky, too — know what I'm saying? — depression and all that, only me mum chucked him out. He was getting a bit rough with me and me bro," Speed said, clenching and unclenching a fist.

"I'm sorry to hear that," Mrs. Burrows said.

Speed ran his eyes over Mrs. Burrows again, lingering on her new sneakers. "Wicked," he said, obviously impressed with them. "You're looking sharp, Mrs. B. Been workin' out?"

She nodded.

"You back here for Will, am I right?" he asked. "Lookin' for him?"

"Yes, I'm just on my way to yet another briefing from the police. They won't have anything new to say — all the usual excuses. It's like dealing with the Keystone Cops."

Speed shook his head empathically. "What are they gonna tell you? Nobody talks to them. They're the last to know what's going down."

Speed seemed on the point of saying something more, then shut his mouth.

"You haven't seen him, have you?" Mrs. Burrows asked. "There were a couple of unconfirmed sightings of him around here before Christmas."

"I . . . ," he started, then seemed to change his mind. "Smoke?" he offered. In a flash Bloggsy was there with an open pack of Marlboros. Mrs. Burrows took one, and Speed lit it for her before he lit his own.

Mrs. Burrows drew hard on her cigarette. "Listen, anything you tell me, it'll stay between you and me," she promised. "No police."

"No police," Speed repeated. He looked up and down the street, then leaned in toward her, dropping his voice to a confidential whisper. "November time, he was back here in Highfield with a younger kid —"

"Mini-Me . . . and that monster pit bull," Bloggsy chimed in.

Speed gave him a harsh look and he immediately fell silent.

"— a younger kid who looked just like him, and, yeah, he also had a seriously massive canine with him. They were on their way to the Tube when me and Bloggsy bumped into them. Y'know, Will and me were never mates, so we didn't exactly stop to chat."

"So you only saw him the once?"

"Yes," Speed confirmed. "Word on the street is he's got some really heavy geezers on his case and he's gone to ground, but he's coming back soon to sort them out. And we say respect to him for that."

"Respect," echoed Bloggsy.

"And if you do find Will, you tell him from me," Speed said, stabbing the air with his cigarette to emphasize what he was saying, "that we didn't always see eye to eye, but that was then. If he wants help, he knows where he can come."

"I'll do that. Thanks," Mrs. Burrows said, watching as they both ambled away, hands in pockets.

And through the window in the rear door of an old and battered van parked up in the square, Mrs. Burrows herself was being watched. Drake increased the magnification on his monocular, zooming in so he could see her face more clearly. "Careful who you talk to, Celia. You never can tell," he said under his breath. "Not until it's too late."

Mrs. Burrows took a thoughtful drag from her cigarette, then studied it in her hand.

"You're not going to finish that," Drake predicted. "Reminds you too much of your sister Jean. You're not like her."

Mrs. Burrows raised the cigarette to her lips, but seemed to think better of it. With a shake of her head, she carefully dropped it down a drain at the curbside, then began to move off.

"Good woman," Drake said. He put away his monocular and got ready to follow her.

Everything had lost its meaning for Will. Playing chess was out of the question — he couldn't begin to concentrate on it — and he realized he hadn't as much as opened his journal for weeks. He could hardly bring himself to eat the food Martha put out for him. He was finding it difficult to sleep — every time he lay down, he felt as if his head was going to burst. And every time he was with Chester, the unspoken question hung between them. *Should we go? Should we go?*

As for Elliott, he wondered at what point the cutoff came, the point at which she would be too ill to be moved. Watching her in the throes of a fit like that had been the last straw. He felt so powerless to do anything to help her.

He'd begun to ask himself whether he and Chester should leave Elliott at the shack with Martha and set out by themselves, but he couldn't see how that would work. What if they were successful and came across something or someone, but couldn't find their way back to the shack again? Or what if they found help but it was too far away, and they didn't arrive back in time to help her? Or what if, by some stroke of luck, they found a route out of the Pore — would they take it, then come back down again? No, Will decided, the only way it would work was if they took Elliott with them.

But he couldn't bring himself to tell Chester it was time — and he wasn't sure how Chester would react if he did.

The only part of his old routine he clung to was rummaging through the trunks of salvaged items.

Now, as he wandered around to the rear of the shack with Bartleby lolloping along at his side, Rebecca called out to him.

"How's Elliott? Any better?"

Will glanced at Rebecca's hut, seeing her face through the open doorway. "No, she's —" he began to answer, then caught himself. He'd been so preoccupied with his concerns that he'd forgotten who was addressing him. "Don't talk to me," he scowled. "It's none of your business!"

Entering the outbuilding, he stood before the trunks and chests in one of the corners that he hadn't yet investigated. He sighed, thinking that he didn't have many more to go before he'd finish the whole lot. Clambering up on a few trunks so he could reach the top of the corner pile, he stretched across and took hold of a wooden casket. He lifted it down, placing it on the small patch of ground in the middle of the hut he kept clear for sorting the items. As he knelt before the casket and swung the lid up, Rebecca deigned to speak to him again.

"Are you looking for something, Will?" she said.

Will stopped what he was doing and stood up, wondering if Rebecca could see him through chinks in the sidewall of her hut. The construction of the log store in which Martha had put the twin was the same as all the other outbuildings; ancient timber planks had been nailed to thick beams, but these planks were so warped and worm-eaten that he guessed the twin had found a crack to watch him through. *How very like Rebecca. Always snooping.* His resentment built. This was the one place he could get away from it all and lose himself in the task of sorting through the trunks. The last thing he wanted to do was get into a conversation with the Styx girl.

"Just leave me alone, will you?" he snapped.

As he knelt down before the box again and turfed out some pieces of lead sheeting, he came across a small plastic container. Inside was what appeared to be a set of relatively modern graphic pens — the type that draftsmen or cartographers use.

There were five in the container, all with different nib sizes. He twisted the lid off one and tried it on his palm. The ink had long since dried out, and he immediately wondered if Martha had anything he might be able to use instead. "Finders keepers," he said as he put the set aside. Just then Rebecca called out again.

"Whatever you're looking for, I guess it must be important if both you and Martha are hunting for it."

"I told you to sh —" he started, but didn't finish the sentence. Getting up, he left his hut and strode over to where Rebecca was shackled. "What did you just say?" he demanded brusquely.

"Well, Martha's been in there, too, rooting around. I thought —"

"Nah," Will said, shaking his head. "Martha's not interested in that old stuff — it's been there for ages." He began to walk away. "You're mistaken."

"No, Will, I'm not," Rebecca insisted. "I swear she's been in there . . . oh, three or four times . . . moving things around and even chucking some of it away."

Will hesitated, turning his head to the twin. "Chucking it away?" he repeated. "What sort of things?"

"I couldn't see exactly what it was, but I did hear clinking."

"Really," Will said, thinking it was strange Martha hadn't mentioned anything to him about it. He gave a small shrug, telling himself that it all belonged to her, anyway, so she could do what she wanted with it, but his curiosity got the better of him. "Where did she take these clinking things?"

"Up past Bartleby. I definitely saw her digging there, and she threw something into the hole."

Will glanced to where Bartleby was rolling on his back, making a series of satisfied piglike grunts. He'd taken so many dust baths in the same spot that there was a large impression in the soil.

"Past Bartleby," Will said thoughtfully.

"Yes. I assumed she was giving you a hand with whatever you're doing."

"Sure, that's right — she's been giving me a hand," Will mumbled, trying to pretend to Rebecca that what she was saying wasn't news to him. But as he ambled back toward his hut again, he knew he had to take a look for himself. He continued straight past it and toward the wriggling cat, trying to be as casual as he could because he suspected Rebecca's prying eyes were still on him.

"Keep going — it's a bit farther," Rebecca shouted helpfully, confirming his suspicions.

"Good grief, what am I doing?" Will grumbled under his breath, annoyed that he was allowing himself to pay any heed to what she'd said. Nevertheless, Will kept going, passing Bartleby, whose head perked up as he saw him there.

Reaching the area Rebecca had indicated, Will stepped slowly around the bare ground, inspecting the surface. It felt firm underfoot, but then his heel sank into a loose patch. He immediately dropped into a squat and began to scoop away the soil. It had been dug recently and it wasn't difficult for him to re-excavate the hole.

Will noticed that Bartleby was watching him intently, head

to one side. "Just looking for my favorite bone," Will joked to the cat. It wasn't beyond the realm of possibility that Bartleby himself had dug the hole, and Will was just as prepared for the discovery of a half-chewed rodent or something equally disgusting at the bottom.

He'd reached more than a foot and was leaning into the hole when he spotted what looked like small, light-colored beads in the dirt. At first he just assumed they were insect eggs or seeds, but as he looked at them more closely, he found they were, in fact, pills. He carefully picked them out of the soil, identifying three distinct kinds: Two types were white, but different in size, and the third was pink. Each of the three types had different letters pressed into them, although they didn't spell out full words.

Then, as he dug down a little deeper, he heard something rattle.

"What have we here?" he said to Bartleby as he came across three glass bottles. They were each about two inches long, and their tops, screw-on metal caps, had been removed, but he also found these in the soil at the very bottom of the hole. He emptied one of the bottles of dirt and, locating the right cap for it, replaced it. It reminded him of the sort of bottle his parents kept in the bathroom cabinet — prescription drugs that nobody ever bothered to throw away.

Making snuffling noises, Bartleby stuck his nose into the hole as Will tried to read the printed label on the bottle. There was a long word on the label, with several letters that weren't in the English alphabet. Despite the fact that Will couldn't understand what it said, he had the strongest sense that the bottle had originated from the surface. Then he noticed a date at the bottom of the label.

"Two years old!" he gasped, and immediately checked the other labels. He found that they had approximately the same dates on them, give or take a few months.

He sat back on the ground, dumbfounded, as several thoughts ricocheted through his head. He felt a surge of hope, because the very existence of these bottles demonstrated that even down here there were medicines to be had (modern ones, no less), which might help Elliott overcome the fever.

But he was also deeply disturbed by the discovery. If Martha had known about these medicines, why hadn't she said anything to him about them? Worse still, why had she been skulking around behind his back and *hiding* them from him? He couldn't begin to comprehend why she would do that.

He gathered up more of the loose pills and put them in the other bottles, then screwed on their tops. Deep in thought, he tucked all three bottles into his pants pocket.

"C'mon, boy, time to get back," he said to Bartleby. To avoid getting into further conversation with Rebecca, he marched quickly past her.

"Find anything?" she called out.

"Nah, nothing," he grunted, keeping his eyes firmly on the path in front of him.

"You're just in time for supper. I made us some broth," Martha said as Will entered the shack. She had her back to the room as she stirred a pot on the hearth, while Chester was seated at the table and already tucking into his food.

"Did that Styx snake tell you anything else?" he inquired, not looking at Will as he drained his spoon of broth.

"Yes, she did," Will answered. "Something very weird." He didn't sit down but began to take the bottles from his pocket, placing them in a row on the table.

"She's a lying little viper, just like the rest of them," Chester said scornfully, lifting his spoon to his mouth but not quite reaching it as his eyes fell on the bottles.

"She's not the only one who's lying," Will said in a low voice.

Martha had been halfway to the table with a bowl of broth for Will. There was a crash as she simply dropped it, splashing broth all over the floor.

Except for the odd crackle of the fire, there was absolute silence in the room.

Chester looked from Will to Martha, who was holding mouse-still, her head down. "What the heck is going on here?" He pointed at the bottles with his spoon. "And what are those, Will?" he asked.

"Medicine, apparently. Look at the date," Will said, rolling one of the bottles across the table to Chester.

Chester picked it up and studied the label. "Two years old," he said. "And the label's in Russian."

"Russian," Will said. "Really?"

"Sure. My grandmother was from the Ukraine. She taught me a few words," Chester said, his expression one of complete bewilderment. "But what's going on? Where did you get these?"

Will snatched up another of the bottles and shook it so it rattled. "They had pills in them. At least they did until Martha sneaked them out of the trunks and buried them by the cavern wall. She buried them so I wouldn't find them." He glowered at Martha, who remained staring at her feet, then he suddenly clapped a hand to his forehead. "Of course, the stethoscope!" he cried. "It's recent, too, like the pills! Tam was trying to tell me! He told me to listen to my heart. He meant the stethoscope!"

Chester was on his feet now, eyeing his friend with alarm. "What? What are you saying, Will? Have you completely lost it? How can Tam have spoken to you? He's been dead for months!"

"Forget it — that's not important," Will said, his voice more controlled, although husky with anger. "What's important is that Martha knew there was some medicine. Maybe some anti-biotics that we could have used on Elliott. And she hid them from us, Chester," Will said, facing the woman. "Why did you do that, Martha?"

She remained silent, her head bowed.

"Martha?" Chester mumbled. "Is this true?"

Martha shuffled unsteadily to the chair at the head of the table and sank into it. She said nothing for a moment, sliding her thumb repeatedly in the palm of her other hand. When she spoke, her voice was barely audible.

"When Nathaniel came back with . . . with cracked ribs . . . and the fever set in, he got worse and worse —"

"Yeah, we know all that," Will interrupted, no longer able to feel much sympathy for the woman.

"I told you he found a metal ship. It's about eight days away in the farthest of the Seven Sisters. While he . . . ," she said, her voice petering out.

"Yes," Will pressed her.

"While he could still speak, he gave me directions so I could fetch some apothecaries' supplies from it."

Will and Chester exchanged glances.

"You mean medicines," Will said.

"Yes, medicines," she confirmed timidly. "But it's a long journey and I strayed off track. I also lost some of the medicines when the Brights attacked. They nest by the ship and I only just made it out of there."

"Brights?" Chester mouthed silently at Will, who just jerked his head in response.

"Go on," Will urged her.

"Nathaniel was dead by the time I came back," Martha sighed. "But even if I had been in time for him, I couldn't tell what the medicines do, or how to use them."

"Yeah, but maybe Chester and I can," Will said sharply. "And you still haven't explained why you lied to us, Martha."

"Because . . . because I didn't want you to get hurt. I couldn't lose either of you, not like I did Nathaniel. I couldn't go through that again," Martha croaked, on the verge of tears.

Will pointed in the direction of Elliott's room. "In there, our friend is fighting for her life, and your lies might very well have killed her," he said. Then he addressed Chester. "OK, this is what we're going to do — we're leaving right now for the metal ship." He went over to where Martha had left her crossbow and snatched it up.

Martha had seen what he'd done from the corner of her eye. The act in itself was significant enough — he didn't need to add anything. She sighed again. "I'm sorry, Will," she said. "I won't let you down again."

"Chester, why don't you get Elliott ready," Will suggested. "Martha, I want you to pack up all the food you've got in the place."

"I need to pick some Aniseed Fire from my garden," she said, rising slowly to her feet, then going to the front door. The boys watched her as she stopped halfway down the garden path and began to harvest her plants. As she lopped their stems, the vivid blue glow the Aniseed Fire emitted was instantly dulled, slowly fading away to nothing.

"That was awful," Chester said. "But I can't believe she lied to us."

They continued to watch the rather forlorn and lonely figure as she bent over her plants, dressed in her threadbare apron, with her red, straggling hair flopping over her face.

"Just a sad old lady," Will murmured. He pulled his shoulders back as if trying to put the whole episode behind him. "Why don't you try to read what was in the bottles," he said. "I'll get our kit ready, then we're making tracks."

"And Rebecca?" Chester asked. "What do we do with her?"

"Count me in — I'd love to help," Rebecca said as she mounted the steps of the front porch and entered the room. Will immediately looked down at her ankles and saw that she'd removed her leg irons. "You know I'm really good at organizing things, don't you, Will?" she added gently.

Shaking his head in disbelief, Will took a moment to answer. "So . . . so you could have escaped whenever you wanted. But you didn't."

"Why would I want to do that?" she replied. "There's nowhere for me to go."

Will noticed Chester had clenched his fist, and was worried what he might be about to do. Just then an amazingly powerful gust of wind swept through the garden, ruffling the plants in their beds.

"Feels like a Levant's blowing up," Rebecca said.

As a shutter banged somewhere in the shack, Will spoke quietly. "Every time one of those winds comes along, something terrible happens."

"Oh, great," Chester muttered.

The wind raged around Dr. Burrows and the Rebecca twin. Caught in an exposed position in the middle of a wide tunnel, there was nowhere they could go to escape it as it grew more and more fierce. The small campfire between them was almost extinguished by the violent flurries, but they were hardly able to see this, anyway, as a sandstorm of black dust suddenly enveloped them.

Dr. Burrows had rolled onto his front and wrapped his arms around his head to protect his face from the dust. As he lay there, spitting grit from his mouth, he finally admitted to himself that he'd had about all he could take from the Styx girl. The pressure from her to come up with results was relentless. He couldn't just snap his fingers and somehow find a feature that tied in with the map on the stone tablets. It made him livid. He was an archaeologist, not some scout in the mold of Davy Crockett.

And to cap it all off, Dr. Burrows felt thoroughly intimidated by the Styx soldier. Just under the surface of everything the girl said was the veiled threat that the ghoulish soldier was going to do him harm. To say that it made Dr. Burrows feel extremely uneasy was an understatement.

Talk about a complete reversal of the parent-child relationship: Now Rebecca was the one calling all the shots — he had no real say in anything. No. It had all become too much for Dr. Burrows. So much so that he was willing to take his chances on his own. And, most important to him, Rebecca had forgotten to take the tablets away from him for "safe-keeping," as she put it. He patted his pocket to assure himself they were there, and smiled.

Knowing the impenetrable dust cloud would mask his movements, he began to crawl slowly along the ground and away from the fire. He made sure he hooked the water bladder as he went — he would need it to keep himself going.

After a short while, he stopped crawling. He still couldn't see very far in front of him, and the wind filled his ears as he listened. Deciding that there was no way his departure could have been observed, he got up and began to walk. Nearly bent double from the force of the wind, he walked straight into what felt like . . . a man.

Next to the man was a vague smear of light, and in this light, between the thick swirls of dust, he glimpsed a face.

"Did you get lost?" Rebecca yelled over the squall.

Dr. Burrows had walked smack bang into the Limiter, and the Styx girl was standing right next to him.

Grabbing his arm, she spun him back in the direction he'd come from. "It's not wise to move around in this," she added. After a few steps she sat down, pulling him with her. "Don't want to get yourself hurt, Daddy, do you?" she said.

15

WILL WAS PACKING the last of his kit as Chester came out onto the porch.

"It's the weirdest thing . . . ," Will started to say, looking mystified.

"What?"

"Well," Will continued as he pulled his headset from a side pocket of his rucksack and regarded it, "I just tested this to make sure it's ready . . . and it's completely dead."

"Are you sure?" Chester asked.

"Absolutely. Not even a glimmer," Will replied.

"Maybe you left it on or something, and the element burned out," Chester suggested.

"No, I've taken really good care of it," Will answered. "I hope your rifle scope is OK — at least one of us needs to have night vision."

Chester fetched his rifle and pointed it down the garden.

"I can't believe it!" he exclaimed, lowering the weapon to examine the scope. "It's not working, either." He turned the knurled focus ring on the scope and tried it again. "Nope. Zilch!" Frowning, he looked quickly over at Will. "You don't think the Rebecca twin . . ." He trailed off.

Will considered this for a moment. "Nah, it can't have been her. I know she's been off her tether, but my headset was in Elliott's room, and there's always one of us in there."

"Well, if it wasn't her," Chester said, shaking his rifle as if it might make the scope function again, "aren't these things powered by light orbs and meant to last for years? Isn't that what Drake said?"

"I think so," Will exhaled, shutting his eyes for a second. "Typical — just when we need them." He snapped his eyes open. "Let's just hope that we don't run into any trouble along the way." As they returned inside he glanced at the pill bottles on the table. "Any luck with those?"

Chester went over and took one of them in his hand. "Yes, this had aspirin in it," he said without any hesitation.

"Wow! That's just incredible!" Will exclaimed. "You can actually read Russian! I'm impressed!" Then he noticed that Chester was smiling at him.

"Will," he said, directing his friend to the very bottom of the label, "if you look down here — in among the Russian words — it says *Aspirin*. In English."

"Right . . . missed that," Will mumbled, feeling more than a little foolish.

From the lettering on the pills, it didn't take long to identify which of them were the aspirins. Then Will and Chester debated whether it would be too risky to give them to Elliott, particularly since the pills had spent a good week in the soil and some of them had begun to go a little fluffy as they were affected by the moisture.

In the end, they decided that the aspirins might do more

good than harm and help take the edge off her fever. And if it prevented another of the spasmodic fits, then they felt they had no option but to give it a shot. So they dissolved a few of the pills in a canteen of water and made Elliott drink it.

The Levant Wind had all but died down by the time they went through the barricade, with just the odd gust blowing on their backs. For several hours, the tunnels were wide and relatively level. Will prayed that the whole journey would be this easy.

Because she knew the way, Martha took pole position. Next came Chester and Will, carrying Elliott between them on a makeshift stretcher. Elliott was swaddled in a blanket and tightly bound to the stretcher so that she could be hauled up vertically if the situation demanded, but for now the boys were trying to keep her horizontal to lessen the trauma of being moved.

Will glanced back at Rebecca, who was bringing up the rear with Bartleby loping alongside her in his long, loose gait. At her own insistence, Rebecca was carrying a huge proportion of their provisions and water in two rucksacks, one on each shoulder. Given her slender frame, this would have been a tall order on the surface, but the lack of gravity meant she could manage it without too much difficulty. Nevertheless, Will still couldn't help noticing how her limp seemed to be more pronounced.

"I'm not sure how she's coping," he said quietly to Chester.

"As well as can be expected, I suppose," Chester responded as he looked down at Elliott.

"I meant Rebecca," Will corrected him.

"Oh, *her*," Chester replied peevishly, his whole manner transforming in the blink of an eye. It was obvious he couldn't care less. "Will, don't be taken in by her. I tell you, it's all one big act."

Will thought for a second. "If it *is* some sort of trick, what could she possibly want from us?"

"I've no idea," Chester said. He was on edge — he didn't like it that Will was giving the girl free rein. Will knew that if Chester had had his way, she would have been chained up again — properly this time — and left behind to rot in the log store.

"I don't think she's up to anything," Will said after a few paces. Although he wouldn't have dreamed of breathing a word to Chester, he was incredibly confused about his feelings. Since she'd turned up at the shack, Rebecca hadn't shown any of the brutal characteristics of her people. In fact, she seemed to be distinctly vulnerable, and a world apart from the Styx and their insectlike cruelty.

He so wanted to believe that everything she'd told him was true — that she'd been forced to follow orders on pain of death. Maybe he wanted to believe her a little too much. Rebecca had been a godsend to Will before they'd left the shack, helping him plan what they needed to take and organizing the rucksacks to the nth degree in that efficient way only she could. It was as if he'd done a backflip over all the atrocious things he'd experienced at the hands of the Styx in the Colony and the Deeps and somehow his sister had been restored to him, the sister he knew from the good times home in Highfield.

Admittedly these were few and far between — and perhaps they were all the more intense in his memory exactly because of that. And perhaps he also wanted to believe in her because, with his father gone, she was all that remained of his Highfield family. Apart from Mrs. Burrows, of course, who was a vague and distant figure on the fringes of his recollections.

"Right now, I'm more worried about Martha," Chester said, breaking into Will's thoughts. They both peered at her rotund outline up ahead. "She's not herself at all," Chester continued. "She's hardly said a word since we left the shack. I know it was wrong of her to lie to us, but I can kind of understand her reasons."

Will gave a half articulated "yes" in response. He wasn't going to forgive the woman in a hurry. "What she did was self-ish. She chose our lives over Elliott's. How can that be right?" he said.

"It's not," Chester replied slowly, as if he was still weighing whether to remain angry with Martha.

"Speaking of Elliott," Will said, "isn't it time for another dose of aspirin?"

"I'm sure we could all do with a pit stop," Chester agreed.

Having shouted to Martha to come back to them, Will slipped off his rucksack and extracted the canteen containing the aspirin solution. He passed this to Chester, who shook it thoroughly, then removed the top and began to tip a few mea-sures into Elliott's mouth.

"It's definitely doing the trick," Chester said, placing a hand on her forehead as he poured a little more of the fluid between her cracked lips. "She's much cooler."

They all froze as they heard a screeching in the distance — the call of the spider-monkeys.

"That's all we need," Will said, as his eyes met Martha's.

"It's her," she whispered, pointing at Elliott. "I told you . . . they can sense weakness. She's drawing them to us like a magnet."

"We'll just have to use the Aniseed Fire and keep going," Will said flatly.

"I want my crossbow back," Martha demanded abruptly, staring at the weapon and the quill of bolts slung over Chester's shoulder along with his rifle.

Getting to his feet, Chester looked at Will for guidance, but he remained silent. He wasn't in favor of the idea.

"Um . . . ," Rebecca said softly, then shut her mouth.

"You were going to say something," Will prompted her.

"Well . . . it's just that Martha's the only one of us who's familiar with the terrain and the sorts of dangers we could face along the way. She really should be armed, because if you lose her, you lose your guide, and you'll never find the ship."

Will looked undecided.

"Hey, it's your show, Will, but that's how I see it," Rebecca said almost apologetically.

"No, good point," Will conceded. He turned to Martha. "So . . . do I have your word that we can trust you?"

Martha nodded grimly.

"Then you can have your crossbow back," Will said.

"Oi! Hold on a sec!" Chester exploded furiously. "You'll listen to what that bloody Styx has to say, but you don't want my opinion?" He gave Rebecca a resentful glance.

"Chester, I'm sorry," Will said. "Go on . . . tell me what you think."

Chester dithered for a moment. "Yes . . . she should have it back."

Will shrugged one shoulder. "So you're agreeing with the 'bloody Styx,' anyway. So why did you make such a fuss?"

Chester turned away, mumbling. "I should have my say — that's all."

"First you're all gung ho for searching around the Pore, then — I'll be blowed — it's all changed and we're following *him*," Dr. Burrows said, pointing his thumb at the Limiter up ahead. "Anyway, where the heck does he think he's going? Aren't we getting ourselves completely lost?"

"Not as long as he's finding the signposts," Rebecca replied.

They had just turned into a new stretch of tunnel, and she was scanning the ground for one of these "signposts" she'd referred to.

She spied the three small pieces of fungus arranged in a line to her right, counted ten paces in her head, then played her light on the other side of the tunnel floor past where Dr. Burrows was walking. There at the base of the opposite wall, and easily missed unless you happened to know the Limiters' operating procedures, were another three objects — small rocks this time. These markers were the confirmation sequence that the first Limiter had left behind so the one leading them could follow in his tracks.

Dr. Burrows was, of course, unaware that there was a second Limiter working behind the scenes, and so was thoroughly confused.

"Signposts? I haven't seen any signposts," he said.

"Trust me," the Rebecca twin replied.

Martha made them stop at regular intervals to eat and rest. She built small campfires from material she'd collected along the route, using them to heat up the provisions, and kept them alight as she and the boys took turns sleeping. And she would always sprinkle a few sprigs of Aniseed Fire around the edges of the fire, so it burned slowly and filled the air with its pungent odor.

On the fourth day, as they were walking, Will noticed how all of a sudden it felt very different underfoot — it wasn't the crunch of gravel or the springiness of the fungus, but something softer.

"Mulchy . . . like old leaves," he said as he sniffed deeply, trying to identify the different smells. Then he noticed something else — movement on the wall next to him. At first he assumed his eyes were playing tricks because he was so tired. Then he saw that the movements were real and coming from all over — not just the walls, but on the roof and the floor of the tunnel as well.

"Wait!" he cried, drawing to a halt and forcing Chester to do the same at the other end of Elliott's stretcher. Squinting, Will saw many white wormlike things on all the surfaces. Then one crossed the ground just in front of his boot. Around four inches long, it was like a thin, perfectly white snake and didn't appear to have any eyes. With some sort of sucker at each extremity, it moved by turning end over end, as if it was continually performing cartwheels.

"Yeuch!" Chester exclaimed. "Monster maggots!"

Bartleby pounced on one, trapping it under his paws. Snapping at the worm, he managed to nip one end between his teeth. Its other end began to spiral around, faster and faster as it tried to extricate itself from this unknown predator. Bartleby's eyes rolled in their sockets as he tried to follow its helicopter revolutions, and he was soon dizzy with the effort. Then the creature stopped wheeling around and planted the sucker on its free end straight onto Bartleby's nose. With a shocked squawk, the cat shook his head frantically and released it from his jaws. That was enough for Bartleby — he looked decidedly uneasy as he surveyed the sheer number of cartwheeling worms all around him, and made small leaps to avoid them, as if he was a pony jumping fences.

Martha heard the commotion and came back to the boys. "Loop Snakes. They won't hurt you," she informed them as she began to pluck them from the walls and stuff them into a sack.

"I'm sorry, Martha, but if the idea is to eat those things, you can count me out. And no way am I sticking around here," Chester said decisively, shuffling to one side to avoid a snake that was trying to attach its sucker to his toe cap. He made a guttural sound deep in his throat to demonstrate his absolute disgust at the creatures, then set off at a brisk pace, yanking the stretcher and Will along with him. "C'mon, Will, we're going!"

Will was reluctant to follow, impeding Chester's quick get-away as he looked at the ground in fascination.

"Buck up, Will!" Chester yelled as he pulled at the stretcher. "I'm not in the mood for a nature class!"

As they left, Will peered behind and saw Rebecca put down her rucksacks. She began to help Martha harvest the Loop Snakes. Then he saw Martha say something to Rebecca, who stepped quickly away from the woman. Rebecca hoisted on her rucksacks again and came running down the tunnel.

Will didn't see any more because Chester broke into a jog, forcing him to move at the same speed. And it wasn't difficult to see why Chester was in such a rush. The number of Loop Snakes had increased until it was as if they were passing through an unbroken carpet of waving white fingers. They were everywhere — some even dropping from the roof above and landing on Elliott and the stretcher. The boys couldn't avoid crushing them under the soles of their boots. The snakes burst with an off-putting squishing sound, and a luminous fluid squirted from their bodies so that the boys left softly glowing patches in their wake.

Eventually they came to a stretch of the tunnel that was free of Loop Snakes, and they waited for the others to catch up.

Rebecca came along first.

"What happened back there . . . with Martha?" Will puffed, still out of breath.

"Nothing," she mumbled, not looking him in the eye.

"That's rubbish," Will said. "I was watching. I saw her say something to you."

"I tried to give her a hand with the Loop Snakes . . ."

"Yes . . . and?" Will urged her.

"She told me to get lost and that she was going to kill me," Rebecca said, keeping her voice low.

"Did she, now," Will growled. "Don't worry, Rebecca — she'll have me to deal with if she tries anything."

"Why do you keep calling her that?" Chester piped up. "It's not her name."

"Don't you start," Will warned him.

"No, really, I'd like to know what her name is. *Rebecca* was given to her by Topsoilers, so it can't be her real name. Besides, there can't be *two* Rebeccas, can there? So what is your real name?" he demanded of the girl.

"It wouldn't mean anything to you," Rebecca replied. "It's in my language."

"Try me," Chester insisted.

Rebecca uttered a short word in the Styx's nasal tongue, which sounded uncannily like a hyena's bark.

"No, you're right," Chester said, shaking his head. "Don't expect me to call you th —"

He fell silent as Elliott began to writhe against her ties on the stretcher. "I don't think anyone should speak Styx around Elliott," Chester observed. "Seems to upset her."

By the seventh day of the journey, the boys were feeling the strain of carrying the stretcher, despite the assistance from the reduced gravity. Will had no idea how many miles of tunnel they'd trudged through, or how many vertical descents they'd made, but he hung on to the thought that Martha had said they should reach the ship at some point during the next day. That was, if she could remember the rest of the route correctly.

They'd backtracked on several occasions when Martha realized she'd taken the wrong turn, but this had cost them a few hours at most. She didn't use a map or compass (and Will wasn't sure that one would work down here, in any case), but instead seemed to have all the directions committed to memory.

The most difficult and perilous moments were when they lowered themselves down huge crevasses, particularly because they had to be so careful with Elliott. But with all four of them on the ropes, they managed to get Elliott and the stretcher down time after time without mishap. And any hostility between Martha and Rebecca was put aside on these occasions, since they each had a part to play.

At other times they had to worm their way through hundreds of feet of horribly claustrophobic passages, dragging their kit behind them because the ceiling was so low. It took much pushing and pulling to get Elliott through these stretches.

Then they suddenly came upon an area where the air was so arid that they were all panting and loosening their clothing. As they descended a steep incline, it became unbearably hot. Will was peering at the way ahead when he noticed it seemed to be glowing with a dull redness. It looked ominous, and he wasn't at all surprised when Martha called a halt.

"What's up?" Chester asked.

Martha didn't reply, but instead produced two full bladders of water. Then she beckoned Rebecca over.

"Styx, get some more water out," she ordered bluntly.

As Rebecca did what she was told, Martha explained. "Through here the lava flows close to the rock. It's very hot, and very dangerous."

"So what do we do?" Will asked.

"Can't we go a different way?" Chester asked at the same time.

Martha shook her head. "There's no way around. Just don't stop for anything — do you understand that? If you do, you'll die."

Chester smiled. "Death by barbecue," he commented, then stopped smiling because he realized it wasn't funny at all.

Martha helped Will wrap some rags over Bartleby's paws and secure them in place with twine. The cat seemed to enjoy the attention from Will, and was purring away merrily until Martha tipped water all over his legs and his new cloth booties. He growled indignantly at her, and Will had to hold him in place so she could finish the job. Chester had been tasked with sousing both the stretcher and Elliott with water, and was halfway through when he suddenly stopped.

"Will," he said.

"Yeah, what?"

"You know this is Elliott's?" He indicated the backpack secured on the stretcher just below the girl's feet, which he had insisted they bring with them.

Will's eyes widened. "Explosives! And there's ammunition in our rifles! Martha, what if it gets so hot it all goes off?"

"The rifles should be fine — just make sure that rucksack's soaked," she advised, upending the bladder and tipping water all over herself, directing most of it over her legs and feet. Once the boys and Elliott were similarly drenched, Martha called them together again.

"Remember — whatever happens, don't stop. Not for anything. Otherwise the heat will get you," she said.

Then they were off, dashing down the rest of the incline and into the blistering air. Everything glowed red. Will had a glimpse of the heat haze just before they hit it — it appeared to be almost solid, as if they were about to crash straight into a mirror or some kind of transparent layer of mercury. The boys felt as though flames were licking their faces.

"It's like a crucible!" Will croaked, hardly daring to draw breath. It reminded him of the inside of the little ceramic pots they heated up with Bunsen burners in their chemistry classes at school.

The rock all around them and under their feet seemed to be shot through with veins that glowed a bright orange-red. Will and Chester instinctively tried not to step on the veins as they ran — it was like some nightmarish child's game of avoiding the cracks in the sidewalk. Will smelled burning, and immediately wondered if the soles of their boots would withstand these temperatures.

He also felt his clothes drying out, and saw that the same thing was happening to Chester, who was leaving streams of vapor in his wake. Bartleby had stuck dutifully to Will's side, but as his booties began to sizzle, he decided he wasn't going to hang around for the humans. He bolted off into the distance like a frightened horse.

"How much farther?" Chester cried as he and Will puffed away, finding it difficult to keep a grip on the stretcher as their palms became slick with sweat.

Then they were through to a cooler section of tunnel, where Martha and Bartleby were waiting. They flopped to the ground.

"Phew!" Will exhaled. "Talk about taking a sauna. Reckon I've lost a few pounds." He took off his rifle and slid the cutlass from his belt. "Why did I bring all this stuff? I'm carrying too much weight," he panted.

"Never know when it might come in handy," Chester commented, then took a large swig from his canteen.

"You sound exactly like my dad. He never threw anything away — used to drive Rebecca nuts." Will chuckled as Chester passed him the canteen. He began to drink, but then spewed out a mouthful of water, some of which splashed over his friend. "Wait! Where *is* Rebecca!" Will spluttered as he realized she hadn't come through yet. "Wasn't she right behind us?"

"I thought so," Chester confirmed.

They took a few paces back toward the incline and waited, but still she didn't appear.

"Maybe it was too much for her and she did a U-turn," Chester said.

Will suddenly upended the canteen over his head.

"What do you think you're —?" Chester shouted, but didn't finish the sentence as Will lobbed the empty canteen over to him. "Will!" Chester screamed as his friend tore back into the heat.

Will hadn't gone far when, through the quicksilver air, he made out something huddled in the middle of the tunnel. Small wisps of smoke were rising around it. As he skidded to a halt, he saw Rebecca slumped on top of the rucksacks, which were beginning to smolder. He shook her, yelling her name. She lifted her head weakly and tried to reach for him.

Sweeping her up, he threw her over his back, then hesitated for an instant. "No! Can't leave them!" he gasped, barely able to see what he was doing as he tried to grab hold of the rucksacks by the straps. He swore as his hand came into contact with the glowing floor, but still he managed to gather up both packs. Then he ran as quickly as his legs could carry him, moving so fast he was almost flying. The heat was merciless — he was breathing in tiny breaths as the air scorched his lungs.

Chester had ventured as far forward into the heat as he dared and was waiting for Will. As Will hurtled toward him, he yelled, "To me!" and grabbed the rucksacks from him.

Reaching Martha, Will quickly put Rebecca down next to Elliott. He seized one of the bladders and poured water over the girl, whose head rolled drunkenly on her shoulders. Then he made her sit up and drink a little of it. In no time at all, the water seemed to revive her, although she was still a bit groggy.

"What happened?" he asked.

"I tripped. Couldn't get up," she answered, clutching her forehead as she had a coughing fit. Then she raised her eyes to him. "Thank you, Will," she said.

"It's nothing," Will replied awkwardly as he got to his feet. Feeling his hand where he'd burned it, he turned to see what Chester and Martha were doing. Chester was shaking his head slowly as both he and Martha regarded Will with identical expressions of disapproval. Will looked past them to where Chester had left the rucksacks. "Hey! You idiots! They're on fire!" he shouted as he spotted that both packs were quietly smoldering. "Quick!"

Chester and Martha immediately set about rubbing handfuls of dirt on the burning bags.

"Are they OK? Have we lost anything?" Will asked, worried that their contents might have been damaged.

"Nah, I don't think so," Chester replied, opening one to check inside. He glanced up at Will. "You shouldn't have gone back. Not by yourself."

"I had to," Will said.

Chester wasn't convinced. "It was a crazy thing to do," he said.

Martha glowered at Rebecca. "And because of that Styx and her antics, we're going to be short of water until the next spring." She turned to face down the tunnel. "We should go."

Several miles later, Martha started to slow down. She approached the tunnel wall, fumbled with something, then swung open a rough wooden door.

"What's this place?" Chester asked as she stepped through the timber doorway.

"They're called the Wolf Caves — it's a bolt-hole Nathaniel found. He kept some spare spider traps here."

With Elliott between them on the stretcher, Will and Chester followed her in and found that it was a reasonably sized space with a floor of soft sand. The tunnel seemed to extend farther, but Martha didn't make any move to go down it, instead dumping her kit on the sandy floor. Rebecca and Bartleby had also come in, although Rebecca, still not fully recovered from her ordeal, simply lay down on the ground.

"Why the *Wolf* Caves?" Chester inquired as he and Will found a level piece of ground on which to place the stretcher.

"Because of the wolves," Martha said matter-of-factly.

"Wolves?" Chester spluttered nervously. "I haven't heard anything."

"You wouldn't." Martha made sure the door was shut and secured, then continued to talk as she went about the business of preparing them some food. "They move like specters, hunting in packs of three or four. They usually pick off stragglers and avoid larger groups of people." Sitting on the floor with her legs stretched out before her, she sliced the ends off the Loop Snakes, then peeled the pale white skins from them. "I only just managed to escape them the last time I came this way. So if you ever get separated from the rest of us, remember where these caves are."

Having asked the boys to light a fire, Martha suspended the skinned Loop Snakes over it. When they were cooked, she distributed tin dishes of them to everybody, and Chester seemed to forget his earlier promise that he would never eat them.

"So, what do you make of it?" Will asked as Chester nibbled at a long strip of yellow-white meat.

"Bit like jellied eels," Chester reflected as he chewed. "But they don't taste of eel, and they're not jellied."

"Helpful," Will replied, taking his first bite.

PART 3

THE METAL SHIP

16

THEY LEFT the Wolf Caves after a few hours, resuming their journey. Will had lost track of how long they'd been walking when Martha indicated that there was something up ahead.

"We're close now," she told them as they came to a rope bridge.

Chester whistled. "I can't even see the other side. How far across is it?" he said.

"Maybe . . . a hundred feet," Will estimated as he regarded the precarious-looking structure that spanned the chasm before them.

"Did you make this?" Chester asked Martha as he and Will put Elliott down. Martha took a step onto the bridge and it swayed and creaked ominously. She took several more steps, cautiously trying each of the wooden slats as she went. "Or was it Nathaniel?" Chester asked, having received no response.

"The boat people," Martha replied, peering anxiously into the darkness above. "I can feel them. They're up there."

"Who?" Will asked.

"We're near the nests . . . where the Brights live." Despite the heat, she shivered. "I can feel them up there — ready to swoop." Her eyes met with Will's. "This is a wretched place.

We're not meant to be here. It's *their* place." Her gaze drifted from Will as if she was seeing something behind him, but there wasn't anything there.

Will realized that she must be exhausted. Although he and Chester had grabbed the odd nap on the unforgiving ground along the way, they'd found the journey tiring enough. Martha rarely seemed to allow herself even that. She'd been in an almost permanent state of vigilance for the week since they'd left the shack, watching out for dangers and navigating them through the labyrinthine tunnels with phenomenal accuracy.

Her clothes, never clean at the best of times, were stained and filthy, and her face was lined with fatigue. Will watched as her eyes slid shut.

"Hey, Martha," he said gently.

Her eyes flickered open and she turned to the bridge. "We cross one at a time. And no talking—we have to keep the noise down from here on in." She took out some Aniseed Fire, but didn't make a move to light it. "Save it," she said, as if reminding herself what she ought to be doing. Then she edged forward, the bridge rocking as she began to cross it.

It was Chester's turn once she was safely on the other side. The boys had decided between them that since Chester weighed the most, he shouldn't attempt the crossing with Elliott. Instead he just took one of the lighter rucksacks with him.

"I'm not happy," he grumbled as he started across. "Not happy at all."

"Safe as houses," Will told him confidently.

"Oh, brilliant, that's the kiss of death. I'm doomed for sure now that you've said that," he groaned, raising his eyebrows at Will, who gave him a nod to wish him luck.

From where he was standing, Will could see that Chester's weight was making the bridge sag. And even though Chester was taking it slowly, the bridge swayed alarmingly and made such loud creaking noises, Will thought the whole thing was going to come crashing down at any moment. But the boy stopped frequently, allowing the bridge to settle down before he continued again, and eventually made it safely to the other side.

Then came Will's turn. Picking up Elliott and the stretcher, he ventured forward. He'd gone twenty steps when he had to stop. He stood as rigid as a statue. There were two guide ropes on either side of the bridge at waist height and Will longed to grip one of these, but he couldn't because his arms were full with Elliott.

"It's a long, long way down," a voice in his head boomed so loudly he flinched. Just the thing he didn't want to happen happened: The irrational urge was back, and it was as if he was suddenly under the control of some puppet master. He could so vividly picture himself pivoting over one of the guide ropes and tumbling into the velvety, welcoming darkness below. Somehow, it made such perfect sense. For several seconds he wasn't aware of anything else, just the overwhelming attraction of the empty air below him as it tried to suck him down. He hadn't a thought for Elliott, who was totally at his mercy, or for Chester and Martha on the other side of the crevasse; there was only him, and the persuasive, irresistible pull. Then, in that small portion of his brain that was still cogent, he forced

himself to consider Elliott and how wrong it would be to take her with him. But it wasn't enough — the compulsion was too strong.

"Please," he whimpered. "Please, no."

Then something nudged him from behind, and he swiveled his head stiffly around to see what it was. Bartleby stood balanced between the slats, his big eyes peering at Will with incomprehension. The cat had obviously decided that it was time for him to cross, and couldn't understand why Will was stationary and blocking his way. As Will locked eyes with the cat, the animal gave a low meow — with an intonation that made it almost human; he could have been saying, "Why?"

Will blinked, and the urge flickered like a candle flame in the wind, and then was extinguished. He swung around to see Chester poised at the other end of the bridge. Will began moving forward again, the cat treading softly behind him, nudging the boy when he thought he was stepping too slowly.

Since Martha had told them not to speak, Chester didn't say anything when Will was back on terra firma again, but his concern showed in his eyes. Will stumbled a little way down the tunnel, where he lowered Elliott to the ground, then slumped beside her, his head in his hands.

Once Rebecca had joined them, they were ready to move on. They hadn't gone far before they noticed that they were walking on fungus again, and then they were almost immediately faced with the prospect of three successive vertical drops. Will was still feeling drained after the incident on the bridge, and the thought of carefully lowering Elliott and the stretcher down each of the three declines was almost too much to contemplate. It wasn't another outbreak of the urge that troubled him — for some reason, that didn't reappear — it was the amount of planning associated with each maneuver. And the slippery surface of the fungus only added to their difficulties. By the time they'd finished the third and final descent, Will was fit to drop. But Martha, by her frantic pointing and gesticulations, wasn't allowing them a second's rest.

Half an hour later they entered a sizeable cavern. Will had just detected the distant sound of falling water when Martha slowed to a crawl. Following the beam of her light, Will saw why. Protruding at an angle from the swells of fungus was some kind of small tower, maybe a hundred feet tall. Only its upper half was visible — its dark surface smooth, with a metallic sheen to it — while the rest was encased in swells of fungal growth.

"The metal ship," Will whispered, his face breaking into a grin.

They'd finally arrived at their destination. He wanted to shout with joy, but knew he couldn't. Chester was jabbing his finger frantically to draw Will's attention to the area underneath the tower, and to the left and right of it. Their lights didn't penetrate very far into the darkness, and it took Will a few moments to see what Chester was so excited about. The form of the fungus suggested there was more to the tower than immediately met the eye, and whatever it was, it was big. It seemed to be cylindrical, and Will immediately tried to work out what sort of ship it could be. He'd never been terribly interested in them, except for those of historical importance, like the *Cutty Sark*.

Martha hurriedly shepherded them to the base of the tower. The boys had to keep shielding their faces as strong squalls blasted showers of water at them. *Salt water*, Will thought to himself as he tasted the tanginess on his lips.

Beyond the tower nothing was visible, just a gaping blackness. Will immediately assumed that the ship was poised on the very edge of another of the Seven Sisters. At first glance it could have been the Pore itself, but the never-ending roar of falling water, like faraway thunder, set it apart.

They climbed up the curved surface of the ship with some difficulty, slipping and sliding as they went, then gathered together at the base of the tower. Martha was using a knife to poke around in the fungus, evidently searching for something. As the knife grated against metal, Martha thrust her hand into the fungus and pulled hard, grunting and straining, until a few links of rusted chain were visible. The fungus growth had clearly enveloped the chain, as it had just about everything else in the vicinity.

With a last effort from Martha, the chain suddenly came free, tearing a line all the way up the fungus sheath. As it rattled against the exposed metal at the top of the tower, Will saw it was secured to something up there. Grabbing hold of the chain, Martha wasted no time heaving herself up. It occurred to Will that they weren't attempting to jump to the top because of the risk of missing it and ending up in the void.

Chester climbed up next, then lowered a rope to pull up Elliott and the stretcher. After Rebecca had ascended with the rucksacks, it was Bartleby's turn. The cat was none too happy when Will looped a rope around him so that Martha could hoist him up. Once this was done, Will heaved himself to the top. And found only Martha.

He didn't have any time to take in where he was, or where the others had gone: A high-pitched wail cut through the air.

"Brights," Martha said, her voice not much more than a whisper. In a heartbeat, her crossbow was raised and cocked. As Will craned his neck to peer above, he glimpsed dim lights, but these were so vague and undefined it was as if he was viewing fireflies through a mesh screen.

Had he blinked? Suddenly a large object was within the limits of Martha's light. It seemed to come from nowhere, and Will found it difficult to take in what he was actually seeing.

His first impression was of its color — it was almost pure white. Its wings, nearly thirty feet from tip to tip, were stretched wide. Between these, its body was the size of a full-grown man's, but there was nothing remotely human about it. Will recognized straightaway that it was some kind of insect from the arrangement of its head and thorax, and from its strange abdomen, which seemed to be split, as if it actually had legs. But as it hovered, Will saw that these twin prongs were not limbs, and were covered in downy feathers, or perhaps moth-like scales. And clinging to its forked abdomen were many small black entities — arachnids. Tiny versions of the spider-monkeys, he guessed on the spur of the moment.

There was something very batlike about the angular outline of the creature's wings, and this impression was further enhanced as it flapped them once and Will heard their leathery beat.

The bolt hissed as Martha fired straight at the creature. Yet the shot encountered nothing but air. Although no more than

fifty feet above the tower, and well within Martha's practiced range, the creature had simply disappeared.

"What!" Will exclaimed. He was sure he *hadn't* blinked — and even if he had, these creatures were preternaturally fast.

He heard another beat of its wings. It appeared again, this time to the left of the tower, and closer. And this time Will had his lantern up. The creature was caught in the full glare of its beam.

Its head was not dissimilar to the size and shape of a football, with a small coiled proboscis dead center, beneath which lay a mouth packed with rows of savage-looking, pearl-white teeth. And right above its proboscis were a pair of silvery disks — Will knew that these probably weren't eyes, but something like the "ears" Martha had shown him on the dead spider-monkey.

Will was so surprised that, this time, he did blink, but the creature was still there when he opened his eyes. The oddest thing was that its features so strongly suggested a face. And stranger still, on the very top of its head was an oscillating disk — a circular structure emitting a light that seemed to pulse in intensity. Will instinctively knew this must be some kind of lure, to draw its prey to it in the darkness.

With this glimpse of the creature, Will also saw that it had its wings drawn back, as if in a dive.

A dive toward him and Martha.

Will was rooted to the spot by the apparition, but Martha again fired her crossbow. For a second time the creature simply vanished, leaving Will staring at thin air. It took a frantic shout from Martha to bring him back to his senses.

"Get in!" she screamed, bundling him into the opening by her feet. His lantern spun out of his grip, falling below, where he heard it clatter. Will, too, would have fallen, if he hadn't by sheer luck caught hold of a metal ladder. He managed to climb down a few rungs before Martha, descending with all the delicacy of a stampeding hippo, trod on his fingers.

"Ow!" he cried, extricating his hand as she slammed the hatch shut above them and secured it by turning the circular locking mechanism.

"What in the world was that out there?" he exclaimed, flexing his fingers to ease the pain as he scanned around the confined space he found himself in. "No way was it a spider-monkey!" he added as he realized he was now inside the "tower" of the ship. It was oval-shaped, and numerous pipes and conduits ran down the sides.

". . . A Bright," Martha said breathlessly. "I told you they nest here. They're a very different kettle of fish from the spiders — they can fly."

"You don't say," Will mumbled to himself as he descended to the bottom of the ladder, passing through another hatch on the way. As he dropped lower, he noticed the air had a staleness to it, and he smelled traces of mold and mildew. His feet clanged down on a metal-grilled floor. It was at an angle, and he assumed that was because of the way the ship had settled when it had fallen down the void. As he stooped to retrieve his lantern, Chester rushed up to him.

Will tried to tell him about the flying creature. "You'll never —"

"Will! Will!" Chester interrupted, gabbling in his excitement.

"This isn't any old ship! It's a freakin' *submarine*. And a new one at that!" He raised his light so Will could see what lay around him.

"Wild!" Will said, laughing with the strangeness of it all. It reminded him of a scene from a movie. He looked at the panels of electronic equipment, all completely dark and dust-covered. And although it appeared very modern and complex, there were stubs of burned-down candles on some of the flat surfaces. Around them there were pools of melted wax, which had formed long strings as it had dripped to the floor. "They didn't have any power," he noted, then stepped to the center of the space, in which there was a column that could have been the periscope, and a small desk above which a Perspex sheet was suspended in a frame. It had contour lines drawn on it as if it was a map, although the sheet was shattered and some of the map missing.

"A submarine," he echoed, not really taking in what he was saying. "So we just entered through what must be the conning tower. And this is the control room or . . . or the bridge, or something like that. Is that right?"

"S'pose so, yes." Chester shrugged.

"But how could a submarine get all the way down here? How could that happen?"

"What about that stuff you were telling me about moving dishes?" Chester suggested.

"Moving plates," Will corrected him. He strolled slowly around, inspecting the sophisticated array of equipment. "Yes, plate tectonics. Some sort of seismic shift on the seabed . . . perhaps the submarine just got sucked in." Then he reached where Chester had left Elliott, still on her stretcher. It brought him back to the reason they had come there. "We need those medical supplies. Martha, which way are they?"

"Here," she said, already heading through a rounded doorway with a raised threshold, then along the gangway on the other side. As they passed a cabin with an open door, Will spotted objects floating in dirty water. Because of the angle of the hull, the water rose above the height of the floor grille down one side of the ship. He saw clothes, a single deck shoe, and some sodden cardboard boxes partially immersed in it, white tendrils of mildew growing over them.

"Hold on a second — there's something here," he said as he stooped to pick it up.

"A newspaper," Chester observed. Will opened it out. Half of it had been turned to a soggy pulp by the water, but the rest was still legible. Will saw a picture of a man with a large moustache; the print around it was in Russian.

As Chester looked over his shoulder, Will pointed to the top of the page. "You're right — it could be a Ruskie newspaper . . . but can you read what that says? Is it a date?" he asked.

"февраль," Chester said, struggling with the word. "Um . . . I'd have to try to remember what that means — it must be the month — but look here at the year. It's less than a year old!" Then he frowned. "I don't even know what the date is now."

"I've no idea, either," Will said. He bit his lip as something occurred to him. "You know, I suppose I could even be fifteen by now. I might have had a birthday." Then he chucked the paper down. "But none of this is going to help Elliott. Come on."

They continued along the gangway and through several bulkhead doors until Martha came to a cabin. She seemed reluctant to enter it. Chester looked at her questioningly. "Too many bad memories," she whispered.

Will had already poked his head inside the cabin. "It's a mess in there."

Martha nodded. "It was like that when I found it," she said.

"But what about the people — the crew? Was there any sign of them when Nathaniel first came here?" Chester asked.

"None. And from the looks of it, they left in a hurry. Now, if you don't mind, I'm going to crawl away someplace and get some sleep," she said, staggering wearily back along the gangway.

Will and Chester set about searching the cabin, in which there was an examination table and a light on an adjustable stand. There were also several medical posters of the human body on the walls. Many metal-framed chairs were heaped in a corner as if they'd just been thrown there, and a good deal of broken glass and medical instruments were strewn across the floor. But what immediately caught the boys' attention was that one whole side of the cabin was taken up by tall cabinets. They quickly began to open these, finding numerous drawers inside them, all lined with foam inserts. Will clucked as he found only empty impressions in the foam of the drawers he was searching, but Chester was having more luck, coming across numerous bottles of pills and liquids.

The boys worked together, taking everything out and placing it on the examination table. In the process, Chester remarked on the dark patches all over the melamine surface of the table. "What do you think this is?" he asked, gingerly touching one of them.

"Could be blood," Will said, frowning at the thought.

Chester stared at it uneasily for several seconds. "So what *did* happen to the crew?"

"Who knows? Maybe they were all wiped out by those flying things I saw," Will replied. "Why else would they leave so much kit behind?" He sniffed, then sniffed again. "Do you smell that? There's something sort of sour in here."

"Hope it's not me," Chester said earnestly, lifting up an elbow to sample his armpit.

Will smiled. "No, I don't mean us. It's a chemical smell. Like chloroform or something."

Chester rubbed his forehead, his expression one of concern. "I was thinking . . . what if the very thing we need — the antibiotics — have already been used up by the crew, or even taken by Martha when she came here before? She did say she lost a load of stuff on the way back to Nathaniel." He thought for a second. "And you do know that antibiotics go bad if they get too warm, don't you? When I had some pills for an ear infection, my mum kept them in the fridge."

Will was undeterred. "Look, there's got to be something here . . . anything . . . that can help Elliott. We can't have come all this way for nothing."

With all the medicines they could find spread out on the examination table, Chester began the arduous process of trying to decipher the labels, as Will held the lantern. They became increasingly despondent; either the words were way beyond Chester's limited knowledge of the Russian language or, even if they were in English, they didn't mean anything to either of the boys.

Fretting to himself, Chester was checking through all the bottles a second time as Will scoured every inch of the cabin to see if they had missed anything. As he began to pull the chairs from the corner, he spotted something.

"Wahay!" he exclaimed, quickly hoisting it out and putting it on the table.

It was an orange plastic case. He undid the catches and raised the lid. There were quite a few medicines piled inside, which he and Chester immediately began to scrutinize.

"Amoxicillin!" Chester exclaimed, holding up a bottle of pills. "I recognize this! The doctor gave it to me when I got a cut on my knee and it got all puffed out with pus."

"Amoxicillin? Are you sure?" Will asked him.

"One hundred percent. And the *Use By* date probably isn't that long ago. I bet it's still safe to take," Chester said. He suddenly grabbed Will's arm. "Wait, what are we doing?! Rebecca! We left Elliott with Rebecca!"

Will tried to calm him down. "Cool it — we're going back there right now. I'm sure everything's fine."

"I don't care what you think! She's alone with Elliott! And I left my flipping rifle there, too!" Chester cried, launching himself through the doorway. Out in the gangway, he was moving so fast that he walloped his forehead against an oil lantern hanging from one of the overhead pipes, but still he didn't slow down.

With Will close behind him, they burst onto the submarine's bridge. Chester went straight to his rifle and snatched it up. Elliott was still lying on the stretcher where he had left her, but her bindings and blanket had been removed.

"What have you done to her?" Chester demanded furiously, pointing at Elliott.

Rebecca backed away in alarm at Chester's outburst. The fact that he had his rifle in his hands made him all the more threatening.

Kneeling beside Elliott, Chester put his ear to her face. Then he took hold of her wrist. "She's still got a pulse," he told Will.

"I cleaned her up. That's all. I found a tank of water up front. And a bottle of iodine to sterilize it," Rebecca explained. "You shouldn't drink it, but it's OK for washing."

"I think Elliott's all right," Chester said to Will, as if he hadn't heard a word Rebecca had been saying.

"Chester," Will said, "she's wearing fresh clothes. Her face has been washed. Look at her!"

"I haven't done anything to hurt her," Rebecca insisted, almost in tears. "I was just trying to help."

Chester caught sight of a small fire burning in the corner of the bridge. "Then what the heck is that? What's your game?"

"I'm heating up some broth for Elliott," Rebecca replied quietly. "Thought you might like some, too."

Chester caught his breath, looking a little sheepish as he realized that Rebecca hadn't been up to anything sinister. "Right . . . good," he said, adding a gruff "thanks" as he rose to his feet.

"My pleasure," Rebecca said, then noticed the bottle in Chester's hand. "You found something!" She turned to Will. "Can I see it?" she asked him eagerly.

"No, you can't," Chester replied automatically.

"Oh, come on. Let her," Will said. "I mean, what harm can it do?"

Chester reluctantly held the bottle out to Rebecca, who took it and studied the label. "Amoxicillin . . . Yes, it's an excellent general antibiotic. These are two hundred and fifty milligram pills, so give her a larger dose to begin with . . . say, three or even four a day. That should do the trick if the fever's caused by a bacterial infection, but of course they won't make any difference if it's viral."

"How do you know all that?" Chester asked in astonishment.

Shaking his head, Will gave a dry laugh. "If you're going to kill a few hundred million Topsoilers, I suppose you might want to know a bit about the medicines they use, don't you think, Chester?"

"Yeah, silly question," his friend conceded.

17

ELLIOTT RESPONDED immediately to the anti-biotics, and it was quite something when she opened her eyes three days later and was able to hold a conversation with the boys. They'd put her in what had to be the captain's cabin, judging by the slightly wider bunk, the oak desk and chair, and the framed photographs of submarines and battleships that adorned the walls.

Although she was still very groggy, the boys propped her up with rolled blankets, and it was a minor miracle to watch her as she drank some water unaided. Their spirits buoyed by her recovery, Will and Chester began to tell her everything that had happened since the moment they'd fallen down the Pore, but it was rather a lot for her to absorb in her weakened state. Her attention seemed to wander as she just gazed around the cabin, so they decided she'd had enough excitement for the time being and should be left to rest.

A day later she was awake and Chester was sitting with her when Rebecca flitted past the doorway on her way down the gangway.

"Who was that?" Elliott demanded.

"The Rebecca twin," Chester said. "Don't you remember we told you she turned up at —?"

"She's a Styx!" Elliott shrieked. "No! No, not here! Don't let her in here with us!"

Will heard the shouting from the bridge and came running in. By the time he arrived, Elliott was hyperventilating and completely beside herself. Chester was holding her, trying to calm her down.

"What happened?" Will asked. "Why's she like this?"

"She saw Rebecca and just went loopy. She doesn't seem to remember anything we told her yesterday," Chester said, as Elliott simply sagged in his arms, falling back into deep slumber.

Rebecca appeared at the door.

"Haven't you done enough already?" Chester snapped at her.

"This is to be expected," Rebecca declared. "Because her temperature was high for so long, it's like her brain has been in a slow cooker. . . . It's only natural that she's acting a bit weird."

"So there's nothing to be worried about?" Will shot back at her.

"No, I wouldn't say so, although we don't know yet whether there's any lasting damage from the fever. But I checked her pupils and the dilation response is normal, and her glands are down."

"You did?" Will asked.

Rebecca nodded. "And as far as I could tell there's no residual inflammation of any of her major organs. We need to keep her on a steady dose of antibiotics and just let her settle down over the next week."

"You sound just like a flipping doctor," Chester said, but Will could tell he was grateful that Rebecca seemed to know what she was talking about.

"We can't stay another week," Martha said, stepping out from behind Rebecca. "There's the minor matter of food and water. I can just about keep our water supply topped up from the spring outside, but we need more food."

This came as no real surprise. Except for Elliott, the rest of them were already on reduced rations. Martha was doing her best to make their stocks last, and they hadn't found anything on the submarine, other than some sucking candies stuffed into the toes of a pair of sneakers in one of the lockers.

And because the Brights presented such a danger, Martha wouldn't let any of them put as much as a foot outside the submarine, not for any reason. Every so often she asked Will or Chester to man the hatch while she went off to the nearby spring to fill the canteens with fresh water, protecting herself from the Brights with smoldering sprigs of Aniseed Fire. And for an hour every day she'd prop the hatch open to allow some fresh air to circulate into the submarine, but she was always there guarding it with her crossbow. At all other times she insisted it be kept shut, with the wheel turned so that it was locked down tight.

No one had said anything, looking at each other for a decision until Martha spoke again. "There's always the cat."

"We can't let him go outside to hunt for us — won't the Brights get him?" Will asked immediately.

Chester inclined his head a little as he spoke. "Will, I don't think that's what she means."

"The only way we can get through another week is if we eat the cat," Martha confirmed.

"Eat Bartleby?" Will choked, although he still wasn't sure if she really meant it. "Absolutely not! No chance!"

"Then we have no alternative but to go back to the Wolf Caves . . . or the shack," Martha said.

Will rubbed his chin as he considered the situation. "Well . . . we can carry Elliott on the stretcher like we did on the way here. That wouldn't be a problem. Once we're in the Wolf Caves, we can decide what to do next. Happy with that, Chester?"

"Sure," Chester agreed. "Just let's not hang around here so long that we're eating soggy cardboard to stay alive. If we're going to go, let's do it soon."

They resolved to set out for the caves in twenty-four hours.

Leaving Chester to watch Elliott, Will went off to check the kit in the rucksacks in readiness for the journey. Once he'd finished, he wandered aimlessly around the submarine, eventually heading to the rearmost and by far the largest compartment in the vessel. It was occupied by the submarine's twin propulsion units, huge chunks of engine in polished steel casings. It wasn't that easy to get around in this compartment because most of the metal grilles composing the gangways had been removed. Obviously it was where Martha's son had obtained the metal sheeting he'd taken back to the shack.

Immediately preceding the engines were two sealed areas which, from the elaborate locking systems, resembled some kind of strong rooms. Will discovered that their doors required special keys to open them. However, he had no intention of attempting this because of the radioactivity warning signs plastered all around them.

As he made his way back to the other end of the submarine, he passed Martha, who was sound asleep, a hand on the crossbow beside her on the mattress.

Will had just passed Elliott's cabin when he heard a noise and turned to see Rebecca following quietly behind him.

"How's it going?" he asked, a little surprised that she was there, and wondering what she wanted.

"Fine," she answered sweetly.

With Rebecca still in tow, Will reached the door that led to the bow section of the submarine. He looked through the thick glass porthole at the mass of tangled metal inside. It must have borne the brunt of the impact when the submarine first crashed down the void.

"Bet there are torpedoes in there," Rebecca said casually, standing on tiptoe to see over his shoulder. "Probably with nuclear warheads."

"Really," Will replied, wiping the glass with his sleeve to get a better view. "Just the sort of thing your people would love to get their mitts on," he added as an afterthought.

She laughed, but her eyes were cold, as if Will had offended her. "No, not our style," she said crisply as she lounged against the sloping sidewall. "We want to mend the planet, not turn it into a wasteland where only rats and cockroaches can live. But you Topsoilers seem to be bent on doing just that. You don't care that you're polluting and ruining it, bit by bit, day by day. Not as long as you have your three square meals, your TV, and your nice warm beds." She was speaking with the spiteful assurance that he knew from the Rebecca of old, with the hardness that he so detested, and it riled him.

"Don't blame me for what's going on," he objected. "If it was up to me, I'd do something to stop all the pollution and global warming."

"Oh yeah? How? You're just as much to blame as any one of those other seven billion people crawling over the crust like greedy dung beetles," she said, with a glance upward. "Don't you see what you've done? You've tried to make the world a 'better' place for yourselves. . . . You've tried to control everything that shouldn't be controlled. And now that it's all gone horribly wrong, you're forced to try to control it even more. But you can't, and you won't. If you try to bend nature to suit yourself, nature's going to bend you back. You and all the rest of the Topsoilers are fast approaching the end of the road . . . just as the *Book of Catastrophes* foretold."

Will didn't much care for the way she was lecturing him, and was only just managing to keep his temper. He couldn't believe the transformation that had come over the girl, as if she was letting her true colors show through. Then, just as abruptly, her whole demeanor changed, and she smiled. Uncrossing her arms, she waved something in front of him.

"I thought you might be interested in these. I found them tucked down the side of a bunk," she said pleasantly. She offered him a handful of photographs, all the size of holiday snapshots.

A little disarmed by the change in Rebecca, he took the photographs and began to look through them. There were ten in all, black-and-white and spotted with patches of mold or perhaps oil. The images were a little fuzzy and reminded him of those vintage instant photographs — *Polaroids*, he thought they were called — that his father had shown him of when, long before Will was born, Dr. Burrows had trekked along a section of Hadrian's Wall.

But these were of groups of clean-cut men in dark sweaters, some wearing military-style caps. The photographs had what looked like Russian words written on them, scratched into the glossy surfaces of the prints with a blue ballpoint pen.

"The crew?" Will said, glancing at Rebecca.

She nodded.

In the first photographs, the men were on the upper deck of the submarine, the open sea behind them. They were all smiling, and their eyes were as bright as the sky above. Then, as Will continued through the pack, he came to some in which the contrast was much higher — they had clearly been taken with a flash, either in the submarine itself or underground. But still the men looked to be in good shape.

However, the last photographs told a very different story. In these there were far fewer men, and they looked a world apart from the young sailors in the earlier pictures: their bearded faces now gaunt and grim, and their eyes haunted.

"Poor sods. You can tell they had a rough time of it," Will commented.

Rebecca didn't reply immediately. Pushing herself away from the wall as if she was about to leave, she lowered her voice. "Will... there's something...," she began, then seemed to hesitate.

"What?" he asked, tearing his gaze away from the photographs.

"Have you ever stopped to ask yourself what became of all those guys . . . what *really* happened to the crew of this sub?"

Will shrugged. "Either they went off somewhere, or the Brights got them?"

Rebecca stared at him, unblinking. "Martha's son salvaged a ton of stuff from here before he came down with the fever."

"So?"

"So did he really lug all that metal back to the shack by himself? Or did some of the men go with him? Did they help him get it there? And, if that's the case, what happened to them?"

Will looked askance at her. "Are you saying that he . . . or Martha . . . did something to the survivors?"

She shrugged.

"Are you saying they killed them?" Will asked. He happened to look at the next photograph, and it took his attention away from what Rebecca had been saying. The men appeared to be standing next to a tall boulder with a symbol on it. Will stuck his head closer to the print, trying to make out what the symbol was. He saw three single lines that splayed out, like the top of a trident. He immediately touched his chest, feeling the pendant under his shirt that Uncle Tam had given him, and which had exactly the same symbol on it.

"What's going on in this one?" he asked, holding up the print. "I know this sign."

Rebecca was dismissive in her answer, perhaps a little irritated that Will had been distracted from what she'd been saying. "Oh, sure, you find it carved on stones in the Deeps."

"But none of the people from this submarine are likely to have been to the Deeps," Will reasoned, "so they must have come across it down here somewhere."

"As I was saying, Will, just keep your eyes open," Rebecca said.

"Martha isn't like th —" Will began, about to defend the woman.

Rebecca gave a harsh guffaw. "Martha and her brat were renegades. They're capable of just about anything. And you didn't investigate the graves behind the shack, did you? . . . You didn't see how recent some of them were?"

"No . . . did you?"

Ignoring his question, Rebecca continued, "You *know* she can tell a porky when it suits her. You caught her out big time when she fibbed about the medicines. She won't forget you did that in a hurry. The only one of us she gives a jot about is Chester."

"Yeah, but —" he started to say.

"Keep the photos — they're yours," Rebecca said. She turned on her heel and strolled away from him, swinging her hips as she went. There was no longer any sign of her limp. She lingered for a moment on the threshold to the next compartment.

"Watch your back, Will," Rebecca said ominously, then snickered. "Because if we run low on meat, she might just *eat* it. And that's all I'm saying." Then she was gone, leaving Will with the photographs in his hand, and serious doubts in his mind.

Will found it hard to sleep after the conversation with Rebecca. Every time he shut his eyes, he saw the haggard, desperate faces of the submarine crew. But worse even than that, his imagination was working overtime as he pictured Martha digging new graves behind the shack and rolling bodies into them. He tried to dismiss the image. His faith in Martha had been largely restored after she'd helped them find the submarine, but now that was being undermined.

Rebecca was right — Will had gone up against the woman when he'd caught her in a lie. *Would she eventually dump him, keeping Chester as her surrogate son?* Will could easily see that happening. And Martha had nursed Elliott, but he was sure that this was only because the girl was important to Chester — he didn't get the feeling Martha really gave two hoots about her. *Would she somehow engineer Elliott's disappearance, or death, too?* And as for Rebecca, she was a foregone conclusion — Martha wouldn't think twice about using her for crossbow practice.

If Martha was really that ruthless, then Will had to be prepared for the eventuality that she might make a move against him, or any of the others. He had to try to second-guess her, and his mind churned with all the possible outcomes.

Will tossed and turned on the narrow mattress in the lower rankings' quarters, where the bunks were three high against the wall. He was in the top bunk, while Bartleby had curled up in the bottom one and was snorting like an angry warthog, his limbs twitching as he had one of his feline dreams. Yet again, Will wished he could trade places with the animal and have a simple, uncomplicated life.

18

AS **THEY ALL CLUNG** to the ladder in the conning tower, Martha lit a large bundle of Aniseed Fire. She lifted up the outer hatch, lobbed the smoldering plants outside, and then slammed the hatch shut again. "We should give it a couple of minutes," she said.

As they waited for the go-ahead from Martha, it seemed to Will that Chester was studying her, as if he was weighing what he thought of her. Perhaps this was all in Will's mind, because he'd told him what Rebecca had said about the woman. Will had expected Chester to dismiss it out of hand — not least because he didn't trust Rebecca as far as he could throw her — but the instant rebuttal from his friend never came. Instead, Chester just looked confused and murmured, "I don't know," several times.

As the seconds ticked by in the conning tower, Chester broke the silence with a cough, and shifted on the ladder. It was obvious that he was itching to get going but, equally, was extremely nervous about what was waiting for them on the outside. "These Bright things — are they really that danger-ous?" he asked Martha.

"Yes," Martha confirmed. "That dangerous."

"You didn't see it, Chester," Will put in. "It was really nasty-looking."

"But the Aniseed Fire will protect us, won't it?" Chester asked.

"It's better than nothing," Martha replied.

"It works with the spider-monkeys, though," Will said.

"The Brights are a different story. Once they've picked up your scent, they're like stalkers — they don't give up." Her eyes became unfocused, as if she was remembering something. "Every so often a Bright would pop up in the Deeps, but they're heavier there, so they're slower. One had been shadowing us for mile after mile as we moved across the Great Plain, and we knew we had to get it before it got us. I eventually brought it down with a lucky shot. I tell you, even when it was grounded, its body all broken up, it refused to die. It was crawling toward us and snapping at us until the last drop of blood had pumped out of it." She shook her head. "I don't know any other animal that can match its hunger."

"Horrible," Chester said, shivering.

Martha touched the point of the bolt slotted in her crossbow. "Some say they're as old as the hills . . . that they ruled the skies long before there were any Topsoilers."

Elliott moaned, tossing her head, the only part of her body she could move now that she was trussed up again in a blanket and bound to the stretcher.

"That should be long enough," Martha decided, placing her hand on the underside of the hatch. "Everyone ready?"

The boys answered, although Rebecca remained silent.

"Once we're away from the ship, we move as a group. And remember — keep the noise down."

She pushed open the hatch and they climbed out onto the observation platform, then abseiled down the side of the conning tower using the chain.

"Easy, boy," Will whispered as he released Bartleby. But rather than scampering off as he usually did, the cat didn't seem to want to move. His large ears were twitching like animated satellite dishes, as if they were homing in on something. Martha had been checking the darkness above the submarine for any sign of the Brights, but now she wheeled around to face the cavern. Raising a hand to indicate they should all stay put, she continued to scrutinize it, tilting her head as if she was straining to hear something. Will couldn't understand what she was doing. *Weren't the Brights the biggest threat right now? Why wasn't she leading them away from the submarine as she'd said she would?*

Will and Chester glanced at each other, wondering what was wrong, when they both heard the murmur of distant voices.

A light flickered from the mouth of the tunnel at the far end of the cavern as two figures wandered out from it. Will couldn't see them clearly, but one of the figures was taller than the other, and he heard a voice — it sounded angry.

Martha had remained statue-still. Hardly moving her lips, she spoke to them. "When I tell you to run, break in that direction. There's a passage there," she said, glancing briefly to their left. "And don't wait for me." She brought up her crossbow.

As the two figures came closer, making absolutely no attempt to conceal themselves, Will was able to hear what the voice was saying.

"What's with all this stop-start business, anyway?" it demanded. "We bat along for mile after mile, then—for no apparent reason—you say we've got to wait. We've wasted days just twiddling our thumbs. We could have used all that time for something constructive."

"Dad?" Will gasped, loudly enough for the others to hear. "Is that my dad?"

"Can't be," Chester said, shaking his head in disbelief.

Will instinctively knew it *was* Dr. Burrows, and his natural impulse was to run toward him, but for reasons he couldn't explain to himself, he found he was checking that his rifle was loaded. Perhaps it was because he'd spotted Rebecca dumping her rucksacks and edging stealthily forward, as if she was about to make a break for the center of the cavern. Or perhaps it was because he also instinctively knew who the smaller figure accompanying his father had to be. An alarm bell was ringing in his head, and it was growing louder by the second.

The taller of the two figures came to a standstill. Will saw the glint of his glasses.

"Dad?" he yelled. "Is that really you?"

The figure started with surprise.

"WILL!" it cried, beginning to walk quickly toward him. "*WILL!*"

"Oh no," Martha breathed, switching her head from one side to the other.

At either end of the submarine stood a man. With their tall, thin bodies they were unmistakable. They were Limiters. Emerging from the shadows, they were standing to attention like Topsoil soldiers, their spears held ready.

"We're in big trouble," Will said.

Bringing his rifle up, Chester made a whining sound.

"We're in deep pooh," he muttered.

Dr. Burrows was about a hundred feet away from the submarine when the smaller figure at his side shouted. "That's far enough!" it ordered him. Will had seen by now that it was indeed the second Rebecca twin who was accompanying his father. She seized Dr. Burrows by the arm, bringing him to an abrupt halt, then aimed a kick that struck him just behind the knee. His leg buckled and he dropped into a kneeling position. Before he had time to react, she had looped her arm around the top of his head and pressed a scythe to his neck.

"What are you doing? Stop this nonsense, Rebecca!" he cried. "Stop it this moment!"

Will still hadn't moved a step, but when he saw that the Rebecca twin behind him had begun to creep forward again, he acted immediately.

"Not so fast," he said. She shrieked as he caught her by the hair and swung her in front of him, forcing the rifle muzzle up under her chin.

"Will! No! Please let me go," she begged. "It's her you want . . . not me!"

"Yeah — like I still believe you! You told me you were alone down here," Will growled. "Chester was right — it was all a big act."

Her whole demeanor changed in an instant. "You have to admit I was rather good, wasn't I? Had you eating out of the palm of my hand," she said smugly. "Drama always was our favorite subject at school."

The fact that the twin had stopped the pretense didn't make Will feel any better about the already horrendous situation. It was clear that the twins thought they had the upper hand once again and could do as they pleased.

"Another Rebecca?" Dr. Burrows gabbled, having registered the second Styx girl beside Will. "How —?"

"Poor old Dr. Buckwheat," the twin at his back cooed. "You always were a bit slow on the uptake."

"But how?" He tried to get up but she dug the scythe sharply into his neck.

"Stay put," she snapped. "You stupid old goat, we've played you right from the start, right from that day we sent Oscar Embers into the museum with the luminescent orb. We wanted to get you on the hook, knowing how it would play out. Knowing that sooner or later it would flush Sarah Jerome into the open."

"Sarah Jerome?" he said, not knowing who the twin was talking about.

"We didn't give a toss about the rest of you. You're all expendable," the twin said, then turned her attention to Will. "But isn't this nice?" she sneered, her voice dripping with insincerity. "The gang's all here. And Daddy's with his little boy — all together again."

The twins began to speak in the Styx tongue.

"Shut up!" Will yelled, pressing the rifle muzzle hard into his twin's throat. "Or I'll shoot you."

"What, are you going to put a bullet in my head? I don't think so, somehow," she said in a strangled voice. In complete defiance, she began to speak in Styx again.

"I mean it," Will said. "I'll do it!"

"No you won't," the other twin behind Dr. Burrows shouted. "You're a big wuss. You haven't got the guts."

"Will, *what* are you doing?" Dr. Burrows exclaimed. "You can't —"

"Stay out of it, Dad," Will cut him short. "You've got no idea what's going on." Will then addressed the twin behind his father. "What do I call *you*? You can't both be *Rebecca*."

"Whatever," she replied curtly.

"OK, um . . . *Rebecca Two*, looks like we've got a standoff here. What do you want to do?"

"For starters, you can give us those phials back. And we'll also take the old woman," Rebecca Two announced.

"Why her?" Will said, asking himself how she could know that he had the Dominion phials.

"Because she's the one with the knowledge of these parts."

Will caught Martha's eye. She had one hand on a bundle of Aniseed Fire stuck in her belt. She looked at Will questioningly. Will gave a shake of his head and she took her hand away from the dried plants. Then she flicked her eyes upward, indicating the area above them. Will nodded. He knew precisely what she was trying to tell him. All this noise was going to bring the Brights down.

And right now, maybe that wasn't such a bad thing.

"Come on, we'll do swapsies with you — we'll trade your father for Martha and the phials," Rebecca Two continued. "The rest of you can go. She's the only one we want."

"You're forgetting I've got your sister here, too," Will countered. "Doesn't sound like a fair deal to me."

Out of the corner of his eye, Will saw Martha very slowly draw her knife. She ran the blade along her forearm, cutting deep into it. Then she lowered her arm, dripping blood over the ground.

"My sister's not part of the equation. Do what you want with her," Rebecca Two continued, tossing her head impatiently. "Why don't you listen to what I'm saying? We'll swap your father for Martha and the phials. Then the rest of you can go free."

"Hah! You must think I'm stupid," Will spat.

"Not stupid — just weak," the girl came back. She gave the Limiters a signal with her eyes, and they immediately began to advance. "The cards are stacked against you, Will, so I suggest we agree that we're going to agree on something." She laughed, but it was unpleasant and throaty.

Rebecca One suddenly babbled again in Styx.

"Don't do that! I warned you!" Will shouted, yanking her hair. He heard growling by his side. He gasped in surprise. Bartleby was several feet away from him and crouching low as if he was about to attack. "Bartleby!" he yelled. "What are you doing?"

"What I told him," Rebecca One said.

The cat's nostrils were flared and his claws drawn.

"He's just trying to protect me," Will said, although he didn't sound too confident.

"Want to bet on that?" Rebecca One cawed. "Remember I told you I looked after him back in the Colony? Well, I gave him some extra*special* training. And he's not the only one," she snickered. Then she spoke in Styx again, and the cat edged even closer to Will.

"You . . . you traitor!" Will yelled at the cat, almost lost for words. It was as if Bartleby didn't recognize him at all. Like a coiled spring about to snap open, the cat crouched even lower and hissed at him. Bartleby's eyes were crazed and wide, as if filled with bloodlust.

"Don't have many friends, do you?" Rebecca One said. "A single word from me and nice kitty will be at your throat."

"If he does, so help me, you're dead meat," Will said grimly, maneuvering her body so it shielded him from the cat.

There was a sudden cry to Will's left, and he saw the Limiter burst into action.

"An angel!" Dr. Burrows exclaimed.

The large white creature fell thrashing to the ground before the Limiter. With both hands on his spear, the soldier repeatedly drove the point into the Bright until its movements ceased.

Will caught Martha's eye again. Her plan was working — the smell of her fresh blood was drawing the Brights like moths to a flame. There was another squeal and she spun around, firing a bolt. It swished into the darkness, but the Bright was gone. It wasn't a perfect plan by any means — the Brights were just as much a menace to her and the boys as they were to the Styx.

There were more eerie squeals from the darkness of the void, and dim lights streaked around like shooting stars.

"It starts," Martha said under her breath.

"Interesting pets you've got down here. I'd like one," Rebecca Two said, but she didn't sound quite so sure of herself now. "Perhaps we should conclude our exchange quickly, Will, and get out of the open?"

There was a flurry of activity from the other Limiter, but this time the Bright was the victor. They all watched as the soldier was whisked off his feet by the creature, which had its barbed legs wrapped around the man's head. Creature and man simply vanished in a blur. The Limiter hadn't even had time to cry out. The only evidence that he'd been there was his spear, which toppled to the ground.

There were a few seconds of astonished silence; then only Chester's voice was heard.

"That evens out the teams a little," he said.

"Very funny, fat boy," Rebecca Two snarled through her clenched teeth. "When I get Topsoil again, I'll be sure to pay your mum and dad a visit . . . in person."

"Uh . . . I . . . no . . . ," Chester gulped, the blood draining from his face.

"We don't have time for this," Martha warned as she glanced upward, her face anxious. "Do it, Will. Do the exchange," she urged him.

"Are you sure?" Will asked her.

"Yes," she confirmed. "The Styx need me alive. I'll be fine."

Will knew that none of them had much chance if they remained where they were, not with the Brights on the rampage.

"All right, Rebecca Two," he yelled. "Let my dad come over to me here, and Martha can come to you."

"No way. Martha stays exactly where she is. I'll come to her," Rebecca Two barked. "You can collect Dr. Buckwheat from here. Got that?"

"How do I know you won't just open fire on us?" Will asked.

"Because we don't have two rifles and a crossbow like you do, meathead," Rebecca Two jeered.

Checking that the remaining Limiter was sufficiently far away and not about to ambush them, Will nodded.

"Right," Rebecca Two announced. "Musical chairs. Let's all begin walking — nice and slow."

Reluctantly, Will relinquished his grip on Rebecca One, who shook her head to straighten out her hair, then glowered at Will.

He glowered back at her. "I should never have bothered to save your life," he fumed.

Knowing that he'd have to take Elliott with him, Chester was just turning to pick up the stretcher when something spun straight between his legs. A black canister. It rolled over the ground toward Dr. Burrows and Rebecca Two, but came to a stop in the middle of the cavern. Will recognized it immediately. It was one of the explosives Drake and Elliott used in the Deeps. But this was a seriously big one, the size of a can of paint.

"It's a twenty-pound charge — with a twenty-second fuse. And while I was at it, I primed all the others," Elliott said quite calmly, throwing her rucksack on the ground beside her. She was sitting up on the stretcher, and looking very much herself again. During the standoff, she'd freed herself from her bindings, and everybody had been too preoccupied to notice as she'd retrieved her rucksack full of munitions from the end of her stretcher.

Will and Chester stared at her, dumbstruck.

"Sixteen seconds . . . BANG!" she said to them, throwing her arms out demonstratively. .

"No!" Will yelled, thinking that the fever must have loosened a couple of her screws. "Why've you done that?"

"Because they're planning to kill all of us, anyway. I heard them say so," Elliott replied.

Will exchanged glances with Chester and was just about to speak when the other boy beat him to it.

"But . . . how can you know what they're saying?"

"Because I'm half Styx. My father was a Limiter. I can speak their language," Elliott said. To prove the point she uttered a couple of nasal and completely unintelligible words.

"Thirteen . . . almost twelve seconds," Rebecca One translated.

Elliott had the Rebecca twins' undivided attention now.

"Eleven seconds," Elliott announced through a yawn.

"Have you really set the explosives?" Will asked her, still unable to believe what was happening.

Elliott nodded. "Ten seconds," she said. And suddenly everyone was galvanized.

Chester snatched up Elliott, and Martha yanked both of them, not toward the cavern but to the left of the submarine and in the direction of the alternative passage she'd indicated.

Although Will had his rucksack on his back, he hesitated for a split second, debating whether to retrieve the other two that Rebecca One had discarded behind him. The memory of how he'd wandered the lava tubes in the Deeps without food or proper equipment was still painfully fresh in his mind, and there was no way he wanted a repeat of that. But there just wasn't enough time, so instead he put his head down and thundered toward his father with all his might. He saw Bartleby pounce at him.

"Geddoff!" Will bellowed, lashing out at him with the stock of his rifle. Possibly because he was confused and couldn't understand why everyone was haring off in different directions, Bartleby's attack lacked its usual intensity. The rifle struck him on the shoulder, and he yelped and curled into a ball as he was sent spinning away.

Will kept on running. He was heading straight for Rebecca Two as she tore in the opposite direction toward the submarine. Rebecca One was already at the base of the conning tower with the Limiter, who was fighting off an attack from another Bright.

By now, Dr. Burrows was up on his feet and yelling, "Will, stop that Rebecca! Get my tablets from her!"

The urgency of his father's shouts got through to Will, who aimed himself directly at Rebecca Two, knocking her to the ground.

"Left-hand jacket pocket! Get my stone tablets!" Dr. Burrows yelled as Will stood over the dazed Styx girl. He immediately dug into her pocket and found a small bundle wrapped in a grimy handkerchief. As she was beginning to come to her senses and hit out at him, he didn't try to search her further. There just wasn't time.

"GET OUT OF HERE!" Will yelled at his father, who showed no intention of moving to safety as he shouted back:

"Did you get them? Did you get them?"

Pounding toward Dr. Burrows, Will built up so much speed he was virtually airborne by the time he reached him. His momentum was enough to carry both of them not to the main tunnel, but toward a small passage at its side. Everything was happening so quickly that Dr. Burrows didn't have any say in the matter as his son swept him away and out of the cavern.

Will kept going. The countdown in his mind reached zero, then passed beyond it, but still nothing happened. He was beginning to ask himself if Elliott had actually set the fuses or whether it had all been a bluff when there was the most almighty explosion.

The ground bucked under his feet as if he was in the midst of an earthquake.

He and Dr. Burrows were flung on their fronts, pelted by a hailstorm of fungus pieces.

Although the tremors were relatively short-lived and the ground settled down again, the sound of the explosion seemed to go on forever. Echoes reverberated from the walls of the void beyond the submarine. As the last report finally faded, Will moaned and began to stir. Pushing aside slabs of fungus, he rolled over and sat up. His ears were ringing, and he swallowed a couple of times until they felt more normal.

"Dad," he called, his voice sounding so small and remote. He staggered to his feet, blinking to clear his eyes of the stinging, stinking liquid. He shrugged off his rucksack, felt around for his lantern until he found it, then began to search for his father.

There was no sign of him, and Will became increasingly worried until he spotted a boot sticking out from under a heap of fungus. Dr. Burrows was almost completely buried, but Will quickly hoisted him out. He knew his father wasn't too badly hurt when he began to spit brown glop from his mouth, issuing a torrent of curses simultaneously. His glasses were missing, but he didn't seem to be the slightest bit concerned about this.

"Where are my tablets? Give me my tablets!" he demanded, blinking myopically at his son.

"You mean these?" Will asked, wondering what was so vitally important about the bundle as he took it from his pocket and passed it to his father.

Dr. Burrows fumbled it open and, one by one, felt the flat pieces of stone. "Thank goodness they're all right. None of them are broken or lost. Well done, Will. Really well done!"

"Good, no problem, Dad," Will said, still at a loss to know why his father was showing more concern for some little pieces of stone than he was for anything else. More even than for Will.

"Now where are my glasses?" Dr. Burrows said, and immediately began to crawl on all fours to locate them.

"But, Dad, I can't believe this!" Will gushed, as the realization sank home that against all odds they had been reunited. "We're back together again! It's so brilliant to see you when —"

"Yes, but I can't *see* anything!" Dr. Burrows snapped at him in a bad-tempered way, still looking for his glasses.

Will hovered by his father for a moment, torn between staying with him or finding out if Chester and the others had escaped the explosion. "Dad, I'll be back in a minute. I'll help you find them then," he told his father, not waiting for a response as he whisked around and began down the tunnel.

Although it wasn't very far to the entrance, the pieces of fungus made the going tricky. Due to the slick of oily fluid in the bottom of the tunnel, the larger slabs of fungus slid from under him as he climbed on top of them. And at one point the tunnel was completely obstructed and he was forced to clear away the debris with his bare hands before he could proceed. As he hefted sizeable chunks of fungus aside, he realized that it had probably saved their lives — not only had it absorbed the blast, but it had also cushioned their landings.

When he finally reached the mouth of the tunnel, he was met by the strangest calm. He was just about to step out when he happened to glance down. He gasped, stopping himself in the nick of time. There was nothing before him but a huge gaping hole. The entire floor of the cavern had completely disappeared. Although he couldn't see the bottom, the cavern walls were illuminated by the small fires, like candles in the niches of a church grotto.

Dr. Burrows appeared beside his son, having retrieved his glasses. For a while they simply stared into the cavern, watching as rocks and pieces of fungus detached from the roof and dropped into the blackness. Then they heard a low grinding sound.

"The submarine," Will whispered, seeing it judder, then settle down again.

"Submarine?" his father asked, as if he hadn't appreciated what was there before.

It was quite something to behold; fires burned all over the vessel and the fungus coating had been blasted away, so its streamlined hull was clearly visible. But something more was happening to it.

A tremendous cracking sound made both Will and his father flinch. More grinding sounds followed. The submarine shook and dropped a small distance, then, as they watched, it seemed to be toppling sideways, but in slow motion.

"It's going! It's falling!" Will exclaimed. The explosion had evidently destroyed either the fungus or the bedrock on which the hull had been lodged — or both — and now there was nothing to prevent the vessel from continuing on its way down.

With a last tremendous groan, it tipped over, completely vanishing from view and leaving just the blackness of the void in its place. Will and his father heard distant crashing sounds as the sub collided with the sides as it descended.

"I wonder if the Rebecca twins were on it," Will said quietly. "They so had it coming."

Dr. Burrows fixed his eyes on his son. "You're going to have *some* explaining to do, my boy," he declared solemnly.

"Huh?"

"I just hope you know what you've done," Dr. Burrows said, his voice grave as he waved his hand in the direction of the crater. He shook his head, his roughly cut hair, soused in fungus juice, sticking up in spikes as if he was some middle-aged punk rocker. He looked quite ridiculous.

"You what?" Will spluttered. "I don't know quite how we managed it, but we just got out of there *alive* . . . and you're acting like some stupid schoolteacher. You have got to be joking!"

"Of course I'm not joking," Dr. Burrows retorted sharply. "You're going to be in big trouble for your part in this."

That did it for Will — he began to snort, then burst into a full-bodied laugh. "Big trouble," he repeated, his voice squeaking with incredulity. Catching his breath, he glanced at his father to make absolutely certain he was being serious.

"That's right," Dr. Burrows confirmed. To his continuing surprise, his son dissolved into howls of even more uproarious laughter.

"I'm in big trouble!" Unable to stop himself from laughing and going weak at the knees, Will looked for a place to sit down before he fell over. But the tears in his eyes were making it hard for him to see. He chose a particularly greasy piece of fungus and slid right off it. But this still didn't stop him. Rolling on the ground, he continued to laugh so much he had to hold his sides.

19

AFTER A SHORT WHILE, Will's laughter petered out and he fell into a sullen silence. Asking himself what he had found so funny, he ignored his father as he made several attempts to climb down from the mouth of the tunnel. The blast-damaged fungus simply peeled away in his hands as he tried to grip it. And even with the fungus removed, the rock beneath was slippery and treacherous due to the grease slopped over it.

"This is hopeless," he mumbled, staring over at the space where the submarine had been. He sucked in his breath as he caught a glimpse of a Bright streaking across the void, and thought how much it resembled a shooting star. "Make a wish," he said forlornly. It seemed everything was stacked against him.

Then he leaned as far as he could into the new crater, his lantern in his outstretched hand. If he had spotted an outcrop or ledge to jump to, he might have taken advantage of the low gravity and chanced it. But the crater appeared to be so deep, it would have been tantamount to leaping into the void itself.

What now? he asked himself. He needed a way to reach Martha and the others. He was counting on them to have made it to the side passage she'd indicated. That's unless their way had been blocked by a Bright.

"Plan B . . . I need a Plan B," he thought aloud, as he leaned out and peered along the cavern wall to his left. If he could somehow get across to the main tunnel through which they'd first entered the cavern, then he might be able to find his way back to the Wolf Caves. But this plan appeared to be equally impossible — aside from the fact that there was no way to climb the wall to reach it, he couldn't even see where the entrance had been. The explosion had concealed it altogether. And in the back of his mind Will was also concerned that he might have another of his strange episodes. Perched on a ledge next to a sheer drop wasn't exactly the best place for him to be right now.

He shrugged. "Plan C, I suppose," he mumbled under his breath. At the very best he had to try to communicate with Martha and Chester, even at the risk of attracting the Brights. He began to call out to them, pausing now and then to listen.

Dr. Burrows didn't offer any sort of help as he lingered at the mouth of the cave and watched his son. Indeed, Dr. Burrows wasn't talking to him at all. Since Will was getting no response from his friends and his voice was becoming hoarse, he gave it up as a lost cause. Leaving his father, he turned and went back down the passage, clambering over the fungus until he came to where he'd left his rucksack. Hoisting it up, he went even deeper into the passage, in search of a clear area of ground. There, he'd begun to unpack his rucksack when he suddenly stopped.

"The virus!" he burst out. With everything else going on, he'd completely forgotten that he'd had the phials on him through all the shenanigans with the Rebecca twins and the subsequent explosion. "Oh God, please don't let them be broken," he said quietly, as he slid the burlap package from the leather pouch. He sighed an enormous sigh of relief when he saw the phials were intact. Putting them away again, he continued to unpack his rucksack, taking an inventory of what he had left. There was a small amount of food, but not enough to last two people for more than a few days. In a side pouch he came across the bar of Caramac he'd taken from Cal's body. Although Will had hidden it from Chester, he'd been planning to share it with him when there was something to celebrate.

"Not today," he said disconsolately, tossing the bar onto the pile of food.

As for water, he had a full canteen on his belt. At these temperatures it wouldn't last terribly long, but he wasn't too concerned, because Martha always seemed to find fresh sources wherever they'd gone. As he moved his hand away from his canteen, it encountered the cutlass still tucked in his belt. He drew it out and then slumped down on the ground, slapping the flat of the blade against his palm as he contemplated the situation.

It didn't look very promising.

It may have been because of this, or because the adrenaline was wearing off, but he found himself overwhelmed by intense feelings of hopelessness and futility. Even if it was possible to get to the main tunnel again, he didn't feel very confident that he'd be able to find his way back to the Wolf Caves. He knew that was where Martha would expect him to go. Then he thought about the shack. He shook his head. No, he'd never be able to remember the route, and in any case, the food would run out long before they reached it.

His thoughts turned to Chester. He should have listened to his friend and not allowed himself to be won over by Rebecca One. He kicked himself for having been hoodwinked by her. Maybe Rebecca Two had been right when she said he was weak — maybe the twins would always triumph over him.

Will's roll call of self-recriminations didn't end there; he shouldn't have doubted Martha as he had, either. Yes, she had withheld information from them that proved vital in saving Elliott, but it was through a misguided desire to protect both him and Chester; and in the end she had led them safely to the submarine.

As for Bartleby . . . even Will's faithful companion had turned on him.

And then there was Elliott. She was half Styx! He should have seen that one coming — the girl had all the skills and stealth of a Limiter. The more he thought about it, the more obvious it had been. She'd never actually said why she'd left the Colony, and though she'd talked about her mother, her father had never been mentioned. And she bore such a striking physical resemblance to the Styx: sinew-thin, yet so strong. *Of course she had Styx blood in her.*

Somehow these deceits and revelations didn't touch him as much as they should have. Maybe nothing could really touch him anymore — not after all he'd endured.

But, as he reflected further, there was one thing that *had* shaken him to the core, making him feel like he should just give up. The day he'd long dreamed of, then had come to believe would never arrive, was finally here.

He'd been reunited with his father . . . and it couldn't have been more of an anticlimax.

His father was just another stupid, bumbling grown-up who had no idea what was going on around him, just like all the others.

"What's the point?" Will murmured, fighting back the tears as he sunk lower into his despondency.

Dr. Burrows cleared his throat to let Will know he was there. "I've got this," he said, tugging a small package wrapped in grease-stained paper from his pocket. "It's meat. I managed to tuck some of it away when nobody was looking — in case of emergency." He made a big show of adding it to the pile of food, but Will didn't say anything. In the ensuing silence, Dr. Burrows hovered there, making clicking noises with his tongue.

"Was that really a submarine?" he finally asked.

Will didn't look up as he answered. "A modern one . . . Russian and nuclear-powered, but there was no sign of the crew."

Dr. Burrows whistled. "How did —?"

"It must have been sucked down one of the voids. . . . Maybe it was drawn in as a plate shifted in the seabed somewhere. Who knows?"

"Voids?"

"There are seven of them . . . called the Seven Sisters. We fell down the one known as the Pore," Will informed him, his voice flat. "Martha took us to another she called Puffing Mary."

"Puffing Mary," Dr. Burrows repeated, nodding. "And those flying creatures?"

"The Brights. They're insects or arachnids or something," Will said, his head still bowed as he jabbed the point of his cutlass into a slab of fungus.

"Do you know," Dr. Burrows began hesitantly, then took a breath. "Do you know, when it just appeared from nowhere like that, I actually thought it was an *angel*," he admitted, giving an embarrassed laugh. "The suggestion just popped into my head . . . and I call myself educated."

"An angel?" Will mumbled.

"Yes. I suppose because of its white coloration and its wings, and most of all because the light above its head looked uncannily like a halo."

Will nodded, drawing the blade of his cutlass from the fungus with a slurping sound. "Martha said they were around on the surface long before people were."

"How very interesting," Dr. Burrows said as he found himself a small boulder to perch on. "Imagine . . . imagine if everything we associate with the archetypal image of an angel derives from a prehistoric insect . . . and if the remote memory of those creatures has been assimilated into our religious iconography and has remained ingrained deep within our culture." He chuckled. "So Gabriel and Peter on either side of the Pearly Gates could actually be inspired by giant carnivorous insects."

"Or arachnids," Will said.

"Or arachnids," Dr. Burrows conceded, then didn't speak for a few seconds.

"Look, Will," he eventually said, "there's a lot I don't know about what's gone on. I mean, it was a bolt out of the blue when I found out your sister was a Styx. And also that you're a Colonist. I really had no idea. And then that Rebecca had an identical twin — well, good grief!" He blew through his lips. "And maybe I'm not thinking straight because you're here . . . because you followed me underground when you should be back at home with your mother."

"Except she's not my mother," Will mumbled, but Dr. Burrows either didn't catch the comment or chose to ignore it as he went on.

"Exactly how you got all the way down here with Chester . . . well, I haven't the foggiest how you managed it. I never in a million years wanted you to be put in danger like this. You've probably had a tough time of it, just like I have, and I was wrong to say what I did back there. It was rash of me — I made a snap judgment, without being in possession of all the facts."

Will raised his head to look at his father, then gave him a single nod in acknowledgment. It was the closest Will was going to get to an apology, unless his father had changed dramatically in the past six months. In any case, Will wasn't going to bear a grudge, not when there were more pressing matters to deal with right now, such as trying to stay alive. "Things don't look great, Dad," he said. "We've got next to no food or water, and I haven't the faintest idea if this tunnel leads anywhere, and, even if it does, which way we should go."

"I'm afraid I'm not going to be of much help there," Dr. Burrows said. "I was brought here through miles of tunnels by Reb — the Styx girl you called Rebecca Two, and the soldier. Couldn't find my way back to the Pore in a month of Sundays."

"We're stuffed then," Will concluded.

"Totally," Dr. Burrows agreed, but he didn't sound in the least downhearted. "So let's get ourselves unstuffed. On your feet, Will, there's no point in hanging around here." He came over to Will and gave his shoulder a squeeze. The Burrows family had never been either very demonstrative or tactile in their emotions, so this small gesture was significant to Will.

"Sure, Dad," he said, suddenly filled with optimism. This is how he'd always imagined it would be with his father — the two of them facing impossible situations and working together to overcome them. He immediately set about repacking his rucksack, then they started out along the tunnel.

They quickly found it wasn't so much a tunnel as an inclined seam, over a hundred feet across at its widest point. As they came to a small offshoot on their left, Will insisted they explore it. He was hoping it might meet up with the passage where Martha and the others had been heading. Will had gone no more than fifty feet into it when he spotted movements. Dark shapes were scuttling across the walls and the roof, and wispy lengths of what could have been the remnants of broken spider-webs waved slowly in the breeze.

"Spider-monkeys," Will warned his father in a whisper. These were smaller and obviously much younger versions, but Will wasn't going to take any chances. He took out his few sprigs of Aniseed Fire and the lighter he had ready in his pocket, but refrained from igniting the dried plants. He only had the handful, and the creatures didn't seem to be following as Will and his father backed out of the passage.

"I reckon that lot were baby spiders — that must be why they didn't go for us," Will said. As they returned to the inclined seam, he told his father how he'd seen these smaller spiders clinging to the Bright's abdomen when it had attacked him and Martha outside the submarine's conning tower.

"So either these smaller spiders are a subspecies of the larger ones, and may be parasites on the Brights . . . or perhaps they are just infants and eventually metamorphose into the flying creatures," Dr. Burrows speculated. "Like caterpillars into butterflies."

"Yes," Will agreed, catching on to what his father was saying. "And these passages could be where the baby spiders grow up?" He looked around warily. "We could be on the nursery slopes?"

"Quite right," Dr. Burrows confirmed. "This could very well be where all the arachnids are born — their breeding ground. Then they spread out through the rest of the tunnel system as they hunt for food."

Twenty minutes of trudging up the incline brought them to another side passage, but again they discovered it was occupied by the smaller spiders.

"How are we ever going to meet up with the others?" Will asked.

"I don't know. I suppose we just carry on up the main haul instead," Dr. Burrows said, trying to sound positive about the situation.

"But one of these might take us through to Martha and Chester," Will responded, wondering how much of a risk the smaller spider-monkeys really were. In the end he decided it wasn't worth blundering into one of the fully-grown ones or, worse still, a Bright, so they just stuck to the seam itself, climbing higher and higher.

They swapped stories as they went. Will began by telling his father how he and Chester found his tunnel in the basement and how, by re-excavating it, they had eventually entered the Colony and been arrested. He spoke about the meeting with his biological father and brother, and the moment he'd learned that he'd been born in the Colony himself.

"Rebecca told me that," Dr. Burrows said.

At times Will found it painful to relate what had happened, occasionally lapsing into silence until he felt he was able to resume his story. He talked about the Styx and how brutal they were.

"I never saw that side of them," Dr. Burrows said categorically. "They didn't treat me badly. They let me go where I wanted. In fact, my worst experiences were at the hands of the Colonists, particularly in the Rookeries, where I got a nasty beating from the thugs living there. If the Styx are sometimes harsh, then it's probably for the good of the Colony, with those sorts of malcontents hanging around."

"Harsh? Oh, get real, Dad!" Will said, raising his voice in exasperation. "The Styx are evil. . . . They're murderers and torturers! Didn't you see what they were doing to the Coprolites and the renegades in the Deeps? They were killing them by the dozen."

"No, I didn't. How do you know it was the Styx and not simply a breakaway band of renegades? By all accounts they're a pretty lawless bunch."

Will just shook his head.

"You have to respect other cultures, and never attempt to judge them by your own values," Dr. Burrows said. "And don't forget you're the outsider — it's *their* world you crashed into, uninvited. If they've treated you badly, then all I can say is you must have done something to offend them."

Dr. Burrows's pronouncements rendered Will momentarily speechless. He made a series of *pfuu* sounds, as if he was spitting feathers. "OFFEND THEM?" he managed to get out in a furious croak when he was finally able to speak again. "OFFEND THEM?" He took a breath to calm himself. "You're being a complete ignoramus, Dad. Haven't you listened to a thing I've been telling you?"

"Take it easy, Will," Dr. Burrows urged. "The way you're behaving is typical of all those times you'd fight with your sister and suddenly flip your lid."

"She wasn't my sister," Will countered angrily.

But Dr. Burrows wanted to make his point. "You were always at each other's throats, constantly squabbling. Nothing changes, does it?"

Will realized that it was futile trying to reason with his father, and decided the only way to convince him was to tell him the rest of the story. He related all the events that took place in the Deeps, while his father listened intently.

"Deadly viruses, shootings, and a mother you'd never known. That all makes for one whale of a tale," Dr. Burrows said, assuming his son had finished. But Will wasn't quite done yet.

"Dad, something's been bugging me ever since you left."

"What's that?" Dr. Burrows said.

"That night back in Highfield, when you rushed out of the living room — what were you arguing about with Mum?" he asked.

"I tried to tell her what I was planning to do, but she didn't want to know. . . . She was glued to some program on the goggle box. Your mother's not an easy person at the best of times, and I have to confess my patience was wearing thin."

"So what happened? Did you tell her where you were going?" Will asked.

"Yes, I did, as far I knew myself. The only way I could get her attention was to switch the television off so she'd listen to me. Then she really let fly on me."

"You switched the telly off," Will said, then whistled expansively. That was the one thing you never did to Mrs. Burrows. It was rather akin to breaking the first commandment in the Burrowses' house: *Thou shalt not interrupt my viewing.*

"I only wanted to explain to your mother what I was intending to do," Dr. Burrows said weakly, as if he was trying hard to justify what he'd done.

"Dad, there's something else, too. . . . You keep saying she's my mother. She's not my real mother, and you're not my real father, are you? Why did you never tell me I was adopted?"

Dr. Burrows remained silent for several paces. As they walked side by side, Will felt the tension between them, and wondered if his father was going to answer him. He did finally.

"When I was young, my parents had a friend who used to visit," Dr. Burrows said. "He was called Jeff Stokes, but to me he was Uncle Stokes. He was married to some woman who owned a stables outside London, and he had a couple of kids, but he never brought them with him." Dr. Burrows smiled. "He was a fascinating character, and both my mother and father loved his company. There was a ripple of excitement in the place whenever he turned up, always in the latest model sports car or on a massive motorbike. And for me it was extraspecial, like Christmas or a birthday, because he never came empty-handed — he always brought me the most wonderful presents. A magic set or some Matchbox cars . . . he even gave me my first microscope, in a little wooden case with slides of crystals and butterfly wings. I can't tell you how much those presents meant to me, particularly as my parents never had much money for things like that."

"Cool," Will said absently, not knowing where his father was going with this.

"I must have been around nine when he brought me two white mice in a cage. My parents had never allowed me to have any pets, so I was over the moon. I stayed up late into the evening, just watching my mice, until my father packed me off to bed. When I woke up in the morning, first thing I did was rush over to where I'd left the cage. It wasn't there. I couldn't understand it. I tore all over the house looking for it, but I couldn't find it anywhere. My father came downstairs because I was upset and crying so much. He told me I must have had a dream because there never was a pair of white mice in a cage. He said I must have dreamed the whole thing. And my mother gave me exactly the same story."

"So they lied to you," Will put in.

"Yes, they lied to me. My mother had a chronic fear of mice, and my new pets had to go. But at the time I really believed what they'd told me, and it wasn't until years later that I put two and two together and figured out what they'd done. However, I didn't resent them for it. It was kinder to let me think it had all been some dream, rather than make me surrender my beloved mice." Dr. Burrows cleared his throat. "Will, your mother and I were going to tell you that you were adopted. But we wanted you to be old enough to deal with it, to understand what it meant. I promise you that." He met his son's eyes. "And now that you know, does it really make any difference?"

Will didn't answer straightaway. "Yes, I think it does," he said eventually. "Deep down I always had this feeling that I didn't quite fit in with you and Mum, and certainly not *ever* with Rebecca . . . I mean the Rebeccas. I tried to make myself fit . . . make myself feel I belonged . . . I suppose I *forced* myself to believe that I did. . . . But that's not right, is it? Even if this stuff with my real family in the Colony and the Styx had never happened, I was still living a lie, wasn't I? Even if it was my own lie?" Will took a breath to try to steady his voice. "And that wasn't right, was it?"

"No, it wasn't, Will. We should have told you before," Dr.

Burrows agreed. Then he changed the subject altogether. "We seem to have been walking upward for a very long time."

"Well, the explosion's completely plugged it up," Martha said as she returned down the passage to Chester and Elliott. She looked at the girl, who was sitting cross-legged on her stretcher, chewing on a piece of biltong made from dried spider-monkey meat and sipping from a canteen.

"Sorry," Elliott said, flicking her eyebrows apologetically. "I couldn't see any other way out."

"No, you did the right thing," Martha assured her. "If it was a toss-up between who got us first — the Brights or the Limiter — I'd already put my money on the Limiter. He wasn't going to let us get away with our lives."

"That vile Rebecca twin we had with us!" Chester growled, then made a *pah* sound. "I just knew she was lying through her teeth, but Will didn't want to know. The Styx are all foul liars, with no exceptions!"

Martha cleared her throat, and Chester slowly turned to Elliott as he remembered what she had revealed back in the cavern. He shifted awkwardly where he sat. "Er . . . no offense meant," he mumbled at her.

Elliott had stopped chewing and was staring at the boy. "Topsoil filth," she said through her tight lips. Chester's eyes opened wide with surprise, until she suddenly burst into laughter. "Only kidding, Chester! My father may have been one of them, but I hate them as much as you do."

Chester swallowed, trying to summon a smile but still looking a little shaken.

"My mother served in the Garrison in the Styx Compound, where they met," Elliott explained. "When she found she was with child, she moved as far away as she could to the West Cavern. To say it was a difficult situation would be putting it lightly — she would have been Banished and he executed if anyone had discovered their secret. So he didn't have an awful lot to do with me while I was growing up, but he did come and visit us whenever he could. Then, when I was nine years old, the visits suddenly stopped. Word was he went missing in action — on some Topsoil operation."

"But don't you feel a bit funny about it?" Chester ventured. "I mean, you speak Styx, you're half Styx, and yet you've fought and . . . and you've killed Styx, haven't you?"

"No, look, I'm a Colonist through and through, like my mother. She brought me up as one, and I saw how the Styx treated my people. I loathe them as much as anyone else," she answered.

"So why did you leave the Colony?" Martha asked.

"Somehow, someone found out who my father was and tried to hold it over my mother. I don't know who — she wouldn't say, but she was going mad with worry. So I thought if I went, it would stop."

"Did it?" Martha said.

"I don't know," Elliott said, her voice sad. "I haven't had any contact with her since I left."

There was a short silence, which Martha ended. "We can't hang about here. We're deep in spider country."

"But what about Will?" Chester asked, frowning. "When I saw him he was moving like the wind. Do you think he's OK?"

Martha took a deep breath. "Even if he did get clear, he's not going to be able to follow us into here. I say we try to get to the Wolf Caves," she said, staring into the tunnels behind them. "If we reach them, we can wait for him there."

"What do you mean *if*?" Chester said.

PART 4

THE UNDERGROUND HARBOR

20

THREE DAYS LATER and with the food nearly exhausted, Will and Dr. Burrows were badly in need of rest. The inclined seam had been interrupted by a number of vertical faults, which meant they had to make it across some terrifyingly deep ravines in order to continue their journey. If these ravines had been on the surface, they wouldn't have stood a chance of crossing them, but in the low gravity environment they could simply leap from one side to the other.

They had just traversed another ravine when Dr. Burrows began to whistle random notes through his teeth. He was pottering along with his chin in the air, exactly as if he was out for a Sunday stroll. It irked Will that his father appeared to be so relaxed about their situation. But within less than half a mile, they came to the top of the seam and found themselves squeezing through an extremely narrow passage, a rock corridor with jaggedly uneven sides.

Dr. Burrows ceased his whistling and was instead making a series of grunts as he struggled through the claustrophobic space.

The whistling had been bad enough, but the grunts were getting to be too much for Will to bear. All of a sudden he stopped, forcing his father to pull up sharply behind him in the corridor.

"What am I doing!" he blurted, kicking out at a loose rock. "Why am I even here with you?"

"Something on your mind?" Dr. Burrows asked.

"Yeah. Other than being totally knackered and starving, I've made a terrible mistake. I should have found a way back to Chester and the others. I didn't try hard enough. I just know they'll be waiting for me at the Wolf Caves."

"We did try," Dr. Burrows replied evenly. "There wasn't a safe way through."

Will shook his head. "We should've just taken the first passage we came across, the one with the young spiders in it, and chanced it. I bet it would have been OK. And we didn't really explore whether there were passages off the other side of the seam. What if there was one that led straight to the Wolf Caves?" He kicked at another rock, which rebounded off the walls of the corridor. "Stupid, stupid, stupid!"

"Will, we did look for passages on the right, and we didn't find any, did we? Just calm down," Dr. Burrows urged him.

"No, I won't! What if they were hurt in the explosion? Chester might need my help."

"I'm sure he's fine. The renegade woman will look after him, and that girl with all the explosives — she was no shrinking violet. Bet she knows the ropes down here," Dr. Burrows said.

"Her name is Elliott," Will fumed, throwing his father a look of irritation. "And she's just as lost down in this place as we are. And at this rate *we're* going to get ourselves doubly lost."

"I think not," his father countered.

Will was about to vent more of his frustration when he stopped himself. "Why do you say that?"

"Because if you had been paying attention for the last couple of miles, you would have observed those." Dr. Burrows shone his luminescent orb on an area higher up the wall. Although the paint was faded and had peeled away in places, a red triangle was immediately above where Will was standing, one of its tips pointing in the direction they were heading. "There were just a few at the beginning, but now they're running at about five-hundred-yard intervals."

Will was instantly curious. "Do you think the crew from the submarine left them?"

"Possibly," Dr. Burrows said. "But we're going to find out for ourselves what's at the end of the trail."

"No way. . . . I've got to go back for the others," Will insisted, but his words had lost some of their conviction, and his eyes widened as his insatiable thirst for discovery took hold. "Though . . . I suppose it wouldn't do any harm to follow the signs for a bit."

Without further ado, he pushed on into the narrow chasm.

"That's my boy," Dr. Burrows said under his breath.

They struggled through the claustrophobic corridor for several more miles. Then, suddenly, the reports of their footfalls seemed to have a different quality to them, the echoes indicating that they were coming to a much larger space.

"Light — more light," Dr. Burrows ordered as they stepped from the corridor and found to their surprise that they were on some sort of level platform. Will turned up his lantern several clicks. "This is concrete!" Dr. Burrows said, grinding his heel into the surface. Then he dropped onto one knee to examine it more closely, all the time wittering to himself. "Concrete . . . probably cold-poured."

But Will was so excited he wasn't listening. "Look! There's a line!" he shouted as he directed his lantern before them. Its light revealed a thick white line, running straight across the way ahead. And just beyond the line, something glinted darkly, giving the impression of movement.

Father and son immediately advanced toward it, trying to make out what was there.

"Careful," Dr. Burrows warned Will.

"It's OK, it's just water," Will said as they came to the line and stopped. The line marked the edge of the platform, and as they both peered down, they could see there was a drop of several feet to where the expanse of water began. Although it appeared to be quite deep, it was clear enough that rocks were visible at the bottom.

"Yes, some sort of subterranean pool," Dr. Burrows confirmed. "I wonder what else is here."

Will immediately began to shine his beam out over the gently lapping surface. As he did this, shifting crescents were thrown against the far wall to the left of the cavern. They both squinted at it through the murky gloom.

"This place is enormous," Will said unnecessarily. He switched his lantern to its full setting so he could see farther along the cavern wall.

"It is," Dr. Burrows murmured, although he still seemed to be more interested in the platform underfoot, turning his attention to it again. "What's a great big slab of concrete doing down here? What the dickens is it for?" he posed to himself as he scraped his boot slowly across its surface.

"I'm going to check up here," Will said as he followed the white line where it ran to the left. Finding that the platform terminated at the cavern wall, he shouted, "Nothing doing — dead end!" He went back to where his father was standing but didn't stop, passing behind him. He thought he'd reached the other end of the platform as he came to a large pile of rubble, but as he climbed over it he found the concrete extended far into the darkness, its level surface only interrupted by the odd crack or pieces of rock strewn across it.

"There's more here!" he reported to his father, then discovered that the platform, still edged with the white line, turned a corner. "Hurry up, Dad! Come and look at this!" he yelled. Dr. Burrows caught up with him and, side by side, they began to make their way down the new stretch.

Then Will pointed his lantern at the way ahead. A lighter patch stood out in the distance, and as they came closer to it they saw a definite shape.

Will held the circle of light steady.

"What is that?" Dr. Burrows asked with bated breath. He and Will froze. There was a suggestion of something regular over by the wall — a building. Dr. Burrows immediately stormed toward it.

As the structure loomed out of the darkness, Will wasn't so quick to follow. The idea suddenly popped into his head that stumbling across such a place might not be such good news.

"Hey, Dad," Will shouted weakly, as he remembered Cal's description of the Bunker in the Deeps. Although Will hadn't seen it for himself, he recalled that it, too, was made from concrete, and it occurred to him that this place could also have something to do with the Styx. Maybe it was one of their outposts. In the same instant he realized how improbable that was. Martha had been emphatic that the Styx's preserve didn't extend this far down. Will shook his head, dismissing the concern. No, this wasn't something the Styx had put here.

"What is it, Will?" Dr. Burrows finally responded.

"Nothing," Will said as he hurried to catch up with his father.

The building consisted of a single story in which there was a row of square windows, ten in total, and beyond these a door. Will was at the door in an instant. It was painted gray-blue, with the occasional brown streak where rust had begun to etch into its surface. And in the center of the door was a wheel — clearly some sort of opening mechanism. Dr. Burrows hung his luminescent orb around his neck and tried to rotate the wheel. He swore as it refused to move.

"You'll have to help me," he mumbled to Will, who clipped his lantern to his jacket and joined his father in trying to turn the mechanism.

After several attempts, they gave up.

"Blast!" Dr. Burrows exclaimed, then drove his heel into the wheel several times in an attempt to loosen it.

"Hang on," Will said as he spotted a length of metal tubing lying at the foot of the wall. He snatched it up and stuck it through the spokes of the wheel.

"A lever! Good thinking!" Dr. Burrows praised him. They leaned on it with all their weight. As the wheel turned, the tubing slipped from the spokes and fell onto the floor, filling the cavern with clanking echoes. Will went to retrieve it.

"Don't bother," Dr. Burrows said. "I think we've got it now." He grunted as he rotated the wheel. There was a solid *clunk* as it reached the limit of its revolution. "Open, Sesame," he announced, and heaved on the door. It swung out a little until its base grated loudly on the concrete platform. "This is a heck of a door — it's nearly two feet thick!" Although he continued to heave, the door wouldn't move any farther. "Let's get all this out of the way," he suggested, kicking at the pieces of rock under its edge.

Will helped him, sweeping aside the larger debris with his boot and then getting down on his knees to brush away the gravel with his hands.

"That should do it. Let's have another go," Dr. Burrows suggested. There was enough of a gap for him to poke his fingers inside the door and get a good grip on it. "Ready . . . steady . . . go!" Dr. Burrows shouted as he used all his strength to yank on the door. With Will simultaneously pulling on the handle, the door opened a little farther, providing sufficient room for them to squeeze through, which they did with breathless anticipation.

Stepping inside, they found a rectangular chamber around thirty by sixty feet. In the center was a small campaign table surrounded by some folding chairs.

"Hey, Dad, get a load of this!" Will shouted excitedly. On the wall directly opposite the door was a complicated-looking panel of dials and switches. "What on earth is it?"

"I haven't the foggiest, but that door certainly did its job and kept the damp out. There's no sign of any corrosion at all," Dr. Burrows noted as he and his son's gaze both fell on the lower corner of the panel, where there were five large breaker switches. The words MAIN POWER CONSOLE were written above them.

Dr. Burrows began to whistle in his usual atonal way, which usually meant he was deep in thought. Then he spoke. "All these handles are up, which means that no connection is being made . . . so they're in the *Off* position." It was as though a silent and irresistible invitation had been issued to try them. Will nodded, fascinated to see what his father was going to do next.

Dr. Burrows was reaching for the first of the handles when Will spotted some words stenciled in red on the wall to the side of the panel. "Hey, Dad — *To Be Operated By Authorized Personnel Only*," he read out quickly.

This caused Dr. Burrows to hesitate, holding his hand a few inches away from the handle. He hummed undecidedly as he rubbed his thumb against his fingers.

"Well, are we going to try it or not?" Will said.

Dr. Burrows drew in a breath, then let it out with a contemplative hum.

"All this looks like it came out of the ark," he said. "It probably won't work, anyway . . . so I don't see why we shouldn't give it a shot."

"Yeah, do it, Dad," Will urged him.

"Yeah," Dr. Burrows echoed, although he never normally used the word. He took hold of the first handle and swung it down so it clicked firmly into place. They peered around the room, the light of Will's lantern slashing through the gloom, but nothing appeared to have changed. They could hear water dripping outside, but all else was silent.

"Do you really think —?" Will said, as he began to ask himself if they should find out what the switches were for before they went any further.

But Dr. Burrows had already gripped the second handle and whipped it down. There was a large blue flash as the contacts met, and a sizzling sound. Father and son jumped back in surprise. The room was immediately flooded with illumination from an array of wall-mounted bulkhead lights.

"Ohh, that's bright!" Will exclaimed, shielding his eyes.

Although it took them awhile to get used to the brilliance, they now had a clear view of their surroundings. Dr. Burrows tried the other switches and found that two of the remaining three were working, as they crackled with blue sparks. On the panel above, the needles in the circular dials twitched and clicked under their hazy glass. Right in the middle of the panel, a pointer crept across a large rectangular gauge.

"That must be the overall power level," Dr. Burrows said, wiping the dust from it.

"How do you know that?" Will asked, fully aware that his father found any gadget more complicated than a toaster a challenge.

"Educated guess," Dr. Burrows said with a smile. He indicated the row of figures under the needle. "This scale seems to be in megawatts, so I'm probably right."

Will nodded as he began to study the room more closely. It had a low ceiling and unpainted concrete walls, and other than the metal table and chairs it was completely empty. "Over there," Will said, pointing. At the far end of the room was a door that was easily twice as wide as the one they had come through.

"Leave it for the moment," Dr. Burrows told him, still examining the vacillating needles in the smaller dials. "This switching panel has to be decades old, so the power can't be coming from batteries or any sort of stored charge. The state of this place — good as it is — doesn't really lead one to believe that it's been maintained, and batteries would have run out by now. That leaves a connection to the grid above, which is also impossible, bec —"

"Because we're too far down for that?" Will cut in.

"Precisely," Dr. Burrows continued, scratching his whiskery chin. "So it's either geothermal or hydroelectric power. Given the water outside, I'd put my money on hydroelectric."

"One thing's for sure, this has nothing to do with the Colony, does it?" Will asked.

"No, it's ours. It's surface technology," Dr. Burrows said, wiping more of the dust from the dials with his thumb. "But from yonks ago by the looks of it." His hand hovered over a bank of chunky switches under the heading EXTERNAL, each labeled with a letter from A to K. "In for a penny!" he declared before clicking them all on. The dial on the large central meter swerved momentarily to the left, then crawled back to the center, where it seemed to settle down again. Dr.

Burrows twisted around to the dust-filmed windows. "Yes, I think that's done the trick," he muttered as they both went to the windows and saw the glow outside.

They hurriedly exited the building through the partially opened door. Glaring lights hung down from rails strung across the roof of the cavern, revealing the full extent of the platform, and that a pier — also constructed of concrete and approximately fifty feet long — branched off it and out into the lagoon. Down both sides, this pier had rusted iron bollards set into its surface, several of which had chains hanging from them, although it wasn't obvious what these were for since they trailed into the water. Will ran to the side to see them more clearly.

"Dad, what are those down there? Boats?" he asked, spying several vessels — basic-looking dinghies — attached to the chains but lying on the bottom of the lagoon. They were either made of plastic or fiberglass, and were all in varying stages of disintegration. Others were completely broken up, and now the cavern was so well lit Will could see their remains scattering the far bank among the craggy rocks.

"They certainly are. And see over there, Will!" Dr. Burrows shouted. "It's a barge!"

As he peered into the far corner of the cavern, Will spotted a long vessel in the water, its sides mottled with a patina of rust. It appeared to have broken free from its mooring and drifted to its current position, its bow touching the cavern wall. At the helm there was a small cabin, and the rest of the vessel was open, with metal crates stacked in it.

"Will, can you believe it, this is some kind of underground

harbor!" Dr. Burrows said, his words clipped by his sheer excitement. He immediately began to survey what was on the rest of the quay, which continued for several hundred feet from where they were standing. As he and Will spotted more build-ings along the base of the cavern wall, they broke into a run to reach the nearest of them. The first had a door with another rotating handle in the center, and Dr. Burrows wasted no time tackling it.

"Want me to have a go?" Will offered as his father struggled with it.

"No, leave it to me," Dr. Burrows replied as he spat on his palms and resumed his efforts. He strained hard and the handle finally began to move, then he pulled the door open. There was a hiss as air was released from inside.

"Oh, yeuch!" Will gasped, wrinkling his nose as they both ventured in. "Dad, that wasn't you, was it?"

"Most certainly not!" Dr. Burrows huffed indignantly. "Smells a little like swamp gas . . . like methane. There must have been a buildup of it in here."

"Sorry," his son mumbled, throwing himself into an exam-ination of the interior to mask his embarrassment. With its three-foot-thick walls, the concrete cabin had the same internal dimensions as the first building, but was windowless. The lights didn't seem to be working, so Will used his lantern to explore it. Three sizeable engines were mounted in pits sunk into the floor, rainbow-crazed pools of fluid around their bases.

"Generators?" Dr. Burrows said. "Yes. See the fuel lines going into them, and the electrical conduits and switching gear on the wall over there?"

"Um . . . I think I've found what smells so bad," Will announced from a corner of the cabin. His lantern revealed a thermos flask with a faded tartan pattern on it and, beside it, an open-topped plastic box, inside which was something black with rot.

"Somebody forgot their lunch." Dr. Burrows grinned.

"It's a bit more than that, Dad," Will said as he peered into the box. "There's a rat in here, too . . . and it's been dead for a very long time."

"Probably got locked in and that's all it had to eat," Dr. Burrows suggested as they left the cabin to try the next building.

In this one they found that the walls were lined with sturdy metal shelves, on which were a number of wooden crates. Dr. Burrows heaved at one of these, not anticipating just how heavy it would be, and he found he couldn't support it once he slid it off the shelf. "Blast!" he yelled, jumping back, as it crashed to the floor and broke open. Assisted by Will, he lifted the pieces of crate aside to uncover something large, wrapped in oil-stained cloth, which ripped as they tugged at it.

"What is it?" Will asked.

"An outboard motor, I think," Dr. Burrows said as he slid a finger over the marine screw. With the grease removed, the metal shone brightly. "Yes. And in top condition, too!" He turned to his son and grinned. "This is all incredible. Let's see what else is here." They both returned outside.

Moving down the quayside, they reached the next building, but Dr. Burrows didn't stop, jogging past it and several others along the way. He seemed to be in a tearing hurry, as if he'd spotted something just beyond them.

Two substantial cylindrical tanks were set into the cavern wall, nearly a hundred feet high and with pipe work and taps at their bases. Dr. Burrows tried one of these, allowing a little of the fluid to gush out.

"Gasoline," Will said, immediately identifying the smell.

Dr. Burrows was careful to turn the tap off. "And this one," he pronounced as he rapped on the second tank with his knuckles and it gave a dull ring, "is diesel. For the generators, maybe."

"You can smell it?" Will asked, impressed.

"No — see the big *D* painted on it? Follow me!" Dr. Burrows shouted. He was waving his arms frantically as words tumbled out of his mouth. Will hadn't seen him quite so animated in many years. But as they began to jog along the quay again, Dr. Burrows became more coherent. "Whoever built this . . . it must have been a heck of an undertaking. . . ."

He paused next to a small crane bolted to the surface of the quay, its single arm reaching out over the water. Like everything else on the quayside, it was badly rusted, and a halo of gray-blue paint lay scattered around its base. "Yes . . . a jib crane . . . to winch raw materials shipped down here in the barges . . . ," Dr. Burrows burbled. "And, of course, an overhead gantry to move goods along the quay," he said, pointing upward. Will turned and saw a chunky-looking rail affixed high above their heads. "Yes . . . but . . . all this . . . and they never completed it!" Dr. Burrows shouted breathlessly, throwing a hand at a partially constructed building as they passed it. "I wonder why?"

Will spotted a rusted cement mixer, mounds of sand, and long-since-hardened bags of cement, their paper sacks in tatters around them. "Air filtration units, I'll wager," Dr. Burrows said as he flew past stacks of wooden crates on pallets. Some of the crates were so badly rotted that the corroded blocklike machines they'd contained had slid out, and sat in a heap on the platform. "For hydroelectric power . . ."

"Yes?" Will panted, trying to keep up.

"You need turbines and . . ."

"Yes?" Will yelled, bursting to know more.

Dr. Burrows stopped abruptly. "Hear that, Will?"

"Yes!" Will said, catching the rumbling sound.

"Fast-flowing water!" Dr. Burrows shouted as he began to run again. They came to the end of the quay and went under a reinforced arch at the mouth of the harbor.

Before them was a channel at least a hundred feet wide, down which swept a rapidly speeding river. Bulkhead lights were dotted around so that everything in the area was visible to them.

Will looked to their left, where the river was flowing and where Dr. Burrows's eyes had come to rest. At an angle, and nearly spanning the full width of the channel, was a metal grille in a sturdily built housing. There was a great deal of froth and flotsam trapped against the grille, but no suggestion as to what lay behind it other than a constant humming noise. It was loud enough to be heard over the roaring water.

"Voilà! The turbines!" Dr. Burrows yelled, nodding energetically. The river was throwing up a considerable amount of spray, and he fell silent while he took off his glasses to wipe them.

Will swung in the opposite direction, then took a few steps along the gangway as he tried to see where the river was flowing from. But the lights didn't extend very far up the channel and the darkness beyond was impenetrable. "What's all this for?" he asked, shouting to make himself heard. "Who built it, Dad?"

"Don't worry about that for the moment," Dr. Burrows snapped. "Can't you see what we've got here?"

"What?" Will demanded, frowning in his confusion.

"If, and it's a big *if*, we can find an intact vessel — something that floats — and we can get an outboard motor to work," Dr. Burrows said, turning to look upstream, his hands on his hips, "we're in business."

Will just stared at the rushing water. He'd all but given up trying to understand what his father was rattling on about.

"Well . . . ," Dr. Burrows shouted, as he swiveled to face his son, "you do want to go home, don't you?"

21

"**I THOUGHT** you might be here," Mrs. Burrows said as she came across Ben Wilbrahams in his usual place, at one of the reading desks in the Highfield library.

"Yes, too many distractions at home," he replied. "I see your ankle's better."

Nodding, Mrs. Burrows handed Ben Wilbrahams a shopping bag, which he took but didn't open, looking at her inquiringly. "The other night," she said, "when you were telling me about all the strange incidents in Highfield, you asked me about Roger and what I thought he'd been up to. I'm sorry, but I wasn't exactly forthcoming."

"About what?" Ben Wilbrahams asked, testing the weight of the bag in his hands.

"I've been thinking about it a lot, and I've decided you should know everything. In that bag is my husband's journal. It covers the days just before he went off, and I'd like you to —"

Hearing a hiss, she stopped abruptly. She wheeled around to see an old man in a shirt that was too big for him, and a correspondingly massive bow tie. He was shaking his head disapprovingly. Putting his finger to his lips, he hissed again, like an asthmatic turtle.

Mrs. Burrows took the chair next to Ben Wilbrahams. "Go on — take a look," she urged him.

He opened the bag and took out the journal and read it all the way through, then and there, as Mrs. Burrows watched him.

"Fascinating stuff," he said as he closed the covers.

"You know . . . when I stepped out in front of your car, I believe —" The old man across the way hissed at her again as she was talking, but she studiously ignored him. "— I believe a couple of those pallid men — or *men-in-hats*, as Roger also referred to them — were after me."

"You're sure?" Ben Wilbrahams asked.

"Pretty sure — I got a good look at them. But couldn't you use that incident and what's in this journal as material for one of your TV programs?"

Ben Wilbrahams rubbed his temples thoughtfully.

"Look, Celia, it's one thing to dredge up oddball newspaper reports from years ago, but I'd be pushing it if I were to include anything about you — or these things your husband's written," he said, holding up the journal. "And he's the subject of an ongoing police investigation, so I also might land myself in hot water if I make any unsubstantiated claims." Ben Wilbrahams was thoughtful for a few moments as he considered the label on the front of the journal. "But I'd still like to hang on to this, chew it over. OK?"

"Of course. And now I've got to get to work — they're short-handed this afternoon." Mrs. Burrows rose from her chair and, as she was passing the old man, she leaned over and snatched hold of the pencil he was using. She snapped it in two, the loud *crack!* filling the library, then dropped the pieces in his lap.

"'Shhhh' yourself!'" she said, and promptly left.

"The cheek of it!" the old man complained loudly, as Ben Wilbrahams hid his smirk behind his book.

Will and his father investigated every inch of the harbor. In another of the squat sheds they found a fiberglass launch in a wall rack, which looked to be serviceable.

"So, maybe we *can* get this show on the road," Dr. Burrows proclaimed, rubbing his hands together. He was whistling madly as they strolled down the length of the quay to return to the building with the switching panel in it. Once inside, they both glanced at the flickering needle on the main dial before they made their way to the large door at the end of the room.

Dr. Burrows considered it for a moment. "I'd hazard a guess that this is a blast door."

"A blast door?" Will repeated. "Wh —?"

"Let's just see what's inside, shall we?" Dr. Burrows interrupted him.

"Fine," Will said a little tetchily, throwing his father a look. "Is it my turn to open it, then?" he asked as he took hold of the wheel-like mechanism.

"Be my guest," Dr. Burrows replied, touching the uppermost of the three massive hinges. He watched as his son spun the wheel around and around, until it *clunked* and Will found it wouldn't go any farther.

"Heavy," Will observed as he yanked on the large door, which wouldn't shift even the smallest degree.

"Blast door," Dr. Burrows said again, as if he was teasing his son. "I'll give you a hand."

They pulled together and it slowly began to open, issuing a low groan. A *whoosh* of air escaped, as if the pressure inside was higher.

The two Burrowses nodded at each other and stepped inside. The first surprise was that a passageway stretched before them, its curved roof about fifty feet high.

"A tube tunnel?" Will murmured.

It was lined with what appeared to be superheavy oblong iron plates, each one bolted to the next, and with something like black tar sealing the gaps between them. A row of continuous lights hung down its center, fully illuminating the passage; and to either side of the lights was a variety of cables and pipes, the thickest of which had offshoots that ended in grilles, where fresh air seemed to be coming in. Will could feel the down draft on his sweat-covered face as he stood below one of them. And considering that the massive door must have been airtight, the atmosphere didn't seem the least bit stale to him.

"Linoleum," Dr. Burrows said as he took a few steps on the gray and shiny floor. "And look . . . There's hardly any dust in the place at all." He had gone a little way down the passage when he stopped, then glanced over his shoulder at his son. "If you think about it, we're now moving beyond the edge of the cavern wall." He turned and held up his hands, his palms outward, to indicate where he thought the wall should be. "So, while the cavern outside may be a natural feature, I'd say that this passage has been hollowed into the bedrock itself."

"Yeah," Will said, "but I wonder what's in these." Down one side of the passage were a series of small cabins with metal doors. Dr. Burrows and Will explored the first of these. The walls were painted with a dark gray gloss up to waist height, above which the remainder of the walls and the ceiling were a dirty ivory color, but the cabin was completely empty.

They backed out of it and into the passage again.

"*Radio Operator*," Will said, reading the stenciled letters on the door of the next cabin down. As they opened it, they discovered a chart on the back of the door, with several months mapped out in a grid and names allotted to specific hours within each day. Neither Will nor his father made any comment as they entered the room itself. It was approximately twice the size of the first cabin, with a bench that was covered with all manner of electronic equipment against the longest wall. Dark gray metal boxes with numerous dials trailed wires down below the bench, where they were bound together into a thick snake of cables that fed into a duct in the floor.

"What are those?" Will asked, pointing at the intricate glass bulbs that protruded from the tops of some of the boxes.

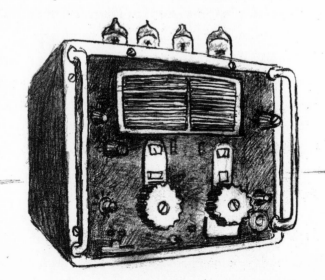

"Radio valves. It's pre-transistor technology," Dr. Burrows said. "And to complete the picture, here's a microphone," he added, pushing aside one of a pair of metal-framed canvas chairs so he could pick up the chunky black object at the front of the bench. He weighed it in his hand, then reached for a pair of headphones that lay beside it. Will opened a loose-leaf binder on the bench and flicked through the laminated pages, upon which were matrices of numbers and letters. "Maybe they're codes?" Dr. Burrows suggested.

But Will was more interested in an old television monitor mounted on the wall to their left. He tried its various switches, but nothing happened. "What does that mean?" Will asked, noticing the word **ROTOR** printed on a map beside the screen. The map outlined the British Isles, over which scores of overlapping circles had been superimposed.

Dr. Burrows shrugged. "Doesn't ring a bell with me. Maybe it's an acronym?"

"No . . . I bet you the letters stand for something," Will suggested, missing the fleeting smile on his father's face. "Look! Telephones!" Will exclaimed as he spotted the red and black telephones mounted on the opposite wall, next to an old switchboard with a tangle of leads dangling from it. "Should we try to ring someone?" he proposed.

"Don't waste your time — I doubt they've worked in years," Dr. Burrows said. "Come along," he laughed, waving Will out of the room.

The next cabin had the same dimensions, but was an Aladdin's cave of military equipment.

"An armory!" Dr. Burrows said as soon as he stepped

inside. All the wall space was taken up with rough wooden racks. He bent to peer at a stubby weapon on the one closest to him. It was obscured by thick gobs of dirty grease, but this did nothing to impede Dr. Burrows. "It's a Sten gun," he decreed as he took it from the rack. "A submachine gun first issued to British troops in the nineteen forties. They were made in Enfield and were known as the *Plumber's Nightmare*. You can see why. Ugly-looking thing, isn't it?"

"Yeah, really ugly," Will said, but his voice was full of wonder.

The rest of the room was crammed with military equipment, either neatly slotted into the racks or in metal crates stacked high against the walls. Each crate was stenciled with numbers and letters, and occasionally with the name of what was inside them.

Will busied himself by throwing open the lids to some of the crates. The first revealed more guns, entwined with heavily greased sacking, side by side with bundles of magazines for the weapons. He unwound the sacking from one of the weapons and passed it to his father.

"Another Sten gun. They're all in mint condition," Dr. Burrows said, wiping the grease from the barrel with his sleeve to reveal the perfect sheen of the bluing on the weapon. "Good as new."

"We could help ourselves to a couple," Will proposed.

"I think not," Dr. Burrows said, giving his son a stern look as he returned the Sten to him. "Put it back exactly where you found it."

The next crate revealed similarly preserved handguns stamped with BROWNING, and many oil-soaked cardboard boxes of rounds and spare magazines. "Browning Hi-Powers,"

Dr. Burrows said, peering at the handguns. "Follows — they're from the same era as the Stens."

"*Two-Inch Mortars*," Will read, staring at the largest crates in the corner of the room. He moved along to a pile of boxes. Many were narrow and contained ammunition, but then he came to some squat crates. Upon opening the lid of one of these and removing a layer of sacking laid on the top, he found row upon row of hand grenades. He whistled in amazement, and was just reaching in to pick one up when his father stopped him.

"Don't, Will," Dr. Burrows cautioned. "Better not mess around with those."

"Huh?" Will frowned.

"I know it's dry in here, but explosives can become unstable over time. And we don't know who all this belongs to, although it certainly looks like they just left it here."

"But who? And why?"

"I don't know yet," Dr. Burrows replied, "but there's enough in here to start a small war." He rubbed his forehead, leaving streaks of black grease across it in the process. "See the little symbol spray-painted on all the crates — the arrow with the line above it?"

Will nodded.

"That means these belonged to the Ministry of Defense . . . or the army, so this might have been a government installation, or it might have been something else altogether."

Will shrugged. "What, like Dr. Evil's secret lair?"

Dr. Burrows shook his head as if his son was being ridiculous. "No. Anarchists . . . the far right . . . or the far left . . . what have you." He frowned. "But whoever it was, all this looks pretty official to me. They've gone to a huge amount of effort and expense." He blew through his lips in an exaggerated way. "I mean . . . just the construction of a hydroelectric plant at this depth in the earth is an incredible feat of engineering, all on its own. And everything I've seen — the whole installation — was built to last. I'd put my money on it being . . ."

"Yes?" Will pressed him, becoming impatient with his father's musings.

". . . a deep-level military shelter . . . a fallout shelter . . . maybe dating back to the Cold War."

"The Cold War?" Will asked.

"Yes . . . it's before your time, Will, in the fifties and sixties. It wasn't a proper war, as you'd think of it . . . just a load of absurd posturing between America and the Soviet Union, really. But people genuinely thought the world was going to be torn apart by a nuclear war. So each country had its own contingency plans, which included building fallout shelters . . . even here in England," he said, then turned to go through the door. Will trailed after him, still clutching a Browning Hi-Power pistol. Dr. Burrows was on a roll with his theory, gabbling away ten to the dozen. "And if this *is* a fallout shelter . . . that would mean it would be self-sufficient, with its own water supply, and there'll probably be living quarters down here, somewhere."

They ignored the remaining cabins and cranked open the door at the end of the passage. As it swung back they were greeted by another blast of air. It was dark inside until Dr. Burrows located a row of switches by the side of the door. He flipped them all up with the side of his hand.

Banks of lights flickered on in sequence.

"My word . . . ," Dr. Burrows gasped.

Although the ceiling was at a lower height than the passage, the area was immense. And row upon row of bunk beds were arranged regularly throughout the space.

"I bet a hundred men could have been billeted here!" Dr. Burrows exclaimed.

Will ran to the first bunk and touched the pillow. Like all the other bunks around him, it was made up with white sheets and coarse brown blankets. "A real bed!" He put his head back and gave out a *whoop*, which echoed through the floor. "I can sleep in a real bed tonight!" Then he was running between the bunks to reach the rooms that lay around the outside, each one with a gray-painted door and a number stenciled on it.

"Showers!" he yelled, leaning inside the first room. Then, as he inspected the next, "Lavatories!" Several rooms farther along he was screaming, "Food! There's food in here!" as he vanished into it.

Dr. Burrows jogged over to join his son.

It was a kitchen area, with a bank of ovens and a long grill, like one might find in a large restaurant. But what interested Will more than anything else was the huge quantity of tin cans on the shelves and in the cupboards.

Will picked out a large rectangular can — it didn't have a label stuck on it, but the contents were printed on the outside in small blue letters. "*Corned Beef,*" he read. "Do you think any of this is still OK?"

"Might be," Dr. Burrows replied, as he took the tin from his son to check it for any signs of rust or leakage. "Will, have a mosey around for a can opener, will you?"

22

"**WATCH OUT!**" Chester spluttered, gesturing frantically at the shadows behind Martha as she entered the section of the Wolf Caves where he and Elliott had been waiting for her. Snuffling, Bartleby came into view, his head down as if he was ashamed of himself. "It's that darn cat!"

"It's all right," Martha said, beckoning the cat over. He sat by her feet, looking up at her. "I couldn't just leave him out there, at the mercy of the spiders and the wolves."

"But he was about to go for Will! He was going to attack him," Chester said, his rifle ready in his hands. "We can't be sure of him."

"You heard what the Rebecca twin said. It was the Styx," Elliott said casually as she bit off another mouthful of spider meat.

"What do you mean?" Chester asked.

"They used the Dark Light on him," Elliott replied. "He had no choice but to do what the Rebecca twin ordered. With the Dark Light, the Styx can break the minds of the strongest men and make them their slaves, and Bartleby's only a dumb animal. Anyway, he might come in useful," she added.

"I reckon *I'm* the dumb animal," Chester grumbled as he lowered his rifle, still regarding the cat with misgiving. "We should have had Bartleby burgers back on the sub."

Martha stroked the cat's bald pate, which was still stained with fungus juice from the explosion. "No, Elliott's right — he *is* a Hunter. He might yet come in handy," she said.

As his father entered the radio operator's booth, Will was lounging in one of the canvas chairs, his feet on the bench. He stuck a fork into the large can of pineapple chunks in his hand and, spearing several pieces, crammed them into his mouth. "Mmmm . . . rather good. This is the life, isn't it, Dad?" he said as he munched on them.

"Don't overdo it with that fruit — your body won't be used to it," Dr. Burrows advised him, placing an army mess tin on the bench. Reaching into his pocket, he produced a few small foil-wrapped packets. Will sat up, immediately interested.

"Brought you some crackers," Dr. Burrows said.

"Great. And what's in this?" Will asked as he regarded the steam rising from the mess tin.

"Tea," Dr. Burrows said. "Try some."

"It looks about the right color," Will observed. He took a sip, then stuck out his tongue. "Urgh . . . that's foul! Far too sweet!"

"That'll be the condensed milk. I loved it when I was young — we used to have it on peaches. . . ."

Taking the chair next to Will, Dr. Burrows began to reminisce about some great-aunt Will had never met, at the same time flicking the switches on the various boxes on the bench. Finally, as Dr. Burrows was waxing lyrical about the steak-and-kidney pudding this great-aunt would make especially for him, he pushed a button on the largest device, and a large dial in its center was instantly suffused with a pale yellow light. Several of the valves on the top of the unit also lit up, emitting a pinkish glow. From a small speaker mounted high on the wall came a sudden burst of static, which gave way to a sound that seemed to ebb and flow. It wasn't that dissimilar to the sound of waves breaking on a distant beach. By now Dr. Burrows had fallen absolutely silent.

"Finally!" Will muttered under his breath, relieved that his father had curtailed his incessant reminiscing.

"Yes, indeed — at last some hope of . . ." Dr. Burrows trailed off in thought, not realizing the real reason for his son's remark. He swiveled the dial in the center of the main unit. But this only had the effect of producing further bursts of static, and after several minutes he stopped, shaking his head. "I expect some of the valves must have blown," he said, pointing at the glass tubes on the top of the unit that had remained unlit.

"Could we try to fix it?" Will suggested.

"I saw some spares in one of the storerooms, but I wouldn't know where to start. It's all a bit beyond me," Dr. Burrows grumbled, as if annoyed with himself. He sighed and sank back into his chair, playing with a packet of crackers. "Anyway, I haven't a clue what all these settings mean or how any of this equipment works," he said regretfully. He got to his feet and clicked his tongue against his teeth distractedly. "It might be a waste of time, but while you're in here you could try to sweep through all the wavelengths, Will. This equipment was probably only for communications around the harbor, and since there's no one else down here but us . . ." He didn't bother to complete the sentence, instead leaving the room.

Will took over, turning the main dial slowly and trying different combinations of switches. As he did this, he repeated, "Hello, hello, anybody there?" into the microphone, although the question was barely intelligible because he was still gorging himself on pineapple chunks. As his efforts only seemed to be resulting in the odd crackle of static from the speaker, and he'd also had enough of the fruit, he eventually gave up.

"No," he said to himself disconsolately. "It *is* a waste of time." Tearing open the packet, he nibbled on one of the dry crackers as he contemplated the rest of the room. His gaze settled on the pair of telephones on the wall. He stood up and lifted the receiver from the nearest, the red one, and put it to his ear to check for a dial tone. He couldn't hear anything, so he pressed the tabs on the top of the phone and dialed random numbers to find out if that made any difference.

"The Bat Phone's out of order," he grumbled, still hearing nothing, and he eventually replaced the receiver. He chuckled to himself as, on a whim, he picked up the receiver from the black phone next to it and began to call the number of his house in Highfield. Sticking his finger in the rotary dial, he dragged it around. It took ages for the dial to spin back so he could dial the next digit. "Why did anyone put up with these?" he wondered. He thought about how strange it would be if his mother were to answer. *That* would be a conversation in a million.

He closed his eyes and began to imagine how it might go.

Click!

Hi, Mum, it's Will.

She would undoubtedly be furious with both him and his father. *Where in the world have you been all this time? You've no idea what you've put me through, have you? You couple of selfish snots — GET YOURSELVES HOME RIGHT THIS MOMENT!* she would bellow at the top of her lungs.

Er, Mum, that's not so easy. We're thousands of miles below the surface, in some sort of secret government installation. . . .

He abandoned his imaginary conversation as silence continued to reign in the earpiece. "Nobody home, nobody home . . . ," he muttered, and was about to replace the receiver when he decided to try again.

He managed to remember his mother's cell phone number, although she rarely had it switched on. As he finished dialing, he strained to listen. A burst of white noise made him start.

In the solicitors' office where she worked, Mrs. Burrows was at her desk typing away furiously. Wearing a headset, she was listening to the Dictaphone and transcribing a letter from one of the law firm's partners. It had to do with a couple in divorce proceedings who were wrangling over custody of their five-year-old daughter. As she imagined the heartbreak and upheaval that lay behind the dry legal language of the letter, Mrs. Burrows was finding it really quite upsetting.

Thinking she heard her cell phone, she tore off her headset and snatched up her handbag. The phone was still ringing as she got it out. Answering it, she put it to her ear and heard a loud crackle. "Hello?" she said, just as the line went dead. She studied the number. She didn't recognize it — it certainly wasn't a London number. "Another annoying telemarketer," she said, slinging the phone back into her handbag and resuming her typing.

After another, much louder burst of white noise, Will had whipped the receiver away from his ear and ended the call. "What am I doing?" he asked himself, but nonetheless resolved to give it one last go. On the spur of the moment, his mind went blank and he couldn't think of a single number to try. He didn't know the numbers for Chester's parents or Auntie Jean's apartment, and as a last resort he thought about just trying to call emergency services — as if he could order an ambulance to the underworld.

But, in a flash, the number that Elliott had been babbling over and over again in her feverish state suggested itself and, knowing it by heart, he immediately dialed it. Again he didn't seem to be getting any sort of connection — in fact, there wasn't even the smallest crackle in the earpiece this time — so he announced, "This is Will Burrows. I'm calling from deep within the earth and I *will* be back soon. Thank you — good-bye!" before he slammed down the receiver.

Gnawing on one of the dry crackers, he went to find out what his father was up to.

"Don't know how you can drink that stuff," Will said as he approached. Taking occasional sips of tea from his mess tin, Dr. Burrows was hunched over a table he'd set up in the main dormitory area. Around the legs of his chair were an assortment of folders, boxes, and wads of loose papers — he'd clearly gathered together everything he thought might be useful and was now sifting through it.

Some kind of plan, so large that it covered the entire surface of the table, was spread open. It was of graying paper, with the odd area of pastel color. As Dr. Burrows finished with his tea and put his mess tin down on the plan, a section close to the tin caught Will's eye. It stood out because it was so heavily shaded. From its shape, Will knew immediately it must be the harbor and the complex where they were right now. Other than the river, which looked like a pale blue ribbon draped across the surface of the plan, small yellow lines radiated off from the harbor cavern, studded every so often by red triangles. Will assumed these were distance markers that corresponded to the triangles they'd seen painted on the walls in the fissure, which had led them to the harbor in the first place.

"Anything interesting?" Will asked, inclining his head toward the plan.

"Not really," Dr. Burrows answered distantly. "Just that they were surveying the surrounding area for freshwater springs."

It was then that Will spotted the small stone tablets nestling in a grimy handkerchief, and was immediately interested because he'd only had a brief glimpse of them before. Dr. Burrows had one of them in his hand and was examining it closely.

"Can I take a look?" Will said.

"Just don't drop them," Dr. Burrows mumbled as he jotted something illegible on a pad.

Will reached over to the handkerchief and took a tablet in his hand.

"Wow! You said the carving was tiny, but I didn't think it was *that* tiny!" he marveled, squinting at the intricate inscriptions and minute diagrams.

"No matter how long I spend on this, I just can't get anywhere with the script. I'm completely stumped." Dr. Burrows exhaled, sitting back in his chair with a resigned expression. "I can remember a few of the words, but not enough of them. I need someone trained in code-breaking to help me decipher the whole caboodle."

"Want me to have a go?" Will offered enthusiastically.

"No, it's too involved," Dr. Burrows said. "It would only frustrate you, too."

"What do you think this map's of?" Will asked as he took a second stone tablet from the handkerchief and began to compare it with the first.

Dr. Burrows turned to a clean page in his pad, on which he began to scribble wildly. Then he twisted it around so that Will could see it. He'd drawn a circle with tiny stick men walking inside its circumference, and a stylized sun right in the center of the circle with jagged rays issuing from it. "This is a mural I discovered in an ancient temple in the Deeps. It depicts a world within a world," he said, then sighed.

"Yeah, I saw your drawing of that," Will remembered.

"What?" Dr. Burrows shrieked, knocking the chair over behind him as he jumped to his feet. "How in the world could you have?"

"I told you, Dad — we found some of your pages by the Pore," Will said.

"Yes, but I thought they were illegible. I thought they'd been ruined by water!" Dr. Burrows cried.

Will looked completely taken aback. "I didn't say that. Some of the pages had been soaked, but most of the ones I managed to pick up weren't too bad. I could read them, anyway."

Dr. Burrows tottered slightly, as if he'd just been struck on the back of the head. He attempted to sit down, stopping himself just in time as he realized the chair wasn't where it should be. He seized it up impatiently and righted it, then sat down and began to scrawl on a blank page like a madman. Seconds later, when he was finished, he shoved the pad in front of Will.

"Was there a drawing like this in with them?"

Will contemplated the outline his father had sketched and the three blocks of text within it. The way Dr. Burrows had reproduced them, the quickly formed letters rather resembled swatted mosquitoes. "Yes, I definitely had that page, with the three areas of writing on it," he said.

"And, pray, where is it now?" Dr. Burrows demanded.

"I put it in a safe place, in Martha's shack."

"In . . . Martha's . . . shack . . . ," Dr. Burrows repeated slowly, emphasizing each word. His face was already white from months of living underground, but it seemed to Will that it had now completely drained of blood.

"Why — is it important?" Will asked tentatively.

"I need that page with the Burrows Stone to translate these tablets. Yes, it's important."

Will frowned at the mention of the Burrows Stone, then shot his father a brief look to see if he was being serious. Turning his attention back to the tablets, Will helped himself to another one from the handkerchief.

"The *Burrows Stone* is like the *Rosetta Stone*," Dr. Burrows explained. "It has three distinct areas of writing on it, all saying the same thing, but one is in Phoenician. That enables me to translate the other two languages, neither of which I believe has ever been seen on the surface. If I had it now, I could translate these tablets and . . ." He trailed off.

"What?" Will said as he looked from one tablet to another.

"And I think it might be the route map to this inner world the ancient civilization believed in. The *Garden of the Second Sun.*"

"The second sun," Will repeated absently.

Dr. Burrows was surprised by the lack of reaction from Will, but his son's attention was elsewhere. He was moving the tablets around on the tabletop and helping himself to more from the handkerchief until they were all laid out, apart from the one his father had been working on.

"Can I have that?" he asked, indicating the tablet in his

father's hand. Dr. Burrows passed it to him, and Will turned it one way, then the other, as he examined the edges, before placing it carefully down with the rest.

"Dominoes," Will said, "they're like dominoes. The edges are quite worn, but didn't you notice the little notches on them? Look," he said, choosing one to show his father. "This has four notches on the end, and so it fits with the next, which has the matching four notches." He put it back into place and straightened up.

"Genius!" Dr. Burrows yelled, studying the arrangement intently, but then his shoulders sagged again. "So now I've got the sequence, but it doesn't really make any difference. I still need the Burrows Stone to decipher the engraved script. And we also don't yet know where the route starts from."

Will held up his hands. "I've got something else for you! Wait here!" he exclaimed, tearing over to his bunk, where he'd left his rucksack.

"I'm not exactly going anywhere," Dr. Burrows said bemusedly.

Will ran back to his father with something in his hand. But before he showed his father what it was, he drew his attention to the stone tablet that came first in his new arrangement. "Look at this, Dad. See the sign . . . right here?" He pointed at the three-pronged symbol carved minutely into the very top left-hand corner of the tablet.

"Sure," Dr. Burrows shrugged, as if it was nothing exceptional. "I found quite a few incidences of that symbol in the Deeps," he added as his son shuffled through the pack of photographs Rebecca One had given him.

"These belonged to a sailor on the sub. Just look at the last of them." Will slapped the photograph down in front of his father. "The same symbol," he announced. "The sailor must have taken that photo somewhere near the sub, near enough that he managed to get back there without being picked off by the Brights."

"No!" Dr. Burrows shouted. "So without knowing it, I could have been in the right place all along!"

"Then . . . then we've got to go there, now!" Will cried, matching his father's enthusiasm.

But Dr. Burrows just shook his head. "No, Will, we can't."

"Why not?" Will asked.

"Because it's important we establish a way back to the surface that we can use. Because I don't want us to become cut off from civilization again, in case there's any sort of emergency. If we can navigate to the top of the river, then it's going to be a cinch to get down here again. We can just let the river carry us." He was about to say something else, but instead rubbed his forehead. When he finally spoke again, his voice was almost a whisper. "And I have to see if your mother is all right. She must be worried sick by now — after all, it's not just me that's gone missing — there's you and Rebecca, too. She's all alone up there."

Dr. Burrows wouldn't meet Will's eyes, which made him instantly suspicious. His father had never seemed overly concerned about his mother before, and Will wondered why he should start now.

"Besides," Dr. Burrows blurted, as if it had only just occurred to him, "I thought you had to get that virus to someone on the surface. You said it was vital that you did?"

"S'pose so," Will said, feeling as if he'd just been dragged back to reality. He had been so carried away by the prospect of new adventures with his father that he'd pushed the Styx plot to the back of his mind. His father saw the turmoil on his face.

"What's the matter?" Dr. Burrows asked.

"Only that it might not actually *be* the Dominion virus," Will replied. "It might all be a waste of time."

"Why do you say that?"

Will frowned even more deeply. "Because just about everything else the Rebecca twins have done or said has been either a trick or a lie, and I still think it's weird that Rebecca One gave the phials to me. It's even weirder that Rebecca Two knew she had — remember she asked me for it at the submarine?"

Dr. Burrows thought for a second. "That aside, it seemed important to them to get it back, so maybe it is the real McCoy? And if you really believe it's so pandemically dangerous, you *have* to give it to the authorities and let them take care of it."

Will nodded in resignation. His father was absolutely right. As long as there was a chance, however slim, that the Dominion virus was in the phial, it was his responsibility to make sure it was put in the right hands so the Styx plot could be neutralized. "OK . . . but once we're Topsoil and I've dealt with the phials, I *will* be coming back with you, won't I? I want to help you see this through, Dad," he asked, his voice wavering slightly.

"Of course, of course," Dr. Burrows replied, still avoiding Will's gaze as he stooped to retrieve a black file by his feet. "But, right now, I've got something else for you to do."

Will took the folder and studied the plastic cover of the file, which was cracked where it hinged. The front was plain except for some letters and numbers, so he flipped it open. He was greeted by an exploded schematic of a piece of machinery. "What's this?" he asked, and then, as he thumbed back to the first page, he read, "*Outboard Motor Operation Manual*? Are you expecting me to read this or something?"

"You know I'm useless when it comes to anything mechanical. Perhaps you could bone up on it while I get the boat ready. If it's the wrong manual for the outboard we found, there are others in a bookcase in cubicle twenty-three, along with a whole load of novels by Alistair MacLean . . . and some weapons manuals."

Will's ears perked up at the mention of the weapons manuals. "I'm your man," he said.

Will spent the next forty-eight hours reading about how to prime and operate the outboard motor, occasionally nipping out to the quayside where he and his father had dragged it. Unbeknownst to Dr. Burrows, Will also sneaked into the armory to help himself to a selection of the guns, which he taught himself to fieldstrip on a blanket laid on the floor of one of the side rooms in the fallout shelter.

At the same time, Dr. Burrows was doing his bit. He'd used a rusting trailer to haul the fiberglass launch to the quayside and then put it on the water. Making sure it was tied securely to the pier, he proceeded to load it with provisions. He was just returning to the stores when he bumped into Will at the main blast door.

"Hot water's on," Will announced. His hair was slicked back and his face — for the first time in a long time — was clean from the shower he'd just taken. He was also wearing a fresh change of clothes: an olive-green shirt and matching cargoes.

Dr. Burrows stared at him, openmouthed.

"You want cubicle thirty-one for the quartermaster's stores and the clothes, and cubicle twenty-seven for the showers. I've left some shampoo and soap in there for you," Will merely said, continuing on his way outside. As Dr. Burrows watched him go, he spotted the Browning Hi-Power tucked down the back of his son's pants.

"Will! I told you not to —"

"It's not loaded," Will replied without missing a step. He grinned to himself as, once out of his father's sight, he threw the carton of rounds into the air and caught it. He knew that Dr. Burrows was unlikely to hear the gunshots from inside the fallout shelter. "Practice makes perfect," he said to himself.

The next day they lugged the outboard motor over to the launch and Will managed to bolt it in place. Getting it started was more problematic. The engine would catch and run for several seconds, then splutter out. Will tried to start it with the handle-pull so many times that he didn't have any strength left in his arms and Dr. Burrows had to take over. Sweating and coated in grease and grime, they eventually succeeded, the engine pouring out black smoke for several minutes as it ran unevenly. Then it stopped misfiring and settled into a regular throb. His father gave him the thumbs-up, his laughter lost in the noise of the engine. Will tilted the outboard so the screw just touched the water, then he revved it. A torrent sprayed out behind the launch.

"Job done," Will concluded as he cut the engine and the last reports of its deafening roar resounded in the cavern.

"Excellent!" Dr. Burrows congratulated him. "Remind me to stow some extra fuel on board before we set off." After they had climbed out of the boat and onto the pier, he looked at his son. "Teamwork," he said, patting him once gently on the shoulder, then together they walked back to the dormitory area.

After a good sleep and some breakfast, they both made their way out of the shelter and along to the pier where the launch was tethered.

"Cool coat, Dad," Will said as he admired the old duffle coat Dr. Burrows had found. With a hood and toggles up the front, it was made of a very heavy-duty, fawn-colored fabric, so stiff it looked as if it could stand up by itself.

"It's a classic Montgomery, made out of Fearnought blanket material. My father had one just like this, which he bought at an army surplus shop. I remember him wearing it when I was young," Dr. Burrows said affectionately. After he'd finished admiring his new coat, he looked up and noticed the two bulky khaki-colored holdalls his son was carrying. "Got enough in those?"

"I picked us out a couple of sleeping bags and some other gear that might come in handy," Will replied immediately, trying his best not to let his father see how heavy the holdalls were.

"I suppose it's a good idea to have a bit of ballast in the bottom of the launch — in case the going gets rough," Dr. Burrows said.

Will glanced down at the breast pocket of the combat jacket he'd requisitioned. "The only thing I'm really worried about is the Dominion phials. We can't lose them. Not at any cost."

They walked a little farther down the quayside, then Will spoke again.

"Dad, you do know the phials are the only reason I'm coming with you? Otherwise I'd have gone straight back to Chester and Elliott. And I will be going back for them once I've handed the virus over to someone."

Dr. Burrows came to a sudden halt. "Will, you've made that perfectly clear to me. And you don't really think I've finished down here, either, do you? I've only just scratched the surface." He shook his head. "No, I'm definitely coming back to see through what I've begun."

As they walked the remaining distance to the launch, his father muttered under his breath, "If we make it home."

They stowed all the equipment in the launch, then Dr. Burrows turned to him.

"I nearly forgot." He tugged a pair of black woolly hats from his duffle-coat pocket, and they both put them on. "Help to keep the chill out."

"Good idea, Dad," Will said, grinning wryly at his father. With his hat pulled down low over his head and his straggly growth of beard, Dr. Burrows really looked like some gnarled old sea captain.

"Onward and upward!" Dr. Burrows proclaimed as Will

started the outboard motor. They took the launch for a few laps around the harbor. Once Will had got the hang of how it handled, he did what his father had suggested and built up speed before he steered under the arch and out into the river channel. Dr. Burrows's suggestion was right on the money — and Will found he had to open the throttle even further in order to make any headway at all against the oncoming water.

As they left the illuminated section of river channel behind them, Dr. Burrows was positioned at the bow with the lamp so he could light the way. He acted as the pilot, shouting to Will if there were outcrops of rock to avoid or sharp turns in the channel. The ride was rougher than Will had expected. As the launch bounced along, both he and his father were very soon soaked to the skin by the spray from the icy-cold river and the occasional sheet of water that broke over the bows. Will was grateful for the woolly hat and the extra layers of clothing he'd donned for the journey.

The river seemed to go on forever, snaking up through the guts of the earth for mile after mile. The only sign that man had ever been there before came in the form of large white circles daubed on the rough walls — these were markers to show which direction to go when the river forked, as it did many times. So as Dr. Burrows kept an eye out for them, Will steered the launch upward, always upward, to the source of the river.

When Will was so tired he was finding it hard to control the outboard, his father swapped places with him at the helm. Although Will could have done with some sleep, this was impossible: Someone needed to be at the bow with the lamp, or else they would be sailing blind in all the confusion of the spray. While it wasn't any warmer there, at least it gave Will an opportunity to rest his aching arms.

They carried on without stopping because there was nowhere they *could* stop that would give them protection from the continuous onrush of water. It must have been almost a day later, in which time Dr. Burrows had repeatedly managed to refuel the outboard engine as it still ran, when Will spotted a different type of sign — a white circle, but this time with a black square within it. He gestured to his father to steer toward it. As they followed more of these signs around a bend, they found that the channel widened out considerably, so that it was at least a half mile wide.

In these less turbulent waters, they noticed something pale in the distance and Dr. Burrows steered the boat toward it. It turned out to be a metal pontoon, which must once have been painted white, although it was now largely discolored by rust. Just beyond it, they spotted a pier jutting out into the water and a small, man-made quay. Dr. Burrows cut the engine and they drifted into the side.

"Got it!" Will shouted as he caught hold of a metal railing, and brought the launch to a stop. After he'd tied up the bow rope, they clambered out.

"Good to be back on dry land again," Dr. Burrows said as he stamped his feet, taking pleasure in the solid ground beneath them. He pulled off his woolly hat and wrung it out while Will took a quick look around. The quay was a fraction of the size of the one they'd departed from, and he was back within a few minutes.

"Nothing much here, Dad. Just some fuel tanks and a small building that's completely empty except for a telephone."

"Thought as much," Dr. Burrows said. "This is probably a refueling stop — a kind of way station, where the barge and the boats could take on more gas. Good thing, too, as we've already gone through a couple of the spare cans. I was beginning to wonder if we'd have enough to make it to the top."

"Better check if there's any fuel in the tanks, then," Will said, and began to go off when he stopped and turned. "Dad, are we nearly there?"

Dr. Burrows chuckled, ramming a finger into his ear to try to get out the water. "You'd ask me that in the car when we used to go on our fossil-hunting trips. You couldn't wait to get there. Remember?"

Will smiled. "Well, *are* we nearly there?"

"Difficult to say, but I'd estimate we haven't gone a third of the distance yet," Dr. Burrows said. "Maybe less." He flapped his arms several times, then jumped up and down.

"Why are you doing that?" Will asked, intrigued.

"Notice how when you move it feels sort of sluggish?" He took hold of the kit bag he'd brought with him from the launch, then slowly lifted it up. "Even this feels heavier. By the time we reach the surface, we're going to feel as if we're made of lead."

"Yes, back to full gravity again. I hadn't thought of that," Will said, then sighed. "We're not going to have our superpowers anymore."

They set up camp in the building, lighting an oil stove in the doorway to warm themselves and dry their sopping clothing and boots. With some hot food in them, they crawled into

363

their sleeping bags and were sound asleep within minutes.

Will was woken by his father passing a mess tin of steaming hot fluid in front of his nose.

"Yuck! Not more of your *tea*," Will said, then groaned. "Can't I have another hour's kip? I'm wrecked."

"Stir yourself, lazy bones. Let's get this journey whipped," Dr. Burrows said, sitting back on his haunches.

Despite Will's protests, he got up and they soon set off in the launch again, coming upon several more refueling stations before, finally, a day and a half later, they pulled into a place that was far more substantial.

"I think we might be there," Dr. Burrows yelled from the helm.

23

ON THE OUTSKIRTS of Cardiff, a man unlocked his front door to let himself in. The house was in complete darkness, but he left the lights off as he put his umbrella on the hall table and made his way into the kitchen. Still without any illumination, he went over to the electric kettle and, checking it was full, flicked on the switch. He seemed to stare at the red light at the base of the kettle as the water heated up and made bumping sounds, until he reached over to a kitchen cabinet to get a mug.

"Sam," Drake said from the darkness.

The man gasped in surprise, dropping the mug, which fell to the floor and shattered.

"For the love of . . . Drake! Is that you, Drake?"

"Hi, Sam," Drake said. "Sorry to give you a fright like that, but if you leave the lights off . . ."

"I thought you were dead," the man said, barely taking a breath before his voice turned to anger. "What are you doing here? You shouldn't come anywhere near me. They might be watching."

"No, I made sure it was safe."

"It's never safe," Sam snapped.

"You always were a little jittery," Drake said, shaking his head. "How's the family, by the way?"

"I don't know — you tell me. I can't see them anymore — I had to walk out on them so they wouldn't be at risk." Sam moved toward the sink, his feet crunching on the broken mug. "I just hope you weren't spotted coming here," he said, still clearly very nervous. "You know *they* took the network apart, don't you? And that most of the old teams are dead, or buried so deep they might as well be dead?"

"Yep," Drake answered casually, which seemed to infuriate the man even more.

"Oh, sorry, I didn't realize this was a social call. I'd offer you some coffee, but I just broke my only mug."

"I need some help," Drake said.

"How do I know they haven't got to you?" Sam demanded. "You've been gone . . . what is it? Four years? They might have sent you here. How do I know I can trust you?"

"I could ask you the same thing. How do I know if I can trust *you*?" Drake shot back.

"You don't need to — my days of skulking around are over. I'm not that person anymore, and you're on your own, pal," Sam said, then sighed deeply. "I don't know how we ever thought we could win. They're just too cold-blooded, too shrewd, and too well established. It's an impossible contest."

"Be a man about it, Sam. Can't you call them by their name? You're talking about the *Styx*," Drake growled.

The man didn't speak as he shuffled another step toward the window and leaned against the sink. The light from outside was bright enough that Drake could see his profile; he was wearing dark glasses.

"Is something wrong with you?" Drake asked.

"They blinded me, Drake. I can't see a thing."

"How? What the heck happened?"

"I think they're using subsonics — similar to the Dark Light technology, but on a much larger scale," Sam replied. "I was driving to a rendezvous point north of Highfield when I stopped at a crossing. I heard a low, deep sound, as if I was underwater — it felt as though there was a vibration right inside my head. I couldn't move, not a muscle. I've no idea what happened next, but I came to a couple of days later in the hospital, with a bandage around my eyes. The *Styx* took my sight," he said, using their name for the first time, spitting it out as if it was poison in his mouth. "I'm still astounded they didn't just kill me."

"Maybe they were sending a signal to the rest of us," Drake said softly. "A warning."

"Maybe," Sam repeated. "But I can't go back to active duty, not the way I am now, Drake. Even if I wanted to."

"I only just surfaced from the Deeps. I'm sorry I didn't know about any of this."

"No, how could you have," Sam said emptily.

"I wonder who they grabbed Topsoil to help them develop the subsonic technology," Drake pondered.

"Perhaps it's homegrown — perhaps the scientists in the Colony did it all by themselves."

Drake cleared his throat. "I should go," he said.

"One thing before you do — I assume you remember the facility I set up on a remote server at the university when we first came together as a network? The secure message exchange that no one was supposed to know about?"

"Sure," Drake confirmed.

"Well, somebody does," Sam said.

"What do you mean?"

Sam rubbed his brow. "I don't know why I never took it offline when everything fell apart, and I still check it every so often. A couple of days ago there was a message for you. It's got a lot of noise on it, but it seems to be from someone called Will Burrows. Does that name mean anything to you?"

"Will Burrows . . . ," Drake repeated in a low-key way, not reacting to the information, although his heart skipped several beats. "No, doesn't ring a bell, but thanks all the same. I'll dial in to the server and have a listen," Drake said. "And I'm sorry I crashed in on you like this. Good luck, Sam."

"Before you go, can I do anything for you? Do you want something to eat?" Sam offered.

But Drake had already left.

"The river continues up there," Will pointed out to his father as they trudged down the long quayside, their soaked clothes dripping with water and their boots squelching. "So shouldn't we follow it along?"

"It might never hit the surface," Dr. Burrows said, shrugging. "Besides, look at all these buildings . . . and the crane." He and Will stood and contemplated the structures in front of them. "This place has to be a loading bay for the journey down. Especially given *that*," he added, pointing at a large arch at the end of the quay, its edges painted white.

They both approached it.

"Large enough to drive a truck through," Dr. Burrows observed.

"Not now," Will said as he knocked on the brick wall that completely sealed it up.

But Dr. Burrows was already striding purposefully off into the shadows. As Will caught up with him, he found his father next to a large double-sized doorway. Like the arch, the cast-concrete frame around it had been painted white.

"Personnel entrance, most likely," Dr. Burrows suggested. It had also been blocked up, and he pressed a palm to the surface. "Cinder blocks," he said. He tested several sections of the mortar, which oozed from the joints between the gray blocks and looked a little like dried toothpaste, tugging at a piece of it until it came away in his fingers. "Sloppy workmanship. This was done in a hurry."

"So what now?" Will asked.

"Unless we can find an alternative way out, it shouldn't be too difficult for us to knock through here."

After a quick search of the buildings and the rest of the quay, they realized that this was their only potential exit.

Dr. Burrows clapped his hands together. "Fetch the tools, will you?"

Will returned to the launch and clambered down into it. He considered his two holdalls of equipment. If his father wanted to knock a wall down, he could think of a quicker way to do it. Messier, but quicker.

"The tools!" Dr. Burrows yelled impatiently, and Will told himself it might be wiser to keep quiet about the explosives he'd squirreled away. Climbing out of the launch, he rushed over with the old canvas bag of tools that Dr. Burrows had helped himself to from the quartermaster's stores back in the fallout shelter.

Dr. Burrows rooted around inside it until he found a long crowbar. He immediately began to work on the wall, using the tapered end of the crowbar to chisel out the mortar in the joints between the blocks. "Soft as frosting," he mumbled to himself, as it proved rather easy to dislodge. Having cleared enough of the mortar from around one of the cinder blocks, he rammed the crowbar under it and began to lever on it. "Here we go," he said when the block finally came loose, dropping at his feet. "We're through! And it's only one layer thick!"

With Will at his side, he held his luminescent orb up to the opening. All they could see was blackness on the other side.

"We need to widen this," Dr. Burrows declared, thrusting the crowbar into Will's hands. Before Will had an opportunity to reply, his father muttered, "And I need some quiet time to think," then abruptly turned and left.

"Think about *what?*" Will called after him, but Dr. Burrows pretended not to hear. As he squelched off into the darkness, Will knew that his father was just going off to take a nap, and that he would be left to do the donkey work by himself.

"Nothing changes," Will complained as he started to work on the next block. "Nothing ever changes."

Will cleared a hole wide enough for them to get through, then went to fetch his father. He found him stretched out next to the oil stove, half asleep.

"How's that thinking going?" Will asked.

"Umf . . . good," Dr. Burrows said drowsily. "What about the wall?"

"It's done. There's a room on the other side."

At Dr. Burrows's insistence, they unloaded everything from the launch, then hauled it out of the water and onto the quayside. After they'd organized what they needed to take with them, they approached the opening Will had made.

"Be my guest," Dr. Burrows said.

His father behind him, Will climbed through the hole in the wall into what turned out to be a corridor filled with empty drums and some old planking. They soon came up against a sturdy metal door, two handles on one of its sides. With a combination of pulling, kicking, and bad language, they managed to get both grips into the open position, then heaved on the door.

"Not more water!" Will cried as a deluge of the most foul-smelling soupy fluid surged around them. Gasping from the stench, they waded into a room that was around fifty feet wide, with banks of lockers on either side. At the far end there was another door, but it was so badly rusted that they eventually gave up on it. They were also beginning to feel a little light-headed from the stench.

"Dad!" Will said, his voice muffled because he was holding his nose. He'd found out that what had appeared to be a cupboard was in fact an alternate entrance. The side room was about six feet square, and there were wide rungs set into the wall. Will raced up these, and smashed his way through some rotten planks at the top.

"Watch it!" his father shouted as pieces of timber landed on him, but Will didn't care — he just wanted out.

He forced his way through a bramble bush, then scrambled to his feet.

He was in the open.

"Topsoil," he gasped. He tottered slightly as he put his head back and took in the wide-open sky above. For some reason he felt an impulse to duck — it was just too much to take in.

"Wonder what time of day it is? Dusk?" Dr. Burrows pondered as he straightened up beside Will. "Or dawn?" he added, his voice downbeat as he peered at the dark, cloudless sky. Will turned to him.

"Dad! We're out! We did it!" he cried. He couldn't believe that his father wasn't over the moon. "We're home again!"

Dr. Burrows didn't answer immediately, and when he did his voice oozed with disappointment. "It's not exactly the *grand retour* I had in mind, Will. After all the things I saw and all my work down there . . ." He pressed the ball of his foot into the long grass in front of him. ". . . I wanted to come back with something that would wow the world. . . . I wanted to knock the socks off the archaeological community." Drawing in a breath, he held it for a few seconds. "Instead, all I've got to show is a bag of tools from the Cold War . . . ," he said, slinging it to the ground with a clatter, ". . . and one of the worst haircuts in history. No, without my journal, my esteemed colleagues would just have to take my word for the whole shebang, for everything I saw . . . and . . . well . . . that just ain't going to happen, is it?"

Will nodded, now understanding the reason for his father's

pessimism. He wondered if he should broach the subject of the Styx again. His father was in for a rude awakening if he thought that he'd have a free hand to publish all his secrets, because many of those were the Styx's secrets, too. They would never allow him to do it. But Will knew if he mentioned this it would most likely result in another argument with his father, and he wasn't in the mood. He was just too dog-tired to get into that now.

Instead he plucked a leaf from a small sapling and crumpled it in his hand, smelling it, smelling the *greenness* of it. It had been awhile since he'd encountered anything remotely like it. "Where do you think we are?" he asked.

"Well, one thing's for sure — it's not an extinct volcano in Iceland," Dr. Burrows smirked as he shone his light around, the beam catching the foliage of the mature trees that seemed to be everywhere.

Will took a few steps. "It might not even be England. We've come such a long way."

"I sincerely doubt we've gone *that* far."

In the failing light, they began to explore, pushing their way through the undergrowth.

There seemed to be many abandoned buildings concentrated within a relatively small area. And what could have been a roadway ran between them, although so many bushes had encroached on the asphalt surface, it was difficult to tell it apart from the surrounding vegetation.

The buildings were brick-built, either one or two stories high, and nearly all had broken windows. It was no problem for Will and his father to gain entry; all the doors were open or off their hinges. Inside, paint chips that had peeled off from the ceilings speckled the floors, giving the impression they were covered in snow. Will and Dr. Burrows were exploring the first floor of one of these buildings when, in the distance, they spotted the twin headlights of a vehicle lancing through the rapidly amassing darkness.

"I don't know who they are," Dr. Burrows whispered, "but I don't want to tangle with them. I say we get our heads down for a few hours and check the place over first thing in the morning."

"Sure," Will agreed, hoping his father was going to suggest just that, because he was dropping on his feet. They found themselves a dry corner in one of the ground-floor rooms, and slid into their sleeping bags.

They left the luminescent orb on the floor between them, half covering it so that the light wouldn't alert anyone to their presence. Through his weary eyes, Will watched the branch of a tree that had grown in through one of the broken windows. When he finally couldn't keep his eyes open any longer, he let them slide shut, and filled his lungs with the cool air. It might have been because of his roots in the Colony, where his real family had come from, or because he'd been underground for so long, but he found that he was incredibly sensitive to the rhythms there on the surface. And it wasn't the chirping insects or the occasional call of birds on the wing, but the silent rhythms, the rhythms of nature. He could almost feel the vegetation around him as it grew.

But more than this, he missed the rhythms that had been so much part of his life deep in the earth — the almost imperceptible settling of rock and soil, and the odors that somehow interacted with the base of the nose, that felt primal and basic and safe. Although he wouldn't have said anything about it to his father, he was already missing his subterranean existence. And with that thought fading in his mind, he drifted into a dead sleep.

Will rolled over onto his back and fluttered open his eyes.

He cried out as the bright dawn light burned his retinas, and he quickly jerked back into the shadows, holding his eyes. After much blinking, he slowly emerged into the light again, still shielding his face. As he wriggled out of his sleeping bag and put on his boots, he felt as though every move he made was incredibly leaden, then realized it was the effects of the gravity. Normal gravity.

"Morning," his father said cheerfully, crunching over broken glass as he entered the room.

"Morning," Will replied, then yawned cavernously.

Dr. Burrows glanced at him. "Feeling rough?"

"Yep," Will said through another yawn.

"You might be suffering from a form of jet lag. *Subterranean lag*," Dr. Burrows said with a laugh as he lit the stove and put a pot of water on it. He checked his watch and then glanced at Will. "You've no idea how long you've slept, or what time it is, do you?" He didn't wait for his son to respond. "You do realize you've probably been operating on days of more than twenty-four hours? Your circadian rhythms will be all over the shop."

"What do you mean?" Will asked, not because he was really interested, but because his father expected it of him.

"In the absence of daylight, the melatonin level in the brain doesn't follow normal patterns. It should rise as the sun goes down, so you feel sleepy." Dr. Burrows reached over to pick up the luminescent orb, examining how the fluids inside had turned oil-black in the presence of daylight. "Underground, all we've got is these. The light they emit is close to sunlight, but it's always on, and doesn't follow the night-and-day sequence we're used to up —"

"Oh, Dad, can you tell me about this another time?" Will pleaded with him. "I'm not really taking it in."

His father fell into a peeved silence, which continued as they drank their oversweetened tea.

"Right," Dr. Burrows began, "if you're quite ready to listen to me now."

Will mumbled a yes.

"We're in an abandoned air base — I'm not sure where, exactly, but it's definitely England — and there seems to be a security patrol, but they're not soldiers. Probably a private contractor. So, come on, pack up what we need to take with us, and hide the rest of it here."

"Why? What's the big hurry?" Will asked.

"Because we're going to London," Dr. Burrows said.

They took a quick look around the base, as Dr. Burrows rambled on about what he thought each building was. One of them had earth banked up around its walls and also a thick wall just in front of its entrance — Dr. Burrows said it was to protect it from bombing. The interior had been stripped, except for an antiquated air-conditioning system and yards of electrical cable running everywhere — Dr. Burrows said he thought it was a control center. On the opposite side of the building was another entrance, but this place turned out to have a more macabre purpose. They found themselves in a long room with a series of metal racks against one wall. Each rack had three tiers, and each tier had a number stenciled on the whitewashed wall at the end of it.

"Disinfectant," Will announced, sniffing the air. "Was this a hospital or something?"

"Probably a morgue," Dr. Burrows said.

"What — for dead bodies?" Will asked.

His father nodded as they emerged into the daylight again. He pointed to a church spire in the distance.

"Let's head for that — there'll be a road nearby."

They came to a huge stretch of tarmac, cracked and covered with piles of broken-up concrete.

"S'pose this was the runway?" Will asked, scanning it up and down, and squinting across at the large warehouselike structures beside it.

"They're called *C-Class hangars*," Dr. Burrows said, noticing where Will was looking. "All this is postwar, like the deep-level shelter they built below."

Crossing a field, Will and Dr. Burrows went through a hedge, then scrambled down a sparse verge to find themselves on a single-lane road, which they began to follow. It took them to a tiny village, and Dr. Burrows made a beeline for the only shop there, a combined post office and convenience store.

Before they entered, Will clapped a cautionary hand on his father's arm.

"Money! We haven't got any money!"

"Oh, haven't we?" Dr. Burrows replied. With great ceremony he unbuckled and took off his belt. There was a zipper on the inside of the belt, which he opened; then he pulled out a polyethylene bag with a rubber band wound around it. Inside this bag was a roll of bank notes, which he counted and stuffed into his pocket. "We need to make sure we've got enough to pay for any traveling expenses, so don't go wild in there, Will," he said.

A bell rattled above the door as they entered, and a portly man bumbled out from a back room. Will selected himself some potato chips and a soda from the fridge, while Dr. Burrows only had eyes for the display of chocolates, adding a newspaper as an afterthought.

"Looks like it's going to be a nice day," the man said congenially, wheezing a little as he spoke. He was dressed in a brown checkered shirt and a woven tie, which looked as though it was made from material better suited for a pair of socks.

"It does," Dr. Burrows agreed. He cleared his throat, then said, "Can I ask where, exactly, this is?"

"Where this is?" The man had been totting up the items but stopped to run his eyes over Dr. Burrows.

"The name of the village?"

"West Raynham," the man replied, a little flummoxed.

"West Raynham," Dr. Burrows repeated several times, as if he was trying to remember if he'd heard of it before. "And what county is this?"

"Norfolk . . . North Norfolk," the man replied, now giving Will a curious look.

"Been on the road a long time," Dr. Burrows explained.

"Ah," the man nodded, ringing up the till.

"And if we wanted to go to London, what would be the best way?" Dr. Burrows asked as he handed over a creased twenty-pound note.

"By car?" the man said, as he straightened out the note between his stubby fingers and held it to the light to check the watermark. He seemed satisfied with it and placed it under the tray in the till.

"No, by bus or train."

"Then you'd be wanting the nearest town — Fakenham — about six miles away." The man pointed out the direction, then put his hand to his mouth as he coughed. He drew in several asthmatic breaths before he went on. "You can get a bus from there into Norwich and catch the train. Or there's the coach twice a day from Fakenham to London — it's slow, but it's cheaper."

"The coach it is, then," Dr. Burrows decided. "Thank you very much," he said as took his change.

Will was holding the door open for his father, who suddenly stopped, frowning as if he'd forgotten something. He turned to the man, who was still behind the counter. "By the way, there hasn't been an epidemic here in England, has there, in the last couple of months?"

"Epidemic?" Will heard the man ask.

"Any outbreak of disease, with people dying?" Dr. Burrows clarified.

"No, nothing like that," the man replied in a considered way. "Nasty stomach bug going around, that's all."

"Thought not. Thanks again," Dr. Burrows said. As the door swung shut behind them, he leaned toward Will. "So much for a *Styx plague* cutting *swaths* through *the population*," he whispered theatrically, as if he was daring to mention some terrible secret.

"I didn't say it had happened yet," Will defended himself. "And it won't if I have anything to do with it, and I have, with the phials I've got."

"No, quite," Dr. Burrows said, without any conviction. "Still time to save the world."

Will let his father's comments go, and they sat on a wall outside the shop, enjoying their purchases. As he savored every mouthful of the chips, washing them down with his Diet Coke, Will closed his eyes in bliss. "Never thought I'd miss the little things like this so much," he said.

Dr. Burrows was silent as he ate his bars of chocolate. "You can say that again," he said as he swallowed down the last of them. Then he leaped off the wall. "Chocks away, old chap!" he announced exuberantly, sweeping his arm through the air. When Will just looked at him, he grinned idiotically, and added, "I'm joking, Will — don't you get it? Chocks away — we were on an airfield — that's what they do with old aircraft — take the chocks away from the wheels — and I've just eaten choccy! It's a joke."

"Are you feeling all right, Dad?" Will asked. His father was behaving very oddly, and wasn't usually one to make jokes.

Dr. Burrows frowned. "I think I just had a sugar rush," he admitted. "Might have overdone it."

"I think you might have," Will said, easing himself off the wall.

But Dr. Burrows was still buzzing and staunchly refused to investigate whether there was a bus they could catch to the nearby town. "Walk'll do us good. Forward to Fakenham," he declared bombastically, striding off through the rest of the village.

When they finally arrived in Fakenham, hot and tired, they found it was market day. The traders were setting out their wares on their stalls and standing around sipping tea from styrofoam cups. Dr. Burrows found the stop where the coaches departed from, and scanned the timetable for the next one to London. They had a couple of hours to kill, and loitered around the main square as more and more people arrived for the market. As the area became increasingly crowded, Will felt decidedly uncomfortable. He kept looking over his shoulder, trying to check everyone out. But there were just too many of them.

"Dad," he said, flicking his thumb at a café up the road.

"Why not? I'd kill for a cup of coffee," Dr. Burrows agreed. He hesitated. "Will, be careful what you eat. You saw what happened to me," he advised soberly. "We should avoid too much sugar or fat because we're simply not used to it." And despite Will's pleas to have a full English breakfast, they only ordered toast and something to drink, then took a table in the corner of the café.

People at other tables were glancing warily at them, not because of their olive drab army uniforms, which actually weren't that out of place in the town, but because, Will assumed, of their extremely dirty and rather odd hairstyles. Will twiddled one of his white dreadlocks between his fingers as he studied his father's spiky hair. Dr. Burrows did look like a time-expired punk rocker as he sat there, engrossed in his paper. Will leaned over to him. "Do you think we should do something about our hair? I reckon we might stick out a bit, and we don't want the police on our backs, do we? Don't forget we're missing, as far as they're concerned."

Dr. Burrows contemplated his son's suggestion, then nodded. "Not a bad idea, Will," he concluded. He went over to ask the lady behind the counter where the nearest barber's was, and they headed for it.

Will wasn't too sure when his father asked the barber for a short back and sides for each of them, and even less so as he watched his long hair being shorn off in the mirror. However, when they were both done, their tidy new haircuts went quite nicely with their military clothing. The coach was on time, and they boarded it. But the journey was incredibly protracted; the coach seemed to be stopping at every town on the way, although Will and Dr. Burrows used the opportunity to catch up on their sleep. As they became stuck in traffic on the approach to London, Will half opened an eye and surveyed the rows of stationary cars and trucks in the other lanes, and the skyline of the city in the distance. "Too many people," he mumbled drowsily, then went back to sleep.

By midafternoon, the coach finally pulled up and the door opened with a pneumatic hiss.

"Euston Station! Everyone out!" the driver shouted.

"I'm never going to get used to this," Will muttered as they made their way to the concourse at the front of the station, where hordes of people were milling around and they could hear the constant rumble of traffic from nearby Euston Road. Dr. Burrows didn't seem to be concerned by it in the slightest.

"Quick — that bus! It'll take us to Highfield!" he exclaimed, pointing. Then he looked confused. "But where are all the double-deckers?"

PART 5

HIGHFIELD AGAIN,

24

AS THEY DISEMBARKED from the bus in Highfield, Dr. Burrows unexpectedly turned down Main Street rather than up it. "Just want to take a quick look at the museum, Will," he said.

"Dad . . . it's not safe. I don't think we . . . ," Will started to object, but from the determined way his father was striding along with his chin in the air, he knew he was wasting his breath.

Reaching the museum, Dr. Burrows went up the steps and pushed his way through the door, Will trailing a couple of paces behind.

Will was just thinking that the main hall looked more brightly lit than he remembered as his father took a few steps, then stopped in his tracks. Dr. Burrows surveyed the scene in a somewhat proprietary manner until his gaze alighted on a far corner.

"What's all this over here?" he exclaimed, and immediately strode off again.

His boots squeaked on the polished parquet flooring as he drew up sharply in front of a tall glass display case. In it, a mannequin sporting a Second World War infantry sapper's uniform stood in all its glory. "But what's become of *my* military display?" he muttered, casting around for the pair of battered showcases in which he'd arranged a disorganized jumble of tarnished buttons, regimental badges, and rusty ceremonial swords.

Will made his way to a bank of new displays behind the mannequin. "*Remembering Highfield's Finest,*" he read out loud as his father joined him. Together, they leaned over the sloping tops of the glass cases to study the ration and identity books, the gas masks and other wartime items, all beautifully labeled with names and explanations of their uses.

Sucking in his breath, Dr. Burrows turned to regard a TV screen set into a brilliant white melamine console by the side of the new glass cases. "*Press to activate,*" he mumbled as he read the instructions on the screen and thrust a finger at it. It immediately began to play a sequence of black-and-white films, which looked like excerpts from old newsreels. The first scenes were at nighttime and showed firemen with hoses battling to put out blazing houses. "*I remember those days so well, as though they were yesterday,*" began an elderly, wavering voice. "*My father was one of the first in Highfield to volunteer as an Air Raid Warden.*"

Will watched as scenes of the aftermath of the raid came on. In hazy sunlight, men in dusty uniforms were frantically picking over rubble strewn across pavements and the front gardens of houses. The commentary continued: "*The heaviest bombing came in February 1942, when there was a direct hit on the Lyons Tea Rooms in the South Parade of shops. I remember it was packed with people having their lunch when the Germans dropped a land mine. It was just awful . . . the injured and the dead, everywhere. And there was another raid that night, even worse than the first.*"

Then Will watched a clip of a pair of old men just sitting on a couple of chairs in the remains of the ground floor of a house, staring blankly at the camera as they smoked. They looked exhausted, and defeated. He tried to imagine their suffering — not only had they lost their homes and all their belongings, but their wives and children had probably perished in the bombing. All of a sudden their plight touched Will — he found it very poignant, and was struck by the realization that whatever he'd gone through, it couldn't be worse than what these men and many hundreds of thousands of others had faced in that war. He concentrated on the commentary again.

"My father worked for two whole days and nights to find —"

Dr. Burrows stopped the film with a jab at the screen.

"I was watching that, Dad," Will said. His father clucked and gave him a frosty look before stumping off toward the door at the far end of the hall, beyond which lay the archives and his old office.

But just as Dr. Burrows reached the doorway, a young man stepped out and blocked his way.

"I'm sorry, sir, you can't go in there. It's off-limits to the public," the man said pleasantly but firmly. "Museum staff only, I'm afraid." He was dressed in a smart blue suit with a lapel badge identifying him as CURATOR. He looked very young, even to Will's eyes.

"I am —" Dr. Burrows began and immediately halted as, unseen by the man, Will nudged his father in the small of the back.

Dr. Burrows grunted, and the man took a step back. Will realized how odd his father must appear to him, with his old

Navy duffle coat done up the neck, and the woolly hat pulled down low over his head.

"Can I be of assistance, sir? I saw you were admiring our new interactive display — I'd be delighted to give you a guided tour of our other exhibits." The young man glanced around the floor of the museum and lowered his voice as if he was confiding some vital secret to Dr. Burrows. "I'm afraid that many of them are rather unexceptional. You might have noticed that this museum is a little, er . . . how shall I put it . . . in need of modernization. It was badly neglected by the previous management." He drew in a long breath as if preparing himself for a massive task. "But now that I'm at the helm, I intend to revamp the whole place with the help of some p-r-e-t-t-y substantial funding I've secured."

The man smiled, expecting an enthusiastic response from Dr. Burrows, but his smile evaporated as he got something altogether different.

"I like it precisely the way it is," Dr. Burrows said as if someone was strangling him.

Will's heart went out to his father. All Dr. Burrows's work at the museum had been belittled in a few throwaway sentences. As Will watched him, Dr. Burrows's head lowered and he seemed to deflate. Will wanted to say something, but he couldn't think of the right words. What was so ironic was that his father had absolutely nothing to be ashamed of.

With all the innumerable and outstanding discoveries he'd made in the Colony and the Deeps, Dr. Burrows would one day be lauded as a great explorer and scientist, perhaps the greatest of the century. But none of that seemed to matter to him right now, as he stood there, his shoulders bowed with disappointment. Will couldn't understand why his father still seemed to care so much about this rather third-rate place, which could never hope to compete with the wealthier museums in central London.

"A lot of time and effort was put into all these displays, you know," Dr. Burrows said. "I think they're very effective."

"Well, to each his own," the young man replied defensively. "These days it's a different game entirely. It's all about interactivity and community involvement. The trick is to give the kids some buzzy new technology to get their attention, and also to pull in the local people by inviting them to participate in time capsules and the like. Yes, Interaction and Involvement spells Interest and Income. The 'four *I*'s' principle."

As Will scanned the hall, he wondered if the new curator's vision would prove to be successful in Highfield. Perhaps this rather dusty and neglected museum was a true reflection of the heart of the borough.

"So, do you live around here?" the curator asked, breaking the silence.

"Sort of," Dr. Burrows replied.

"Well, if you're interested, I'm always on the lookout for people to assist me with the running of the museum, you know, to help on —"

"Weekends," Dr. Burrows cut in. "Ah, yes, the Saturday squad."

The curator's mood changed and he grinned, imagining he'd found a new recruit.

"I assume you've got Major Joe signed up, and then there'll

be Pat Robbins, Jamie Dodd . . . ," Dr. Burrows said, ". . . and, I'll bet, Franny Bartok."

The curator nodded at each name as Dr. Burrows reeled them off. Will had stepped to his father's side and saw the twinkle in his eye as he continued to speak. He was definitely up to something.

"And how could I forget the one and only Oscar Embers," Dr. Burrows ended his list.

"Oscar Embers?" The curator stopped nodding. "No, I don't recall anyone of that name."

"No? Are you sure . . . he was a retired actor and always the most passionate and committed of the bunch."

The curator couldn't help but notice the look that passed between Dr. Burrows and Will.

"No, I've never come across him," the curator said categorically, then narrowed his eyes as if he was becoming suspicious. "And can I ask you, sir, how you come to be so knowledgeable about my volunteers when I've never met *you* before?"

"I was . . . ," Dr. Burrows began, but was interrupted by Will, who coughed loudly to warn his father not to say any more. ". . . I helped out your predecessor when he was here and, er, got to know him well."

"Ah, that would be Dr. . . . ," the curator said, then frowned as he grasped for the name. "Bellows or Bustows, or something like that."

"Burrows, Dr. Burrows," Dr. Burrows snapped.

"Yes, that's it. I assume you know the poor chap went missing — it was before I took over the reins here, so I've no idea what he was like."

"A very impressive man," Dr. Burrows said tersely. "And now, I regret to say, we have to be on our way."

"Are you sure I can't give you a quick tour around the new exhibits?"

"Maybe another time. Thank you, anyway, and good luck with your plans," Dr. Burrows said as he turned smartly. He was muttering to himself, but it wasn't until he was outside that he really let loose.

"Interactive! Bah! That young just-out-of-university novice will burn buckets of money, and all for nothing. Then the museum will run short of funds and probably be closed down, and my collection will be mothballed for all eternity." He stamped his foot on the pavement with such force that it echoed across the road.

"Dad, just cool it, will you?" Will urged him, concerned that his father's behavior was attracting unwanted attention. "I know why you were asking about Oscar Embers," he said, attempting to distract his father by getting him on a new tack. "It is really weird that the curator hasn't heard of him. He was always hanging around, wasn't he?"

"Yes," Dr. Burrows agreed, "very strange."

"So that twin was probably telling the truth about him being a Styx agent, and we should get the heck out of here. I tell you — we're not safe in Highfield."

Dr. Burrows pursed his lips thoughtfully and suddenly stuck his finger in the air. "I know! Oscar must have died, before that new doofus took over," he declared cheerfully. "After all, Oscar was no spring chicken! And there's one way to find out if that's what happened."

"How?" Will tried to ask, but his father strode off at full speed again.

They headed up Main Street, pausing outside a shop that was in the process of being gutted by a team of builders. Dr. Burrows surveyed the old green-painted shelves, which had been torn out and piled on the pavement in front of the shop.

"Clarke's has gone. Is nothing sacred?" he said, referring to the old fruit and vegetable shop that had been there since anyone could remember. "That's the supermarket chains for you!" he fumed. Will guessed immediately that there was more to the shop's closure than that. He was on the point of telling his father about the Clarke brothers' special relationship with the Colony, but decided against it. Dr. Burrows was having a hard enough time coping with what he already knew — Will didn't want to make it any more complicated for him.

Turning off Main Street, they marched past the old convent and very shortly came to Gladstone Street, where Dr. Burrows paused in front of a row of almshouses.

"What are we doing here, Dad?" Will asked.

"Checking the facts," Dr. Burrows replied as he advanced toward a narrow alleyway between two of the small houses. He seemed to know exactly where he was going as he disappeared into the darkness. Will followed a few paces behind, anxious that he couldn't see anything at all around him. He slowed for a second as his foot clipped an empty milk bottle, sending it rattling over the cobblestones.

As he emerged into the light again, Will saw that the alley was bordered on both sides by garden walls, and that it was sealed off at the end by an old factory building with tall windows. There seemed to be no other way in or out of the alley except the way they'd entered. Will couldn't for the life of him think why his father was interested in this place. Then Dr. Burrows went up to the wall on their right and peered over it.

"Who lives here?" Will inquired, joining his father at the wall and looking at the unkempt garden. A plump cat padded over the patchy grass, carefully avoiding the numerous plastic bowls of filthy water that seemed to be everywhere. Then Will remembered what he'd read in his father's journal, which he and Chester had found all those months ago. "This is where the luminescent orb was discovered, isn't it?"

"Yes — this is Mrs. Tantrumi's house."

Will shrugged. "So what are we doing here?"

"She was a friend of Oscar's," Dr. Burrows told him.

"So, what, are you going to ask her what happened to him?"

"Yes, that was my intention," Dr. Burrows confirmed decisively. "And there was more than just the luminescent orb here."

Will looked searchingly at his father. "What do you mean?"

"The orb was found in the basement just beyond those steps over there," Dr. Burrows told him, glancing at the dark doorway. "There was also a wardrobe downstairs, stuffed full of Colonists' coats."

"Colonists' coats," Will repeated, then realized what his father had said. "Dad, what are you thinking!" he burst out. "You must be going mad!" He was looking nervously around now. "This is probably a route down to the Colony — there could be Styx in that house."

"No, just a sweet old lady," Dr. Burrows told him.

"But, Dad," Will whined, stamping his foot. He was so frustrated that his father wasn't listening to him, he suddenly felt like he was a child of five years old again, not getting his way. He seized hold of Dr. Burrows by the arm as if he was about to drag him forcibly away from the wall. "This is just crazy. We've got to get away from here," Will pleaded. "We have to!"

Dr. Burrows turned to give him a stern look. "Unhand me, Will."

Will did as he was told and released his father's arm. He recognized the resolve in his father's voice as he spoke. "I've spent too much of my life hanging back from what I should've done. It's all too easy to find an excuse to put things off until another day. Heaven knows, *I* should know. But right at this moment, I need to investigate what your sister . . . ," he faltered for a beat, ". . . that twin said. I have to find out if Oscar really was some sort of Styx agent. I have to check the facts for myself."

"I suppose you're right, Dad," Will agreed reluctantly.

"Good," Dr. Burrows said, straightaway hauling himself on top of the wall, then jumping down the other side. As he landed in the mud, his feet slid from under him and he sat right on top of one of the numerous bowls. The sharp crack of breaking plastic resounded around the garden, and in the ensuing silence Dr. Burrows swore and hauled himself to his feet, wiping the algae from his duffle coat. "Not again," he muttered to himself.

Full of misgiving, Will remained where he was, watching as his father went to the back door and knocked on it gently.

"Mrs. Tantrumi," Dr. Burrows called. "Are you there? It's me . . . Roger Burrows."

The door opened a crack and an enormous ball of black-and-white fur bolted out. It flew straight between Dr. Burrows's legs and into the garden. Startled, Dr. Burrows muttered "Cat?" as he tottered back a couple of steps.

A wrinkled face peeped shortsightedly through the gap.

"Hello? Who's that?"

"Mrs. Tantrumi, it's all right. It's only me, Roger Burrows."

"Who?"

"Dr. Burrows. I . . . um . . . dropped in to see you last year about the luminescent orb that Oscar Embers brought to me. Do you remember?"

The door opened fully. The old lady had wispy white hair and was wearing an apron that wasn't tied properly, so that large yellow and white flowers ran at rather an odd angle across her body. She also appeared to be very unsteady on her feet, and was hanging on to the doorjamb as if she needed it to support herself. She adjusted her glasses, clearly finding it a struggle to focus on Dr. Burrows. "Yes, of course I remember you," she eventually answered. "You're from the museum. You wrote me that lovely letter."

"Yes, that's right," Dr. Burrows said in a relieved voice.

"How lovely that you've come to see me again," she grinned, her lined face lighting up. "You must join me for a cup of tea."

"That would be very nice," Dr. Burrows replied warmly as the old lady waddled back into the kitchen.

Dr. Burrows remained by the open door, stooping to stroke an ancient and painfully thin ginger-colored cat. To his surprise, the cat hissed and lashed out at him.

"Orlando! Mind your manners, you naughty boy! I'm so sorry, Dr. Burrows. He's not used to strangers. I hope he didn't scratch you."

"Not badly," Dr. Burrows said, rubbing his finger where a claw had caught the skin. He narrowed his eyes angrily at the cat, which was still standing there with its scraggy ruff up, like a feline guard dog. "Mrs. Tantrumi, I actually came here to ask you about Oscar Embers. Is he all right?"

Mrs. Tantrumi stood up from the sink, the tap running on full as she gripped the handle of the kettle so tightly Dr. Burrows could see her knuckles drain of blood.

"No, he's not. Poor soul tripped on the pavement and broke his arm." She stared at the water swirling around and dwindling down the drain as she spoke. "Then he picked up a nasty infection in Highfield General Hospital, and was terribly ill. He did get better, but they said he couldn't look after himself and packed him off to a nursing home, so I don't see him anymore."

"Do you know which nursing home he went into?" Dr. Burrows inquired.

"No, I don't, and I can't visit him, anyway, not with my hips the way they are," she said mournfully. "I do miss him so. He was a good friend."

"I'm very sorry," Dr. Burrows said, rather unconvincingly. "But you must have *some* idea which home he's in."

"No, dear, I don't," Mrs. Tantrumi replied, finishing the

task of filling the kettle, then swaying over to the stove with a series of *"oohs"* and *"aahs,"* as if each step was causing her considerable discomfort.

"Poor old Oscar," Dr. Burrows said distantly, turning to regard the doorway to the basement. "Would you mind if I took another look down there, where the luminescent orb was found?"

"Ludicrous orb, dear? What's that?" she asked, squinting at him.

"The object you very kindly donated to the museum. Do you remember?"

Mrs. Tantrumi thought for a second, her frail hands trembling. "Oh, of course, I know — the glass ball. Yes, please do have a look, if you want." She took a large tin from the kitchen counter. "Would you like a biscuit first?" she offered, as she struggled to get the lid off.

Clutching his Garibaldi biscuit, Dr. Burrows glanced at Will, whose head was just visible as he peered over the garden wall from the alleyway. Dr. Burrows raised his eyebrows at Will, then made his way down the mossy brick steps to the basement. Once there he went straight for the area that lay toward the front of the house. All was silent in the darkened basement, except for the sound his feet were making in the dirt.

As his eyes adjusted to the gloom, he saw that the wardrobe wasn't where it had been before. In fact, there was no sign of it anywhere. "What the blazes!" he muttered. "Somebody's nicked it!"

Still muttering to himself, he took a moment to give the old piano another quick inspection. Moldering against a damp wall, it appeared to be in an even worse state than the last time he'd seen it; one side had become detached and the instrument sat lopsidedly, as if it was at the point of collapsing altogether. Lifting the lid, Dr. Burrows found that many of the keys now didn't make any sound at all when he played them.

Stamping his feet on the ground by the base of the walls, he made a complete circuit of the basement, certain that somewhere he was going to find a trapdoor. But the ground felt solid enough, and he'd just decided to check the walls themselves when he heard a noise behind him.

He wheeled around.

Silhouetted in the light coming from the garden stairwell, a figure lurched at him. It was wielding something in its hand, something that glinted like polished steel.

"YOU'VE MEDDLED ONCE TOO OFTEN!" the figure shrieked.

"Mrs. Tantrumi!" Dr. Burrows cried as he recognized his assailant.

The speed at which the old lady was moving took him completely by surprise. Her face set in a vicious snarl, she lunged at him with the knife, not showing any trace of the frailty she'd exhibited before.

All of a sudden there was a resounding crash, and Garibaldi biscuits and custard cream cookies flew everywhere. Mrs. Tantrumi stopped dead in her tracks, the knife fell from her hand, and she keeled over.

"Will!" Dr. Burrows gasped. His son stood over the crazed old lady.

"I couldn't decide whether to use this," Will said, holding up the dented and now empty biscuit tin, "or a flowerpot to wallop her one."

Dr. Burrows's face was a picture of confusion as he attempted to deal with what had just taken place. "She . . . she was going to *stab* me." He looked gratefully at his son. "Thank you, Will."

"No problem."

They both peered down at Mrs. Tantrumi, who was lying on her side. Although she'd been stunned by the blow, she seemed to be recovering quickly. She rubbed her cranium with an aggrieved expression, then immediately tried to get the knife again.

"What do we do now?" Dr. Burrows asked, as he watched the old lady's hand snaking toward the weapon.

"Stop her from killing us?" Will suggested. He took a step toward her and, without applying much pressure, placed a foot on her wrist to pin it to the ground.

"Gerroff!" She seemed to have all her strength back now and, behaving like one of her feral cats, she proceeded to hiss and spit at Will and his father. "Your time is coming!" she ranted. "Nobody escapes the Colony!"

"Just a sweet old lady, huh?" Will said.

Shaking his head, Dr. Burrows watched the old woman with horrified fascination as she strained to free her hand from under Will's foot. "I don't believe it," he murmured.

"You'd better," his son told him.

"But—"

"No, you listen to me, Dad: They have people all over. Granny Gruesome here is obviously one of their agents, so it follows that Oscar Embers was, too, just like the Rebecca twin said. The Styx even have people in the police and in the government, so we can't trust *anybody*. From now on, we tread really carefully. Got that?"

"DEAD! YOU ARE BOTH DEAD!" Mrs. Tantrumi screamed as Will stooped to pick up the knife, still not releasing her hand from under his foot.

"I don't think so," Will sneered back at her. "And we're going to put a stop to you and your foul friends if it's the last thing we do."

"IT WILL BE!" she screeched. "THERE ARE TOO MANY OF US!"

"Come on, Dad, let's get away from this stinking old witch." Curling his lip in disgust, Will slung the knife through the doorway behind him. There was a startled meow from outside in the garden.

"Oops, think I got one," Will said. Mrs. Tantrumi exploded into such language and at such volume that Dr. Burrows covered his ears.

Will took his foot off Mrs. Tantrumi's wrist and backed away quickly, closely followed by Dr. Burrows, who had no intention of being left alone with the frenzied woman. As they climbed the steps to the garden, squinting in the bright light, a figure leaped from the top of the wall and landed on the muddy lawn, deftly avoiding the many plastic bowls of stale water.

"What happened in there?" it demanded in an urgent whisper.

Will couldn't believe his eyes.

"Drake!" he exclaimed.

"Drake?" Dr. Burrows repeated.

"Tell me what just happened," Drake demanded again, jerking his head at the basement. "Who's in there?"

"A Styx agent," Will answered. "I can't — I've got — you have to — the virus — how did you —?" he gabbled, everything he wanted to say to Drake coming out in an incoherent torrent.

"Not now," Drake cut him short. He whipped out a handgun and offered it to Will. "Take this. The safety's off."

"It's all right — I've got my own," Will said, hooking his jacket aside to show Drake the Browning Hi-Power tucked into his waistband.

Dr. Burrows clucked with disapproval at his son, but Drake flashed him a brief smile. "Cool. By the way, love the new look," he said, as he took in Will's short hair and combat fatigues. Then Drake was in action again, slipping past Dr. Burrows and cautiously descending the steps.

"She's an old woman, but she's vicious," Will tried to warn Drake, but he'd already disappeared into the gloom of the basement.

"What's he going to do? Put a bullet in her?" Dr. Burrows said.

"I would if I could, but she's bailed," Drake rumbled, over-hearing the remark as he stormed out of the basement. "So now the White Necks will know you're back in circulation, and the heat will be on."

Will was astounded. "She's gone? But she can't have!"

"There's no way out of there," Dr. Burrows added, giving Drake a skeptical look. "I checked it myself." He made as if he was going to go back into the basement, but Drake grabbed his elbow and spun him around.

"No, you don't. It's a waste of time — you'll never find it," Drake growled at him. "I heard there was a portal somewhere around here." He shot a glance at Will. "Someone told me about it."

This wasn't lost on Will, who looked at him questioningly.

"We need to get away from here, and pronto," Drake said to Dr. Burrows, then he stepped toward Will and his face crinkled into a grin. "I can't tell you how good it is to see you again, Will. In fact, I'd say it's a miracle! So you did the impossible — you all made it out of the Pore?"

"Yes . . . no, we —" Will began, but gasped as in the blink of an eye Drake had dropped to one knee and brought his handgun to bear on the kitchen door. Will also drew his Browning Hi-Power, although he was far less practiced than Drake and it took him a great deal longer. The door to the kitchen, which Mrs. Tantrumi had left ajar, moved the smallest fraction. Will was holding his breath as a mangy black cat stuck its head out and gave them an indifferent look before it ducked inside again.

"Yes, you've got to watch out for her pussycats — they're vicious brutes. One gave me a really nasty scratch," Dr. Burrows declared drily as he surveyed both his son and Drake poised with their weapons.

"Can't be too careful. This place is riddled with Styx," Drake said as he straightened up again. He regarded Dr. Burrows rather coldly before addressing Will. "I presume this is your father — the intrepid explorer?"

Will nodded.

"And you've come back to Highfield to see your mother," Drake said.

"My wife — yes, of course we have," Dr. Burrows jumped in before Will could answer.

Drake put away his handgun. "Well, if you thought you'd find her in your old house, you're wasting your time. She's sold it."

"She did what!" Dr. Burrows said, aghast.

Will's mind was beginning to function after the shock of seeing Drake again, and something didn't quite add up. "But, how did you know we'd come here? How did you know that I was even still alive?" he asked.

"When you rang that number, your message was logged on a secure server in Wales."

"Number? Message?" Will said, then the realization hit him: It had to have been one of the calls he'd made on the old telephone in the fallout shelter. "So the line wasn't dead! And that was *your* number all the time!" Will said, shaking his head. "I had no idea what it was for."

"You can only have got it from Elliott, so I assume she's still alive, too. Is she OK?"

Will nodded. "I hope so. We got separated after she set off a huge explosion."

"Typical," Drake chuckled. "And what about Chester?"

"He should be with Elliott, but Cal . . . something terrible —"

"I know about Cal," Drake interrupted softly. "I was there. I saw the whole thing."

"You were there?" Will sputtered. "At the Pore?"

"Yes. With Sarah . . . for her last moments . . ."

"No," Will said. "She's dead, then?"

Drake glanced away from Will, as if he knew how painful what he was about to say would be for the boy. "Will, she threw herself off the edge, taking the twins with her. I reckon she did it because she'd messed things up so badly with you, and it was all that was left for her."

"Oh God," Will gasped. He'd hung on to the hope that somehow she might have survived, but now that had been dashed by what Drake had told him. Will tried to speak, to ask more about what had happened, but his throat had tightened to such an extent that Drake couldn't hear him.

Dr. Burrows was completely ignorant of Will's feelings, and of how both Cal's death and now this account about Sarah's final act of self-sacrifice struck him to the very core. Still put out at being manhandled by Drake, and even more so by the discovery that he was now homeless, Dr. Burrows spoke with uncharacteristic boldness.

"Hey, gunslinger — whatever your name is — you said we shouldn't hang around here?"

Drake didn't shift his gaze from Will as he answered, but a slight movement of his eyes betrayed his irritation. "It's Drake, and yes, I did say that, didn't I? I'm going to take you somewhere to lie low for a while, and maybe you'll get a chance to see your wife at the same time."

"You know where she is?" Dr. Burrows asked immediately.

"Come along, Will," Drake said softly, placing a hand on the overwrought boy's shoulder and steering him toward the garden wall. "We've got a load of catching up to do, but not here. Let's go."

"Excellent," Dr. Burrows declared to their backs as they moved away. Even if he didn't admit it to himself, he was more than a little resentful that he seemed to have been supplanted in Will's affections by this rather imposing stranger, who evidently had such a strong bond with his son.

25

DRAKE WENT AHEAD to check that the road was clear, then waved Will and Dr. Burrows out after him. As the renegade escorted them away from Mrs. Tantrumi's house, Will thought how good it felt to be back with him. He'd had no idea how he and his father were going to cope, particularly since Dr. Burrows had seemed so unwilling to accept that the Styx were a very real threat. He just hoped that the incident with Mrs. Tantrumi would open his father's eyes.

Drake used a hand signal to tell Will to stay back as he moved to the end of the road. Slowing, he glanced around the corner, then disappeared from sight. He was being every bit as cautious as he had been in the Deeps.

"Is all this cloak-and-dagger stuff really necessary?" Dr. Burrows grumbled to his son. "I mean, what can anyone do to us here? This *is* Highfield, for goodness' sake!"

"They tried to snatch me and Chester on the way home from school, and that was only a couple of Colonists. If the Limiters come for us . . . ," Will said, but didn't finish the sentence.

Dr. Burrows mouthed a silent "pah!" as he and Will hurried to catch up with Drake, who showed them through an iron gate, then led them down a narrow alley.

"Martineau Square. That's where you're taking us, isn't it?" Dr. Burrows asked, as he saw that the alley extended behind a row of Georgian terraced houses.

"Yeah, but not the front way," Drake answered.

Both sides of the alley were bordered by tall redbrick walls, and it was paved with tread-worn cobblestones, between which grass and weeds grew in abundance. Clusters of old trash cans and heaps of empty cardboard boxes impeded the trio's progress, particularly when Dr. Burrows lost his footing on a soggy pizza carton and fell over. "Get a move on," Drake urged, as Dr. Burrows picked himself up.

Drake stopped at a wooden door coated with chipped black paint, its bottommost edge rotted away. They slipped through it, finding themselves in a small backyard, a concreted area with what looked like the original outdoor privy still in one corner. Drake used a key to let them through the back door of the house and into a hallway, which was a dismal dark brown color. From the state of it, Will reckoned it hadn't been decorated for many decades.

They climbed several flights of stairs with cast-iron metal banisters, the treads creaking with every step, and at the very top Drake ushered them through a doorway so low they had to duck to get through it. They found themselves in a dingy room, the only light filtering through a small cobwebbed window. Will knew they must be in the attic of one of the terraced houses that lined Martineau Square.

Drake shut the small door and drew two bolts across, then skirted swiftly over the bare floorboards to the window. He stopped short of going right up to it, instead peering at the view outside through the dusty panes.

"What's there?" Dr. Burrows asked as he ambled straight up to the window and pressed his face against the pane. In the blink of an eye, Drake had hauled him back.

"Blast it, man, don't show yourself like that!" he growled.

Dr. Burrows made a sharp movement, shoving Drake's hand away, then squared up to him. "Don't you *dare* touch me!" he simmered. "I don't know what your game is, but if you do that again, you'll be sorry."

Will had never seen his father like this before — he had always gone out of his way to avoid even the mildest confrontation. Dr. Burrows was several inches shorter than Drake, and it was difficult to imagine him faring well in a fight against anyone, let alone this man who regularly came up against Limiters, and won. Nevertheless, Dr. Burrows's whole body was quivering like a bantam cockerel about to attack.

As Dr. Burrows's and Drake's eyes remained locked on each other, the two men radiated an angry calm which seemed to fill the small room. Will had the weirdest sensation that he was back with Chester and Cal again. Time after time they had rubbed each other the wrong way and he'd been forced to smooth things over. Now Will didn't like the way things were going between these two grown men, and felt compelled to intervene. "Dad, you've got to be careful. Remember what just happened with that old woman. She was going to stab you."

His upper lip curled with anger, Dr. Burrows turned his head stiffly from Drake and toward his son. "You don't really know who this person is, or what he's done. Remember what I told you about strangers — you should never tr —"

"He's not a stranger! He saved my life in the Deeps!" Will burst out. "He looked after us there. He knows what's going on."

"Dr. Burrows, what will it take to convince you that our lives are at risk?" Drake asked in an even voice.

"Please just listen to him, Dad," Will implored his father.

Dr. Burrows *humphed*, then withdrew to a corner of the attic, where he sat down heavily on an old trunk.

Drake didn't appear to be the slightest bit fazed by the confrontation, and turned immediately to Will, smiling.

"Right, bring me up to speed."

"OK," the boy replied, throwing a glance at the shadows where his father was sitting in a brooding silence. "I've got something for you."

"Make yourself comfortable first. We've got a lot to talk about," Drake said, lowering himself to the floor, where he sat cross-legged. Will did likewise, then delved inside his jacket pocket and brought out the leather pouch containing the two phials. He unwrapped the burlap from around them.

"Those aren't what I think they are, are they?" Drake said in amazement.

"Supposedly are. This one," Will said, grinning as he held up the phial with the black stopper, "is the virus."

Drake took it from him with the greatest care. "Dominion," he said softly, lifting the phial so it caught the dim light filtering through the small window. "So the other one must be the vaccine?" he asked.

Will nodded as he also passed the white-stoppered phial over to Drake, who gently placed it on the floor beside him.

Dr. Burrows cleared his throat loudly, making Will start. "So, Drake, I take it you believe this whole dastardly plot routine is for real, then? You actually think the Styx are intending to wipe us all out with a lethal virus?"

"No, not all of us," Drake replied. "They just want to depopulate the surface, and then move in on what's left."

"I've never heard such a load of claptrap," Dr. Burrows countered from the shadows. "Tell me you don't really believe that."

"While you were underground, you missed the whole Ultra Bug episode. That was the Styx limbering up for something far nastier and far more serious. For this, for Dominion. And it's a killer clever plan. By using a biological reagent, they can exterminate Topsoilers but leave the infrastructure intact. You see, all the buildings, roads, railways — everything they need — will be there for the taking. And when they do march in, there won't be enough of us to put up any resistance."

"But why now?" Will asked. "They've been underground for centuries, haven't they?"

"I've got two theories about that. Either their numbers have grown so much that it's time for them to move on to greener pastures . . . ," Drake answered.

"Or?" Will prompted him.

"Or because — and this is the more likely explanation — with all the development going on in Highfield, the Colony is losing air channels by the dozen as the old buildings are torn down. And at the same time as that's happening, it's upping the ante that someone will rumble what's down there — the Discovery, as the Colonists call it."

"Yes, the Discovery," Will mumbled, remembering the first time he'd heard about it from Grandma Macaulay.

"But spreading a deadly virus, like terrorists?" Dr. Burrows said, shaking his head. "Have they got the capability for that?"

"Sure. It's nothing new — the Styx have pulled the same stunt a couple of times down the years," Drake said. "You're aware of all the major epidemics — the outbreaks of Asian and Spanish flu, and the Great Plague of 1665 — they're all the work of the White Necks."

"I like a man with a good imagination," Dr. Burrows laughed cynically. "But this is too much!"

"In a way, the Styx themselves are not that different from a virus." Drake was thoughtful as he continued to dangle the glinting phial in front of him. "Know much about viruses, Doc? Do you know their MO?"

"Can't say I do," Dr. Burrows said sneeringly.

"Well, they're tiny organisms, so small that you need special filters to trap them. They're like nothing else on earth. In fact, they resemble miniature space rockets, and they can even be crystallized — it's debatable whether they're alive, in the sense of the word you or I understand it. And it's a heck of a job to identify a new one when it does pop up."

"So how, exactly, are they like the Styx?" Dr. Burrows interjected.

Drake continued as if he hadn't heard him. "They attack a host cell by anchoring themselves to its membrane. Then they shoot their genetic material inside and hijack the cell. They use its internal machinery to reproduce themselves like billy-ho, until there are so many of them the cell bursts. Then millions of identical viruses flood out in search of new hosts to infect." The Dominion phial swung gently as Drake touched it with his pinkie finger. "The rats sink the ship."

"But you're talking about organisms that *kill* people," Dr. Burrows said, outrage in his voice. "You sound as though you actually admire them."

"I admire their simple, uncluttered intent to survive. Their objective isn't to kill — in fact, if the host loses its life, that's not good for business. The smart viruses keep their hosts alive . . . because they're dependent on them."

"What are you trying to say — that the Styx are like viruses because they use people . . . use people for their own ends?" Dr. Burrows asked, flicking his eyebrows as if he was buying none of this. "Interesting concept, I suppose, but hardly credible."

Drake had evidently tired of the exchange with Dr. Burrows, and turned to Will.

"All I can say is that I'm impressed," he told the boy, then frowned deeply as if suddenly troubled by something. "Wait — the only place you could have got these phials is from —"

"From a twin," Will finished the sentence for him. "That's right."

"So . . . so did you take them off her dead body?"

"No, she gave them to me," Will said, his voice beginning to waver. "The Rebecca twins did try to get them back at the submarine, but I wasn't about to let them have them."

"But these are the Styx you're talking about, and all that sounds way too easy. Are you absolutely sure these phials contain genuine Dominion virus?"

"Well, I hope so," Will replied earnestly.

"You need to tell me everything, right from the moment you fell into the Pore," Drake said. "And take your time — we're in no hurry."

26

WILL AND DRAKE talked for several hours, until Drake finally got to his feet and stretched his legs.

"So you didn't see what actually happened to the Rebecca twins, or the Limiter," he said with a grimace. "I don't like it. It's too open-ended."

Will was unsettled by his response. "Well, either they were blown to smithereens or, if they did manage to make it inside the submarine, then they're a long way down," he said. "I just hope Martha got Chester and Elliott to the other—"

"Oh, come on, enough of this! You were going to show me where my wife is," Dr. Burrows demanded tetchily. He hadn't moved from the trunk since the set-to with Drake, but now stood up.

"Yes, I was, wasn't I?" Drake replied. He took a stepladder from the wall and set it up in the center of the room. Mounting it, he pushed open a hatch, then climbed through. Dr. Burrows and Will followed, finding themselves on an area of leaded roof, the darkening sky over their heads.

Dr. Burrows ignored the view of the square below, apparently more interested in the thick chimney stack at the side of the roof. He stood on tiptoe to touch one of the large terra-cotta chimney pots.

"I was working on a theory that there are ducts built into these, for the Colony's air supply," he said, as if talking to himself.

"Then you'd be spot on," Drake confirmed. "The Fan Stations blow stale air out of some of them, while others are intakes for fresh air. In fact, the whole square and many of the other buildings in the older parts of town were erected by Martineau's men, and disguise all sorts of things. But this square — Martineau Square — is Styx Central."

"If that's true, then why in the world have you brought us here?" Dr. Burrows asked.

"Other than that it's the last place they'd think of looking for us, the reason I've brought you here is . . ." Drake trailed off. He'd raised his hand to point, but now lowered it as he watched Will intently. "Don't get too close to the side — you might be seen," he warned the boy.

As soon as Will had laid eyes on the edge of the roof, he'd been seized by the overwhelming desire to go toward it. That other self, who was so strong and domineering, was taking control of him again. It drove Will to take a few steps, but then he managed to stop himself from going any farther. "Help me," he whispered as, breaking into a cold sweat, he sank down suddenly on the lead flat.

"What's up?" Drake asked as he quickly went over to Will. "I didn't know you had a problem with heights."

"I don't," Will croaked. "Or I didn't." He looked beseechingly up at Drake, trying not to cry he was so frightened. "This is something else. I keep getting this feeling like I want to . . .

like I *have* to jump. I don't know what's wrong with me."

Drake crouched beside him, his eyes full of concern. "When did this start?"

"Not long ago. It's like I want to kill myself! Am I going mad?"

"What is it, Will?" Dr. Burrows said, now standing helplessly by his son's side. "What's the matter?"

"I think I might know," Drake said as he gently took hold of the boy. "They used the Dark Light on you, didn't they?"

"Yes," Will answered, his body trembling violently as he still struggled with the urge to get up and throw himself off the roof. It was as though there was a battle taking place in each of his limbs, the muscle groups straining against one another in some sort of antagonistic contest to vanquish its counterpart. "In the Hold. A lot," he gasped.

"Then this is not you. The Styx have done this to you," Drake said.

"They did what?" Dr. Burrows shouted.

"Stay out of it and keep your voice down!" Drake snapped at him. "Will, they implanted this in you. You've been conditioned . . . brainwashed, if you want to call it that. When they were interrogating you, they probably left something in your preconscious, like a poison pill, that would become active if you left the Colony."

Will stared at Drake, unable to grasp what he was telling him.

"It's not you — remember that. They did this. And you can fight it. Come with me." He helped Will up and, looping an arm around his chest, supported him to the very edge of the roof. Drake kept hold of him as they stood there together, a three-story drop below them.

"Is that such a good —?" Dr. Burrows began to object.

"I said keep out of it, Doc," Drake growled at him. "Will, look down there, at the road. You've got a picture in your mind, haven't you? A really vivid picture?"

Will nodded, unable to stem the tears.

"I'd guess it's the image of you lying broken on the pavement. And it feels so right, as if it's the answer to everything."

"Yes," Will replied in a hoarse voice. "But how do you know that?"

"Doesn't matter. Will — you need to stay with me and listen to what I'm saying." Drake placed the palm of his hand on Will's forehead for a moment. "You have to realize there's something intrinsically wrong with the picture that they've stuck in your head. You can't feel the pain . . . you can't feel anything . . . you can't feel any loss, can you?"

Will shook his head. "No, nothing."

"The Styx rewired your mind — they've made you think this way. It's wrong. Resist it, resist the vision. It's false. Instead think about how your father and I would feel if you actually did jump. Put yourself in our places and feel what we'd feel. Are you doing that?"

"I'm trying," Will croaked.

Drake took his arm from around the boy and stepped away from him.

"You're on your own now, but *you're* in control, not the Styx. Tell me how that feels?"

"Better . . . Yes, it's like I've got myself back . . . like the voice isn't so strong," Will said as he wiped his eyes. "I can look down now and the picture isn't so clear. Oh, this is all so stupid."

"No, far from it," Drake said as he took hold of the boy again. "We're going to do this over and over again until there's nothing left of their conditioning. I can help you to beat it."

"But I wasn't like this in the Deeps. Why now?" Will asked, his head sagging as if he was completely exhausted.

"It's what they wanted," Drake shrugged. "Probably the Styx's insurance policy in case you went on the run. A fail-safe measure."

Dr. Burrows clucked with disapproval. "What a load of old baloney!" he said. "I think *you* need help, Drake. You're so delusional, it's scary."

Drake swung around to him. "No, you're the one who won't admit what's going on, even though you've seen it with your own eyes. That old woman was set on killing you. How do you explain that?"

"She . . . ," Dr. Burrows began, but then trailed off.

"Mrs. Tantrumi might be a full-fledged Styx agent, or she could have been brainwashed. And if she *was* brainwashed, she's one of many. There are probably thousands of people all over the country who have had varying degrees of conditioning, and some of them hold influential positions — businessmen, members of Parliament, high-ranking officers in both the police and the army. All it takes is a keyword or a signal from the White Necks and these people have no option but to do their bidding."

"Bartleby," Will said. "At the submarine the Rebecca twin spoke to him. He was acting like I was his worst enemy or something. Does that mean it works on animals?"

Drake nodded. "Sounds like it does."

"And Sarah — Sarah Jerome — what about her?" Will asked as the thought occurred to him. "Did they use it on her so she'd come after me?"

"I didn't get that impression in the short time I knew her. I think the Styx recognized she was vulnerable and they tricked her, plain and simple," Drake replied.

"Tricked her?" Will echoed.

"Yes. If they can't coerce people into doing what they want using threats, bribery, or their elaborate lies, then they resort to mind control. But it takes weeks, if not years, of Dark Light sessions to induce anything more than impulsive actions in the average person."

Will frowned, not understanding what he meant.

"Anything more than short bursts of behavioral change — inducing a person to do something in response to a keyword or, in your case, Will, when you are confronted by a steep drop."

Will still wasn't sure what he was talking about. "But can I really stop it?"

"Sure you can. It sounds as though you only had a few weeks of conditioning, so with any luck I'll be able to reverse it. Others might not be so fortunate, and their programming is so deeply ingrained that nothing can be done for them." He took a deep breath. "We're going to stay up here for a while," he said. "Can you handle that?"

"I think so," the boy replied.

They waited for half an hour, Drake perched by the edge of the roof and occasionally glancing at his watch as darkness gathered in the sky above.

Then he abruptly beckoned to Dr. Burrows to come over.

"There's your wife," Drake said, pointing down at a road that joined the corner of the square.

"Celia?" Dr. Burrows said, hastily getting up from the lead flat.

"What's she doing here?" Will asked as he stood alongside Drake.

"See that house three in from the end?" Drake said, glancing at the terrace on the opposite side of the square.

"Yes," Will confirmed.

"Your mother's renting an apartment on the first floor. She's taken a temporary job to pay for it."

"Job?" Will spat as though he'd been stung, his face a picture of incredulity. "You're saying my mum's got herself a *job*?"

"Yes," Drake replied. "And she goes to the gym every morning. . . . Quite the reformed character, as if she's trying to turn over a new leaf. She's also been researching Martineau and Highfield's history at the local archive, to see if there's any connection with your disappearances. She's thorough, I tell you. That's why the Colony is keeping tabs on her."

"Oh, so you're saying the Styx are after *her* now," Dr. Burrows snorted. He and Will watched as she came nearer, noticing that she wasn't alone as she turned into the square. "But she's with someone! A man!" Dr. Burrows said, becoming quite agitated.

"Yes, and he's not to be trusted," Drake informed him.

Dr. Burrows was frantic. "I need to speak to her! I have to go to her!"

"Sorry, Doc, no can do. Not right now," Drake told him in no uncertain terms.

But Dr. Burrows had opened his mouth and yelled "Celia!" before Drake, in the blink of an eye, had bundled him away from the edge of the roof. As Dr. Burrows tried to fight him off, Drake flipped him onto his back in a single fluid move, putting his head in a lock so he couldn't make a sound.

"Stupid fool!" Drake scowled, then snapped an order at Will. "See if anyone heard that! And if you do anything silly like jumping, I'll kill you myself!"

"Did you hear that?"

Mrs. Burrows had been about to unlock the door, but was now scanning the road around the square and the unkempt garden in its center.

"Hear what?" Ben Wilbrahams asked.

"I thought I heard . . . I thought someone shouted my name," she said, a bemused expression on her face. "It sounded like . . ."

"Well, I didn't hear anything," Ben Wilbrahams said unequivocally. "Other than the wind."

Mrs. Burrows shrugged and inserted the key in the lock to let them in. As Ben Wilbrahams followed her, she was unaware of the tall thin men flooding into the square, and the activity on the rooftop across from her apartment building.

Any problems Will had had with heights were put aside as soon as he saw what was happening below.

"Trouble," Will called back to Drake. "Looks like at least four Styx coming our way, and fast."

"You'd better behave yourself, Doc," Drake warned as he released Dr. Burrows, then joined Will at the front of the roof.

As Will craned his neck to see into the corners of the square, he felt rather than heard something land close to his feet. He looked down. Where the angle of the roof dipped forty-five degrees toward the guttering at the very edge, a neat hole perforated the surface of the lead. The same thing happened again, but this time he was looking down at the roof as another hole appeared next to the first.

"Um, Drake," he said, pointing.

Drake reacted in an instant. "Sniper!" he hissed, quickly pulling Will back with him.

Huffing resentfully, Dr. Burrows had gotten up and was just about to give Drake a piece of his mind when a sharp sound made him flinch. Inches from his face, one of the chimney pots simply exploded, pieces of it raining all over him.

"What the —?" Dr. Burrows spluttered, and flung himself down with his arms around his head. He didn't stay down for long, immediately scrambling back over the roof and scattering fragments of the red chimney pot as he went.

Drake raced to the rear of the roof, where he checked the alleyway behind. "Keep low and stay close," he ordered Will and his father as he scrambled over the brick parapet to reach the adjoining roof.

"Are you telling me we were just shot at?" Dr. Burrows asked, wiping dust from his face.

"Yes, you gave our position away. Can't you ever do what you're told, Dad?" Will said in an exasperated voice as he followed Drake.

Crouching and in single file, they continued to cross from roof to roof as they made their way along the line of houses.

"But I didn't hear any shots," Dr. Burrows whispered as they went.

"They'll be using silencers or some kind of suppressor, and maybe low-velocity ammunition," Will said.

"Go to the top of the class, Will. You really have mugged up on your military manuals, haven't you?" Drake smiled. As they came to the last house in the terrace, Drake crawled forward on his chest and heaved up a hatch in the roof. He swung himself through the opening, crashing into some old cardboard boxes in the attic below. Will and Dr. Burrows dropped in after him.

"So what do we do now? The whole block will be surrounded," Will asked, looking quickly around at the empty attic, identical to the one they'd been in before, as he imagined an army of Styx and Colonists taking up positions outside.

Drake flicked on a small flashlight. Gripping it in his teeth, he went to where the chimney flues ran up the wall and began to tap the brickwork. "Never get yourself into any situation where you haven't got at least two escape strategies," he said out of the corner of his mouth as he worked his way along the wall. Although there was no difference in the appearance of the brickwork, the sound changed — it became hollow, as if the wall was made of metal. He pushed against it and a small trapdoor swung inward. Will and Dr. Burrows were beside him in an instant, peering down into the duct. Inside it a rusted metal ladder was bolted to the wall.

Will was relieved they had a way out. "Now that's a really cool escape strategy!"

"Yes. Thanks to Martineau," Drake said.

"Sir Gabriel Martineau?" Dr. Burrows asked.

"Sure. He loved his secret passages, and got his workmen to build them on a whim. And he was usually in such a tearing hurry, he often didn't stop to make records."

"So the Styx don't know about this one?" Will asked.

"I truly hope not." Drake turned to Dr. Burrows. "And, Doc, do you need any more convincing that the Styx are a threat?" he said pointedly to him. "Like a bullet in your head?"

Dr. Burrows frowned, but said nothing.

"Good. Now pick up your kit and get down the ladder — and take a left at the bottom," Drake told them.

Will and his father descended the old ladder, then began along the stone-lined passage, which was high enough that they could both stand. A small stream of brownish water trickled down the center of the passage, and its sides and roof were covered in glistening black slime. As they walked, the light from Dr. Burrows's luminescent orb revealed there was more to the walls than they had first noticed.

"Look! A mural!" Will cried. "A man with a boat!"

"Noah and the Ark, I'd say," Dr. Burrows proclaimed as he inspected the image under the garlands of black algae and pale smudges of limescale. "But they're not murals, they're carved in relief, cut into the stone."

"And here's one of a man and a woman," Will said, squinting at the other side of the passage.

"Adam and Eve, probably," Dr. Burrows said. "They're all Biblical scenes, sculpted into the limestone with such skill. The artistry is just breathtaking. Remarkable!"

Drake seemed to be taking his time to close the trapdoor, but as he slid down the ladder and caught up with father and son, he found they were both so captivated by the murals that they had hardly gone any distance at all.

"I told you two to make tracks!" he snarled.

"But this is an important discovery," Dr. Burrows insisted. "Why on earth would anyone have put these down here?"

Drake glanced warily down the passage behind them. "Three centuries ago this led back to Martineau's house, so he could walk to church without getting wet when it was raining." Drake took Dr. Burrows by the arm, guiding him on. "And now, if you don't mind, please can we wind up the sightseeing tour for today, gentlemen."

They moved at a fast pace, finding the passage was beginning to rise. Then it split and they took the left fork, but after several hundred feet they appeared to have hit a dead end. Drake went to the front and, handing Will his flashlight, felt around until he located two blocks of stone that were slightly recessed.

"Bet you there's a hidden catch or something for another secret door," Will whispered excitedly to his father.

But to Will's surprise, Drake braced himself, then aimed an almighty kick at the recessed stones.

"Hidden catch, huh?" Dr. Burrows whispered back, as Drake took several more kicks, driving the heel of his boot into the stones with all his strength.

A whole section of the wall crumbled away with a crash. Drake retrieved his flashlight from Will and played it through the opening. As the dust settled, the first thing Will and Dr.

Burrows laid eyes on was a skull. Then they saw a jumble of decayed bones on the ground, where the old lead coffin Drake had dislodged had fallen and broken up.

"Where are we?" Will asked in a hushed voice as he climbed out behind Drake.

"It's all right, you're not going to wake 'em up," Drake told him, making no effort to keep his voice low.

As they moved farther into this new area, something crunched under their feet.

"Ye gods!" Dr. Burrows gasped, examining the mass of human remains scattered across the floor. Then he raised his light and spotted other intact coffins on stone ledges around the walls. He and Will saw they were in a space about thirty feet square, but the ceiling was far above them, as if they were in some sort of well. "We're in a burial chamber!" Dr. Burrows realized.

"You got it, Doc. After Martineau decided he didn't need his personal subway, he gave it over to an industrialist friend to use as his family mausoleum. Looks like they're all in here." Drake crossed to the opposite wall and began to climb the ledges until he reached the uppermost one. "Give me some light," he said as he edged along what Will thought was a stretch of stone wall. He located a short bar of rusted iron attached to it, then pivoted it to the vertical.

"Is that a door?" Will asked, shining his lantern up.

"Sure is. Luckily for us, it can be opened from the inside," Drake said. "I suppose it was in case any of these guys wanted out!"

Putting his shoulder against the heavy stone door, Drake applied his weight. With a low grinding sound, it slowly swung away from him. "Well, what are you two waiting for?" he said to Will and Dr. Burrows as he slipped through the open door. Will was a little uneasy about where he was putting his hands as he clambered up the ledges. Quite a few of the caskets seemed to have fallen apart and their contents spilled out, and he didn't fancy touching the slime-covered bones.

Reaching the top, Will stepped outside the mausoleum. He breathed in the night air as he took stock of where he was. Before him he saw row upon row of headstones, dimly lit by the streetlight seeping over the cemetery wall. A building loomed before him. "Highfield Church," he muttered under his breath.

"This way," Drake said. They wove their way through the thickets of small trees and knee-high tangles of horsetail to another part of the churchyard. "Make yourselves comfortable, gentlemen — we're stopping here for a second," he told them. Perching on a large slab of moss-covered stone, Will and Dr. Burrows were grateful for the opportunity to rest — and now that they were experiencing earth's normal gravitational pull again, theirs felt like quite a considerable weight.

"Did you know that's actually the Martineau family grave?" Dr. Burrows informed Will, pointing at a tomb with small stone statuettes of a pair of men, one holding a pickax, the other a shovel, at its apex. Will had explored the graveyard before, but never after nightfall. But now, as he looked where his father was indicating and felt the damp, cold stone under his palms, there was something strangely familiar about the spot. Stirring deep within him was a memory, so distant that as he tried to remember more he might as well have been attempting to catch a wisp of smoke in his hands. Shrugging to himself, he began to hum as he scratched at the moss with a fingernail.

"So what did you make of the journal?" Mrs. Burrows asked Ben Wilbrahams as he shifted two piles of books from the armchair and onto the table to clear a place to sit. "Sorry, they're my husband's," she apologized as Ben Wilbrahams studied the spine of what was obviously a self-help book from its cover.

"*The Power of ME — Exercises in Self-Belief,*" he read, raising his eyebrows quizzically.

"Well, a few of them are mine," Mrs. Burrows was saying when a blinding flash of light filled the room, followed by the most incredible explosion. One of the curtains billowed out as if the wind had caught it, followed by the tinkle of glass.

"What on earth —?" Mrs. Burrows cried, racing over to the window and yanking the curtains aside. The roof on the end of the terrace opposite was completely wrecked, flames leaping from the remaining timbers. Car alarms cried out as tiles and pieces of the roof rained down throughout the rest of the square.

"Somebody might need help," Ben Wilbrahams said. "I'm going down there."

Mrs. Burrows was scanning the pavement in front of the house. "I don't think anyone's been hurt. But what in the world could have caused that?" she asked, noticing that the blast had shattered a pane in one of her windows.

"I don't know. Maybe a gas leak," Ben Wilbrahams replied, slipping on his jacket as police and ambulance sirens sounded in the distance.

■ ■ ■

"I don't get it," Dr. Burrows had been saying to Drake. "With what you know about the Styx and the Colony, you could give the whole game away. Why don't you just go to the authorities?"

"You really aren't grasping the scale of it, are you, Doc? The wolf is inside the house, and has been for centuries," Drake replied. "They've got their claws into people at all levels of the police *and* the government."

"Then go straight to the newspapers and make them run the story," Dr. Burrows suggested. "Make it all public."

"It's been tried. Any proof mysteriously goes missing, and people end up getting killed," Drake said. "Good people."

At that moment there was a tremendous explosion. Will and Dr. Burrows jumped to their feet. They could see that an area of the night sky was suffused with light.

"Is that coming from Martineau Square?" Dr. Burrows asked.

"Yes, I rigged a grenade on the door into the duct," Drake told him.

As the light faded away and the sky returned to darkness, there was a quiver in Dr. Burrows's voice. "But . . . you can't go around blowing things up . . . this is Highfield . . . this is *London* . . ."

"No, Doc," Drake said. "This is a war zone."

27

DRAKE TOOK WILL and Dr. Burrows to a drab semi-detached house in a neighboring borough. Although it was a short journey, Will and his father were both so exhausted that the motion of the vehicle had lulled them to sleep. They came to as Drake parked the car behind a tall hedge. There were no lights on in the property as he shepherded them inside. The interior was dirty, with only a stained carpet and a few pieces of battered furniture.

"You don't live here, do you?" Dr. Burrows asked, a little taken aback as he dragged himself lethargically into the scruffy living room and dumped his kit bag on the floor.

"I don't live anywhere," Drake said, already making toward the door. "It's just somewhere for tonight. There are blankets and a sleeping bag on the sofa, and you'll find food in the fridge."

"Want some help?" Will volunteered through a gaping yawn.

"No, that's fine, thanks. I'm going to call in an old favor and get the contents of these phials checked," Drake said, patting his jacket pocket.

"But after everything that's happened, is this place safe?"

Dr. Burrows exhaled as he flopped down on the sofa.

Drake nodded. "Yes, it's all right for a while. Just keep the curtains closed," he said. He was about to leave when he snapped his fingers. "Will, while I think of it, give me some of that plant . . . what was it called? . . . Aniseed . . ."

"Aniseed Fire," Will reminded him.

"Aniseed Fire," Drake repeated. "I'll get it analyzed at the same time."

"Right," Will said, frowning, because he wasn't sure why Drake should consider it important. He began to unpack his rucksack, careful to put the box of ammunition for his pistol out of his father's sight. Then he pulled out the night-vision device.

Drake smiled. "Ah, there's an old friend — my spare headset. Did Elliott give you that?"

"Yes, but it's stopped working."

"Has the element been exposed to bright light?"

Will shook his head. "No, nothing like that. I didn't use it for a few weeks, and when I tried it again, it was completely dead," he said as he untangled the cord from around the headband to which the flip-down lens was attached.

"Let me take a look," Drake said, and Will handed it to him before returning to his rucksack. He'd just fished out a few sprigs of Aniseed Fire when he spotted something in the bottom of his pack. "What an idiot I am!" he cried.

He plucked out his camera and swiveled to face his father. "I totally forgot about my camera!"

Dr. Burrows sluggishly raised his head. "Your what?"

"My camera! I took some pictures of the Colony and the

Deeps, but more important . . . some of them are of the pages from your journal. I finished the last of the roll at Martha's shack, and I'm sure your drawing of the Burrows Stone is on it."

Dr. Burrows took a second to grasp what Will was saying, then he leaped to his feet. "Will . . ." He almost couldn't talk, he was so overjoyed. "You really are a genius!" He laughed. "Well, a dimwit for not remembering until now, but a genius all the same."

"Can we get them developed?" Will asked Drake. "And blown up?"

"I should think so," Drake replied. "Anything else I can do for you? Want your combats pressed and your shoes shined?" he smirked.

After Drake had gone, Will made a beeline for the fridge, helped himself to a couple of sandwiches, and swigged milk from one of the cartons. He returned to the living room to find his father ensconced on the sofa, a blanket spread over his legs as he examined the stone tablets in his lap. "I might just make sense of these yet, Will," he said.

"Good night then, Dad," Will grumbled, surveying the floor.

Will and Dr. Burrows slept well into the next morning, and were woken by Drake's return.

"Bacon rolls," he said, putting a paper bag and three styrofoam cups on the table.

"Groovy," Will said, worming his way out of his sleeping bag. As he padded barefoot to the table, he suddenly remembered the reason Drake had gone off the previous evening. "Did you get the phials tested?"

Drake looked done in as he blew on his tea. Will wondered if he'd got any sleep at all. "No, it'll take a few days," he answered.

Dr. Burrows appeared beside Will, dipping into the paper bag for a bacon roll, which he immediately began to wolf down. "Any joy with the photographs?" he asked.

Drake handed him a packet. "Ten by eights — hope that'll do you?"

In a mad rush, Dr. Burrows tore open the packet and riffled through the prints, sorting out any that were of his journal. He stopped suddenly, bending his head to study one of them more closely. "Yes," he muttered, sticking his head even closer to it. "Yes!" he said again, holding up the photograph of the Burrows Stone so Will could see it. Without a word of thanks to Drake, he retired to the sofa with the print and the remainder of his bacon roll. "With a magnifying glass, this might just do it," he mumbled.

"I suppose you want me to go out and buy you one of those, too?" Drake asked.

"Yes, soon as you can," Dr. Burrows replied, completely engrossed in the photograph. "And some pencils and more paper."

"Your wish is my command," Drake said sarcastically.

Will began to examine the photographs his father had discarded on the table. The uppermost one had been taken in the Jerome house — it was of Cal sitting on his bed with a big smile on his face. It was difficult for Will to look at it, and he quickly moved on to the next. It was of the street in the Quarter on that day so long ago when he and Chester had first gone down the tunnel under his house. Then, in the next photograph, the entire frame seemed to be filled with a single giant eye. Will chuckled, then stopped himself. "I shouldn't laugh," he said.

"What's so funny?" Drake asked, leaning forward so he could see the print.

"The Second Officer. I used the camera flash to blind him when I got Chester out of the Hold."

"No, I really do need a magnifying glass," Dr. Burrows suddenly piped up from the sofa. "And what day is it, today?" he demanded.

"Friday," Drake replied.

"Will Celia be at work?"

"Yes," Drake answered.

"Then I'm going to see her tomorrow when she's home, and you're not going to get in my way this time," he announced defiantly.

"I wouldn't dream of it, Doc," Drake said. "But I thought you might want to go this evening?"

"No, tomorrow will be fine," Dr. Burrows replied, whistling through his teeth and already beginning to make some notes as he glanced from the photograph to one of the stone tablets and back again. It was obvious where his priorities lay.

"Busy, busy, busy," Drake said, opening a newspaper and beginning to read it.

"I've done it," Dr. Burrows bellowed the next morning. Will had been catnapping on the floor as his father rushed over to him. He was clutching a sheaf of pages, which he shook in Will's face. "I've got my route — now I just need to find the starting point."

"My route?" Will asked. "You said *my* route."

"I . . . of course, I meant *our* route," Dr. Burrows said shiftily. "Hey, Drake!" he called. "I want to see my wife now."

Drake wandered in from the next room, rattling his car keys. "Let's go, then," he said.

As they stepped outside the house, the morning sun was so fierce that Will and his father were forced to shield their eyes.

"Takes a bit of getting used to again," Drake commented as he unlocked the car and they got in.

"I've never got used to it," Will complained.

Drake made a call on his cell. "Fine," he said, flipping the phone closed. He turned to Dr. Burrows, who was sitting beside him in the front of the car. "She's over at Wilbrahams's place."

"She's what?" Dr. Burrows exploded. "You have to take me there! Right this moment!"

"Sure, Doc," Drake replied, then took a pair of sunglasses from the glove compartment. "Put these on. Don't forget the police would be very interested if anyone clocked you. And if the police get you, then so do the White Necks." He adjusted the rearview mirror so he could see Will in it. "And keep your head down in the back."

Even before the car had come to a stop outside the Victorian house, Dr. Burrows had leaped from it and was running up the front steps. He hammered on the door until a bemused

Ben Wilbrahams opened it. Dr. Burrows barged him aside and went in.

"Do you think this is such a good idea?" Will asked Drake from the backseat.

"Apart from knocking your father out cold, I'm not sure what I could have done to stop him," Drake replied, scanning the street ahead.

Less than a minute later, Dr. Burrows stormed out, Mrs. Burrows in hot pursuit.

"It's Mum!" Will told Drake in an excited voice as he slid across the backseat to get a better view of her. "Wow — the new streamlined Mum! She looks really different. . . . She looks great!" Will could hear his mother's tirade through Drake's open window. "But she doesn't sound very happy."

"Think you can just turn up, then skip off again? Where've you been all this time? Where are the children? . . . Where are Will and Rebecca? What have you done with them?" she was shouting furiously at Dr. Burrows, following him as he thundered back toward the car. Ben Wilbrahams came to the front door, but made no move to go after her.

Will got out of the car. "Mum! Mum!" he yelled.

Mrs. Burrows stopped on the spot, her mouth clamping shut. She looked stunned. Then she dashed over to Will and threw her arms around him.

"Oh, Will! I didn't believe him! You *are* here!" she cried.

Will was completely taken aback by this extravagant display of affection as she squeezed him tight. The old Mrs. Burrows was remote and uninterested. Not only did his mother look like a completely different person, she was behaving like one, too.

Dr. Burrows had already got back into the front seat as Drake leaned out of his window to speak to Will and his mother.

"We can't hang around here."

"Who's this?" Mrs. Burrows demanded as she eyed Drake suspiciously. "Is this the man who kidnapped —?"

"No, he saved my life, Mum," Will said, cutting her short.

"Get in, both of you!" Drake snapped. "This is no place for family reunions."

Drake drove them out of London and deep into the countryside. The bright sunlight flickered through the car windows, making Will blink as he talked nonstop to his mother. Except for the occasional gasp, she listened intently without interrupting him. But she couldn't keep quiet when Will told her of Rebecca and the Styx's cruelty, and how it had been revealed at the Pore that, all along, there had been two Rebeccas.

"My Rebecca . . . two of her . . . liars . . . *murderers*? No! How can that be?" she said in a strained voice as she flitted between disbelief and acceptance.

Finally, when Will paused to take a drink of water, Mrs. Burrows let out a long breath and glanced at her husband in the front seat, who was maintaining a stony silence, his arms crossed belligerently across his chest.

"Unless you've all gone completely mad and this far-fetched story is something you've dreamed up between you, I have to assume it's all true," she said, then frowned. "It isn't some crazy stunt you're trying to pull on me, is it?"

"Oh, dear me, she's seen through us, Will," Dr. Burrows declared, his voice dripping with sarcasm.

"What did you say?" Mrs. Burrows asked, although there was no way she could have missed it.

"Yes, it's all a complete fiction. I went to Disneyland for five months while you flogged my house and made a new friend," he said.

Will noticed Mrs. Burrows's eyes had narrowed to slits, and knew that it wasn't a good sign. He was right. She clenched her fist and, without any warning, she leaned forward and swung at the back of Dr. Burrows's head, nearly knocking off his glasses. "You stupid sod!" she shrieked. She struck him again, this time precisely on the small balding patch at the top of his scalp.

"Hey, come on, you two!" Drake said, the vehicle swerving as he tried to shield Dr. Burrows from any further blows. "Not in the car, and not in front of Will."

"What was that for?" Dr. Burrows bleated as he rubbed his head.

"What was that for?" Mrs. Burrows repeated twice in quick succession. "You selfish, *selfish* creep! You swan off on some half-baked frolic without a by-your-leave to anyone, and get my son and his friend stuck right in the middle of all this! They might have been killed!"

"Mum, please," Will appealed to her. "He wasn't to know what would happen."

"Really," she muttered, unconvinced. No one spoke after that, looking at the countryside as it rolled past them. Drake eventually turned onto a single-lane road, both sides of which were flanked by wild hedgerows. They drove through a ford, then several miles later Drake slowed to steer the car into a field. Will saw they were at the bottom of an incline covered in lush grass.

As they all got out of the car, Mrs. Burrows collared her husband. "You . . . you're coming with me!" she ordered, grabbing him with such ferocity he cowered. Will made a move to go with them, but Drake headed him off.

"Let them talk," he suggested.

Will watched as Mrs. Burrows frog-marched his father up the grassy incline. He looked like a man being led to his execution. Although Will couldn't hear what his mother was saying, her head was moving as if she was in full flow. "I feel sorry for him," Will said. "The last time they were together in Highfield, before all this started, they had a flaming row. Dad was trying to tell her where he was going, but she wasn't interested — she was too tied up with what was on the TV. That was all she ever did . . . watch TV."

Drake and Will strolled over to the shade of a large oak tree and Drake sat down at its base, using its thick trunk as a backrest. "My parents never once exchanged an angry word in all the time they were together. Not once," he said. "They bottled it all up, and I always reckon that's why my old man died so young." He tipped his head toward where Dr. and Mrs. Burrows were gesticulating wildly at each other on the top of the hill. "At least yours have got some life left in them." Selecting a couple of fallen branches, he took out his knife and began to strip off the bark, then whittled them to sharpen the ends. Will leaned on a low branch and watched him. When Drake had finished, he put his knife away and examined the clean white wood he'd exposed. "What do you get if you rub two Styx together?" he posed, tapping a couple of the smaller branches against each other.

"I don't know?" Will asked.

"Fire and brimstone," Drake replied. "That was something they used to say in the Rookeries . . . and how right it turned out to be. They certainly got their fire. Poor sods." Will saw Drake's eyes were unfocused as he stared past the branches and at the ground.

"Those sticks remind me of when we were on the island," Will said. "Elliott barbecued us an *Anomalocaris* — she called it night crab — and some devil's toenails."

"My favorites," Drake said distantly.

"We were eating living fossils," Will reflected. He chuckled at the strangeness of it all, then he, too, became thoughtful. "It's good to be away from the darkness and the damp — even if it's just for a while. It's funny, but it all seems ages ago now." Letting his eyelids slide shut, he angled his face to catch the warm rays filtering through the leaf canopy, and filled his lungs with the fresh air. "I dreamed about a place like this when I was in the Deeps. There was long grass, wispy clouds in the sky, and the sun was shining just like it is now . . . and it was weird because there was someone with me in the dream — a girl — but I don't know who she was. I never saw her face."

"Elliott?" Drake inquired gently.

"Hah!" Will exclaimed. "That's hardly likely."

"I wouldn't say that. She's very fond of you, you know."

Will laughed. "Well, she's got a funny way of showing it."

"That's girls — women — for you," Drake said, joining in

with Will's laughter. "I know you fell out big time after that patrol on the Great Plain, but she respected you for standing up to her."

Just then, Will and Drake heard raised voices behind them.

Mrs. Burrows was marching toward the tree, Dr. Burrows trailing behind her. She was shouting stridently. "Will! Will, come here! We need to speak to you."

Before he went to meet them, Will whispered to Drake, "Looks like I'm wanted."

"It's nice to be wanted," Drake replied with a nod.

His parents came to a stop under the other side of the tree. Mrs. Burrows's face was flushed and angry, while Dr. Burrows just looked at his feet, browbeaten.

"Your father and I have talked things over, and we've decided we're not going back to how we were before," Mrs. Burrows declared.

"No, we're not," Dr. Burrows said emphatically, still examining his feet.

"OK," Will said, wondering where this was leading.

"Your father thinks he has unfinished business underground, and he's going to return there as soon as he can — by himself, that is."

"No —!" Will began, but his mother spoke over him.

"And we've decided that you're going to stay with me," she announced.

"Forget it," Will growled. "I'm going back for Chester and Elliott. You can't tell me what to do anymore! You've got no idea what —"

"We can find somewhere well away from these Styx people. Maybe down on the coast . . . Brighton would —"

"No way!" Will screamed. "Brighton? Are you kidding me? They'll find us there in two seconds."

Mrs. Burrows bristled. "Don't you dare talk to —!"

This time it was Drake's turn to interrupt. "It's not quite as simple as that, Mrs. Burrows." He touched the top of his head in what was clearly some kind of signal, and a man stepped out from the hedgerow at the bottom of the field. He advanced toward them in rapid, easy strides.

"Who's he? And what's he doing sneaking around here?" Mrs. Burrows demanded.

"He's been with us the whole time, and you can call him Leatherman," Drake said.

"I don't care if he's the King of the Fairies," she snorted. "Where's he from?"

"He's originally from Fiji. He was in my unit for a while."

"What — an army unit or something?" Mrs. Burrows hissed, her lip curling viciously as she became increasingly angry. Will took a step away from her, worried that she might be about to start throwing punches again.

Drake shook his head. "I suppose you could say that we worked for the government, in a sort of unofficially official capacity, until the relationship was disrupted by our dear friends, the Styx. That's all you need to know," he said flatly.

The man drew alongside Drake and stood as if waiting for an order. A full head taller than Drake, he looked about as solid as the trunk of the old oak tree. His short-cut hair was black, and he had a well-trimmed moustache. His skin was burnished, as if he spent all his life in the open, and as Will thought to himself how much it resembled old, tanned hide, the wry suggestion occurred to him that his name was very apt. The man was dressed in a knee-length Barbour coat and jeans and, reacting to a nod from Drake, he opened his coat. Will caught a glimpse of a stubby-looking weapon suspended at his side.

"Assault rifle?" the boy asked.

The man paused to give Will a friendly smile. "Sawn-off twelve-gauge," he said, tugging something from an inside pocket. Some sort of camera.

"You were saying," Mrs. Burrows snapped at Drake, clearly not the slightest bit impressed by the newcomer's abrupt appearance, or the fact that he was armed.

Drake took the camera from Leatherman and flipped open the small screen on the side.

"So, tell me, why can't I take Will off somewhere, away from all this nonsense?" Mrs. Burrows asked impatiently.

"Because of this," Drake said, holding the screen so she could see it.

"Ben? Is that Ben?" she asked. Grabbing the camera from Drake, she peered at the screen as the piece of green-tinted film played back. "It is — you've been snooping on Ben! You've got no right to do that!"

Will managed to see the screen, although his mother's hands were shaking as she held the camera. It wasn't only Mrs. Burrows's friend in the picture — he was with two thickset men in flat caps, wearing dark glasses. And then the screen went blank for an instant and another clip started in which

Will could see Ben Wilbrahams with a single Styx. "So, no question that he's an agent?" he said.

"None. And apologies for the poor quality," Leatherman said, as if it really mattered. "The meetings were held at night, and I couldn't risk getting any closer."

Mrs. Burrows gave Drake a half shrug. "So some people approached Ben. What does that prove? These might have been chance meetings — they could've gone up to anyone," she burbled.

"On six different occasions? In isolated locations?" Leatherman said pithily. "I don't think so, sister."

"I'm not your sister, Mr. Leather-soles or whatever your name is," Mrs. Burrows spat, then peered at the screen again, shaking her head. It was obvious that she wasn't convinced by the films. "Tell me — precisely *when* were these filmed?" she asked.

"I told you — on six different occasions, and all at night-time. The first surveillance was just after you went back to Wilbrahams's house — the evening the Colonists were pursuing you."

"Mum?" Will began with a look of concern.

"You went back to his house?" Dr. Burrows said. "At night?"

Mrs. Burrows gave her husband a frosty look, then closed the small screen and threw the camera back to Drake with unnecessary force. He caught it in one hand. "So if this is all true, you've known about Ben for a while, haven't you?" she accused Drake.

"We had our suspicions," he said.

"And still you let him see my husband and son. You let Roger blunder in to get me, so Ben would know he and Will are back in Highfield."

Drake nodded. "The Styx knew already, but, yes, I took a calculated risk in allowing the Doc to show himself, because I need to lure the Styx out into the open."

"But why?" Will asked him.

Leatherman took over. He raised his hand, the two phials dangling from his fingers by their cords. "Because we drew a blank on these. You've been had, Will. One's full of Ultra Bug, and the other's the vaccine for it. I'm sorry to tell you there isn't a trace of the new virus, not in either of them."

"No Dominion virus!" Will gasped. "So it was a lie right from the very start, and they even kept it going when they said they wanted the phials back at the submarine. Do those evil little cows *ever* stop playing their stupid tricks?"

Leatherman addressed Mrs. Burrows. "It doesn't make any difference whether the Styx know your husband's Topsoil or not, your days are numbered, anyway."

"Huh?" she said, not looking quite so sure of herself now.

"You would have been disappeared before long — you've been digging too deep . . . if you'll excuse the pun," he said without any hint of humor. "But now you've had contact with the Doc and Will, they'll assume you know everything they know, so you're marked. You've got no option — you've got to run. But you don't have the know-how to keep ahead of the Styx and, believe me, they're good. They will catch up to you and kill you. It's only a matter of time." He retrieved the camera from Drake and put it back in his jacket. "That's the way the cookie crumbles, sister."

"So you may as well take your chances underground, all three of you," Drake said bluntly.

"Underground?" Mrs. Burrows echoed, a look of horror spreading across her face. "Me?"

"Great," Will piped up, with a glance at his father. "That's exactly what we wanted, isn't it, Dad . . . to go back."

"Shut up, Will," Mrs. Burrows murmured, in evident distress from the way she was trembling.

"No, Will's right," Drake said. "If he and the Doc were able to hike themselves out of the Pore, then there's every chance the Rebecca twins might do the same. Sure, they could already be dead, but somebody's got to make sure. If they survived Elliott's explosion, they've still got the real Dominion virus on them. And we can't risk that." He looked into the middle distance, as if a thought had just occurred to him. "However, there might be something you could do for me up here, Celia."

"What?" she croaked.

"Well, you're not really cut out for all that grubbing around underground, are you?" he asked.

Mrs. Burrows blanched, and as she tottered on her feet, Will thought she was about to faint.

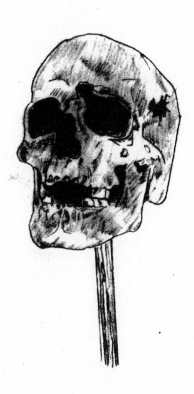

PART 6

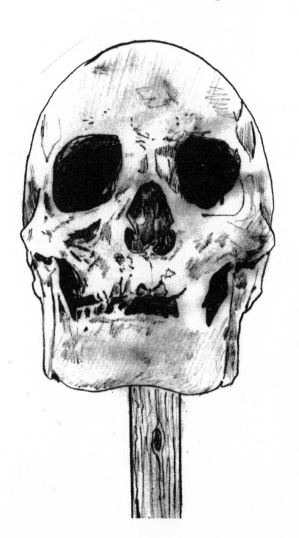

DEPARTURE

28

IN THE LITTLE CHEF restaurant, Will and his
father sat on one side of the table, Drake and Mrs. Burrows on
the other. Their food had arrived, but Mrs. Burrows hadn't touched
hers. She'd pushed away the plate and instead stared at the motor-
way through the window, watching the endless stream of cars.

Drake had told them that when they were finished eating he
was going to drive Will and Dr. Burrows back to Norfolk, and
Leatherman — although he was nowhere to be seen — would
be taking Mrs. Burrows to London. So this was to be the
parting of the ways, the final meal before they went on their
separate paths.

At other tables lone truck drivers sat eating in silence, and
a young couple with their noisy infant in a high chair fussed
in a far corner. There was a loud crash as one of the waitresses
dropped a pile of dishes, and Mrs. Burrows recoiled. It didn't
take much to see that her nerves were strained to the breaking
point. She hastily took a sip of water, her hand shaking as she
replaced the glass on the table.

"You had to meddle in things you didn't understand, didn't
you? If you'd left well enough alone, none of this would have
happened," she said very quietly.

"Who . . . me?" Dr. Burrows asked, his fork poised in front of him.

"Who d'you bloomin' think?" she replied bitterly.

"Please don't start whacking him again," Will said, giving her a wary glance as he pulled his bowl of fries toward him.

Mrs. Burrows rested her head in her hands and sighed. "No, Will, I haven't got the energy to do any more of that." She looked up at him. "And it really doesn't matter about your father or me. We've already had most of our lives and made an abominable mess of them. But you're young. You've got everything ahead of you. I'm so sorry, Will." She reached out a hand and squeezed his forearm. "I'm so sorry you've been dragged into the middle of all this."

Will wiped tomato ketchup from the corner of his mouth. "Mum, *I am* the middle of all this. There was always a chance my real . . ." He trailed off.

"Your real mother," Mrs. Burrows helped him out.

"Yes . . . a chance that Sarah Jerome would show up again. It's what the Styx were trying to make happen." He picked up a fry with his fingers and chewed it slowly. "And I was a problem for them, too. I'd have been grabbed or killed at some point, anyway." Will glanced sideways at Drake. "Isn't that right?"

Drake put down his cup of coffee and nodded. "They play the long game. They would've tidied up sooner or later," he agreed.

The infant began to howl, its ear-piercing shrieks making the truck drivers shift in their chairs and grumble under their breath as if they'd just been roused from a very deep sleep.

"I can't stand this," Mrs. Burrows said suddenly, rising to her feet. "I'm going."

"Once you're outside, walk toward the gas station. Leatherman will pull up beside you in a white van. Get into it," Drake told her.

"So be it," Mrs. Burrows said.

Dr. Burrows and Will also stood up.

Mrs. Burrows offered her hand, and after a split second of hesitation Dr. Burrows took it and they shook.

"Good luck," Mrs. Burrows said.

"Good luck to you, too," Dr. Burrows replied, then promptly sat down again.

It was such a formal act, as if two strangers were bidding each other farewell, that Will didn't know what he should be doing.

He hovered in front of his chair, then Mrs. Burrows stepped around the end of the table to him. "Come here, you," she said, taking him in her arms. She was crying, and it was all Will could do to stop himself from crying, too. She kept on hugging him, as if she didn't want to let go.

"Take care, Will. Always remember I love you," she finally said in not much more than a croak, and strode toward the exit, wiping her eyes.

"I love you, too, Mum," he said, but she was through the door and outside in the parking lot, striding quickly away.

Will sat down heavily in his chair. He glanced at his remaining fries, then looked away from them. He couldn't remember the last time his mother had spoken to him with such affection, or said those words to him. He knew she must have done so when he was younger, but he couldn't remember a single occasion. As the infant in the corner of the room shrieked again, he was hit by the realization that it had taken all the nightmarish events to clear away the chaff that had been their Topsoil lives and reveal how his mother really felt about him. And how he felt about her.

He was overcome both by a sense of moment and a sense of aching loss.

As the waitress came with his order of ice cream, three dollops of chocolate, strawberry, and vanilla, he stuck a spoonful into his mouth, more as a diversion than anything else, because he didn't want his father or Drake to see him choking back his emotions. But the taste of the ice cream just made it worse — a far-off taste of childhood, of lost years. He got up from the table and tore toward the door, wanting to speak to his mother one last time before she went.

But once he was outside, he couldn't see her, or the van Drake had said would be picking her up. He ran over to the gas station to check if his mother was there, then he came back to the Little Chef, where he desperately searched the parking lot. But again there was no sign of her. He was too late.

Drake and his father would be waiting for him in the restaurant but, at that moment, Will felt too upset to face them. Instead, in a corner of the parking lot, he ducked behind a large dumpster on wheels where no one would be able to see him. He looked up into the sky and cried and cried.

By late afternoon, they arrived at the perimeter of the old airfield. Drake steered the Range Rover down a side track and stopped. Will was sitting up front with Drake, while Dr. Burrows was stretched out on the backseat. Will and Drake could hear his steady breathing as he slept.

"Are you OK with everything, Will?" Drake asked him in a quiet voice.

"I think so."

"Once you're back down, your first priority is to link up with Elliott," Drake said.

"I'd do that, anyway," Will put in. "And Chester."

"Yes, of course you would. But when you find her, brief her on what I want done. We have to be certain the Rebecca twins and their remaining Limiter aren't still operative, and that any risk of the Dominion virus resurfacing has been neutralized. You, Elliott, and Chester have to do whatever it takes. Don't let anything get in your way." He stopped speaking as Dr. Burrows stirred in his sleep and made some snorting noises. "Or *anyone*," Drake told Will, and glanced at Dr. Burrows on the backseat to emphasize who he was referring to. Then he sighed. "I'd be coming with you, but there are a few things I have to see through up here."

Will nodded as Drake continued.

"And afterward, if you, Chester, and Elliott decide to return Topsoil, I'm sure we can work something out. I can't say it'll be easy for any of you, but —"

"Thanks," Will said, not needing to hear the rest. "But what about Dad?" he asked.

"I get the feeling he wants to be as far away from the surface as he can get, after the way things have turned out with your mum. I don't think he's planning on coming back for quite some time." Drake consulted his watch. "Right, we'd better rouse Sleeping Beauty so we can get the gear sorted out and you on your way again."

■ ■ ■

On the open tailgate of the Range Rover, Drake checked that they had everything they needed for the trip. He'd brought large military rucksacks for Will and his father, which he referred to as *Bergens*, each holding considerably more than the one Will had been using.

"And now we get to the interesting stuff," Drake announced. He pulled a holdall onto the tailgate and unzipped it. "Here's the headset, Will. It's fully functional again."

"What was wrong with it?" Will asked.

Drake showed him where there was a ring of plastic heat-wrapped around his repair to the cord. "Someone made a tiny incision to sever the circuit. No way was this from wear and tear — it was tampered with."

"Rebecca One," Will said slowly. "Seriously! She must have nobbled both my headset *and* the rifle scope. Chester was dead right to suspect she'd done it. The twin obviously didn't want us to spot that a Limiter was following us!"

"You got it," Drake said, then yanked out a box that contained what appeared to be aerosol cans, although they were plain gray and without any markings. "We ran some tests on the sample of Aniseed Fire and found that on oxidation it releases large amounts of N,N-Diethyl-*meta*-toluamide."

"That's easy for you to say!" Will laughed.

"DEET, for short. It's a common garden insect repellent, but the stuff in these aerosols is industrial-strength. Handy if you come under attack. You could also try spraying your clothes and kit with it. Should keep the spiders at arm's length, and your friends, too. Just avoid getting it on your skin. Understood?"

"Got it," Will said.

"And the fuel for the outboard?" Dr. Burrows chirped up.

"All in good time, Doc — I'm not finished yet." Drake held the holdall open so Will could see what else was in it. "I've given you some climbing ropes. And because you're so fond of your fireworks, I've stuck some emergency flares in here, too, along with some other goodies." Drake pulled a third Bergen toward them and undid the top.

"Explosives," Will said, recognizing the canisters Drake and Elliott used in the Deeps.

"With one difference — it's not my homebrew in them this time, but C4 . . . plastic explosive. This lot is for Elliott, but you have to tell her to be careful how she sets these babies, because they're more potent than anything she's used before. And last, but not least," he announced, and lifted out a shiny black plastic box from a side pocket of the third Bergen. It was the size of a pack of playing cards and had a length of wire trailing from it. "This is a radio beacon," he said, then lifted up the wire so Will and Dr. Burrows could see it. "It puts out a radio signal called VLF, which stands for *Very Low Frequency*. The technology is still in its infancy and nobody knows the extent of its effective range yet, but leave these at strategic points on your route, and it'll help you find your way around."

"Like Hansel and Gretel leaving a trail of bread crumbs in the woods," Dr. Burrows commented wryly.

"Something like that, but these are digital bread crumbs with twenty-year batteries. I've given you fifteen beacons and a couple of trackers," Drake said, then swung around to face Dr. Burrows. "And your spare fuel is already in place for you, Doc.

I had Leatherman move in at night and stow it by the quayside, next to the kit you left there."

"He found his way down there, just like that?" Dr. Burrows asked, amazed.

Drake retied the top of the Bergen and slid it toward Will. "We're not amateurs, you know," he said.

"No, clearly not," Dr. Burrows sniffed, disgruntled. "You've got access to weapons, labs for viral analysis, cutting-edge night-vision equipment, and other technology the likes of which I've never seen before. Just who the blazes *are* you?" he demanded. "You haven't told us."

"Ever heard of the Illuminati?" Drake said.

"Of course I have — the German secret society from the eighteenth century," Dr. Burrows answered with great authority, throwing a sidelong glance at his son to see if he was impressed.

"You got it — the Illuminati were founded by Adam Weishaupt in 1776 in Bavaria," Drake said, then inhaled deeply. "Well, I suppose you might say we have vague parallels with them. We're a clandestine network of scientists, military personnel, and a handful of people in senior government. But unlike the Illuminati, we didn't come together for sinister purposes — far from it. We have a common and single goal: to try to fight the Styx any way we can."

"That doesn't help me very much."

Drake gave Dr. Burrows a wink and lowered his voice to a theatrical whisper. "It's not meant to."

29

THE LAUNCH was carried along at steady speed by the river, needing little assistance from the outboard motor, except when Will blipped the throttle to keep them to the middle of the channel. And although Dr. Burrows had taken up position at the bow, Will now had the use of his headset again and didn't really need any guidance on what lay ahead.

They sailed straight past the first refueling station, but stopped at the second one to dry themselves out and get some rest. They had something to eat, choosing a curry from the impressive selection of lightweight rations Drake had provided for them.

As they lounged around after the meal, warming their hands by the oil stove, Will turned to his father.

"Once we got Topsoil, you didn't have any intention of bringing me back here, did you?" he accused him. "You were going to dump me on Mum so I wasn't around your neck. In fact, that's the *only* reason you wanted to go home, isn't it? You wanted me off your hands. You lied to me, plain and simple. It's that white mice thing again, isn't it?"

Dr. Burrows closed his eyes for a moment, then opened them again. "It was for your own good, Will. I was trying to do what was best for you."

Will gave his father a withering look. "And yesterday you were more interested in working on your precious tablets than seeing poor old Mum. You don't care about her at all anymore, do you?"

"How can I put this, Will?" Dr. Burrows's voice was strained as he tried to explain himself. "It's a bit like my job in the museum. I *had* to do it because I needed to bring in enough money to keep us all afloat, but it was never *me*. All the time I knew I could do something better . . . something exceptional. And sometimes relationships — marriages — are the same. People stay with what they've got, although, underneath, they're not really happy. I'm sorry to say that your mother and I had grown apart. You must have seen it."

"But it doesn't need to be like that," Will threw back at him, becoming very upset. "You don't just give up. You didn't try hard enough!"

"I'm trying right now," Dr. Burrows replied. "I'm trying to do something to make people proud of me. I'm trying to make you proud of me."

"Don't bother," Will grunted disdainfully, pulling his jacket collar up around his neck and crossing his arms over his chest.

They both slept, and barely spoke to each other as they climbed back into the launch to continue their journey. Again they skipped a refueling point, knowing that if they made a push for it and kept going, they should arrive back in the underground harbor in under twenty-four hours.

And so, after a day and a half of traveling, the barrier across the channel that housed the hydroelectric turbines loomed in front of them. Will was at the prow but, due to his fatigue, he wasn't as alert as he should have been. He only spotted it at the last moment, shouting a warning to his father. It didn't give Dr. Burrows much time to maneuver. He had to open the throttle fully in order to power them around the corner and into the harbor. He clipped the wall of the archway as he went, splintering the top of the hull. But the damage wasn't serious and, now in calm waters, he finally cut the engine and they coasted slowly toward the pier.

The brightness of the overhead lights making him squint, Will grabbed hold of a bollard, then leaped from the boat and onto the pier in a single effortless bound.

"Bet you're happier now that you've got your super-powers back," Dr. Burrows laughed, trying his best to relieve the tension between them. "Let's unload all the kit, and then get ourselves dry."

"Dad," Will began, as he squatted at the side of the pier. He might still be angry with his father, but he knew he had to get along with him if they were going to achieve anything. "We've come all this way again, but we don't really have any sort of plan, do we?"

"Sure we do. I've got a set of directions that are almost complete," Dr. Burrows countered.

"But you still don't have any idea where the map starts from."

"The tablets say the route begins in the place *with the falling sea*, and *by the single stone*, if my translation is accurate. And that's likely to be somewhere near the sub, because I believe that 'single stone' could be the one in the submariner's photograph. And also, you think brine — seawater — is falling down the inside of the void. Sounds promising to me."

"Fine, but the submarine's not there anymore, now that Elliott's blown a big part of the void to smithereens, and before I do *anything* else, I'm going to find my friends. And then I need to make sure the Rebecca twins and the Limiter are out of action."

Dr. Burrows looked up at Will on the pier and took a deep breath. "Then we've got an awful lot to do," he said.

Drake held back at the bottom of the steps as Mrs. Burrows knocked on Ben Wilbrahams's front door. He answered, wearing a silk robe and slippers.

"Celia!" he said with surprise. He moved his glasses from where they were resting on the top of his head and put them on properly. "I didn't expect to . . . see . . ." His voice petered out as his eyes fell on Drake, who was staring coldly at him from the pavement.

"Let's just drop the pleasantries," Mrs. Burrows said, her voice uncompromising. She thrust her hands into her leather jacket and turned her head to regard the street, curling her lip with disdain. She didn't bother to look at Ben Wilbrahams as she spoke, as if the sight of him was distasteful to her. "Tell your friends we have something they want. We have information about the twins and the virus they had with them."

"My friends? The virus?" Ben Wilbrahams asked.

"I'm not in the mood to dance with you!" Mrs. Burrows barked, only now turning to look at him. "So don't waste my time. You know precisely what I'm talking about. I'm prepared to make a deal with the Styx. Tell them they can have Dominion *and* the twins, but in return they're to leave me and my family alone. And I'll only do a deal with someone who can give me the right assurances, so I want a parley with their Mr. Big."

Ben Wilbrahams blinked, but didn't say a word.

"I know precisely what the gray-haired Styx looks like, so tell them not to try to dupe us with some dodgy stand-in," Drake added. It was an outright lie, because he'd only seen the old Styx at a great distance, when he was issuing orders by the edge of the Pore. "And they need to get their skates on. In forty-eight hours we put the twins out of their misery and incinerate the virus."

Drake held up the two phials so Ben Wilbrahams could see them, then slipped them back into his pocket.

"If the answer's yes," Mrs. Burrows said, pointing to his brass door knocker, "tie your wig to that. We'll see it and contact you to arrange where and when."

Ben Wilbrahams automatically put his hand to the back of his head. "How did you kn —?"

"Oh, come on, I've seen better rugs down at the local flea market," she sneered, then spun on her heel and descended the steps. As she and Drake walked away, she called back,

"Remember — they've got forty-eight hours to get their act together."

Drake glanced at her as they drove back to the safe house.

"We didn't rehearse half of what you said to Wilbrahams, but that was perfect. I couldn't have done better myself," he congratulated her. "Where did you learn to handle yourself like that?"

"Oh, here and there," she shrugged, peering at a shop window full of televisions as they sped past. "But don't you think this is sailing a bit close to the wind? Now that we've stirred up the hornets' nest, won't they just come at us with all they've got?"

"Sure they will, but if we can draw their Mr. Big — as you called him — out into the open and nab him, that gives us a bargaining chip. At the moment we're playing with an empty hand — we don't have the Dominion virus *or* the twins, but —"

"But they don't know that," Mrs. Burrows cut in. "And what happens if they don't want to meet us?"

"Then it will tell us they've already got the virus and don't need us. Which is the real point of the exercise, because then we'll know we're in trouble, serious trouble."

"I'm with you," Mrs. Burrows said, "but in the meantime I'm the shark bait — or should that be *Styx* bait?"

30

"**DRAKE, IT'S ME.** I just want you to know we've reached the deep-level shelter," Will said into the black telephone in the radio operator's booth. As he stopped speaking, he heard a crackle in the earpiece, but otherwise there was just silence. "And please can you tell Mum . . ." Will's voice became uneven, and he swallowed hard. "Tell Mum I love her all the world and that I'll see her soon." Just as he was replacing the receiver, Dr. Burrows poked his head around the door.

"I thought I heard you talking to someone," he said. "What's going on?"

"I left a message for Drake," Will replied.

Dr. Burrows looked disappointed. "You realize that man's just using us — all of us — don't you? He's got you scampering around after the twins and the Dominion phials, and who knows what he's going to get Celia to do for him. He just uses people for his own questionable ends."

"Drake's my friend. And if it wasn't for him you'd be dead by now," Will snapped, ending the exchange.

They spent the next twelve hours sorting out their equipment and getting some sleep. When they were finally ready to go,

Will and Dr. Burrows pulled the massive door shut behind them, then stopped by the electrical panel.

Will watched the minute flicking of the needle on the main dial as his father reached for the first of the switches and swung it upward. He did the same for the others, and the harbor was once again returned to darkness.

"Do we really need to power it down?" Will asked.

"Always leave a place as you'd wish to find it," Dr. Burrows replied. "You never know when you might need it again."

As they stood side by side in the pitch-black, the luminescent orb in Will's Styx Lantern stirred to life, growing in radiance until the sublime green light was pouring through the lens.

"Here we go again," Will said under his breath as he shone the beam on the back of his hand.

As they exited the concrete building and set off down the quay, they both had the large Bergens on their backs, which held considerably more kit than the civilian ones they'd been toting around before. And despite the fact that Will was lugging two of these rucksacks, one hooked over each shoulder, and also the sizeable holdall, his rifle, and the Sten gun, the lower gravitational pull meant it felt as if he was carrying nothing more than a bag of feathers.

As he thought about this, he turned to his father. "I've got that sick feeling again."

"Yes, I noticed you were looking a bit green around the gills. I've got it, too, just like when I came down the Pore the first time. Nothing to be concerned about — it's because your gut relies on normal gravitational pull to assist it with peristalsis, the mechanism by which the muscles in your duodenum ripple and move your chewed-up food down your —"

"Dad, please, I *said* I feel sick!" Will moaned, holding a hand to his mouth.

As they went into the narrow crevasse, Will planted the first of Drake's radio beacons, lodging it in a crevice high up on the wall.

"Bread crumb number one," he said.

It was late morning and the light streamed into the empty room. Mrs. Burrows was in the middle of her yoga routine when she heard Drake calling her from downstairs. She'd been missing her almost daily visits to the gym and so this was the best she could do, exercising on the floor of one of the bedrooms in the shuttered hotel that Drake was using as a safe house for the time being. Grabbing her towel and bottle of water, she went out into the corridor and hurried down the flight of stairs where Drake and Leatherman were waiting. The hotel lobby was still intact, with a reception desk and a few tables and chairs arranged around the place. Drake and Leatherman were standing just inside the main doorway.

"Hi, guys," Mrs. Burrows greeted them. "What's up?"

"Baldy Wilbrahams just left his hairpiece on the door-knocker," Leatherman said with a straight face.

"He didn't!" Mrs. Burrows said disbelievingly, then burst into a raucous laugh, Drake and Leatherman joining in with her.

Drake held out a cell phone to her. "Then it's all systems go. You need to call him with the time and place," he said quietly.

Mrs. Burrows stopped laughing as she took the phone.

As Martha pounded on the door to the barricade of the Wolf Caves, Chester stirred on the soft patch of ground where he'd been snoozing. He groaned and heaved himself to his feet, then rubbed his back and groaned again. Wiping the side of his face that had been resting in the dirt and scooping his long hair back, he grumbled, "I'm a caveman" to himself as he went to the entrance. He slid out the crossbar from behind the door so Martha could come in. The first thing he spotted was Bartleby lolloping around behind her.

"Keep that mangy moggy away from me," he said in a bad-tempered voice.

Then he noticed Martha was grinning from ear to ear.

"We hit the jackpot," she announced gaily.

He saw what was on the ground beside her and took a step back.

"Urhhhhh!"

Steam rose from a dark, matted fleece. It was hard to make out precisely what it was — it looked rather like someone had discarded an old furry rug there, until Chester caught sight of the thick snout protruding from it.

"That's a wolf?"

"Sure is," Martha said. "Caught it in one of my snares. A real brute — took three shots to the back of the head to kill it."

"Three shots," Chester repeated, not really knowing what he was saying as Martha stooped to take hold of a hind leg and began to drag the dead wolf past him.

Chester watched her, nodding his head. "I *am* a caveman,"

he sighed in quiet acquiescence, and was about to shut and secure the door again when he remembered Bartleby was still outside. The cat's big platelike eyes were fixed nervously on Chester — the animal knew he was still out of the boy's good graces.

With a resentful grunt, Chester waved the cat inside. Bartleby got the message, skulking warily past him, then bounding off into the caves after Martha.

Chester, too, followed after Martha, and found that she wasn't where he expected her to be, in the area with the soft dirt floor that they usually occupied. When he finally caught up with her farther inside the complex, she was already preparing the carcass, and Elliott was watching her raptly.

Martha cut one of the wolf's eyeballs from its socket, made a small incision in it, then put it to her mouth. She squeezed it hard, the fluid from the eyeball dribbling down her whiskery chin as she drank it.

"Gah!" Chester gagged.

Martha then proceeded to hack the second eyeball out. She also gave it a jab with her knife, but this time passed it to Elliott.

"Good source of fluid," Martha advised Elliott as the girl drank hers.

"Ohhh!" Chester moaned, sitting down suddenly.

"That's good," Elliott said, then glanced at Chester. "You must try some next time."

Chester made another gurgling sound, at which Elliott started laughing. It took him a few seconds, but then Chester saw the funny side of it, too. He shook his head as Elliott turned her full attention to Martha, watching how she was gutting the large beast.

Elliott's recovery had been nothing short of a miracle. The antibiotics had done the trick and she almost appeared to be back to her old self. Although not quite her old self. There was something different about her. Compared to the taciturn Elliott of the Deeps, Chester had noticed that she was now more forthcoming and even, at times, lighthearted.

Perhaps, as Rebecca One had warned might be the case, the fever had "cooked her brains." But Chester liked to think it was because Elliott was just grateful that he, Will, and Martha had pulled out all the stops and saved her life. Whatever the reason, she made the long days cooped up in the Wolf Caves bearable for Chester as they chatted together and played tic-tac-toe in the dirt by scratching it with sticks.

Elliott also talked to Martha for hours, evidently trying to soak up as much local knowledge as she could. She had insisted that Martha show her how to prepare spider-monkeys for cooking, and became so adept at this that she took over the task each time Martha returned from one of her hunting trips. And now she was learning how to prepare a cave wolf.

There was the most horrific tearing noise as Martha yanked a forelock from the dead beast and blood pumped in little spurts from its torso.

"Martha, why did you come all the way down here?" Chester asked as he turned his head away and instead looked around the unfamiliar part of the cave.

"Because the smell will attract other wolves . . . and the spiders," Elliott answered, taking the severed limb from Martha and placing it on a flat rock. "And if you want to make yourself useful, why don't you get a fire going for us?"

"Sure," Chester said.

The wolf was delicious and made a welcome change from the spider meat, which was all they'd had for days. After eating their fill, they sat around in contented silence. But Chester was finding it hard to relax. With every day that passed with no sign of Will, he had become increasingly impatient to go back and search for him. He chose this moment to tackle Martha about it again.

"So what are we going to do?" he asked her, as she sat propped up against the wall with Bartleby at her side. "We can't stay here forever."

"Now that Elliott's stronger," Martha began, as if she had been expecting the question, "we could go back to the shack. We're low on Aniseed Fire, but if we're careful how we use it, there should be enough for the journey home."

Chester shook his head.

"Will might be there by now," Martha added quickly. "I can't see him surviving for long if he hung around the void."

"He survived in total darkness for more than a day with no food or water when he got separated from us in the Deeps. This time he had his kit with him, and his dad. Will's no pushover," Chester said.

"Well then, we could go back to the void and take a proper scout around the area. You never know, if Bartleby picks up his scent we might be able to track him. But it'll be touch and go whether we do find him, and all the time we're there we'll be exposing ourselves to danger. If Will made it through the explosion, then maybe the Styx did, too, and don't forget about the Brights. I wouldn't —"

"I'm going to look for him, even if I have to do it by myself," Chester interrupted her.

Elliott had come over to listen to the exchange.

"What do you say?" Chester asked her.

"I'm with you. We never leave our own behind," she said resolutely.

At that instant, Chester realized how much like Drake she sounded, and it lifted his spirits that she was so intent on finding Will.

"While there's even a tiny chance he's out there and still alive, we keep looking for him," she added. "He'd do the same for us."

"Yes, he would," Chester agreed. "Good old Will."

"Get a move on, or I'll leave you behind!" Will threatened his father, who yet again had hung back to examine something that had caught his eye. This time it was a mineral formation at the side of the seam.

"These yellowish-white deposits we keep seeing . . . I really do believe it's electrum," Dr. Burrows said, half-turning to Will. "Know what that is?"

"A mineral?" Will guessed, not showing an ounce of enthusiasm.

"Not just any old mineral, my boy. It's an alloy of gold and silver — and there's quite a high proportion of gold in it, at that!"

"We don't have time for this," Will snapped. "Come on, will you!"

Dr. Burrows straightened up. "What's the big hurry all of a sudden? We've been away more than a week. Your friends will be long gone by the time we get down there."

It was very clear that Dr. Burrows couldn't care less about Chester, Elliott, or Martha. Will didn't respond to this, instead showing his frustration by cocking his Sten gun, which he'd decided to use as his main firearm because it was shorter and much less unwieldy than the rifle strapped across his back. He also thought it looked the part with his military getup.

"There's no hurry," Dr. Burrows said again. As he turned his attention back to the mineral deposit and began to whistle in that annoying way of his, Will was only just able to keep his temper.

"Have fun with your electrum," he said through gritted teeth, kicking out his legs as he stormed down the seam. Noticing he was passing the dark mouth of a side tunnel, he checked the aerosol of insect repellent he'd secured to his upper arm with duct tape. What with this, Drake's headset, and the submachine gun, he felt he was ready for anything, with or without his father at his side.

"Hey, Will! Wait for me!" Dr. Burrows yelled, running to catch up with his son.

31

"**I HAVEN'T** been here for years and years," Mrs. Burrows remarked as she and Drake went under the metal arch at the entrance to Highfield Common.

A recent addition to the park, the arch was achingly modern — a rainbow-shaped span of burnished stainless-steel tubing, over which ivy had been encouraged to grow. The combination of the ivy and steel worked up to a point, although the effect was rather marred by the numerous pairs of worn-out sneakers with their laces tied together that had been lobbed over its vertex. And the occasional stray brassiere displayed next to the sneakers only added to the overall impression of seediness.

But Mrs. Burrows didn't notice any of this, her mind somewhere else as distant memories were rekindled. "I used to wheel my kids around here in their strollers when they were small," she said. Then, as the realization hit her, her head came up suddenly and she stared at Drake. "I used to push a young Styx around. No, worse even than that, I used to push two of them around, AND I HADN'T THE SLIGHTEST IDEA!" she exclaimed.

"Easy, Celia," Drake warned her. "We don't want to attract attention." He indicated the gravel path that led up the hill before them, and they climbed it at a leisurely rate, passing on the way a couple of young boys trying to untangle a kite. "Not enough wind for that," Drake commented, and he and Mrs. Burrows instinctively glanced up above, where the clouds appeared to be fixed in the clear blue sky.

"It's funny how you only really appreciate things," Mrs. Burrows said, lowering her eyes from the sky and drinking in the lushness of the grass and the trees, "when you think you're going to lose them." She turned her head in the direction of Broadlands Avenue, where the rooftops of the houses were just visible over the curve of the hill and the intervening trees. "Or you've already lost them."

At the top of the hill, there was a roughly laid area of pavement, in the center of which a Victorian granite drinking fountain stood. Drake went over to it and pressed the tarnished brass button, which once would have produced a jet of sparkling water from the spout in the middle of the recessed bowl. But now nothing happened; no water came into the bowl, where there was just a dark mat of rotting leaves and a crumpled-up Coke can.

"So, about this time tomorrow, I'll be up here waiting for the Styx," Mrs. Burrows said, glancing at her watch. She frowned heavily as she scanned the area at the bottom of the hill. "Are we really safe up here, right now? They might be watching, and decide to grab us or something."

"Unlikely," Drake said. "Too many witnesses."

"But still . . . ," Mrs. Burrows began.

"Relax. They know we wouldn't be stupid enough to have the phials on us, so they won't try anything. Not today, anyway. And it's important that you get the lay of the land, so you feel ready." Crossing his arms, he leaned back against the water fountain. "Don't react to what I'm about to tell you, but Leatherman has already got his men in place. They're in the clumps of bushes around the base of this hill."

"They are?" Mrs. Burrows said dubiously.

"Yes, ten of them," Drake confirmed.

Mrs. Burrows gave the bushes a casual glance. "Men there? Now? How can they be? I can't see them."

"They're in dugouts, probably with their scopes on us this very moment. And we'll have more people carefully positioned at strategic points around the perimeter. I want you to know we are doing everything we can to protect you."

"Can I ask you an obvious question?" she began.

"Fire away," he replied.

"Have the Styx got tunnels under here? From what you tell me, they have a warren of them everywhere."

"We did a geophysics survey and found a few vague shadows. It probably means there were some underground chambers once, but they've collapsed, or been filled in."

Mrs. Burrows smiled. "How very History Channel," she said.

Drake pushed himself off the fountain and they headed back down the hill, still talking as they went. "Look, even if the Styx do try to play dirty, we'll be ready for them," Drake assured her, rubbing his hands together as if he relished the possibility. "No, we're going to have fun once we turn the tables on them and nab whoever comes to the meeting."

"But you don't actually expect their Mr. Big to come, do you?" Mrs. Burrows asked.

"I don't know him well enough to confirm his identity even if he does make a star appearance. But whoever they send, we'll interrogate him. He'll add something to our intelligence about their operations. But that's not the point of all this — the fact that they've agreed to a meeting in the first place tells us all we want to know — it tells us they don't have the virus."

Mrs. Burrows shrugged. "Maybe it's yet another double bluff. Maybe they already have the virus, and they just want to find out how much *we* know, or silence us."

Drake didn't answer as they reached the bottom of the hill.

32

THERE WAS a tightness in Mrs. Burrows's chest as she strode up the hill a day later. She took a series of deep breaths to try to quell her rising anxiety. *You'll be fine. This will soon be over,* she tried to reassure herself. *Yeah, one way or another,* came the unwelcome response from somewhere else in her head.

Although she hadn't said anything to Drake, she was scared stiff. From what she'd heard about the Styx, she knew she was up against an adversary capable of the most savage acts imaginable. An adversary that would think nothing of killing anyone that got in its way. And she felt thoroughly unprepared, as if she'd been dropped between the battle lines of a war in some foreign land and hadn't the slightest idea where the enemy was lurking.

She consoled herself that at least she was doing her bit to help Will. He was probably already deep in the bowels of the earth, where he might be facing the megalomaniac twins again. This thought didn't do much to ease Mrs. Burrows's state of mind. She should have fought tooth and nail to stop him from going back. But she hadn't, and her remorse was so strong it was like a physical pain in her gut. It had been criminal to ask so much from someone so young, and she found that hard to live with.

A small yapping dog drew Mrs. Burrows's attention and she looked down the slope to the base of the hill. She sought out the animal, then located its owner, who was throwing a ball for it. As she continued to walk briskly up the gravel path, she ran her eyes over the rest of the scene, scrutinizing the other people there that afternoon.

About a hundred feet away, two teenage girls were sitting next to each other on the side of the hill, a blanket spread beneath them. They didn't show any interest in Mrs. Burrows, or anyone else for that matter, their noses buried in their books. Then she caught loud voices and located a trio of tramps on a bench down by the east side of the hill, which was just now coming into view as she continued up the slope. They were passing around a half bottle of something and smoking. Drake had told her the Styx sometimes posed as vagrants, so she kept her eyes on them for several seconds. She remembered the images of the thin Styx and stocky Colonists caught on Leatherman's surveillance films. No, the tramps appeared to be the real thing. Indeed, no one looked out of place, no one looked suspicious.

She checked the time.

2:55.

Five minutes to go.

Perhaps she was just working herself up over nothing. Maybe the important Styx whom Drake was hoping to grab had rumbled what he and Leatherman were up to and wasn't going to make an appearance. *So be it*, she told herself. If this operation was all a waste of time, then she should just try to enjoy a pleasant afternoon in the setting of the Common as best she could. But as she closed her hand around the phials in her pocket, she found it impossible to relax.

The situation was far too fantastic for that.

It was as though her life had been ratcheted up into some hyperreality over the last six months. First her quiet existence had been capsized as her husband had taken off on his wild caper. Then, at Humphrey House, just as she felt she'd been waking from a deep slumber and had the chance to regain some measure of control over her destiny, both Will and her fake daughter — or daughters — had gone missing. She'd been cast into a situation as wild and improbable as the films she used to rent on DVD, but usually discarded before she'd watched them all the way through.

2:58.

"Everything OK?" Drake's voice sounded from the tiny transmitter in her ear, as clear as if he was standing right beside her.

"Yes," she answered as she reached the rough patch of pavement on the apex of the hill. Strolling casually around the drinking fountain, she rechecked the lower ground from her elevated viewpoint. As she peered down the north side of the hill, a man in a skimpy vest and running shorts jogged past the dilapidated bandstand, next to which an elderly couple were standing. It all looked completely innocent. She raised her hand to her mouth as if she was touching her chin, and spoke into the microphone pinned inside her sleeve. "Looks all clear," she reported to Drake. "Nothing. Not a sausage."

3:00.

"And it's the witching hour," she added.

"Just keep your eyes peeled," he said.

By the entrance to the Common, Drake was in a battered van along with Leatherman and two hired hands — former soldiers from Leatherman's old regiment. On the floor of the van there were three black-and-white television monitors with wireless feeds from cameras rigged in the trees around the hill. Leatherman and his comrades were watching them carefully. "Missing the racing on the other channel," one of the soldiers grumbled in phony regret, but his eyes were glued to the grainy picture of Mrs. Burrows on the screen nearest to him.

Drake consulted his wristwatch. "3:02. Looks like a no-show," he said disappointedly.

"Give it a little longer," Leatherman suggested. "Slowly, slowly, catchy monkey."

Drake nodded. "Let the teams know we're maintaining position," he said. Leatherman switched his handheld radio to a different frequency and communicated with the other soldiers in the dugouts, as Drake went back to watching through the rear window of the van with his binoculars.

Mrs. Burrows strolled very slowly around the drinking fountain. She heard a distant droning high above her. A passenger jet was advancing slowly across the sky, leaving a white-crayon trace behind it. *I'd give anything to be on that*, she thought wistfully.

3:05.

A man in a bright red tracksuit shot along one of the lower paths on a racing bike. The elderly couple were on the move, making their way up the hill and toward Mrs. Burrows in shambling steps. She began to pay them more attention. The old woman was pushing a wheeled shopping cart while the man seemed very doddery. He was hanging on to the old woman's arm and also leaning heavily on a walking stick in his other hand. The couple's progress was so labored that Mrs. Burrows crinkled up the side of her mouth. Hardly your typical murderous Styx.

"Got a pair of old age pensioners heading my way. Otherwise as quiet as . . . as . . . as a very quiet place," Mrs. Burrows said into the microphone as she pretended to adjust her hair.

She heard Drake's laugh in her earpiece. "Roger that," he said.

"Leave my husband out of it," Mrs. Burrows replied immediately, chuckling outrageously as she got some of the tension out of her system.

3:08.

A persistent fly alighted on her forehead, and she automatically swiped at it.

She went to the opposite side of the fountain and glanced down the south side of the hill. The man and his dog had moved on from the lower path and in their place she could see someone else strolling along, but he was walking away from the hill. Then she sought out Drake's van. She could just about see the tinted window where she knew he'd be watching. Then she stepped sideways toward the east and looked at the two teenage girls, who were both still immersed in their books. The fly buzzed in her ear, and she wafted it away. She went farther around the fountain. The elderly couple were slowly but surely approaching, the man looking extremely frail, as if he would topple over if it wasn't for the support his companion was giving him.

3:10.

She heard shouting and swearing. She crossed to the east side. Two of the tramps were leaving. The third was still on the bench. All of a sudden he was on his feet and waving his fists threateningly at the others. He followed after them in a reeling walk. She kept her eye on the group as they went past Drake's van. *Not Styx*, Mrs. Burrows told herself again.

She saw a woman on the lower path with two sizeable Afghan hounds — lanky, long-legged dogs that looked as though they were wearing furry pantsuits.

The fly buzzed close to her eye, making her blink.

"Stupid thing!" she exclaimed.

"What was that?" Drake asked, his voice concerned.

"Only a fly," she said.

She heard a *squeak, squeak.*

It was coming from the wheels on the old woman's cart. Mrs. Burrows crossed to the north side of the fountain. The elderly couple was thirty feet away and closing, but at a snail's pace.

Mrs. Burrows walked nonchalantly around the fountain, scanning the slopes again.

3:11.

"Got company — the wrinklies are up here with me now," she said to Drake.

"Yes, we can see them from a tree cam, and two teams have got scopes on them," Drake said. "They're the wrong side of the fountain for me to have eyes on them."

"Don't worry — think I can cope with them," Mrs. Burrows said confidently into the microphone. She lowered her arm as the elderly couple came around the side of the fountain — she didn't want them to catch her having a conversation with her sleeve.

Squeak, squeak. The shopping cart wheels. Accompanied by the steady tap of the old man's walking stick on the pavement.

Mrs. Burrows pulled her shoulders back and inhaled deeply, trying her utmost to look as if she was up there to enjoy the fresh air. Slowly releasing the breath, she gave the elderly couple a sidelong glance, then looked away hastily. The old woman had been watching her. Through the lenses of her spectacles she had hard little eyes.

The fly swooped in front of Mrs. Burrows's face again, but this time she didn't bother to swat at it.

Her senses quickened.

She glanced back at the old woman.

The old woman's white hair was a tangle of tight curls, as if it had recently been permed. She had a small mouth, with a top lip that was overstretched by her false teeth. It made her look vicious and angry. Mrs. Burrows averted her eyes, then raised them again, but this time turned her attention on the old man. He could have been in his eighties, and seemed to have something — Mrs. Burrows assumed they were hearing aids — plugged into both ears. He met Mrs. Burrows's gaze full on. He narrowed his eyes as if he resented her scrutiny. She immediately turned away, then took several unhurried steps as she tried to maintain her façade of nonchalance.

She told herself she was being silly — that they were merely an old married couple out on the Common for their constitutional. Or on their way to bingo, or to the shops. But something nagged at her, and she turned slowly back to them.

The old man was bending over the cart. Now that she was able to see it clearly, it was bigger than she would have expected — far bigger than the average shopping cart wheeled daily along the sidewalks of any main street. It was rectangular, and instead of the usual bright tartan or florid flowery fabric, it was covered in a dun brown material. It also had sturdier wheels than she remembered from similar carts.

The fly settled on Mrs. Burrows's cheek, but she didn't notice it.

She was staring directly at the old woman, who appeared to be putting hearing aids in both ears, just like her partner had in his.

As the old woman finished this, she looked straight back at Mrs. Burrows.

"Good afternoon," Mrs. Burrows said pleasantly, a little embarrassed that she'd been caught so obviously staring at the woman.

"Think you're so clever, don't you?" the old woman snarled. Mrs. Burrows didn't respond. For the tiniest instant, she asked herself if the old woman was addressing the comment to her partner — it was the sort of sour remark that might pass between a married couple of such advanced years.

But then she saw that the old man, still leaning over the cart but with his face toward her, had a finger poised as if he was about to press a button.

Was it a bomb?

There and then, Mrs. Burrows recognized him.

"Oscar Embers!" she gasped. He'd been one of her husband's Saturday helpers at the museum. And Will had said he was a Styx agent. That meant the old woman was probably —

"Tant . . . Tant . . . Tantrum!" Mrs. Burrows choked as she struggled to recall her name.

"Say again," Drake crackled in her ear. "What did you —?"

3:13

"Con . . . CONTACT!" Mrs. Burrows managed to scream at the top of her lungs.

Black-clothed soldiers leaped up from their positions all around the base of the hill.

"Come on, man!" Drake shouted as one of the soldiers fumbled to open the rear doors of the van. Leatherman moved in to take over. He heaved the soldier aside to get at the handle himself, but precious seconds had been lost.

"Fools!" Oscar Embers exclaimed as, smiling, he pressed a button on the top of the cart.

A low tone cut through the air, quickly building in volume.

With Drake's frantic voice in her ear, Mrs. Burrows braced herself. Her first thought was that there was going to be an explosion — it had to be some sort of bomb in that cart. Her second thought was that she was too close to escape the blast.

She was done for.

As it grew so loud that Mrs. Burrows's teeth were vibrating, the tone dropped an octave, then another, then several more, until it couldn't even be heard as a rumble. Her eyes rolled up into her head as she had the sensation that a knife was being dragged down her spinal cord, making each of her limbs twitch uncontrollably. The sound, beyond the limits of human hearing, was unbearable.

Then Oscar Embers hit another button.

The fabric panels on the sides of the cart were blown off, revealing a chunk of machinery. Its sides were gloss-black, inset with concave dishlike hollows of varying sizes that appeared silvery, like liquid mercury.

There had been an explosion, but not one that Drake or the soldiers would have recognized:

Mrs. Burrows was flung unconscious to the ground.

A concussive wave had been thrown out by the device, an invisible wall of subaudible sound that only affected living things.

To a man, the soldiers who had emerged from the dugouts were dropped where they stood. The woman and her Afghan hounds were knocked insensible. The two teenagers reading their books simply keeled over on their blanket. A small flock of starlings fell to the grass around them, caught by the pulse of sound as it radiated skyward.

The few occupants of the houses on Broadlands Avenue at that time of day were similarly affected, collapsing to the floor. And a number of cars within the blast radius either came to a halt or drifted into parked vehicles at the side of the road as their drivers blacked out.

Unable to get the doors open in time, Drake, Leatherman, and the two soldiers lay slumped in a tangle of limbs in the back of the van.

"Enough," the old Styx ordered as he appeared on the top of the hill beside Oscar Embers and Mrs. Tantrumi. Oscar Embers turned off the device. "Get clear before the Topsoil police arrive," the old Styx ordered as he yanked out his earplugs. There was no need for them now.

His ankle-length black leather coat creaked as he stepped over to where Mrs. Burrows lay in a crumpled heap. But he didn't pay attention to her, instead watching the Styx Limiters scuttling out over the areas below like a swarm of cockroaches. Then, as a pair of Limiters ran up the hill toward him, he waved them over to Mrs. Burrows. She was out cold, her head hanging forward on her chest as they hoisted her up between them.

"Wait," he barked. "Search her."

One of the Limiters found the pair of phials in her pocket and held them up so the old Styx could see. He nodded. "Good. Get them tested, and take her to the Hold." Then he walked around the water fountain, monitoring his men's progress as they dragged away the unconscious soldiers. Other Limiters were kicking in the dirt around the dugouts where the soldiers had been hiding, and removing the surveillance cameras from the trees. No trace of the operation would be left by the time they had finished.

Returning to the south side of the hill, the old Styx peered down at the van by the entrance to the Common — the Limiters hadn't got to it yet, but the rear doors seemed to be open. He was sure that they'd been shut before the weapon had been powered down.

Something wasn't right.

And as he watched he could have sworn he caught a fleeting glimpse of a tall, thin figure by the van — it certainly looked like one of his own people, but it was wearing black. He frowned.

That couldn't be.

He was the only Styx there that afternoon not in Limiter combat uniform.

He began to hurry down the gravel path to investigate for himself.

Leatherman had just turned the handle on the rear doors as the wave of sound engulfed the van. Once Mrs. Burrows had used the trigger word, there was no question in his or Drake's mind that they were under attack.

The van hadn't provided any shielding against the subsonic wave. If anything, it had concentrated the effect on its occupants. Within less than a second of Oscar Embers activating the device, Drake had passed out, with Leatherman and the two soldiers dropping beside him.

So Drake didn't see the man wearing the twin earpieces that Mrs. Burrows had mistaken for hearing aids as he wrenched open the doors and climbed into the van. And he felt nothing as this man, who he would have identified immediately as a Styx, located his limp body from among those of Leatherman and the soldiers, and carried him to a waiting car.

And Drake didn't know until later how fortunate he'd been. That he and Mrs. Burrows would be the only two to live out the day.

33

"**HALLEY WAS** the first person to come up with the Hollow Earth theory," Dr. Burrows announced completely out of the blue. "And that was way back in 1692."

"What are you going on about?" Will asked, mopping sweat from his brow as they took advantage of the gradient to maintain a fast pace down the seam.

"Edmond Halley; you know . . . the astronomer who discovered Halley's Comet. His premise was that there are four concentric spheres, one within the other, like those dolls from Russia that fit inside each other. Then, in the nineteenth century, another chap called Symmes resurrected the idea. He — WHUP!" Dr. Burrows cried as his feet slid from under him. He skied a distance in the loose shale covering the slope, then managed to right himself. "Nearly lost it there."

"I think you did," Will muttered.

"Where was I? Yes, Symmes's contribution to the theory was that there were two whopping great holes in each of the planet's poles, and that the gas escaping from these was the cause of the aurora borealis — the northern lights, as they're called . . . or maybe Halley proposed that."

"Dad, I've heard all this before, so why are you banging on about it again now?" Will asked a little tetchily.

"Because those ancient people I was researching in the Great Plain have to have gone *somewhere*. They can't simply have been jumping to their deaths down the Pore or the other voids. This wasn't some flash-in-the-pan aberration that took place one day when an entire race decided to commit mass suicide like a pack of lemmings."

"But that's a lie about lemmings, anyway — they don't commit suicide at all," Will pointed out. "It's a myth."

Dr. Burrows went on, regardless. "No, with these people, it *had* to have been more than that. . . . I mean, they even built a temple in praise of the other world that they believed was deep inside the planet, calling it their *Garden of the Second Sun*. The triptych I saw in the temple clearly demonstrates that they thought it was some sort of idyllic place, some sort of Utopia."

"Maybe the spiders gobbled them up?" Will suggested mischievously.

"That doesn't make sense — they wouldn't have gone to all the trouble of making the map on the stone tablets or carving their three-pronged symbol near the submarine, or wherever it is. No, they were deadly serious about it all. . . . They were on their way somewhere . . . but where?"

Since Will didn't offer any sort of opinion, they walked on in silence until Dr. Burrows spoke again.

"Back in the sixties, some oddball professor claimed that a technologically-advanced race inhabited the inner world, and that they had flying saucers."

Will had just about had enough of his father's ramblings. "Right, so Symmes and the other guys were all nutty professors with wacky theories. Your point is . . . ?" he said brusquely.

"They might not have been that crazy," Dr. Burrows replied.

"Wait," Will said, stopping in his tracks.

Dr. Burrows looked at Will expectantly, thinking that he had just had a brainstorm, that he was about to impart some revelation that would shed light on where the ancient race had gone.

It was as though a battle of ideologies was taking place in Dr. Burrows's head, like a tug of war between two opposing teams. The stronger team, with a gray-bearded Charles Darwin as its captain, was made up of all the scientists, historians, and other great thinkers that Dr. Burrows had looked up to and tried to emulate all his academic and professional life. The opposing team consisted of rather more unconventional figures, including the likes of Halley and Symmes, and their captain was Lucretius, who in the first century B.C. had convinced everyone that the world was flat as a pancake.

As a matter of course, Dr. Burrows would normally have been cheering on Charles Darwin's team, but now, as the rope creaked and the two teams strained, he found himself strangely drawn to the unconventional team. It was as if he was beginning to take the Hollow Earth theories seriously.

"What is it, Will? Have you thought of something?" Dr. Burrows asked with bated breath.

But instead of shedding light on the fate of the ancient people, the only light the boy shed was from his lantern, which he was directing at a nearby passage. It led off to the right of the main trail, and Will was slowly moving toward it. "If we're close to where the submarine was, this might have been one of the tunnels we tried, but didn't take because of the teen spiders?" Switching off his lantern, he flipped the night-vision device down over his eye so he could see farther inside the passage. "Dad, *does* it look familiar to you?" he asked eventually.

"I . . . think . . . it . . . does," Dr. Burrows said slowly, rubbing his chin.

Will was impressed. "Really?"

"There's something about that piece of rock up there at the top — the way it hangs down."

"That's amazing! You remember that?" Will asked.

"Yes, because I noticed it was unusual at the time. It's obviously from the ignoramic class . . . and I reckon it could be stupidite."

"You mean igneous class?" Will whipped his head around to his father. "*Stupidite?* There's no such thing."

"Ha!" his father burst out. He had been profoundly disappointed that his son wasn't taking the Hollow Earth theory more seriously, and had decided to exact his revenge.

"Stupidite," Will repeated, shaking his head.

"Look, Will, I've trogged down more miles of tunnel than I care to remember, and they all look the same, tediously so. Do you really expect me to recognize that particular one from all the thousands of others?"

But Will had tuned out what his father was saying. Turning back to the tunnel, he sniffed the air. "Spiders. I smell spiders." Sliding one of the Bergens off his shoulder, he put it down, untied the top, and then took out a radio beacon. He switched this on and carefully positioned it on a ledge.

"Is that so your chum can find his way?" Dr. Burrows asked snidely.

"Drake?"

"Why else do you think he gave you those beacons? It's so he can follow us down when the mood takes him." Dr. Burrows suddenly leaned over Will's Bergen and snatched out another of the beacons, secreting it in his coat pocket.

"What do you want that for?" Will asked, closing the top of the Bergen and then hoisting it over his shoulder.

"Just want one," Dr. Burrows answered childishly.

"Why?"

"In case we get separated. Then you can find *me*."

Frowning, Will raised his Sten gun and edged slowly forward into the passage.

"Spiders, you say? Can't smell anything," Dr. Burrows said as he reluctantly followed his son in, making a show of sniffing loudly.

They had gone a few hundred feet when something scuttled away into the darkness.

"Yes, spiders," Will whispered. "I was right. And keep that luminescent orb shielded or you'll knacker my headset."

"Let's just go back to the main stem and try the next off-shoot," Dr. Burrows carped. Ignoring what Will had said about shielding his light, he was holding it high above him as he scanned the openings in the roof of the passage, all of which looked ominously spider-sized. "We don't want to get cut off in here."

Something loomed out of the darkness: The first thing Will saw was the glowing lure at the tip of the stalk on the spider's head. In the blink of an eye, it had sprung at him, landing within the limits of the light cast by Dr. Burrows's orb.

"Good heavens!" Dr. Burrows exclaimed as Will opened up with the Sten, shredding the spider with rapid fire. The only problem was that bullets were ricocheting alarmingly off the sidewalls of the tunnel.

"Will! Enough!" Dr. Burrows yelled, and his son released the trigger.

As they stepped over to inspect what was left of the creature, Will was chuckling. "Take that, spidey!" he said as he rammed a fresh magazine into the submachine gun.

"It was a big brute," Dr. Burrows commented, as he nudged part of its hairy body with his toe cap. "Took quite a bit to kill it. At this rate, you'll have used up all the ammo before we've got anywhere," he reflected.

Will nodded. "Yes, that was nearly a whole magazine — thirty-two rounds. Better find out if we can use the repellent on them instead."

"And just *how* are we going to do that?" Dr. Burrows posed.

"Because if I know my spiders," Will said, "the blood from this one will bring a swarm of the things on us."

"Um . . . is that such a good —?" Dr. Burrows began nervously, but didn't finish the sentence as Will drew out his Browning Hi-Power and pulled the slide back to cock it.

"Safety's off," he said to his father as he thrust it into his hands, sounding remarkably like Drake.

"These aren't pussycats we're dealing with here," Dr. Burrows muttered under his breath.

Tearing off the duct tape, Will pulled the aerosol from his arm and held the can beside his Sten gun. Then they waited, searching the darkness before them.

Dr. Burrows was distinctly uneasy. "This is a terrible idea," he complained.

"Shhh!" Will said, as they heard stones being dislodged, then he yelled, "LOOK OUT!" as several glowing lures accelerated at them from the gloom. Will had been right — the scent of the blood from the dead spider had been irresistible to the beasts.

Shouting "EAT THIS!" Will pointed the can directly at the spiders and sprayed frantically. As the spiders hit the cloud of vapor, the effect was instantaneous. The creatures couldn't get away quickly enough, their legs tangling with each other's as they scuttled into reverse.

When all sign of them had gone, Will shook the can and looked at it, a smile on his face.

"Works like a charm," he said. "Nice one, Drake."

The iron door to the cell slammed back against the wall with a skull-shaking crash. A man stood there, his gargantuan bulk almost filling the doorway.

"Rise and shine, darlin'," he said. "No use pretending you're still sparko."

Although Mrs. Burrows had been conscious for some hours, she suspected someone might be watching her and hadn't moved from the damp lead shelf.

The man's tone hardened. "On your feet, Topsoiler. Don't make me drag you out!" he bellowed.

After she'd come to, she had felt incredibly ill, as if all her insides had been mashed up. She wondered what the device in the cart had done to her. She couldn't remember much after it had started to make deeper and deeper sounds and the sides had suddenly flapped open, but one thing was for sure: It had given her the mother of all headaches. With the pain thumping in her temples and a foul taste in her mouth, she'd lain there in the pitch-black of the cell as she tried to take stock of her situation. The more she thought about it, the bleaker her outlook appeared to her — if she had one at all.

From the staleness of the air, there was little doubt in her mind that the Styx had taken her below the surface. This meant any chance of escape was highly unlikely. And the Styx certainly weren't going to send her on her way with a pat on the back. Not after the stunt she and Drake had tried to pull.

Despite the bleakness of her situation, Mrs. Burrows wasn't as frightened as she might have been. It was a bit late now for regrets. She'd agreed to act as the cheese in the mousetrap knowing she might lose her life — the Styx were out to get her anyway, so maybe it had only brought forward her day of reckoning. As she lay on the shelf and took deep breaths, she knew she had no option but to accept whatever fate lay in store for her. There was no use ranting and railing against the inevitable. At the very least, the deep breathing had seemed eventually to rid her of her headache.

"That's it," the monster of a man grunted and began to stomp toward her, his hand extended.

She sat up straight.

"Good morning," she said, seizing his hand and shaking it. "I'm Celia Burrows. What's your name?"

Flummoxed by his prisoner's behavior, the man shook her hand back.

"I'm . . . er . . . the Second Officer," he stuttered.

"I thought you were a policeman," she said, peering at the dull gold star stitched onto his jacket. "From your very fine uniform."

"Why, thank you," he replied, letting go of her hand and puffing out his chest so that he resembled an overinflated hot air balloon.

Then he remembered what he was there for.

"Come on. Get up," he growled.

"There's no need to be so rude," Mrs. Burrows retorted. "Manners maketh man."

"I said —"

"I heard what you said." Taking her time, she rose to her feet, adjusted her clothes, then stepped past him and through the door into the aisle outside. She took in the dim glow of a shielded luminescent orb above a wooden desk at one end of the aisle and the open door at the other.

"Where is this?" she asked, as the Second Officer joined her.

"It's the clink."

"Yes, that much I was certain of," she said, smiling at him. "But are we in the Colony?"

"The Colony is several miles away. This is the Quarter," he replied.

"The Quarter," she repeated. "I think my son said something about it."

"Your son!" the Second Officer hissed, the pale skin of his face suddenly reddening. "Let me tell you about your son, Seth Jerome, or . . . or whatever his Topsoil name was."

"Will," Mrs. Burrows put in. "Will Burrows."

"Yes, Will *bloody* Burrows," the Second Officer said, his voice full of scorn. "That little tyke clouted me with a shovel, he did," the indignant man added, passing a hand over his almost completely bald scalp as if the injury still caused him pain.

"Why? Were you a rude pig to him, too?" she asked, her voice all sweetness and light.

"I . . . ," he began, then his huge face went through a seismic shift and he snarled, "Don't you talk to me like —"

"If you're the Second Officer, where's the First Officer?" she cut him short. "Having a breather back at the primate house?"

The man wasn't sure quite what to make of this, but answered nevertheless. "He's on duty at the front desk. What's a *primate house*, anyway? Never heard of that before."

"No, no reason you should have, but you'd fit right in there. It's a place up on the surface where impressive specimens like you go to eat bananas. And it's very popular — crowds come from all around to watch."

"I like bananas," the Second Officer said, his mood lightening as he smacked his lips together.

"Thought you might," she murmured under her breath.

As they reached the doorway at the end of the aisle, she held back for a second to glance at the other cells.

"Have you got anyone else in here . . . Drake or perhaps Leatherman?"

"No, you're the only one at the moment," the Second Officer said.

Dismayed by his answer and thinking the worst, she allowed herself to be escorted from the Hold and into the whitewashed hallway beyond. Although her eyes were still adjusting to the bright light after the gloom of her cell, she caught a fleeting glimpse of the main entrance of the police station. She saw the front desk, where another policeman, a younger version of the Second Officer, was craning his head to get a look at her. But the Second Officer shepherded her hastily to the right, into a corridor with a row of closed doors.

"My mouth is very dry — I'd really like some water," Mrs. Burrows said.

"Better to have an empty stomach," the Second Officer advised her, nodding slowly, "before the *Dark Light*."

Mrs. Burrows didn't like the sound of that at all. She tried to remember everything Will had said about the Dark Light and his interrogation as they passed down further corridors, the sound of her footfalls on the polished flagstone floors a delicate counterpoint to the Second Officer's heavy clumping steps.

Then she saw an open door up ahead. Light was flooding from the room. She squared her shoulders and readied herself as the Second Officer steered her inside.

The first thing she laid eyes on was a single chair — a chunky affair made of stout, age-darkened timber. It was in front of a table, on which was some type of device that she immediately assumed was the Dark Light itself. But she didn't dwell on this as there were two Styx, in all their frightful glory, standing behind it. She'd seen them in Leatherman's surveillance footage, but she'd never been this close to the people who, according to Will and Drake, were evil personified. Other than the two Rebeccas, she had to keep reminding herself. But these were adult Styx, and she couldn't stop herself from staring at them. She took in their starched white collars atop their coats of the blackest black. She saw the sheen on their dark hair, and their putty-colored faces so gaunt and stern. She saw the eyes that seemed to burn with an otherworld intensity and which froze her blood.

The Second Officer had helped her into the chair and passed straps around both her wrists, securing them to the arms of the chair. She'd been so mesmerized by the strange beings that she only really became aware of what the Second Officer was actually doing as he began to fasten each of her legs in place. She tensed her forearms against the thick leather restraints, realizing that she was well and truly in their power. Then the Second Officer looped a strap around her forehead, pulling her head back against the headrest. Because of the design of the headrests, with two padded clamps on either side, she had no option but to look straight ahead, where the two Styx were waiting on the opposite side of the table.

She heard the Second Officer take his leave and the door close behind him. Then she was alone with the Styx, and the loudest silence she'd ever known permeated the room. The bizarre men simply stared at her, their intent pupils glinting like highly polished black diamonds. She suddenly had the feeling that at any moment someone was going to shout "Cut!" and she'd see the cameras and production crew . . . that none of this was actually happening but was merely a scene in a movie. She caught herself. *No!* The old Celia Burrows was trying to surface — this was precisely the way she would have once dealt with the situation. She had to face the stone-cold reality. She had to face her demons. These demons.

They suddenly moved, swiveling so that their rake-thin bodies were arched toward each other. Gesticulating jerkily, they broke into a language the likes of which Mrs. Burrows had never heard before. The closest thing she could compare it with was the sound of paper being ripped and torn. It was ugly, and set her nerves even more on edge.

"Why don't you just get this over with?" she declared, her tone defiant. "Do your worst, you pair of cadaverous scarecrows."

They ceased their exchange and turned to her.

"As you wish," the one on the left said in a nasal voice, and immediately reached toward the device on the table. His movement was darting, almost reptilian. His pale fingers flicked a switch on a small black box, from which a twisted brown cable ran to an odd-looking device she had assumed was the Dark Light. While this did vaguely resemble some kind of table lamp, the bulb didn't look anything like a normal bulb — it was purple, but so dark as to be almost black.

With a rattle, the box began to vibrate, then settled down again. The Styx adjusted some controls behind the light. As he withdrew his hand from it, Mrs. Burrows was sure there was a suggestion of a smile on his tight lips. She saw the bulb flare a dark orange, then dim again.

Quite abruptly, without either of the Styx moving a muscle, the room seemed to be plunged into darkness. Mrs. Burrows tensed as her ears popped — she felt as if she was descending in an express elevator. *Here we go again*, she thought as her teeth rattled together. She remembered the same sensations when the machine in Mrs. Tantrumi's cart on Highfield Common had been fired up.

Although the Styx were lost in the gloom, she could hear them talking to each other. Then she heard a *click*, as if a switch had been thrown, and before her was a scene in which millions of tiny sparks showered down on what looked like a calm night sea. Were they trying to frighten her with these special effects? *This isn't so bad*, she said to herself.

Then it got bad.

It was as though something was attempting to worm inside her head, like a hungry maggot trying to push its way through the skin of an overripe peach. But whatever it was, it was bigger than a maggot — more like a hedgehog, but a world apart from the storybook Tiggy-Winkle variety found in piles of leaves that have gathered in the garden. No, this one had supersharp steel spines and no compunction about causing pain. And cause pain it did. Mrs. Burrows screamed in agony as it suddenly sunk inside her cranium, bouncing from one hemisphere of her brain to the other and back again. Then it scurried forward to sit just behind her left eye, making her blink involuntarily as her eyelid went into rapid spasm. Then it was back in the very center of her cranium again. She grimaced as her headache returned, worse than ever, and she was sure she was going to vomit.

Both Styx began firing volleys of questions at her.

"What is your name?"

"What is your purpose?"

"Are you with the man called Drake?"

"What was your purpose?"

"Where is Will Burrows?"

"Where is your husband, Dr. Burrows?"

"Where are the girls you knew as Rebecca?"

"Where are the Dominion phials?"

"Name? Purpose?"

"Where are the Dominion phials?"

There was no way she was going to answer, but each question seemed to be launched from afar, as if she was watching a flaming comet plummet toward her from a starless sky. And when it actually struck, she was racked by the most excruciating pain. Her whole body was rigid and straining against the restraints, and she was dripping with sweat.

The Styx kept the questions coming, repeating them in a continuous cycle, every so often lobbing in a fresh one. And when these fresh ones came, it was as though an even larger and fierier comet, a white hot streak of pure plasma, had been shot straight at her.

And all the time, the evil hedgehog in her skull was rooting around and going exactly where it pleased. Memories of various events in her life were flashing up before her: First it was the day when she and Dr. Burrows moved into their new flat in Highfield; then the meal at the local Indian restaurant to celebrate his appointment as the curator of Highfield Museum. She remembered the afternoon they had brought Will home for the very first time — when he was not much more than a toddler — and they put him into his brand-new playpen.

As if a deck of cards was being shuffled, these memories were appearing and disappearing so fast she could barely keep up with them. She wondered if this was her life passing before her eyes because she thought she was about to die. But, no, she realized it was the thing in her head. It was helping itself to whatever it wanted, and she couldn't do anything to stop it. She felt violated.

She attempted to hold on to the thought that at least she'd tried to help Drake, tried to assist him in his struggle against these people and, in so doing, to help her son, Will. She'd failed. But at least she'd tried. She was proud of that, even if she *was* about to die.

34

AS WILL AND his father traveled farther down the passage, they came into a section sheathed in fungus.

"I never thought I'd be pleased to be in mushroom land again," Will said, knowing that it meant they were getting close to where the submarine had been. Then, as they heard the sound of falling water, they finally came to the end of the passage. "The void," Will said.

For a while they both stared out into the darkness, trying to catch their breath. Dumping his Bergens, Will leaned out as far as he dared from the mouth of the passage to investigate what lay below.

"Got anything?" Dr. Burrows asked as Will pulled back.

"No — we're on some sort of overhang, so I can't see much."

"Marvelous," Dr. Burrows complained. "I suppose we're going to have to retrace our steps and try the next offshoot?"

Will was already pulling a climbing rope from one of his Bergens. "This will be quicker," he said, scanning around for something to secure it to. He stepped slowly back from the void and farther into the tunnel until he spotted a boulder. Looping the rope around it, he knotted it. Then he went back to the void and played the rope out.

"You should take this," he said, passing his father one of the aerosol cans. Then he sprayed himself with repellent and retaped his can to his arm. "Still got my Browning?" he asked.

Dr. Burrows nodded.

"Great. Wait for me here," Will said, and started for the edge.

"There isn't going to be any more silliness with — you know — your thing about heights, is there?" his father asked him.

"I wish you hadn't reminded me," Will replied, "but, no, I seem to be OK now."

And he wasn't troubled in the slightest by the irrational urges that had plagued him before. And due to the reduced gravity, it was barely any effort to walk himself down the vertical wall of the void, but the never-ending deluge of water against his face made it difficult to see anything around him. He kept looking over his shoulder in case any spiders or Brights decided to turn up. He estimated he was three-quarters down the length of rope when he caught sight of a passage mouth off to the side. It was level with him, but about a hundred feet farther around the void, and he couldn't quite get enough traction on the fungus-coated wall to reach it without slipping back. He resorted to swinging himself like a pendulum until he was finally far enough over to drop into it.

He held the Sten and the can of repellent ready. The passage seemed clear, but he was just giving it a couple of squirts to make absolutely sure when he heard a sound behind him.

It was the beat of wings in the air.

He turned.

It was a Bright.

About six feet away, with its wings extended and its legs reaching out toward him.

Will yelled out in alarm and, acting purely on instinct, gave it a full burst from the aerosol.

He'd fully expected the creature to zip away, but it didn't. It hung there for what seemed like seconds. Then the strangest thing happened. Will could only compare it to when salt is sprinkled on a garden slug and the poor animal froths up and eventually bursts in a messy splurge. In the same but much more immediate way, viscous fluid oozed from joints all over the Bright's body as it shook frenziedly.

Then, piece by piece, it simply fell apart. Its two-pronged abdomen was the first to go, with a wet, slurping sound. Then its head lolled to one side and rolled off altogether. The thorax with the wings still attached went into a dive, turning end over end as Will watched it vanish down the void.

It took him a moment to recover from his fright, then Will began to laugh with relief. "Well, Drake, A+ for this stuff!" he yelled.

Like a small voice calling through the chaotic fog in her brain, a notion occurred to her. Mrs. Burrows seemed to still retain some control over her breathing, and she began deepening each inhalation, holding it in for longer and longer before she released it. Part of her mind cleared for an instant, as if a wind machine was blowing the fog away, and she grasped at the memory of what her yoga master had taught her. At first it was elusive; then, as she concentrated with every fiber of her body, she had it.

"I pray that I might not let those around me spoil my peace of mind," she began to think or say — she couldn't tell which — over and over and over again.

Her body still felt as though it was a length of wood bowed almost to the breaking point, but the evil hedgehog didn't seem to be quite so energetic or effective anymore.

"I pray that I might not let those around me spoil my peace of mind." As she continued to repeat this mantra and maintain the rhythm of her deep breathing, the strangest thing happened.

Where there had been darkness was light.

It was as though she'd been flipped into a completely different reality, the one she'd left behind as the Styx had activated the Dark Light. For starters, she could see around her, see that she was back in the brightly lit room again. She watched the Styx. One of them was repeating the constant cycle of questions at her while his companion asked about completely different matters. And, to her astonishment, she found she was replying voluntarily to these questions, and in some detail, too. Voluntarily, but involuntarily.

He was asking her everything she knew about Drake; what he had told her when she was Topsoil with him; where he'd taken her; and if she'd met any of the other people in his network.

That's enough of that, the part of her mind that was in the brilliantly lit room decided, and in midsentence Mrs. Burrows stopped what she'd been saying about Drake. Frowning, the Styx looked at her askance.

"Continue," he barked.

"You can sod off! You've got as much as you're going to get from me!" she screamed, then clamped her mouth shut.

The other Styx abruptly ceased the cycle of repetitive questions and they both glanced at each other. Then the Styx behind the light made an adjustment to it, and it flared an even brighter orange. The evil hedgehog swelled to the size of a cat and became more powerful, its spines sizzling with pure energy. As Mrs. Burrows kept the meditation exercise running endlessly through her mind, she felt the presence of the overgrown hedgehog circling around her head. But it just didn't seem to be able to find a way in.

The Styx adjusted the light again so the intense orange flooding out of the bulb was even brighter than before. The hedgehog grew to the size of a dog, but Mrs. Burrows found she could still repel it and stay in the well-lit room at the same time. She had a picture of herself simultaneously riding a bicycle and juggling. *If there's one thing we women are good at, it's multitasking*, she thought jubilantly.

The Styx ramped up the output of the Dark Light several more times, until Mrs. Burrows could stand it no longer.

"*I pray that I might not let those around me spoil my peace of mind*," she enunciated quite clearly — certain that she was actually saying the words aloud this time — then passed out. Every ounce of energy had been drained from her.

In an instant the Second Officer, now accompanied by the slightly younger First Officer, came into the room. The Second Officer began to release Mrs. Burrows's restraints.

"So you got what you wanted?" the First Officer asked, sensing that all was not right.

"She was shutting us out," one of the Styx said, and the Second Officer stopped what he was doing as both he and his colleague stared at the saturnine man.

"But nobody's ever done that before," the Second Officer gasped in astonishment.

The Styx were silent.

"Then you're not finished with her yet?" the First Officer ventured.

"No, and in a few hours, when she regains consciousness, we start all over again. We do it as many times as it takes," the Styx behind the Dark Light said.

"We *will* break her," the other Styx agreed.

"Even if it kills her?" the Second Officer asked.

Both Styx shrugged indifferently.

"So be it," they said, almost in unison.

Having climbed back to where his father was waiting, Will had his work cut out for him persuading Dr. Burrows that they should give the new passage a try. Complaining loudly, he eventually agreed, and lowered himself down the rope.

Will repeated the trip several times to fetch all their gear, then planted a radio beacon before they set off down the passage, only to find themselves at a fork. They chose which way to go at random, and were almost immediately faced with another intersection, then yet more, and before long they had absolutely no idea what direction they were actually going in.

But more significantly, they found that they were encountering some very steep gradients.

"I reckon we've dipped quite some way below the seam now," Will observed as he leaped down an incline.

Dr. Burrows wasn't happy. He hadn't been in favor of leaving the seam so early. "We don't know where we're going, we don't know where we're going," he sang in a bittersweet way.

"We *never* know where we —" Will was just replying when they both heard a low noise, like a murmuring, coming from somewhere up ahead.

Will had the aerosol at the ready in a split second, as Dr. Burrows fumbled the Browning Hi-Power out of his pocket and pointed it nervously at the darkness.

"Hold on, Dad, can't see any creepy-crawlies," Will whispered as he used the headset to scan the stretch in front of them.

They both listened.

It came again. It wasn't just a murmuring, it was a voice, a human voice, and Will immediately recognized whose it was.

"Sounds like Chester!" he said to his father.

"Careful. It could be that Limiter," Dr. Burrows warned in hushed tones. "Might be a trap."

"No, that's Chester all right," Will decided, hardly able to contain his excitement. He dropped his voice several octaves, making it as gruff and manly as he could. "Chester Rawls, is that you?" he called out.

Silence. Then Chester replied.

"Will?"

"Chester!" Will burst out in his normal voice, overjoyed. "Sure *is* me! I'm here with Dad, and we're both OK."

"Thankfully! I knew you'd be all right! Elliott and Martha are with me, and we're all fine, too. But what's with the silly voice, and *where*, exactly, are you? I can't see you, but you sound really close!"

"So do you! I've got my headset working again, so we'll come to you," Will proposed. "Just keep talking so we can find you."

"Got you, loud and clear," Chester confirmed. *"And did those feet in ancient times, walk upon England's . . . ,"* he began to sing, although he was so out of tune it was painful to listen to him.

But as Will and Dr. Burrows moved into the labyrinthine network of passages before them, Chester's voice seemed to fade away, and there was absolutely no sign of him or the others. Flummoxed, Will and Dr. Burrows retraced their steps to the point they'd started from and, sure enough, they could hear Chester again.

"Onward Christian soldiers, marching as to war . . . ," the boy was singing.

"Chester, can you hear me? Stop that awful racket for a second," Will said.

"Course I can hear you. Where've you been? We've been waiting here like a bunch of muppets, and I'm getting a sore throat!"

Dr. Burrows suddenly spoke up. "Chester, Dr. Burrows here. I think I know the reason for this. It might be similar to the whispering galleries you sometimes find in large churches or cathedrals. There's one in St. Paul's. What's happening is that the layout of the tunnels, maybe helped by the fungus lining them, is reflecting our voices. We might be much farther apart than we think — maybe even miles — but our voices are being transmitted by the acoustics."

Martha now joined the conversation, her tone rather terse. "You stay put this time — it's our turn to find you."

It was a good ten minutes before Chester, Elliott, and then Martha stepped out from around a corner and revealed themselves.

"Chester!" Will cried, leaping up as he saw the trio clearly through his headset.

"That was really weird. Mushroom-powered radio! Now I've heard of everything," Chester exclaimed. But when he was close enough to see Will and Dr. Burrows's military garb and their new weaponry, he was speechless, and simply stared at them.

"Chester, you just won't believe where we've been. We found this fallout shelter, and a river, which we took up to the surface," Will replied. "We went back to Highfield. We went *home*."

"Home?" Chester choked, almost unable to take in what Will was telling him.

"Yeah, and Elliott, that number you kept repeating when you had the fever . . . I found out what it was," Will said.

"Number?" she repeated as she tried to work out what he

was talking about. Then it clicked. "The emergency number! So you saw him! Drake's alive!"

Will nodded. "Certainly is. He was waiting for us in Highfield."

As something detached itself from the shadows behind Chester, coming full pelt along the ground, Will yelled, "Watch out!" He gave whatever it was a full burst with the aerosol.

Bartleby stopped in his tracks, a chaos of scrabbling legs on the fungus floor, then bolted back into the tunnel, yowling.

"Thought it was a spider," Will said unapologetically. "So you took the traitor back in."

"He may be a traitor, but he just led us to you," Chester replied. "Besides, you're one to talk — *you* took that lying twin back in."

They locked eyes, their expressions deadpan, then Will said, "Touché," and they broke into laughter.

Chester took two massive strides over to his friend and hugged him. "Will, it's so good to see you," he said. "But I'm not sure I'm ever going to forgive you for grabbing a quick holiday Topsoil, not without me."

"You will when you see the food we've brought back with us. Fancy a curry?" Will said.

"Is the sky blue?" Chester chuckled.

Martha lit a fire to heat the food, and Elliott dived into the Bergen full of equipment from Drake. As Dr. Burrows sat by himself scribbling furiously in his journal, Will told Chester all about the underground harbor and their return to the surface.

"So, we follow these radio beacons, and we can get home

again. Simple as that?" Chester said. "And we don't have to mess with the Deeps or the Colony." He punched the air with his fist. "Result!" he roared.

"Yeah, but don't forget what Drake said — we've got to make sure about Dominion first," Will reminded him.

Chester arched his eyebrows. "And how exactly do we do that? If the Styx didn't reach the sub in time *and* they somehow survived the blast, then they've either been gobbled up by spiders or the Brights, or —"

"Or they're still floating around here somewhere," Will interrupted.

Chester looked doubtful. "They could be miles away by now. And if they *did* reach the sub, then they could be miles *down*. C'mon, Will, the likelihood is that they're out of the running, isn't it?"

"Drake wants us to make sure," Will said.

"Then that's what we do," Elliott put in, her tone resolute. She'd been listening to the boys' conversation as she reverently handled the two spare Sten guns Will had brought with him. "We can have a scout around and see if Bartleby picks up any scent trails. And if the submarine got hooked up somewhere farther down the void, we might not have to go too far to check it out."

"But what if it's all the way at the bottom?" Chester posed.

He never received an answer to his question, and he didn't much mind as right at that moment Martha announced that the food was ready.

With Martha handling Bartleby, who was in full bloodhound mode as he strained on his leash and sniffed away at the fungus floor, they explored the passages. They were making their way lower and lower, until they reached the huge cavern that Elliott's explosion had carved out of the side of the void. Once there, Drake's climbing ropes gave them the means to work their way around to the other side of the cavern, past where the submarine had been, and into one of the tunnels that lay beyond it.

They trekked down this tunnel and, just as Martha was saying that they must be close to the void again, Will and Chester made a discovery that was to change everything.

"Dad, you need to see this," Will called to him.

"What is it now?" he answered cantankerously. He'd been moseying along at the back of the group, supposedly to protect them from any spider attacks to the rear. But he certainly wasn't being very vigilant, his can of repellent stuffed in his duffle-coat pocket. And he'd also been peculiarly uncommunicative for the last couple of hours.

As he joined his son, Dr. Burrows saw that a tall boulder protruded from the fungus, and that the three-pronged symbol was scored into it. "Yes!" he shouted, and hastily removed his Bergen. He delved into it and fished out the black-and-white photograph the submariner had taken.

"Snap! It's the same one," he confirmed as he held up the picture to compare it with the boulder before him.

"And, Martha, you're right — we're at the edge of the void again," Will said. He stared down into the darkness where the showers of water fell, wondering where the submarine was. Then he wheeled around to face his father. "But what does this sign mean, Dad? That we're only at the beginning of the map on your tablets? That doesn't make sense, because it's a heck of a hike from the Pore to get here."

Dr. Burrows didn't answer as he ran his fingers over the three deep notches chiseled into the boulder.

"Dad, if you think about it, how can this be the beginning of the map?"

Dr. Burrows looked up, his lips slowly curving into a smile as he nodded approvingly. "Good boy, Will, you got there, too. After you worked out how to put the tablets in the correct order, I assumed that they were describing the route from left to right. How mistaken I was to use our Western conventions, when I should have been thinking more laterally. The fact is, they describe the route right to left. So my premise that this symbol must be at the *start* couldn't have been more wrong. No, indeed, it marks the *end*."

"If we're stopping here, I could brew up some tea?" Martha offered, but no one took any notice of her, least of all Dr. Burrows, who was putting on his Bergen again as if he was going somewhere.

"I don't get it. If this is the end of the trail, where the heck is the rest of it?" Will asked. "Where did the ancient people go from here?"

"Faith," Dr. Burrows merely replied.

"Huh?"

"Take physics, for example. . . . The lower gravitational pull that we're experiencing down here is the reason that we lived to tell the tale after falling thousands of miles," Dr. Burrows said, lobbing his luminescent orb up and snatching it out of the air by the lanyard as it drifted down. Then he stuck his hand through the lanyard, winding it around his wrist so it was held securely in his palm. "And if one continues to travel toward the center of any massive body — this planet, for instance — then it follows that the gravity will continue to decrease even further. Maybe to nothing. Maybe to a zero gravity belt."

"Sorry, Dad, I don't underst —" Will tried to say.

"But I'm not just talking about faith in the laws of science. I'm talking about faith in one's convictions, in one's beliefs. For far too long, I lacked faith, and faith can move mountains, faith can open your eyes to whole new lands."

"Well, are we going to take a breather here or not?" Martha asked again.

Dr. Burrows was looking only at his son as he spoke. "You think I've been callous and selfish, Will, but some ideas are too big and too important to let people get in the way. I'm sorry if you think I've been a poor father to you, but one day you'll understand." As he stepped slowly toward Will, he felt inside his coat for the radio beacon and, pulling it out, waved it in front of his son's face. "You'll be able to find me, if you want to. It's up to you."

"What do you mean?" Will said.

Dr. Burrows continued past Will, and when he was on the ledge with just the void before him . . . he launched himself off.

"Dad!" Will screamed, lunging at his father in an effort to grab him, though there was no way he could have reached him. Dr. Burrows had gone.

"No!" Chester whispered. Martha and Elliott ran over to watch Dr. Burrows spiral into the vacuum below, the luminescent orb in his hand growing dimmer until there was no sign of it at all.

"He just killed himself," Martha muttered in disbelief. "Is he mad?"

After the initial shock, they all simply stared down into the infinite darkness. Then Will began to whistle through his teeth in that random way Dr. Burrows did when he was deep in thought.

"Dad may be a little crazy, but he's not mad," he replied eventually, with a glance at Martha. "What he was saying about the gravity does make sense."

"Will, are you all right?" Chester asked. He placed a hand on his friend's shoulder, concerned at the detached way he was taking Dr. Burrows's death leap. It wasn't the reaction that Chester would have expected.

"Logically, the gravity should be even less toward the center of the planet, shouldn't it?" Will pondered out loud.

"So what?" Chester spluttered. "We're hardly going to put it to the test, are we?"

Will nodded, not in response to Chester's question, but as if he'd suddenly remembered something.

"Martha, you never told us what this void is called. Don't the Seven Sisters all have names, like Puffing Mary or the Pore?" he asked, as he slipped off his Bergen and began to rummage through it.

Martha shook her head. "Nathaniel and I never got around to it, and I didn't want to have anything to do with the place after he died," she said.

Will smiled to himself. "But it should have a name.

Everything has a name. Why don't we call it *Smoking Jean*, after my Auntie Jean, because her apartment's sort of like a black hole, too," he said. He took several radio beacons and a pair of larger devices, the trackers themselves, from the Bergen before putting it back on. Then he swung around to Chester, Elliott, and Martha.

"Talk to me, Will. What are you doing with those?" Chester asked, frowning.

Will held up one of the trackers. With a pistol grip, it resembled some sort of stubby handgun, but it had a small dish at the front and a dial on the top. He switched it on and aimed it at the void, where his father's signal caused the needle to vacillate and a slow ticking to come from the device. "That's my dad," he said. Then he made a quarter turn, and the needle showed a weaker signal and the ticking came more slowly. "And that's the way to the fallout shelter."

He went over to the tall boulder with the carving. "Let's mark the spot, shall we?" Will said, activating a new radio beacon and then sliding it into a crack in the boulder. "And one for each of you," he added, doling out the other three beacons to Chester, Elliott, and Martha. He did this so quickly, they didn't have time to refuse him.

"Why do I need this?" Elliott demanded, holding her beacon up.

"Will?" Chester said, close to losing his patience.

"Oh, yes, nearly forgot — you'll need this, too," Will added, thrusting a tracker into Chester's hand. "Follow the bread crumbs and you'll get yourself home."

"Don't be stupid. I'm not going anywhere without you,"

Chester growled, now very angry. As he tried unsuccessfully to give the device back to Will, it picked up the signal from the tall boulder and gave a rash of loud *clicks*. "I don't want this!"

But Will seemed to be in a world of his own and wasn't listening to a word that was being said to him. "My guess would be that the twins made it to the sub, and they're down there in Smoking Jean somewhere." He chuckled to himself. "Isn't it funny? The Styx brainwashed me with their Dark Light so I'd jump and kill myself, but Drake helped me to stop it. And now that I'm over it, that's exactly what—"

Chester noticed the glint in his friend's eye, and that meant trouble. "So help me, Will, if you . . . ," he said, interrupting him, but he never completed the sentence.

Will turned the second tracker on and, following in his father's footsteps, he broke into a run toward the void.

And flung himself from the edge.

"Nooooooooooo! You crazy maniac!" Chester screamed, but Will never heard him, his ears filled with the sound of rushing air.

In his time at the station, the Second Officer had seen and heard things a normal person would find difficult to deal with. It was as if he'd become numb, as if he'd erected a barrier around himself so that he could filter out the horror.

Now, as he waited in the corridor outside the closed door, that barrier didn't seem to be working. The screams were chilling—the sound of a human soul being torn in half. And he couldn't understand how they seemed to be sustained for so long, hardly pausing even for breath to be drawn.

Then, all of a sudden, a silence descended, which was even more chilling than the screaming.

He heard the footsteps of the First Officer thudding on the damp flagstones as he approached. But the man had only come halfway down the corridor when he stopped and gave the closed door a quick glance. He grimaced, unhappy that the interrogation was taking so long, then slowly turned on his boot heel and began to walk away again, most likely to return to the front desk. In case any more Styx decided to turn up at the station.

Thankful to be alone, the Second Officer wiped the sweat from his brow. For an instant his face contorted, as if he was about to weep. He didn't know why he should be feeling like this, but perhaps he'd had about all he could take of the misery and suffering that went on in this place. He regained his composure — and just in time, too, as he caught the low rumble of voices and the door swung open.

The old Styx strode imperiously out, accompanied by his young assistant.

"All done?" the Second Officer said.

The old Styx looked up at him, mildly surprised by his interest.

"We got what we needed," he replied curtly. "We always do."

"Er . . . she . . . is she . . . I mean . . . is she still . . . ?" the Second Officer asked.

Arching his brows, the old Styx broke into the policeman's incoherent stream. "If you're asking if the Burrows woman is still alive, her heart appears to be beating and somehow she's breathing," he said, then moved to the side of the doorway. "See for yourself."

The Second Officer stepped into the light flooding from the room. He could see the back of the chair in which Mrs. Burrows was still strapped. One of the Styx had unfastened the restraint around her head and it was slumped forward, unmoving. Beyond her he saw three Styx, who were packing up a whole bank of Dark Lights. There must have been six or seven of these lights on the table, but at that moment the Second Officer was so over-wrought he couldn't even count them.

"She was a tough nut to crack," the young assistant commented. This was said with the detached air of a doctor discussing a patient's case notes. "One of the toughest yet."

"Yes," the old Styx concurred. "Unusually resilient." He swept his hand in the direction of Mrs. Burrows's motionless body. "What you see is merely a husk. I'm afraid there won't be anything much left inside — we had to break *all* the crockery in the shop. It's a shame, because I was rather hoping we might use her again in the future."

"She probably won't last the night," the young assistant said.

"I was wondering . . . ," the Second Officer began, his voice failing as the old Styx's hard eyes switched to him.

"Yes?" the old Styx said.

"If she hasn't got long, I could look after her," the Second Officer blurted out.

The old Styx lowered his head, as if inviting an explanation. To say that the Second Officer's request was irregular would have been a rank understatement.

"I mean, rather than let her die in the Hold. Even though she was a Topsoiler, she . . . she seemed like a good sort to me," the Second Officer gabbled, then shut his mouth and looked at his feet.

For a moment no one spoke, then one of the other Styx came out of the room carrying a Dark Light in his arms, and passed down the corridor.

The old Styx smiled, but it wasn't a pleasant smile. It was the smile of someone who had learned something they could use, and *would* use, in the future.

"Have you got anyone at home, officer?" the old Styx inquired. "She'll need to be cared for while you're on duty."

"My mother and sister," he replied.

"Take her, then, but it's probably kinder just to let her fade away in the Hold," the old Styx said, and began to move off with the young assistant several paces behind him, like a shadow. *"All the king's horses and all the king's men couldn't put Humpty together again,"* he recited without looking back.

The Second Officer waited until they were out of sight, then slid a finger around the inside of his starched collar. It was slick with sweat. He didn't know what had come over him. He should never have spoken out of turn like that. But he'd felt he had to.

He took a deep breath to prepare himself before he went into the bright room.

35

THIS TIME Will was fully conscious.

As he hurtled through the air, he went into an uncontrolled spin, then came out of it only for the same thing to happen again. The G-force was so powerful that his head swam and he thought he was going to be sick. But he quickly found that if he spread his limbs like a skydiver, he could bring himself out of the spins, which made his downward passage far smoother. And by angling his arms and legs, he could precisely direct his flight, despite the encumbrance of the bulky Bergen and the weapons he was carrying, and avoid any collisions with the sides of the void.

He fell and fell and fell, and there was ample opportunity to ask himself if there would ever be an end to it, a *happy end*.

"What have I done?" he shouted at the showers of water that fell with him, licking his lips and tasting their saltiness. He tried to mop the moisture from the lens of his headset so he could see more clearly, but his movements caused an imbalance and his trajectory became erratic. He quickly extended his arms again. His speed was so great that everything was shooting past, a blur, but he was doing his best to look out for the submarine. He had made a commitment to Drake that he would deal with the Rebecca twins and the Limiter, and he wasn't going to let him down.

He could see the needle flickering on the tracker in his hand, and just about hear the *clicks* it was emitting. His father was somewhere below.

His father . . .

What if Dr. Burrows had got it dreadfully wrong? What if the gravity didn't reduce any further, or, more to the point, what if the void wasn't deep enough for him to reach the areas where there *was* lower gravity?

He hadn't thought of that!

It had seemed like the right thing to do when he'd flung himself into the void. . . . He had listened to his father's words about faith, and they'd made sense to him then. For the first time in a long time, Will had really understood why Dr. Burrows had been acting so incredibly selfishly. And Will had wanted to demonstrate that he, too, had faith; faith in his father.

But now . . . Well, he must have been out of his head to jump. Maybe this was one grand gesture too many.

Then he noticed that the onrush of air against his face seemed to be less intense. It wasn't snatching his breath away anymore. And, although it was difficult for him to be certain because the change had been so gradual, he could have sworn that he wasn't falling quite so rapidly.

The tracker continued to click away merrily to itself, but there was still no sign of anything below — just the crimson glow from the incandescent rock on the sides of the void as he plummeted past. He felt the intense heat on his exposed skin for the milliseconds he sped by these red-hot rocks, and heard the hiss as some of the cascades of brine were instantly turned to steam.

Then he was absolutely sure he wasn't falling so fast.

He could mop the moisture from the lens on his headset without going into a helter-skelter tumble. And he could study the sides of the void as he descended, take in the patterns created by the shifting water droplets accompanying him down.

Some time later, he began to feel as if he was actually floating, but he realized that this might be his brain playing tricks on him because he'd been falling for so long. It was also around this time that he began to hear a low rumbling sound. Maybe it had been there from the beginning of his drop but he'd been too preoccupied to notice it.

As he listened further, the sound seemed to be growing louder, much louder even than the rush of air in his ears. He scanned down below him.

What could be causing it?

A bizarre picture of monstrously huge cogs and gearwheels flashed through his mind — maybe it was a vague memory of some children's story he had read when he was young. He tried to laugh it off, but the picture persisted. Perhaps he was heading toward the earth's engine room, full of giants operating equally giant machines.

He shook his head, as if he was trying to shake himself from a ludicrous dream.

Due to the rumbling sound he couldn't hear the clicking

from the tracker anymore, but he could see that the needle was going crazy.

He scanned below him.

There!

In the corner of his eye he caught a tiny pinprick of light far, far below.

As a gust of wind buffeted him and he rotated in his flight, he lost sight of it and couldn't locate it again. Had it really been a light that he'd seen? It wasn't lava, that much was for sure — wrong color.

Then he spotted the light again. And when Will pointed the tracker in its direction, the display seemed to show a higher signal. He angled his limbs and maneuvered his flight path toward it.

As the light grew in size, he became less certain. Was this such a good idea? Although the tracker was indicating that his father's radio beacon was somewhere close to the light, he also couldn't dismiss the possibility that it might be the Styx.

By now his speed had diminished to the point that he hardly felt as if he was falling at all, more like a soap bubble being buoyed along by the wind.

The light grew bigger. It was giving off a blue glow, but he couldn't judge how far away it was.

Making sure he had his Sten ready, he continued to glide toward the blue light.

Just as he made out a long sleek shape below him, it came up much faster than he expected, and he crashed straight into it. It wasn't a hard impact by any means, but he banged his head and felt a little dazed.

Someone grasped his arm and hoisted him to his feet.

"Get off!" he shouted. He tried to struggle with what he thought was the Styx, then saw the glint from a pair of glasses.

It was his father. Will registered the intense blue glow emanating from behind him. Dr. Burrows had evidently set off one of Drake's flares. And it took Will a couple of seconds to realize that he was actually standing on the submarine. He hadn't recognized it right away because it was tipped over onto its side. Will had landed near one end of its hull, although he couldn't tell if it was the prow or the stern.

Not knowing if he felt so euphoric because he was still alive, or because now he wasn't alone in this remote and isolated place at the bottom of the world, Will flung his arms around Dr. Burrows. Even that small movement sent them both shooting along the hull of the submarine for quite some distance. Talk about being weightless!

As Will got back on his feet, he could almost feel himself drifting off the surface of the hull. His father was wagging his finger at him, then put his thumb and forefinger together to form a circle. Zero gravity — that was what Dr. Burrows was trying to tell him. It wasn't quite zero gravity, but Will was going to have to be extremely careful about how he moved around or else he'd float over into the void, like a space walk gone wrong. Will nodded at his father to show he understood, and tried to talk to him, but his voice was lost under the rumbling sound. He realized then just how tumultuous it was.

Still a little dazed, Will allowed Dr. Burrows to lead him to the conning tower, which, because of the way the vessel had come to rest on its side, was sticking out into the void. Then his father was pointing at something far below them. Will leaned over. In the distance, glimmers of light came and went, like lightning on the far horizon during a thunderstorm.

Dr. Burrows attempted to tell him something, speaking directly into his ear.

Will shrugged — the noise was far too great for him to hear.

Dr. Burrows produced a scrap of paper and wrote on it. He showed the paper to Will. It was a single word.

"Triboluminescence?" Will mouthed back at Dr. Burrows, who nodded excitedly. Will knew what that was — his father had demonstrated it to him once using two pieces of rock quartz that he'd rubbed hard together. In the darkened cellar of their home back in Highfield, Will had marveled at the eerie flashes of light suffusing through the milky crystals. Although at the time it had seemed like magic, it had something to do with energy being released when the bonds are broken in a crystal. So below him, unbelievably large pieces of some type of crystal must be grinding against each other. That would explain the sound.

Will wondered if this was it — was this really the center of the earth?

The spectacle of the lights as they rippled in all directions — something like electrified cotton — was hypnotic, and father and son simply stared at it, filled with wonder. But there were other matters on Will's mind, and he eventually pulled his eyes away from the lights and looked down at the thick metal shell beneath his feet. As he contemplated the runnels of water running over its dull gunmetal surface, he was alert to the fact that the three Styx could be inside at that very moment. Inside with the Dominion virus. Perhaps it didn't matter anymore — perhaps there was absolutely no way for him, Dr. Burrows, or any of the Styx to get back up the void again, so the threat had effectively been neutralized. But he was here now, and he had to make sure.

He took out the climbing rope from his Bergen and knotted one end to a metal cleat he found on the side of the conning tower. Better safe than sorry — even a small slip on the wet hull might send him careering off toward the huge crystals below. Keeping a tight grip on the rope, he stepped very carefully to what would have been the top of the conning tower if the submarine had been the right way up.

As Dr. Burrows watched, Will began to lower himself over and into the conning tower. It only required the most minimal effort to make any sort of movement — the pull of gravity was almost nonexistent.

But as soon as he reached the observation platform, he froze.

Not three feet away from him, there was something disturbing stuck to the duckboard flooring, which of course was now vertical rather than horizontal given the orientation of the submarine. Two crumpled white wings waved slowly in the air currents.

"A Bright!" Will said through his clenched teeth. But as he looked further, he saw that its head and most of its abdomen were missing. In rigor, the barbs at the end of its articulated legs still gripped the duckboard, which was the reason it hadn't drifted away.

Will had left his Bergen with Dr. Burrows back on the hull, and with it his cans of repellent. So instead he extended his Sten and prodded the Bright with the tip of its barrel. Nothing. He was pretty sure it was dead — from the Bright's appearance he guessed that the Limiter had made short work of it, hacking the creature apart. Will jabbed it even harder, but there was still no sign of life, so he moved across to the main hatch and tried it. It was firmly shut.

Still giving the Bright carcass wary glances, he began to rotate the wheel in the center of the hatch. As the wheel reached the open position, he checked his Sten to make sure the safety was off. This time he was ready for the twins. This time there would be no hesitation — he was going to open fire the moment either of them, or their pet Limiter, popped their heads up. He closed his eyes for an instant, steeling himself.

Then, just as he was about to yank the hatch open, a small hand seized his wrist, stopping him.

He jerked his head up.

It was Elliott.

He couldn't believe it. Had she followed him down because of Drake's orders? He couldn't imagine any other reason she would have jumped into the void after him. Straightaway he looked behind her to see if Chester had come, too, or Martha for that matter, but neither of them was there.

Indicating to Will that he should move aside, she opened the hatch the tiniest fraction, then ran her fingers around the inside. She was suddenly very still, then shot a tense glance at Will. She delved inside her pocket and took out a length of twine, which she carefully attached to something just under the rim of the hatch. Not paying any attention to the dead Bright, she tied the other end of the twine to one of the slats of the duckboard flooring just beside it. After making sure the twine was drawn tautly, she produced a pair of rusty clippers, which she nosed under the hatch and then used both hands to operate. It was only then that the tension left her face and she allowed herself to relax.

Will brought up his Sten as Elliott very slowly swung the lid of the hatch open. She directed his attention to something just inside it, a package the size of a brick, with a wire extending from it. Or at least what was left of the wire after Elliott had attached the twine to it and cut it, rendering it harmless. Will didn't need to be told that the package was some form of explosive device. The Limiter had rigged up a booby trap, probably putting it together from chemicals he'd found on the submarine. There was no other explanation.

Will followed Elliott inside the conning tower, where she mouthed the words "Wait here," then slipped outside the submarine again. Clinging to the ladder, Will kept on his guard, watching out for the Styx. Elliott was gone for less than a minute, reappearing with both Dr. Burrows and Bartleby, who she was tugging behind her on a leash. She closed the main hatch, and they all crept along the ladder to the submarine's bridge. Now that they were inside, the rumbling sound was considerably reduced, giving them the opportunity to talk.

"That was a close call," Will said, shaking his head. "Another second and I'd have set that bomb off. Thanks."

Elliott held her finger to her lips. "Not so loud," she whispered, looking cautiously up and down the gangways at either end of the bridge. "And don't touch a thing!" she hissed at Dr. Burrows, who had begun to inspect the banks of equipment. "There might be a second trap around here somewhere."

"Chester? And Martha?" Will asked. "They didn't come with you?"

Elliott shook her head. "Just me and the Hunter."

She used Bartleby to make a thorough search of all the compartments, checking for trip wires as she went. Will followed behind, covering her with his Sten. The orientation of the submarine and the fact that they couldn't use the gangways didn't matter, because they were able to float along in midair, like divers swimming through a submerged wreck. As there was no sign of the twins or the Limiter, they made their way back to the bridge, where Dr. Burrows was waiting.

"I never expected you to come after me," Will said to Elliott, in a half question. "You didn't need to."

"Lucky for you I did," Elliott replied, but didn't offer any sort of explanation.

"And Chester — do you know what he's going to do?" Will asked her.

"No, he didn't really say, although I think he might try to go to his Topsoil home. But he did say the next time he saw you he'd knock the living daylights out of you. He said you should've at least discussed it with him before taking a flying jump over the edge like that."

"I was afraid he'd try to stop me," Will muttered.

But Elliott was already thinking ahead. "So the Styx aren't here, but because they rigged the explosive on the main hatch we know that at least one of them survived. So they've either hidden the virus somewhere in this submarine, or—"

"Or they've got it with them," Will interrupted her.

"Correct," she said. "So our job isn't done yet."

"I bet this was one of the new generation of subs with stealth drives the Russians and Americans were both developing," Dr. Burrows suddenly piped up. "Maybe the Russians were using it to spy on England from the North Sea, and as a subsea plate shifted it was sucked down into this void."

"Smoking Jean . . . I've named this void Smoking Jean," Will said.

"After Celia's sister . . . How very appropriate." Dr. Burrows grinned momentarily, then he was off again on his theory. "And maybe no one knows this sub has been lost because the Russian government would hardly want to publicize th—"

"Focus," Elliott cut him off sharply. "We need to focus. There's absolutely no point hanging around here. I'm going to set a charge to blitz everything inside this sub, in case they've left the virus behind. Then we need to find out just where they've gone."

"But how? In this place?" Will asked her, then glanced at Bartleby, who was cleaning his nether parts. "Use *Bartleby the Traitor* to sniff them out?"

She nodded. "We'll do a full three-hundred-and-sixty-degree search around the submarine," she proposed. "It'll be faster if we split up—I'll take the area below the submarine. Will, you can take the shelf and the areas on either side, and—"

"No way," Will countered immediately.

"Why not?"

"Because every time they do that in the movies something terrible happens. We stick together. And we make sure Bartleby stays with us, because whenever the cat runs off and someone has to go and fetch it, that's really bad news, too."

"You're your mother's son," Dr. Burrows commented wryly.

Elliott glanced from Will to Dr. Burrows. "I don't know what you're talking about, but if it makes you feel better, we can keep together," she said with a sigh. "Now make yourselves scarce while I set the charges."

Once she had returned outside, Elliott linked them all together with the climbing rope. Will watched her as she was doing this. Although she had risked everything to reach this phenomenal depth in the earth, and there might be no going back, there was a grim determination about her. She was set on doing her duty and finding the Styx. Will drew strength from this. Maybe he'd acted on a rash impulse when he jumped after his father, but he was proud that he'd also risked his life to do what he had to do. Just as Drake would have expected of him.

They made a thorough search of the fungal ledge around the submarine. Bartleby didn't pick up any trails there, so they began to climb down the inclined side of the void underneath the ledge, on the lookout for any caves or openings, or any evidence that the Styx had gone the same way. As they reached another fungal shelf below, Bartleby was becoming increasingly agitated. Will didn't know if the constant rumbling was putting him on edge, but whatever it was, he didn't seem to be finding any trace of the Styx.

As they climbed still farther down the void, they found that there were no more fungal ledges below them, and were forced to cling to the bare rock face. The biggest risk remained that if one of them made a sudden movement, they might all be sent careering off into the void.

When Elliott's charges in the submarine finally detonated, they had covered quite some distance, and heard nothing of the explosion over the unceasing rumbling. Nevertheless, as they all paused to watch the brief blaze of light above, Will felt a little strange, because with the submarine gutted they now had nowhere they could return to. They were very much alone in this alien environment, where trying to find three Styx was tantamount to searching for three needles in the biggest haystack imaginable, and in the darkest of nights, too.

After a while Elliott drew them to a halt and indicated that they should reverse direction. She obviously thought they'd gone far enough and that it was time to search higher up the void.

It was exactly at this moment that one of the group made an overzealous movement.

Before they knew it, they were sailing away from the wall at some speed and out into the middle of the void. Will could see Elliott's panic-stricken face and her open mouth as she screamed, then he realized he was doing exactly the same. But he couldn't hear anything except the jaw-rattling rumbling, and there was nothing that he or any of the others could do but grab tightly on to each other, with a very anxious Bartleby trailing several feet behind them on his tether.

Eventually their momentum diminished as the air resistance brought them to a halt.

But it wasn't quite a halt. They were still drifting through the nothingness at the center of the void, similar to when the engine of a boat fails and it's left to the vagaries of the currents.

Thoroughly confused, Bartleby hadn't stopped thrashing his long limbs in an attempt to get back to the side. Now Will and Elliott joined in with him, paddling with their hands and kicking out, anything to get themselves into motion again, but it was all to no avail. As the hours passed, the three of them attempted to communicate with each other, but what could they do? There were no fungal ledges to aim for, and even if there were, they had no means of reaching them. And while Will and Elliott remained in a state of panic, Dr. Burrows appeared strangely composed.

They gravitated toward a large boulder, which was spinning slowly on its axis, and were eventually able to seize hold of it. Its surface was pitted and rusty, like that of an asteroid. They clung to it for a while, then, at Dr. Burrows's suggestion, they used it to push themselves off, precisely as though they were three divers jumping into a pool. *Equal and opposite forces*, Will thought as they went one way and the boulder the other — although it really didn't get them anywhere. Using his headset, Will continued to check the space around them, hoping and praying there would be something else to help them. They bumped into pieces of rock and sometimes encountered small cloudlike formations of gravel, but nothing substantial. Will was still scanning all around them when, with a start, he realized he could no longer see the sides of Smoking Jean. They seemed to have disappeared altogether. Looking over his shoulder, he spotted them at some distance behind, growing smaller by the second.

Will knew then that they had gone beyond the void.

He pointed frantically in an effort to tell his father, but Dr. Burrows just shrugged in response. Slowly but surely they seemed to have floated into a totally new area. Into the area where the triboluminescent flashes came and went.

Will broke into a cold sweat as he saw that ahead of them was an infinite darkness. It was as though they had been shot beyond the stratosphere and into outer space, but this was some kind of *inner* space at the center of the earth.

All they could do was watch the triboluminescence as they gradually approached a continuous belt of what appeared to be floating mountains of crystal. As these crystals trundled ponderously around against each other, the evanescent but regular bursts of light zipped through the belt, allowing Will to make out that it stretched as far as the eye could see to the left and the right. The closest thing he could compare it to was the satellite photographs he'd seen of the rings of Saturn. There was a dreamlike quality to the lights, and as he stared at them, he found he was becoming almost mesmerized. This must be one of the wonders of the planet, he thought to himself, knowing that he might not be around long enough to tell anyone about it.

And it was impossible to judge distances. Wave upon wave of nausea washed through Will, and this wasn't solely due to the effect of the zero gravity on his stomach. It was because he had the impression he was falling toward the lights from an incredible height. And at other times his mind played tricks on him; he really believed the lights were in touching distance and would try to reach out to them. They became a string of Chinese lanterns flickering on and off. But as he regained his sense of perspective, he knew that there was probably a vast distance between where he was and where the belt of crystal mountains lay. Will wondered if they would simply die of hunger as they drifted there, marooned in the night-black darkness; or if they ever did get as far as the rotating crystals perhaps they'd be crushed to a paste between them.

Then Dr. Burrows gathered them together and tried to explain something by scribbling on a scrap of paper and motioning with his hands. In the end, he gave up and simply took Will's Sten gun from him. He slipped off the safety catch and, without any warning, he shot it. It was as though a retro rocket had been fired. Bartleby was startled by the muzzle flash from the weapon and Elliott had a heck of a job restraining him, but they were on the move again. The recoil from the Sten had propelled them at some considerable speed — not back toward the void, but deeper into the space where the crystal mountains were slowly turning.

For the life of him, Will couldn't understand what his father was hoping to achieve, but he didn't attempt to stop him. At least he seemed to have a plan. Dr. Burrows continued to fire the Sten, Will and Elliott reloading the magazines for him each time he emptied the weapon. Sometimes the shots made them wheel dizzily around as they went forward, but more often than not Dr. Burrows got them just right and they sped straight ahead.

Will found he'd completely lost track of time. They hadn't eaten anything or slept for what seemed like ages, but the whole scale of the place was so mind-blowing and so terrifying that none of them dwelt on this for very long.

And words such as *up* or *down*, *left* or *right* held little meaning in this place — there was only the crystal belt to orient themselves on.

It may have taken them as much as a day — Will really couldn't tell — but they entered an area where dust particles and water droplets hung in the air, making everything hazy. Many hours later, it seemed to Will, they'd passed through this area and were moving away from the crystal belt. Just as he was wondering if the dust they'd traveled through was at the very edge of the belt, he thought he caught a glimpse of what his father was aiming for.

Dimly visible in the distance, he spotted a beam of light. It was different from the triboluminescence — it was constant. And it gave them all hope.

With each shot from the Sten, the beam of light was coming that little bit closer. And when Will looked back, they definitely seemed to be leaving the crystal belt behind. But as Dr. Burrows fired the weapon time and time again, Will began to worry that they'd run out of ammunition. Then he found they were actually *in* the beam of light. There was a quality to it, a warmth, that prompted him to think it could be sunlight, but that notion didn't make much sense to him.

At one point, Dr. Burrows stopped using the Sten and became terribly animated as he jabbed a finger toward the crystal belt. The column of light penetrated it like a searchlight, enabling them to see that it was not only composed of the huge rotating crystals. No, between them were suspended large bodies of water, like huge raindrops, but these suggested the size of lakes, seas, or maybe even oceans. And in these bodies of water, there appeared to be moving objects. It may have been a trick of the light, but they all swore later that they had caught sight of huge snakelike creatures and fish as large as whales.

Dr. Burrows continued to use the recoil from the Sten to drive them toward the source of the light, which grew so strong that Will switched off his headset. He saw that Elliott was smiling, and then he realized why. They seemed to have left the huge area and entered a new void. The illumination allowed them to see its walls around them. They were still moving toward where the light was originating, moving deeper inside this void. And little by little, gravity was returning. And the rumbling sound was diminishing, too.

It was hard to tell because of its scale, but the new void appeared to be conelike, with steeply angled sides. Dr. Burrows drove them closer to one of the sides, where they could see no sign of the ubiquitous fungus, but something much more surprising. They began to notice small specks of green in among the rocks: alpine plants growing together in clumps in the scree. These specks of green became more numerous the farther in they traveled, until eventually they were joined by gnarled, knotty trees — sorry-looking specimens with twisted trunks and very little foliage that gave the impression they were hanging on to the steep sides for dear life. And when, finally, Elliott spotted a ridge on the sidewall, Dr. Burrows took them over to it.

Like survivors washed up from a shipwreck, they crawled a little way and then just lay there, panting and more grateful than it was possible to express that they were back on terra firma. Elliott had the presence of mind to rope them to one of the trees — the last thing they wanted was to drift off again.

They passed around a canteen of water, and although the rumbling sound was at more bearable levels and they could hear each other, they barely exchanged a word, because none of them knew quite what to say. But they were alive, and as they realized this, their sheer fatigue overtook them and they slept.

"And do the Princes fade from earth, scarce seen by souls of men," the old Styx declaimed as he stood by the very edge of the Pore in the Deeps.

A little distance around the perimeter, ranks of soldiers in formation were lining up and leaping from the edge. As these Limiters deployed their parachutes, they resembled wind-borne seeds drifting gently down into the wide expanse of darkness. Each soldier was loaded with equipment, and a number had large bundles dangling below their feet, which writhed and growled.

"Takin' the dogs with them, too?" said a perturbed voice. "Why are so many of yer soldiers takin' the plunge? Either this is a suicide mission, or yer know something I don't."

"*But tho' obscur'd, this is the form of the Angelic land,*" the old Styx continued. He turned slowly to regard the misshapen human form, its head draped with filthy cloth, that had materialized beside him. "I wondered how long it would take for you to show up, Cox," the old Styx said.

Cox was silent for several seconds, and when he spoke there was indignation in his voice. "Nobody told me 'bout this. What are yer Limiters up to? And what's with the dogs — why do they need stalkers with them?"

"We have recently learned that the twins are still alive."

"Down the Pore?" Cox gasped. "No, can't be."

"It can be — our information is indisputable. So there's every chance we can recover the Dominion phials."

"Ah, that's good. So —" Cox gushed, but the old Styx silenced him with a flash of his obsidian eyes.

"Let me finish. Not only did the twins survive, but also the Burrows child and so, it transpires, did Elliott."

"Burrows? Elliott?" Cox gulped. On hearing this, his head twitched like a bird's and he took a hasty step back from the old Styx. As nebulous as his body was, from the way he was holding himself there was no doubting that this piece of information had made him acutely nervous.

"Yes, they're both down there somewhere," the old Styx said, rubbing his chin absently. "And if I recall correctly, your side of the bargain was to deliver up Will Burrows and anyone who'd had contact with him, and in this you have failed us singularly. And to add insult to injury, Drake is loose Topsoil, where he's been a minor but very real irritation." The old Styx raised his black-gloved hand and a pair of Limiters immediately appeared on either side of Cox, hoisting him into the air between them.

"But I am not without compassion." The old Styx grinned, showing rather too much of his teeth. "I'm prepared to give you the opportunity to honor your commitments."

"No, please, no, no," Cox gibbered as it dawned on him what the old Styx was saying.

"Isaiah, chapter twenty-eight, verse fifteen — *'We have made a covenant with death, and with hell are we at agreement,'*" the old Styx quoted.

"You don't want to do this, not to yer old friend Coxy."

"Deal's a deal," the old Styx said simply. With that the Limiters heaved Cox into the Pore. As he corkscrewed downward, his filthy black stole flapped in the wind behind him, making him look like a particularly hideous warlock short of one broomstick.

"Rough justice — wasn't that what you said, Cox? Rough justice?" the old Styx yelled, his voice echoing around the Pore.

36

WILL OPENED his eyes. He found he was lying on his front, his head resting in the scree, and only inches away from his nose was a most curious sight. It was a slow-moving creature that for all intents and purposes could have been a well-fed slug. But what set it apart from the common garden variety was that it had alternating stripes of light and dark green down its back, which seemed to pulse with iridescent light.

Because he was going cross-eyed, Will pulled himself back so he could see the slug more clearly. It sensed his movement and immediately stopped in its tracks.

"Hello," Will said. As it continued to hold completely still, he puffed lightly on it.

All of a sudden, the slug rolled itself inside out, so that the vivid greens were replaced by a dull gray color almost indistinguishable from the rock it had been slithering across. At the same time it contracted into a ball. If Will hadn't just seen it two seconds before in its glowing green incarnation, he would have assumed it was merely a satisfyingly round pebble.

Since it was insisting on playing dead — or playing at being a piece of inanimate rock — Will blew on it again. This time there was no reaction at all, so he blew even harder.

There was a popping sound and it flicked itself straight up into the air like a flea, then was gone.

"What the . . . ?" Will exclaimed, sitting up sharply.

As he scanned around, he saw that Elliott and Bartleby were still asleep. However, his father was wide-awake, lounging against a small fern tree.

"Did you see that?" Will said to him.

His father nodded, but his eyes were burning with an intensity that had nothing to do with the discovery of a flying slug.

"I've never seen anything like it before . . . must be a completely new species," Will said.

Dr. Burrows held up a hand. "Will, that's really not important . . . not right now."

"What do you mean?"

"Just look around you. Haven't you realized where we are? We made it . . . we're actually inside the planet. We're *inside* planet earth!"

Will didn't answer right away, angling his head to catch the golden light filtering down from above. "But . . . no . . . that's *sunlight* up there," he said falteringly.

"Yes, Will, it's sunlight, but not from *our* sun," Dr. Burrows said. "That ancient race knew a thing or two — they found a way through here, and we've followed in their footsteps. We made it through, just like they did. We've done it!"

Will frowned deeply, struck by a thought. "Dad . . . when we drifted off the side and into the middle of the void, I thought Bartleby had done it — I thought he'd pushed us off." Dr. Burrows held his son's gaze as he continued. "But it wasn't him at all, was it? It was you."

As Elliott mumbled in her sleep, Dr. Burrows touched his finger to his lips. "Shhh — not so loud, Will."

But Will wasn't about to be silenced. "You were making darned sure we *couldn't* get back. And when you were firing my Sten, you didn't know where you were taking us, did you? You had no idea if we'd make it here, or if we'd just die somewhere in that horrific place?"

"No, no idea at all," his father admitted. "It was a shot in the dark." He looked very pleased with himself at this unintended pun, and repeated it again. "A total shot in the dark."

"You — !" Will growled, appalled that his father had been so ready to risk their lives, and then could be so casual about it.

"You're quite right to feel like that, Will, but just *look* at what we've achieved," Dr. Burrows said softly, glancing again at Elliott. "And I'd advise you to keep mum about all this, because now's the time we need to pull together and get ourselves to the top. If you rock the boat with young Ellie over there, it isn't going to help us any."

"Her name's Elliott, and you're a freakin' wacko. You could have killed us with your crazy ideas," Will accused him.

"Well, I didn't, did I?" Dr. Burrows retorted. "And if we'd just hung around at the bottom of 'Smoking Jean,' how long do you think we'd have lasted?" He raised his eyes toward the light. "Look, Will, when we get to the top and there's nothing there but some solar-swept barren desert, then you can congratulate yourself for being right . . . as we all die from starvation and lethal skin cancers." He nodded to himself. "Like Icarus, we will have flown too close to the sun."

Will didn't know how to respond to this. Dr. Burrows had turned everything on its head, so that if Will *was* right, then it sounded as though they were all doomed. Will lay back on the scree, and when Elliott finally woke up he didn't tell her what his father had confessed. Besides, what difference did it make now?

Still roped together, they climbed farther up the interior of the giant crater, and the air became warmer and the light grew brighter. The crater wall inclined at approximately forty degrees, but despite this the going hadn't been too arduous at first because they were still relatively weightless. However, as they rose higher, the increase in gravity began to pull them down, making them feel like they were dragging themselves through molasses. The vegetation also became more abundant, which didn't help matters, either. They were forced to dispense with the climbing rope because it kept getting hung up on the larger trees, but then there were frequent and rather frightening occasions when one of them would lose their footing and start to tumble pell-mell down the inside of the crater wall. The trick, they quickly learned, was to spread their limbs and grab at the nearest shrub or tree to stop themselves from falling farther.

With the light growing in intensity, Elliott was clearly having problems as she groped her way up the incline. It was very different from the catlike nimbleness she usually exhibited, but Will wasn't overly surprised. She'd never experienced anything like these levels of illumination before, and he just hoped she'd be able to adjust to it.

Then they encountered a stretch where nothing grew and a dark brown residue coated all the rocks and saturated the soil.

"Some sort of oil slick?" Will asked his father. He looked ahead, trying to work out where it had come from.

Dr. Burrows rubbed the glutinous dark substance between his fingers, then took a sniff of it. "Yes, in a way. I think it's bitumen," he decided.

"What — same as the stuff they use on roads?" Will said, not liking the sound of this.

"Yes, but this is naturally occurring — it must be flowing out of the strata. One theory is that it's derived from huge accretions of primordial microscopic organisms that, over the centuries, bacteria breaks down to leave just this fraction." Dr. Burrows wiped his fingers on his pants. "By the way, try not to get too much on your skin — it's not unknown to have arsenic and other nasties in it."

"Bit late for that," Will muttered, examining his hands as they set off again.

After what seemed like several days of hauling themselves through the ever more abundant vegetation and further deposits of bitumen, they were finally out of the crater and on level ground again.

"Incredible!" Dr. Burrows cried. "We're here!"

"Wherever that is," Will said under his breath. "I thought we'd *never* reach the top." He stretched his back, enjoying being able to stand up again.

Dr. Burrows slipped off his Bergen. "Don't think I'll be

needing this. Not in this climate," he said as he removed his duffle coat as well. He took out his binoculars. "Just look at this place!" he exclaimed. "It's beautiful."

Squinting, Will began to scrutinize the range of hills that formed the horizon whichever direction he turned, and then he examined the deep red soil underfoot.

Elliott staggered a few paces, and raised her hand to shield herself from the fiery ball of light in the sky. "It's scorching," she puffed.

"That's because the sun is always directly overhead," Dr. Burrows informed her. "Here it's always midday."

"What are you talking about?" Will spat.

Dr. Burrows studied his compass, then looked up. "The earth doesn't orbit around this sun — this second sun is up there in the sky day in, day out . . . in fact, there is *only* day . . . there's no night at all here."

"Only day," Elliott echoed, meeting Will's eyes.

If what Dr. Burrows was saying was right, Will realized how strange this concept must be for her. Her whole life had been spent underground and all she'd known up to this point was the permanent shade of subterranean lands. But the journey through the Crystal Belt and into this new world had taken her from one extreme to the other.

"*The Garden of the Second Sun*," Dr. Burrows proclaimed as he continued to survey their surroundings. "I shall call it Roger Burrows Land!"

Will had heard enough. "Dad, I'm sorry, but I'm not buying this *second sun* stuff," he said, shaking his head. He thrust his finger at the scene before them. "Look at the woodland, or forest, or whatever it is over there on the sides of the hills." He shrugged. "All perfectly normal. How can you say we're inside the planet when it all appears so normal? And tell me something — if you're right, why can't I see the land curve *upward?*"

"Well, even if those hills weren't blocking our view," Dr. Burrows explained patiently, "the massive scale of this second world, combined with the heat haze, would probably make it difficult for us to see very far. But maybe, given favorable microclimatic conditions, we will be able to observe a little more of the other sides of the sphere."

Will shook his head again. "So that big burning thing in the sky is what, exactly?"

"I told you — it's the second sun. It must have been here from the beginning of time, when our planet was created after the big bang. And here it's been for millions upon millions of years, without any of us knowing, spinning away in its own secret existence."

"You're saying it's like some sort of star?" Will ventured, frowning.

"Yes. A cloaked star. I suspect it might not be an isolated case, and there are others out there in the universe, but of course we have no way of seeing them," Dr. Burrows suggested. "And common sense dictates that this sun's far smaller than the one in the middle of our solar system — it has to be in order to fit inside our planet."

"Oh, come on," Will shot back quickly. "Somehow, and I don't know how, we've managed to climb up another of the pores — one that's open at the top — and we're on the surface again. I know the plants are a bit weird . . ." He hesitated as his gaze fell on a large blue flower the size of a beach ball. ". . . but maybe we've come up in Africa or something. Listen to those crickets — don't you get them in Africa?"

Nobody spoke as they listened to the rhythmic clicking sounds coming from all over.

"Cicadas," Dr. Burrows decided. "They sound like cicadas, which you get in tropical areas like —"

"Told you," Will interrupted him. "We're back on the surface."

"Really?" Dr. Burrows said. "If that's so, then what about the gravity? Go on — try it."

"All right, I will," Will replied, taking up the challenge. He bounded up and down several times, reaching unfeasible heights above the ground with each successive jump. As he stopped jumping, he seemed undecided. "Feels lower than normal."

"Thank you," Dr. Burrows said a little scornfully. "In fact, it's much lower. And that's because it's mainly centrifugal force keeping you on the inside of this rotating sphere, which is less than the force of gravity we're used to back on the surface." Dr. Burrows stopped speaking as they heard a twittering noise and a flock of flame-red birds swooped past. They were the size of pigeons, but far more refined in appearance, with fanned tail feathers, fine, curving beaks almost four inches in length, and, most remarkably, two pairs of wings. One of these birds dipped down to the blue beach-ball flower and, hovering by it like a hummingbird, poked its beak deep inside the bloom to collect nectar.

"Ever seen anything like that before?" Dr. Burrows asked his son.

"Can't say I have," Will conceded reluctantly.

As they turned to begin the journey toward the mountains, Bartleby sprang up and grabbed the flame-red bird in his jaws.

"Bartleby! No!" Will shouted, but it was too late.

Elliott led them toward a V she'd spotted in the hills, which turned out to be the right decision because a pass lay there. Although this meant they didn't have to do any more climbing, the "woodland or forest" Will had referred to was the thickest jungle imaginable, and it took them many hours to push their way through the tangle of vegetation and cover even a short distance. When they finally emerged from it, they found they were at the edge of an area of scrubland, perhaps a half mile square. It was bordered by more jungle, which rose to an incredible height and looked even more dense than the stretch they'd just come through.

"I wonder why this area isn't overgrown, too," Dr. Burrows pondered, bending down on one knee and beginning to poke around in the grass while muttering something about "pioneer colonies" of plants.

"Hey," Will said to his father as he spied several herds of animals grazing at the distant reaches of the clearing.

In an instant Dr. Burrows was up and peering through his binoculars. "Buffalo," he said. "But see over there." He pointed to a far corner of the scrubland.

"Zebra?" Will suggested, just able to make out their black-and-white markings.

"They're like zebra, but the stripes stop behind their forelegs. . . . Will . . . I do believe they're quagga!" Dr. Burrows exclaimed, then gave a slightly hysterical giggle.

"Nah. Quagga are extinct, Dad," Will said dismissively. "The last one died in a zoo in —"

"I know, I know — the eighteen-eighties . . . a zoo in

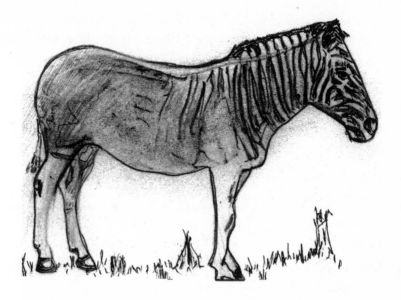

Amsterdam." Dr. Burrows lowered his binoculars. "But they haven't been hunted to extinction here. It's as though they've been given a second chance!"

"You mean *we've* been given a second chance," Will contradicted him.

Dr. Burrows was silent as something else caught his eye and he passed the binoculars to his son. "Just above the tree line — tell me what you see."

"Looks like smoke — a big cloud of it," Will answered.

"Yes, I saw that," Dr. Burrows said. "A bushfire, I'd say. The foliage probably gets so overheated that fires break out spontaneously. From a quick examination of the ground around here, there appears to be a thick layer of ash under the new raft of vegetation." He paused dramatically. "But I wasn't talking about the smoke. Take another look, Will."

Will adjusted the binoculars. He didn't say anything, but

then lowered them and met his father's eyes. "Pyramids . . . two of them."

"Yes," Dr. Burrows said, "and they—"

"—look like Mayan pyramids," Will interrupted him. "The tops are flattened, just like them."

"Yes . . . Mayan pyramids," Dr. Burrows agreed. "But I counted three. We should head for the nearest," Dr. Burrows decided on the spot.

As they trekked across the clearing, the herds of grazing animals seemed not to take the slightest notice of them, as if they held no fear of human beings. But Will was feeling more and more uncomfortable. He held out his forearm to examine it.

"What's the matter?" Dr. Burrows asked him.

"It's the sun—I can't stay in this much longer. It'll burn my skin off," Will said.

Fortunately, they were close to the perimeter of the scrubland, and Will was soon able to take shelter under the thick canopy of trees.

"Happier now?" Dr. Burrows said to him as they stopped to drink some water.

Then they pressed on, battling their way through the jungle, which was almost impenetrable. Dr. Burrows compared it to Amazonian rain forest, telling Will and Elliott that the trees were several times taller than those in any Topsoil rain forests. They had some respite as they came to several stretches where the going was far easier. The leaf cover was so dense above these sections that it was really quite dark on the jungle floor, and much cooler. Little hindered their progress except the tremendously thick tree trunks and a few smaller bushes, from some of which dangled exotic fruit. Now that she was out of the bright sunlight, Elliott seemed to be in her element once more; she took the lead and upped the pace.

They caught fleeting glimpses of what appeared to be antelope and gazelle. Elliott spotted a large snake coiled around a branch high above them, and although it was motionless, they were careful not to walk underneath it. And on the ground, hiding in the leaf detritus, there were smaller reptiles — vividly colored lizards — and froglike amphibians, which delighted Bartleby as he sniffed inquisitively at them and they scuttled or hopped frantically away from him.

Dr. Burrows had been whistling in his atonal, random way as he took in the varied fauna, but all of a sudden fell silent, and strode past Elliott with an air of self-importance. He'd clearly made up his mind that it was his place to lead the party. However, after he nearly blundered straight into a fast-moving river that was completely hidden by a thick mat of vegetation, he dropped back and let Elliott take the lead again. And they all took more care about where they were treading.

Following Dr. Burrows's compass bearing, they finally came to the edge of the jungle. They stepped out into a clearing. Some one hundred feet away stood the nearest of the pyramids.

Will and Dr. Burrows stopped dead on the spot. Through his binoculars, Dr. Burrows examined the edifice, greedily taking in the detail of each of the tiers as he worked his way to the very top.

"By Zeus, just look at that! Do you see all those carvings! It's stunning!" he cried. "And, Will, look at the scale of it! The apex is way up above the trees!"

"What are those?" Elliott said, squinting at the sky. Huge clouds loomed overhead, blanking out the sun so completely it was as if dusk had suddenly come upon them. At the same time the calls of the cicadas and the birds ceased, leaving an eerie silence.

"Don't worry—they're just clouds. You get them Topsoil, too," Will told her just as a blinding flash of lightning split across the sky. In the next instant, they were pelted by a torrential rain.

"It's a monsoon!" Dr. Burrows laughed.

Will held his arms out, letting the rain wash over him. "Ahh, that's just what I needed!" he yelled above the noise of the storm. But a few seconds later, the downpour had grown so powerful it was knocking them off their feet. "Ow! It hurts!" Will cried as they beat a hasty retreat back into the jungle. "That was a bit *more* than I needed," he complained.

As the three of them watched the deluge from the edge of

the jungle, they heard a crashing through the trees: Not far behind, a hefty branch dropped to the ground.

"The trees certainly take a beating," Dr. Burrows said as Will and Elliott went over to inspect the fallen branch. Will frowned, then bent over and, using both hands, plucked something from it.

"An apple . . . as big as a head?" he said, holding up the massive fruit so his father could see it.

It certainly resembled a giant apple, with beautiful rosy patches on its flawless green skin. Using Cal's penknife, Will cut a hunk nearly the size of a slice of watermelon from it.

"Let me see," Elliott asked, and Will passed it to her. At first she simply sniffed it, then she took a bite. "That's good. Have some," she said, and handed it back to Will, who also sampled it.

"Good? It's totally delicious!" he exclaimed, offering it to his father.

"No, we need to take this one step at a time," Dr. Burrows said. "If we eat the same thing, and it doesn't agree with us, it might put us all out of action. After all, this isn't our natural habitat."

"Tastes pretty dang natural to me," Will said, biting off another large mouthful.

As the rain moved away, they emerged from the jungle, marveling at the drops of water that hung from the edges of the leaves and glittered like diamonds in the bright sunlight.

"What a truly, truly wonderful place. It's totally unspoiled," Dr. Burrows enthused. "Like a secret Eden."

"That was a doozy of a storm," Will said, mopping his face. Their footfalls on the lush green carpet made squishing noises as they went, but even now the ground was beginning to dry out again in the intense sunlight.

"Yes — any bushfires would immediately be quenched by precipitation that heavy. Maybe that's how it goes," Dr. Burrows said thoughtfully.

"How do you mean?" Will asked.

"Maybe it's an endless cycle of fire and water, death and regrowth, which probably makes sense, since technically there are no *seasons* in this world. And the only 'night' here is when the cloud cover blots out the sun, as we just witnessed first-hand." He fixed his son with a stare. "So, Will, now do you believe that this isn't the surface?"

"I think I have to," Will concurred.

"Good boy." Dr. Burrows grinned, placing a hand on his son's shoulder. He turned to face the pyramid. "Shall we take a look at what we've got here, then?" he suggested, and with bated breath they approached the base of the pyramid. "The three-pronged symbol!" Dr. Burrows stated abruptly.

"Yeah, I've got it on every level," Will said as he scanned up the tiers of the pyramid, locating the tridentlike motif carved into the facing stones. They were so large that he didn't need the binoculars to see them. He thought again of the pendant with the same symbol on it that Uncle Tam had given him, which even now hung around his neck. He wondered how Tam had come by it, and whether he'd known of this secret at the center of the earth all along. Will certainly wouldn't put it past him.

"So my forgotten people — who predated the Egyptians and the Phoenicians — might have been responsible for this pyramid." Dr. Burrows was thinking out loud. "Maybe somewhere around here is the Lost City of Atlant —" He broke off at the sound of Elliott's birdlike whistle. They spun to where she was standing, by one of the corners of the pyramid.

"What's she trying to tell us?" Dr. Burrows asked.

"Dunno," Will replied. He immediately took his Sten from his shoulder, shook the water from it, and cocked it. Then he and Dr. Burrows went to investigate.

As they approached Elliott, they saw that before her, spiked on wooden stakes, were three skulls. The skulls had no flesh on them, and were sun-bleached bone-white.

"Human?" Will asked.

"Yes, but not recent," Dr. Burrows observed, as if that was any sort of consolation.

"This one has a wound to the temple," Elliott said as she pointed at the middle of the three.

Dr. Burrows and Will circled around it, studying the irregular hole in the side of the skull.

"You can't tell that for sure," Dr. Burrows countered, shaking his head. "Might have been caused by an accident — a fall or something. And this could be some sort of ritual burial."

"It's a bullet hole," Elliott said unequivocally. "There's an exit wound on the other side."

Will glanced uneasily over his shoulder, regarding the dense jungle around them in a different light. "Why were the skulls left here?" he said.

"It's a sign . . . a warning," Elliott replied.

Will immediately swiveled his head toward her and their eyes met. She'd used precisely the same phrase when, back in the claustrophobic confines of the Deeps, they'd stumbled upon the grisly display of the dead Coprolites and renegades, then come within a whisker of being discovered by a patrol of Limiters. Will had been so upset by the incident that he'd lashed out indiscriminately at Elliott, saying things he almost immediately regretted. His words put a strain on their relationship, and nothing he'd done since had succeeded in salvaging it. But it was different now, as if he'd been given a second chance — an opportunity to start over again with her.

Dragging his gaze away from Elliott, Will addressed his father. "Whatever killed these people, Dad, now we know we're not the only ones here," he said quietly. "Could be anyone down here with us — the men from the submarine, pirates from the old galleon, or maybe something far, far worse."

Dr. Burrows arched his eyebrows.

"Maybe this isn't such an unspoiled place after all," Will said to him.

37

"**WILL SAID** this used a ton of fuel to get them home," Chester shouted as he cut the outboard engine and silence returned to the harbor.

"Don't you fret, my precious boy, I'll fetch some more cans for you," Martha offered as she stood on the quayside, gazing lovingly down at Chester as he remained sitting in the launch.

He watched the plump woman waddling off toward the fuel tanks. "Precious boy?" he muttered to himself, shaking his head. She was getting really scary. Without Will around, she seemed to be focusing all her affection on him, and he didn't like it one bit. She was forever gawping at him with those doe eyes, and it filled him with mounting unease.

The worst moment had come when they'd been trekking up the seam, using the signals from the radio beacons to guide them to the underground harbor. As they'd broken off for a rest, Martha offered to keep watch while Chester got some shut-eye for a few hours. But he'd woken up with a start, certain that someone was stroking his hair. Through the slits of his half-closed eyes he caught Martha making a sudden movement as she retracted her hand. He'd been far too embarrassed and, quite frankly, far too disturbed by the whole incident to confront her about it. And as he thought about it again now his skin crawled.

He certainly wouldn't have attempted the journey to the fallout shelter on his own, and there was little doubt in his mind that he needed someone else with him for the next leg up the river. But he also wouldn't in a thousand years have chosen Martha as his sole traveling companion, not with the way she was acting now.

With the launch rocking beneath his feet, he slowly rose up so that he could just see over the pier. He watched Martha's progress along the quay. As soon as she disappeared into one of the buildings, he was on the move. "Go for it," he said, leaping from the boat. He rushed in the opposite direction down the quay and into the fallout shelter. There he made straight for the radio operator's booth and closed the door behind him.

"The black phone . . . the black phone . . . Will said the black phone," Chester gabbled a little hysterically as he snatched the receiver from its cradle. He listened. "No tone . . . but Will said there was no tone," Chester reminded himself, and hurriedly began to dial the number that Elliott had been repeating while she'd had the fever.

In his haste, he misdialed, putting his finger in the wrong hole. As he panicked, he caught sight of a small poster on the wall. In simple, bold letters, black on a white background, it proclaimed KEEP CALM AND CARRY ON. Some wag had added the word DYING at the very end in blue pen, but the original message wasn't lost on Chester. He took a deep breath and redialed.

"Please be working, please be working . . ."

He waited a few seconds just in case it took a moment for the call to connect. Hearing a crackle in the earpiece, he began to speak into the receiver, his words coming out in a gush. "Drake, this is Chester, I'm about to start the journey up the river, and I . . . um . . . you've *got* to meet me at the top," he begged in a strained voice. "You have to," he added, and ceased for a moment as he thought he heard a noise outside in the corridor. He lowered his voice to an urgent plea, "I'm counting on you being there, Drake. I can't handle —"

Now certain that someone was moving around in the corridor, Chester quickly hung up the receiver and dropped himself into one of the chairs. Putting his feet up on the bench, he tipped his head forward onto his chest as if he'd fallen asleep.

The door creaked slowly open behind him. "My precious boy, are you in . . . ah, you *are* in here," Martha said, a little surprised.

Chester stretched out his arms and yawned in a rather stagey manner. "Must have dozed off," he lied.

Martha ran her eyes over the equipment on the bench without any interest. "I've seen to the fuel, and I was wondering if you're ready to eat now," she said, scratching her bottom through her voluminous skirts.

"Er . . . no . . . that's OK, Martha," Chester replied. "I thought I'd check out the supplies myself a bit later on. Really, you just go ahead and have something and don't worry about me."

"Right you are, dearie," she said, not hiding her disappointment as she shuffled off.

Chester remained in the booth, wondering yet again if

there was any possible way he could complete the remainder of the journey on his own. The thought of steaming out of the harbor without Martha in the launch was very tempting, but from what Will had told him, the trip needed two people to take turns on the outboard. Chester swore silently — no, he couldn't see how he could do it on his own.

And he also couldn't see how it was going to work when he actually *did* arrive Topsoil. There would be the ever present risk of the Styx to contend with, but despite this he was determined that he was going to see his parents. He had to let them know he was still alive. However, with Martha in tow, how would that work? It was as if he had somehow collected a third parent, a doting and rather deranged one. All of a sudden a terrible picture forced its way into his head. In this picture, Martha, consumed by jealousy and frothing at the mouth, was about to use her crossbow on his mum and dad.

"No, no, no, no, no." He rubbed his forehead hard. "Will, wherever you are, you've got a lot to answer for," Chester said, and then, for some reason, he began to laugh. "Will, Will, Will," he repeated, shaking his head and still laughing.

38

WILL HAD TO AGREE with his father — they'd found themselves in an Eden of sorts. Although the discovery of the impaled skulls had struck a discord in their otherwise perfect idyll, they put all thoughts of it behind them and immersed themselves in their new way of life. But, more than anything else, this uncomplicated existence offered them all the chance for them to have a badly needed rest, to recover.

On one of their first excursions into the jungle, Will and his father came across traces of a city. Although the land had long since been reclaimed by the prodigious growth of trees, the numerous ruins suggested that the city had been built on an immense scale, covering several square miles. Dr. Burrows was convinced he'd found where his itinerant people — the *Ancients,* as he had taken to calling them — had settled and established a sprawling metropolis. And the friezes and writing on their pyramids demonstrated that they had been more advanced by many centuries than Topsoil cultures if Dr. Burrows's estimate of the age of the ruins was correct. Their achievements in philosophy, mathematics, medicine, and many other disciplines were simply astonishing.

Dr. Burrows's theory was that the Ancients were the basis for the legend of Atlantis. He was certain that somehow Plato had heard reports of this hidden civilization back in the third century B.C. and had written about it in his dialogues, but had never learned of its true location. And so all the centuries of conjecture that ensued — that the city had been on an island or islands in the Atlantic Ocean or Mediterranean Sea, islands which had been swallowed up by the waves — were completely mistaken. Dr. Burrows was convinced that it had been hidden here in the very center of the earth all along. Will wasn't so preoccupied with such matters, more than content to spend his days working closely with his father as they recorded their findings. It was as though Will's dream had finally come true.

Elliott learned to live with the sun, turning as brown as a berry in no time at all — Will attributed it to her Styx heritage, knowing how the Rebecca twins had just as effortlessly adapted to Topsoil conditions.

Not far from the pyramid, she built a shelter up in the branches of one of the giant trees to accommodate them all. And armed with a bow and arrow, she would go off on hunting trips with Bartleby at her side. The Hunter proved his worth in tracking prey after he'd been persuaded not to just sniff out small rodents and reptiles. The girl and the cat would often be absent from the camp for days on end, going deep into the jungle to stalk gazelle and antelope. These provided an ample supply of both meat and hides, which she knew how to prepare from the skills she'd picked up in the Deeps. She also discovered that several major rivers meandered through the jungle;

Will would sometimes accompany her to these and help her to string nets across them to catch any of the many varieties of large fish.

It was on one of these outings that the unexpected happened.

Taking Bartleby with them — because Dr. Burrows refused point-blank to look after him, maintaining he was far too busy with his work and that it was tantamount to babysitting — Will and Elliott had set off to do some fishing in the largest of the rivers. It was a day's walk from the camp, but Will had jumped at the opportunity for a change of scenery, and to spend time with Elliott.

But Elliott spoke little to Will as they went, their feet hardly making a sound as they trekked across the thick carpet of leaf debris covering the jungle floor. It was as though she was unable to refrain from using the field skills that had been so essential to her survival in the Deeps. Will didn't see the need for this constant state of vigilance at all, quite content to stroll along and observe the wildlife, or to lose himself in his thoughts.

Several hours into the journey, Elliott held up a clenched fist — the sign they should stop immediately. Will failed to notice this for a few paces, causing Elliott to make a hissing noise to get his attention. Frowning, he turned to her.

"What is it?"

Taking her rifle from her shoulder, she gestured toward Bartleby.

Will looked at the cat, who had slunk low to the ground, his spindly tail stuck straight out behind him. As he'd been trained to do in the Colony, the cat did seem to be pointing like he'd sniffed something out.

Will nodded. "It's probably just some animal he doesn't know. A Heffalump or a Woozle," he chuckled.

But Elliott was deadly serious. "Don't want him running off—going to put a leash on him," she whispered to Will. Removing her Bergen, she took a length of rope from it, which she looped around Bartleby's neck and knotted. "And get your Sten ready," she ordered.

Will scanned the jungle floor ahead. So thick was the foliage above, only the odd finger of sunlight made its way through. In between the gargantuan tree trunks, these laser-bright beams of light stretched as far as the eye could see, shifting slightly and sometimes flickering out altogether when the wind blew hard and the branches above came together. It all looked so unthreatening and innocent. But then again, Elliott had glimpsed some type of large feline predator just a few days before. From the description the girl had given, Dr. Burrows thought it could be a saber-toothed tiger, much to his excitement. Either way, Will knew that he might be becoming a little too complacent in a world where anything was possible. So with a reluctant sigh, he swung the Sten off his shoulder, checked that the magazine was full, then cocked the submachine gun.

"This way," Elliott whispered, allowing Bartleby to pull her forward.

"Hey, hold on a minute," Will objected. "You mean you actually want to follow the trail? Why don't we just forget it and continue toward the river?"

Elliott shook her head, adamant. "No, we should check for

ourselves what it is. We have to find out all we can about this place if we don't want any surprises."

"OK, anything you say," Will replied, pursing his lips unhappily. The feel of the loaded weapon in his hands already seemed to belong to a different time, a time that he was grateful was behind him. And nothing on earth — or *inside* earth, he thought wryly — would induce him to go back to those fear-filled days.

As Bartleby snuffled away at the leaves, the trail appeared to avoid the vertical beams of light, where flies and other insects buzzed languidly. Soon they could hear a symphony of birdcalls, and the chirping of cicadas also seemed to be growing louder.

"Do you know this area?" Will asked Elliott.

She started because he hadn't bothered to lower his voice, and in response she gave another disgruntled shake of her head. Whether this meant she hadn't been there before, or that she was annoyed he wasn't being quiet enough, he had no idea. But he suspected it was the latter.

Fine, if you want to play soldiers . . . , Will thought to himself. *Stealth mode it is.* Crouching low, he began to emulate the way Elliott was treading lightly on the dry leaves underfoot.

Before long, they started to spot tracts of sunlight on the ground up ahead, which meant they must have been coming to the end of the thicker, tropical tree cover. Indeed, as they reached this brighter area, the giant trees of the jungle were replaced by thorn-covered acacias — far shorter, and with swollen pods dangling from the branches of their less developed canopies. It wasn't all that different in feel from Topsoil woodland.

Will glanced up at the blindingly white sky. As he lowered his gaze, it fell on a sheer cliff face.

"We're not going to climb that, are we?" he grumbled to Elliott.

They both stopped to take in the white stone escarpment, which was well over a hundred feet high. On the top of the cliff, the jungle appeared to resume its prolific growth.

Elliott made a quick assessment of the escarpment through the trees. "It seems to go on," she observed, looking to their left and then their right.

Will immediately knew they must be at some sort of fault line, where there'd been a fracture in the crust. He still wasn't used to the idea that the earth had two crusts — an outer one he'd spent most of his life on, and an inner one, like the white flesh lining a coconut shell. He and his father talked for hours about what else they might find in this new world: Huge mountain ranges? Vast shipless seas and oceans? So, Will decided, the cliff could have been formed as a result of a fault line, and either the land on which he and Elliott were standing had subsided, or the land on the other side of the escarpment had risen up, or possibly both.

Elliott called him over with a whisper, bringing an abrupt end to his reflections.

She was squatting down and studying a patch of mud and rotted leaves. She looked anxious. For the life of him Will couldn't work out what she was getting so wound up about.

She traced out a shape with her index finger, then moved crablike across the ground, putting her cheek almost to the mud to examine an adjacent area. As Bartleby strained on his leash, she ignored him, crawling forward a few feet, still examining the ground. She suddenly looked up at Will. She held up three fingers, then pointed ahead.

It was another of the signs she and Drake had used in the Deeps.

Will knew only too well what it meant.

He felt a rush of adrenaline, his heart beating hard in his chest. Since he failed to react and instead just stood there, Elliott leaped to her feet and came over to him.

"People. Three sets of prints — one adult, two smaller," she confirmed.

He shook his head, not wanting to hear any of this, not wanting to register what she was saying. Wide-eyed, he stared at her, his hands gripping the Sten.

"People?" he asked numbly. "Or Styx? Are you telling me it's the twins and the Limiter?"

Elliott turned to where the tracks led off. "One set is certainly the right size for a man, and his tracks are light — like someone with military training."

"On the ball of the foot," Will murmured, recalling the way Elliott had tried to teach him to move around on the Great Plain.

"Yes," she said. "But the other two sets are much smaller, and identical in size," she went on.

Will swallowed hard. "What do we do now?" he asked.

"What Drake asked us to: Make sure the Rebecca twins and the Limiter are inoperative, and that the Dominion risk is neutralized," she replied succinctly.

"Inoperative . . . neutralized," Will mumbled to himself. Concentrate on the words alone and that all sounded fine — two tidy, detached words like you'd read in a book or newspaper. But this was different, this was real, and in order to achieve Drake's objectives, he and Elliott would have to do things that were far from *tidy*. Will himself would have to do things that he wasn't sure he was capable of, not anymore. Things that would probably change him, forever. Of course, Elliott was right. It was their responsibility to make sure — however they could — that the virus didn't find its way Topsoil. But as he looked at Elliott, at how she was immediately equal to the task, she seemed so clear-cut about it, as if she had no reservations whatsoever, whereas Will's head swam with doubt.

Glancing in the direction they were about to take, he guiltily admitted to himself that he wished the three Styx were long gone and that Elliott wouldn't be able to find them. But as he thought about it, he knew that couldn't be the case — the tracks had to be relatively fresh because otherwise the frequent monsoons would have washed them away.

Elliott tethered Bartleby to a tree, then pulled the rolled-up fishing net from her Bergen and stowed it under some branches. Will knew she was getting herself battle-ready as she checked the equipment in the bottom of her Bergen, then slung it back on. "Single file, four paces behind," she said to Will, as she began to read the tracks and slowly creep forward.

Will regarded their surroundings with mounting dread. The trees and the foliage were no longer benign — each bush harbored a Limiter, and each tree trunk hid one of the malicious girls who attempted to kill him any chance they got. Will's mind hammered with various thoughts, as loud as shouts.

I can't do this anymore. I'm not ready for this. Not now. He felt as if his head was going to rupture.

They came to the foot of the escarpment and looked up. Very little grew on its face — the odd sapling or shrub had managed to anchor itself in the cracks, and across the upper reaches long trailing tree roots and dried-out vegetation hung down, like a pale green fringe.

She led him under an overhang in the escarpment. "They stopped here for a while, maybe to get out of the sun," Elliott whispered into Will's ear after she'd scrutinized the ground. Then Will and Elliott crept along the foot of the escarpment, every so often clambering over rockfalls where the face had crumbled away. Occasionally they came across passages that penetrated into the escarpment, but these were nothing more than narrow corridors, overrun with tangles of thick undergrowth. Elliott didn't bother to go down them to investigate; she could see that the tracks continued straight past.

Eventually they came to another opening in the escarpment, wider than the others, with vertical sides of white rock. Even Will could tell that someone had gone down it, pushing their way through the dense vegetation and leaving footprints behind as they went.

"Stay close," Elliott had said to Will before they started in. He had no intention of doing anything but that.

As they advanced into the passage, Elliott continued to read the ground, finding broken blades of grass and the odd shrub that had been trodden down.

They followed around a gentle curve in the passage, and then Elliott waved Will down. They both lowered onto their chests. She touched her earlobe — an instruction for Will to listen. He wasn't sure to start with, but he thought he might have heard a voice.

A girl's voice.

Elliott began to snake forward very slowly, making sure there was nothing in her path. A snapping twig might give their presence away.

Coming to a halt, she held still for several seconds, then turned her head to Will. She pointed to her eye, then patted the ground beside her. Once Will was level with her, he sought out what she'd spotted.

The passage widened out into a larger, roughly circular space, a hundred feet or so in diameter. Its sides were as steep and the same height as the rest of the escarpment. From what Will could see, it resembled a cove in a coastal cliff, and the passage he and Elliott had come down appeared to be the only way in or out. A sprawling mass of parched vegetation hung down the sidewalls, and all other flora in the circular area also appeared to be desiccated and brown. Will guessed this might be because the space, with its white walls, acted like a sun trap. It certainly felt far warmer there than back in the acacia wood.

Then Will did see something, but it was completely out of place. Near the center of the circular space, there was some type of structure — a small hut with a flat roof, its sides a dark reddish brown and with a number of holes in them, as if they had rusted through.

Corrugated metal?! Will thought. *What's that doing here?!*

Then, above the sound of the cicadas, he heard, quite plainly, one of the Rebecca twins. The voice was nasal — she was speaking in the Styx tongue.

If Will's heart had been beating fast before, it was pounding so rapidly now that his pulse in his ears sounded as loud as a ten-gun salute on repeat.

Then, as he turned his head and tried to get a better view through the vegetation, he located where the voice was coming from. He saw the Rebecca twin's profile as she sat on something slightly raised, maybe a boulder, not far from the hut.

As he was watching, she jiggled her leg, and he heard a gentle splash. Then there was a bigger splash, and the second twin rose up into view, just in front of the first Rebecca. She was dripping wet, her long black hair loose and hanging around her face. She swept it back with one hand, scattering drops of water, which sparkled in the intense sunlight. Were they swimming or bathing in some kind of pool? Will couldn't believe how relaxed they both appeared — but then, they hadn't the smallest inkling that he'd also made it through to this inner world. They'd lowered their guard because they believed there was no threat here.

But where was the Limiter?

Will continued to watch them as the second Rebecca sank back out of view and, he assumed, into the water. Although she was out of sight, they were still talking. He heard a few vague words. They were in English. As the rays from the overhead sun drenched the scene before him and the odd bird twittered, he was transported back to past summers at his home in Highfield. His bedroom had overlooked the part of the garden where Rebecca would often spread a towel on the lawn and sunbathe, while he had to hide himself away from the rays because of his lack of pigmentation. On these days, days when he wasn't off digging somewhere and he lay on his bed and read, her voice drifted up to his window as she sang along to the radio.

With a nudge from her elbow, Elliott brought Will back to the present. She was pointing at something. It was difficult to see them because their dun camouflage merged so effectively with the rusty metal, but there they were . . . two Limiter combat jackets . . . hanging on something at the rear corner of the hut.

The Rebecca twins' jackets.

Will couldn't believe it.

His eyes met with Elliott's. He knew she was thinking the same thing — he was willing to bet that if the twins were taking a plunge in the pool or whatever it was, they would have left the phials somewhere for safekeeping. And where better than their jackets?

He caught himself. Maybe they'd left the phials with the Limiter. *Where the heck is that Limiter?* he asked himself again.

Elliott gave the sign to withdraw, and Will was grateful beyond words that he didn't have to remain so close to the Styx girls or the so far unaccounted-for Limiter. As he edged back, it felt a little as if he'd just put his head in the mouth of a particularly bad-tempered and hungry lion, and got away with it.

Once he and Elliott were around the curve in the passage and far enough from the cove, she quickly took off her Bergen and began to delve in it. She took out two large explosive charges with timers attached to them — they were from the batch that Drake had asked Will to deliver to her.

Then she moved close to Will and again whispered in his ear. "I'm going to set these along here. Go to the entrance of the passage and keep watch. If a charge goes off or you hear shots, clear out — fast. You can come back for Bartleby after."

Will nodded, then crawled off down the passage. Once he was back at the escarpment, he found a sheltered spot behind a tree and watched the passage, waiting for Elliott.

The longer he waited, the more uncomfortable he felt. Elliott's words resonated in his head. It was obvious she was shouldering all the weight of a possible conflict so that Will didn't have to put himself in any danger whatsoever. Indeed, it sounded as if she was ready to sacrifice herself in order to deal with the Styx. As he mulled it over, he realized he couldn't let her do that. It was his battle, too, and it was only right he played his part in it.

To his incredible relief, she reappeared at the mouth of the passage. He had begun to wonder if he'd ever see her again — alive.

She joined him behind the tree and, keeping her voice low, murmured, "Two charges set on twenty-minute fuses, mounted high so I can snipe them if I need to. I'm going to see if I can climb the cliff and get the full view of what's going on."

"Why don't I do —" he began to ask.

"No, better that I try. I know how to use this," she interrupted him, patting her Limiter rifle with the telescopic sight. "I just need you to cover this area."

"What if they come out?" he asked quickly.

"Open fire with the Sten. Whatever you do, keep them pinned down inside the passage. Contain them," she said, glancing over at the opening in the escarpment, "I'm going to see if I can pick them off, starting with the Limiter. Once he's down, the twins should be easier to deal with."

Will nodded grimly, and Elliott immediately moved toward the escarpment, looking for a place to climb.

Finding himself a better vantage point behind the trunk of an acacia, Will lay down. His palms left smears of sweat on the blued steel of his Sten as he adjusted his grip on the weapon. "Keep them pinned down inside," he repeated, staring so hard at the opening of the passage that it seemed to become something unreal, like an illustration from a graphic novel.

He tried to make himself less tense by shifting his shoulders around, but that didn't work. He couldn't stop himself from jumping at even the smallest movement, to the point that he almost fired on a leaf as it dropped from a branch. He could feel the sun heating the shirt on his back as he lay in wait. He was suddenly hit with the realization that this was one of those pivotal moments in his life, one of those moments when he could step up to the plate and prove himself. If he didn't and it all went terribly wrong, then he would have to live with that. And he felt as if he already had far too many regrets in his short life. No, he wasn't just going to sit there and let everything happen around him, like some passenger in a car. He had to do something. He was *going* to do something.

What, exactly, he did not know.

Come on! he said to himself. He began to formulate a rough plan, leaving his position and entering the passage. *Twenty minutes*, he reminded himself as he spotted Elliott's charges where she'd fixed them on the upper branches of the trees on opposing sides of the passage. It was a clever strategy — when they both went off, the passage would cave in and the Styx should be trapped in the circular cove — unless, that was, they could somehow climb the sheer walls.

Crawling slowly, he reached the spot where he and Elliott had been before. He could see that the twins were now sitting side by side. He felt incredibly exposed, and he had an awful sinking feeling in his stomach because he knew he wasn't going to stop there.

Now what? Will asked himself. He assumed Elliott hadn't reached the top of the escarpment yet, and the charges still had a good fifteen minutes left before they detonated.

Then he decided.

Swallowing hard, he began to crawl to his right. Bit by bit, he inched himself forward on a route that would take him around to the rear of the hut. It was a calculated risk, but he figured he could get there without the Rebecca twins seeing him because they were on the other side of the hut. And it also helped that they were distracted as they talked to each other.

Clearing his path of any dry leaves or twigs as he went, he continued to crawl, pausing every couple of feet to check in front. He kept glancing at the two jackets. He fixed in his mind the image of himself reaching them — that was his goal, his reward.

Where's the Limiter? The question nagged at him yet again.

The sweat was running into his eyes, but he didn't wipe them, trying instead to blink it away, because every movement he made was crucial. And every second could mean the difference between success and failure. He kept his whole body low to the ground, all the time checking that he was taking the best route between the shrubbery, one which would provide him with cover in case either of the Rebecca twins decided to take a stroll around to the rear of the hut. Or if the Limiter did.

He kept crawling, closing in on the corrugated hut. He didn't have far to go, but the vegetation was particularly dry the nearer he got to the center of the cove, the walls of white rock focusing the full force of the sun on it. He took even more care to check for twigs — one wrong noise and the jig was up.

Then the jackets were mere feet away from him.

He'd made it this far!

He took another quick look. The coast seemed clear. The twins were still on the other side of the hut, and there was absolutely no sign of the Limiter.

He got to his feet, but remained in a half crouch as he stepped slowly to the jackets and lifted them off a rusty nail where they were hanging.

He wondered if Elliott had managed to get to the top of the escarpment yet and was watching him through her telescopic sight. If so, what would she be thinking right now? Probably swearing like a sailor.

He laid the jackets down on the frazzled grass and, kneeling beside them, quickly went through the pockets, pulling all their contents out. Bits of paper, luminescent orbs, some objects in small leather pouches that he decided to take in case they held the phials. He didn't have time to open them, not there and then.

Then, in an inner pocket, he found what he was looking for. The pocket had a flap over it with a snap closure. It made a tiny *click* as he undid it. He held his breath, waiting and listening for anything, but all he could hear was the murmur of occasional conversation between the Rebecca twins drifting over to him. He felt inside the pocket, and his fingers came across two small objects. He lifted them out. Wrapped in a square of camouflaged material, there were the phials, both of them. He couldn't believe it. He heard the Rebeccas laughing. They wouldn't be laughing much longer, not when they found out what he'd done. He put the phials carefully in his pocket, and went through the rest of the jackets just in case there were any more phials. He didn't want to have done all this only to end up with more phony phials containing Ultra Bug specimens.

He was finished. He felt light-headed, and his face was streaming with sweat as he began to crawl away.

He'd gone about fifty feet, keeping carefully to his original route through the undergrowth, when he heard a shriek. He twisted his head around.

Fear exploded in his mind.

The Rebecca twin was standing where he'd left the jackets on the ground. Dripping with water, her face was pulled into a vile, angry mask, and she was looking straight at him.

"You little creep!" she screamed, holding a scythe high in the air as if she was going to throw it. "This is *it* for you!"

Will flipped over onto his back, whipping out his Sten. His finger was on the trigger. He felt no hesitation. It was as if he was seeing everything in monochrome. He had to do this. He didn't know for sure if he'd got the genuine Dominion phials, so none of the Styx could be allowed to escape. If a single one of them got away, his job wasn't finished.

In his panic, Will began to fire before he was on target. Rounds sprayed wildly, hitting the corrugated metal of the hut and punching more holes in it. As he swung farther around, the twin seemed to go down.

That was enough for Will.

He was on his feet and running through the passage.

He heard another shout.

A man's this time.

Will snapped his head around.

With a spear poised above his head, the Limiter was running like some sort of machine, pounding toward him in huge strides. The soldier shouted again, his words like a call from a bird of prey. They sounded so harsh it was as if they scored the hot air itself, leaving their marks in it.

Will didn't know how far down the passage he'd gone, but he couldn't see the mouth yet. And he still hadn't finished the job.

He skidded to a halt, turning to aim at the Limiter.

Everything was happening so fast it was a blur.

Then there were two sounds that Will couldn't understand. He heard a sharp *crack!* and at the same time, a *swishing* sound. On the top of his head, the Limiter's black hair seemed to fluff up. He was flung face-first to the ground, his legs still running, as if the machine couldn't stop.

And as for the swishing sound . . . Will felt a sudden pain in his arm. His hand twitched, and he dropped the Sten.

Then there was a flash of light, quickly followed by a second, and Will was lifted clean off his feet. Maybe it was the lower gravity, but he seemed to be whisked an incredible distance through the air, smashing through a cluster of thick bushes and tumbling over several times before he finally came to a stop.

He tried to pull himself up, but his arm hurt too badly. He saw that it was covered in blood. All of a sudden, he felt very cold — he couldn't understand why when the sun was still shining. *The sun always shines here* ran through his mind.

He managed to prop himself up on one arm, and looked back to where he thought the passage was.

Fifty feet behind him, all he could see were huge swirling sheets of fire and thick black smoke, the colors so vivid against the white rocks of the escarpment. "Cool," he said, before he lost consciousness.

He came to a little later. He lifted his head, noticing that there was a bandage on his arm.

"You stupid idiot. Only an amateur could have attempted that and got away with it," Elliott said, moving into his field of vision. "Next time, can we please stick to the plan?"

Will looked at her blearily. "Oh great, I haven't upset you again, have I? I always seem to do this with girls, I always say or do the wrong thi —"

"Just shut up, Will," Elliott said.

He tried to move his arm again, but it was too painful. "What happened?" he asked.

"The Limiter clipped you with his spear before I took him out. Sorry, couldn't get him in my crosshairs quick enough," she replied as she knelt beside Will, adjusting the bandage.

"The Rebecca twins?"

"I think you took care of one of them, and the other didn't stand a chance. See for yourself."

Elliott helped him sit up. He recalled seeing smoke and flames before he'd passed out, but down by the escarpment a huge fire was now raging. A plume of smoke snaked above it, like the ones he and Dr. Burrows spotted through the binoculars from time to time in other parts of the jungle.

"After I set off the charges with a shot, the passage collapsed in on itself, and the remaining twin was stuck inside. With all that dry stuff around, the whole place went up like a tinderbox. And even if you only winged the other twin, she was in there, too," Elliott said. "There's no way either of them could have made it out."

"So we did it?"

Elliott nodded.

"And you're not angry with me," Will asked, blinking at her.

Elliott held up the two phials. "How can I be?" she replied, smiling broadly. Leaning forward, she kissed him on the cheek.

Will smiled, too, the pain in his arm forgotten for the moment.

39

IN A SMALL terraced house in the Colony, Mrs. Burrows was propped up in a chair, her legs covered with a thick gray blanket. Her eyes were closed, and cushions had been placed on either side of her head, since she was unable to support it herself. Indeed, she had no control over any part of her body.

In another chair, closer to the hearth where a fire burned, an elderly lady darned a sock as she chattered gently to herself.

"It's a crime what they pay policeman these days, partickly when 'e got his old mother, 'is sister, and now . . . now 'e's got an invalid on 'is back, too." The elderly lady ceased her needlework and peered around at Mrs. Burrows. It wasn't an unkindly look, but the old lady pressed her pale lips together with concern. "I told 'im, I did, it's all well and good playing the Samaritan, but it's like 'aving a new baby to care for, a big new baby that won't never grow up. But 'e don't listen. . . . I think 'e's going soft in his old age." The elderly lady turned back to her stitching. "I don't know where this is all going to end. I don't know 'ow we're going to make ends meet, I don't, not on 'is wages."

Because of the crackle of the fire, and because she was still nattering to herself, the elderly lady didn't hear that Mrs.

Burrows's breathing had changed. It had become deep and forced, as if she was about to try something that, in her state, was a Herculean and almost impossible feat. She maintained the deep breathing for several minutes, building herself up to the task. Then she stopped altogether, holding her breath as she strained.

Like a wild animal in a winter-black cave, she was isolated and cut off from the outside world. Here the darkness was only broken by the odd sparkle as a thought or a desire or a memory coalesced for the briefest moment, then was gone almost the moment it had appeared.

But now she had something she was determined to do. From somewhere the will to survive, to succeed, had emerged.

She made the most immense effort.

She strained even harder, still holding her breath. She managed to raise her right eyelid the tiniest degree, and to keep it raised. The chink of her exposed eye glittered and the light of the blaze registered on her retina, firing off the cells there. They generated minute electrical impulses that were conveyed up her optic nerve to her brain, which struggled to process them. Some of these signals did make it through to her cerebral cortex, and she vaguely sensed rather than saw the rosy glow in the room.

But to her it was everything; it was something from outside her cave. She clung on to the sensation with animal instinct, and it gave her hope.

Then, because the effort had been all too much and had drained every last ounce of energy from her body, the eyelid slid shut once again. Letting out her breath, she sank back into a deep slumber as the elderly lady, none the wiser for the miracle that had just taken place, continued to chatter to herself.

Will and Elliott talked at length about what they should do with the phials. They even went as far as to consider whether they should attempt the journey back through the crystal belt so they could reach Topsoil and deliver the phials to Drake. But neither of them took this suggestion seriously, since they believed the chances of making it through were pretty slim. And the worst outcome would be if there was a mishap along the way in which the phials were damaged and the virus released. Dr. Burrows had warned them about the global system of air currents, saying that, although it might be one in a million, there was always the possibility that the virus could be carried up to the external world.

They couldn't risk this, so instead Will took it upon himself to search for a safe, secure place to bury the phials. His arm still in a sling but healing well, he'd left the camp on his own and was exploring a nearby tract of jungle when, out of the corner of his eye, he thought he saw someone in the shadows cast by a grove of trees. The hairs on the back of his neck stood up, not only because he knew it couldn't be his father or Elliott, but also because the figure looked so much like Uncle Tam.

As he crept toward the trees, he realized that what he'd seen must have been a knot of creepers hanging from a lower branch and that there was no one there. Telling himself he must have conjured up the sighting because Tam had recently been so much in his thoughts, he investigated what lay behind the grove.

He found a small spring bubbling up from between a few gray boulders, encircled by a ring of short-cropped grass. It was such a peaceful and secluded spot that it was here that he decided to bury the phials. He put some of the grass inside one of the medicine bottles he had taken from the submarine's sick bay, then carefully lowered in the phials, packing more grass on top of them. After having dug a hole in the rich soil, Will made sure the lid of the bottle was tightly screwed on before burying it. Then he placed a few rounded stones on top to mark the spot and protect the phials from inquisitive animals.

Following the discovery of the spring, he felt drawn to come back to it. Hardly a day passed when he didn't visit it. The fresh water seemed to attract the most exquisite butterflies and dragonflies, which alighted on the lichen-speckled stones to cool themselves and to drink. It was paradoxical because he knew the Dominion virus, a lethal biological weapon, was buried there, which should have made it a place of death and destruction, but instead he found that the spring filled him with tranquility. It was somewhere he could lower his defenses and allow himself to remember the terrible events of the past. And begin to heal.

On the other side of the spring from the Dominion virus and its small marker of stones, he made three larger piles of boulders. On each of these he erected a cross. Although their bodies weren't there, he carved Uncle Tam, Sarah Jerome, and Cal's names on these crosses. He found it a great comfort to sit in the grass by them, with the glorious display of colors from the butterflies flitting all around him. The Rebecca twins had finally been made to pay, and this felt like the end of a chapter to Will, a resolution. No longer was he living under their shadow, and no longer was he driven by the need for revenge. He felt liberated. He'd wiped the slate clean, and it allowed him to remember the family members he had lost at the hands of the Styx.

One day when he was there, deep in thought, somebody cleared their throat behind him and made him jump.

"I hope you don't mind me coming here," Elliott said. "I wanted to see for myself where you'd put the phials."

Will showed her, but she seemed more interested in the three memorials he'd erected for his family.

"I didn't know you'd done all this," she said quietly. "I . . . um . . . it's a . . . a nice idea."

Will nodded, and they didn't speak for several moments as, together, they gazed at the crosses. For once, Elliott seemed incredibly unsure of herself. In a nervous gesture she swept back her jet-black hair from her face — since they'd left the Deeps, lice were no longer a problem and she'd stopped cutting it. Now it was almost shoulder length, and Will could barely recall what she'd looked like with closely cropped hair.

"I've no idea if she's dead or alive, but would it be OK if I built one of these for my mother?" Elliott asked.

"Of course," Will said, genuinely delighted. He suddenly thought of his own mother, his adopted mother Mrs. Burrows, and hoped that she hadn't come to any harm. But, he reminded himself, at least Drake was there to look after her.

And the next day when he arrived at the spring he found that Elliott had already set up a cross a little distance from his. She came and sat next to him. As Bartleby basked in a patch of sun filtered by the trees and took lazy mouthfuls of grass, Elliott began to open up to Will. There had been a feeling of camaraderie between the two of them after the incident with the Styx, but this was different. She talked about her childhood in the Colony and how she had been forced to leave when her mother had been blackmailed. And then she mentioned her father — the Limiter — and how she knew so little about him.

All of a sudden, Elliott turned to Will. "Do you feel guilty about what we did to the Rebecca twins? Does it trouble you when you think about it?"

The question was completely unexpected, and Will looked at her askance. "Yes, it does. I'm certain what we did was right, but it's not something that you can get out of your head, is it?"

"No," she answered. "It never leaves you."

From beside the spring, Elliott chose two flat stones that had been worn smooth by the water. Taking one in each hand, she weighed them in her palms as if she was working out which of the two was the heaviest.

"Can I ask you something?" Will ventured.

"Sure," Elliott shrugged.

"That was a Limiter you shot, just like your dad," Will said.

He watched as Elliott absently tugged a third polished stone from the soil. Since her hands were already full with the other two stones, she eventually tossed it into the pool of springwater. The splash made Bartleby roll over and sit up, as if he'd missed a fish leaping out of the stream or another unfortunate amphibian to chew on.

"What if it had been your dad? Would you have been able to shoot him, too?" Will asked.

"Never thought about it," Elliott replied quickly. "My father's dead and gone, so it's never going to happen."

In a jam-packed pub in the heart of London's Soho, a man in a heavy overcoat slouched by himself at a corner table. His hair was unkempt and his face ruddy. Obviously the worse for drink, he clumsily examined his glass, discovering that it was empty. He mumbled something under his breath and banged the table with his fist, which sent the glass spinning to the floor, where it shattered. Then he lifted his head. "The Styx!" he spat, and began to shout, his words slurred and barely intelligible. "Sod them!"

The low hum of conversation in the pub continued unabated — nobody appeared to take the slightest bit of notice of him. The man blearily regarded the throng: people having a quick drink after work before they made their way home.

He sneered lopsidedly.

"And sod the lot of you, too! You're all blind to what's going on!"

Again nobody seemed to pay him any heed. Nobody except for a thin man with a sallow, hollow-cheeked face, who was suddenly at his table.

"Pull yourself together, Drake. If you carry on like this, you'll get yourself arrested. And you know what a night in the cells means," the tall man warned in a low growl. He leaned closer to Drake so he couldn't be overheard by those around them. "I helped you because I owed you a debt of honor for saving my daughter, but I'm not your fairy godmother. I might not be able to do it a second time."

Drake wiped the spittle from his lips with the back of his hand. "Sometimes I think Elliott saved *me*," he drawled, his eyes heavy-lidded at he peered up at the former Limiter who had pulled him from the van that day back on Highfield Common.

All at once Drake's belligerence turned to despondency and his head sagged on his shoulders. "The White Necks have me beat at every turn. I let Celia down. I let Leatherman down. I let every one of them down. And, for all I know, the Styx still have the virus. I might as well just throw in the towel. I'm finished — we're all finished." He gave the thin man a desperate look. "What's left for me? What can I do now?"

"Oh, we'll think of something," the thin man said confidently as he helped Drake to his feet. "Now, let's get you home."

40

"I'VE HAD ENOUGH for today," Will decided.

"Really? So soon?" Dr. Burrows mumbled, as he continued to work on a sketch.

"My arm's acting up a bit," Will added, although the injury from the Limiter's spear had long since healed.

"Going back to see Elliott?" Dr. Burrows asked, a knowing tone to his voice.

Will ignored this, raising his eyes to the ever-burning sun. "I just don't want to overdo it again," he said, adjusting the wide-brimmed hat that Elliott had fashioned for him from animal hide.

He and his father were on the side of the pyramid, and while the hat afforded his face a measure of protection from the direct sun, he still had to be careful about the reflected rays in their exposed position.

"No, quite," Dr. Burrows finally answered, looking up from his work.

Will rubbed his eyes and blinked several times. "Of all the places we could have ended up, this one is an albino's worst nightmare. Dad, do you think next time you could find us a world with a few more clouds?" he asked with a smile.

"I'll see what I can do. Off you go if you want to," Dr. Burrows replied glumly. He depended on his son's support for the mammoth task of recording the inscriptions and the scenes depicted on each of the tiers of the pyramid. It was all written in one of the languages on the Burrows Stone, and little by little he was deciphering it. He and Will had started at the base of the pyramid and were methodically working their way to the top, knowing they had another two pyramids to tackle that they hadn't even visited yet.

"I'll see you back at the camp, Dad," Will said.

"Yes . . . ," Dr. Burrows murmured. He watched his son make his way down the successive tiers to the ground, leaping distances that would be unthinkable in the Topsoil world. Then Dr. Burrows resumed his work on a numerical sequence, which was making no sense to him at all.

After a while his concentration was broken by a distant droning. He immediately dismissed it as the wind, telling himself it was another of the violent storms, of which there were many. It sounded as if it was too far away to be a concern, so there was no need to get himself under cover. But then he heard the noise again, louder this time, and it didn't sound anything like the wind. He wiped his brow, then rose to his feet to study the sky.

He couldn't see anything out of the ordinary, but he realized he wasn't in the best position, so he vaulted up the tiers until he reached the very top of the pyramid. There he walked across the level plateau of stone, passing the radio beacon that Will had left the very first time they'd climbed it.

"What a view," Dr. Burrows sighed, never failing to be

impressed, no matter how many times he saw it. From this elevated position, he was a considerable way above the canopy of the rain forest, which stretched out before him like some rolling green sea, broken only by the tops of the other pyramids.

"Where's the storm?" he said to himself, not seeing any clouds as he scanned the horizon on each side.

Instead he spotted something in the distance.

Stepping slowly across to the other side of the pyramid, he shielded his eyes with his hand as he tried to make out what it was.

"What *in* earth is that?"

Something was moving across the clear white sky.

Something that, as he looked further, was terribly familiar.

He reeled, nearly losing his footing at the edge of the pyramid.

And as it changed direction and began to come toward the pyramid, Dr. Burrows could clearly hear the whine of its single prop engine.

"An airplane? Here?" he said soundlessly.

As he strained to see more, he wished he'd brought his binoculars with him.

But there was no doubt.

It *was* an airplane.

And, yes, it was strangely familiar.

He recognized the W shape of the wings. It was still some distance away, but as it tipped into a full dive, he could hear the howl of the siren on the aircraft, issuing one of the most distinctive and most feared sounds of the Second World War.

"A German bomber," Dr. Burrows gasped, nearly losing his footing again. "A Stuka!"

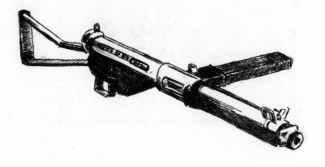

AUTHORS' NOTE

ROTOR, as Will and Dr. Burrows spotted on the map in the radio operator's booth, was an extensive air defense radar system built in the 1950s by the British Government on sixty-six sites in response to the perceived threat from the Soviet Union. It is *not* an acronym, which just goes to show that Dr. Burrows doesn't know everything (even if he correctly identified the Sten submachine gun, pictured above).

People are the walls of our room, not philosophies.
from *Free Fall*
William Golding (1911–1993)

ACKNOWLEDGMENTS

W^E are deeply indebted to: Professor Lidenbrock, his nephew Axel, and Hans Bjelke, naturally; Siobhán McGowan and the team at Scholastic in New York: Starr Baer, Kevin Callahan, Whitney Lyle, Elizabeth Parisi, Jess White, Sawatree Green, Charisse Meloto, Rachel Coun, Jacquelyn Harper, John Mason, Suzanne Murphy, and Ellie Berger; Chicken House in Somerset, especially the one and only Barry Cunningham, our publisher and wearer of many magnificent pairs of shoes; Catherine Pellegrino of Rogers, Coleridge & White; Katie Morrison, formerly of Colman Getty, now at UNICEF; Susan Collinge and Roger Gawn for allowing us access to West Raynham Airfield; Jo Brearley and the pupils of Gresham's School; Simon Wilkie; Karen Everitt.

And George.

Coming Soon!

CLOSER

RODERICK
GORDON

BRIAN
WILLIAMS

The Fourth Book in the *New York Times*
Bestselling TUNNELS Series